MICHAEL JACKSON vs CONRAD MURRAY

THE TRIAL

Richard Collins

2

Michael Joseph Jackson (August 29, 1958 – June 25, 2009) was an American recording artist, entertainer, and businessman. Often referred to as the King of Pop, or by his initials Michael Jackson, Jackson is recognized as the most successful entertainer of all time by Guinness World Records. His contribution to music, dance, and fashion, along with a much-publicized personal life, made him a global figure in popular culture for over four decades. The seventh child of the Jackson family, he debuted on the professional music scene along with his brothers as a member of The Jackson 5, then the Jacksons in 1964, and began his solo career in 1971.

In the early 1980s, Jackson became a dominant figure in popular music. The music videos for his songs, including those of "*Beat It*", "*Billie Jean*", and "*Thriller*", were credited with transforming the medium into an art form and a promotional tool, and the popularity of these videos helped to bring the relatively new television channel MTV to fame. Videos such as "*Black or White*" and "*Scream*" made him a staple on MTV in the 1990s. Through stage performances and music videos, Jackson popularized a number of complicated dance techniques, such as the robot and the moonwalk, to which he gave the name. His distinctive musical sound and vocal style have influenced numerous hip hop, post-disco, contemporary R&B, pop and rock artists.

Jackson's 1982 album Thriller is the best-selling album of all time. His other records, including *Off the Wall* (1979), *Bad* (1987), *Dangerous* (1991), and *HIStory* (1995), also rank among the world's best-selling. Jackson is one of the few artists to have been inducted into the Rock and Roll Hall of Fame twice. He was also inducted into the Dance Hall of Fame as the first (and currently only) dancer from the world of pop and rock 'n' roll. Some of his other achievements include multiple Guinness World Records; 13 Grammy Awards (as well as the Grammy Legend Award and the Grammy Lifetime Achievement Award); 26 American Music Awards (more than any other artist, including the "Artist of the Century"); 13 number-one singles in the United States in his solo career (more than any other male artist in the Hot 100 era); and the estimated sale of over 750 million records worldwide. Jackson won hundreds of awards, which have made him the most-awarded recording artist in the history of popular music.

Aspects of Jackson's personal life, including his changing appearance, personal relationships, and behavior, have generated controversy. In 1993, he was accused of child sexual abuse, but the case was settled out of court and no formal charges were brought. In 2005, he was tried and acquitted of further child sexual abuse allegations and several other charges after the jury found him not guilty on all counts. While preparing for his concert series titled This Is It, Jackson died of acute propofol and benzodiazepine intoxication on June 25, 2009, after suffering from cardiac arrest. The Los Angeles County Coroner ruled his death a homicide, and his personal physician was convicted of involuntary manslaughter. Jackson's death triggered a global outpouring of grief, and as many as one billion people around the world reportedly watched his public memorial service on live television. In March 2010, Sony Music Entertainment signed a $250 million deal with Jackson's estate to retain distribution rights to his recordings until 2017, and to release seven posthumous albums over the decade following his death.

INTRODUCTION NOTE

A life dedicated to work and charity led Michael Jackson to be loved by many generations of fans; and still today these fans keep this memory alive... of an artist who gave his best.

A man envied by predators that turned his life upside down destroying him both morally and physically.

Even suffering from pain he was going to give us a tour, his last one, as he said when he was in London to announce "This Is It".

Once again he would have been able to amaze us, another time... for the last time...

It wasn't meant to happen. As for the rest we keep it safe in our hearts.

A much awaited trial that found Mr. Murray guilty of serious negligence, that right from the start led to his famous patient's unhappy end.

The list that included those who had hurt and betrayed Michael Jackson is rather long, and only time will judge. I hope that this will happen during this life.

In respect to a man who has always protected his image, there will be no pictures in this book of his corpse that were shown during the trial. It will be his hands that will lead us page after page, between sincere testimonies and unconvincing evidence.

Richard Collins

Murray Trial Summaries Day 1 /September 27 - 2011

Hearing started approximately 30 minutes late. Judge Michael Pastor explained the reason as traffic and problem with the elevators.

Trial started with Judge Pastor explaining jurors the process, breaks , taking notes and what is an opening statement.

Prosecution Opening Statement

DA Walgren started his opening statement. He used a presentation to accompany the points he's making. In the presentation he showed a picture of Michael lying in a gurney - most probably taken at the hospital after revival attempts.

DA Walgren "Evidence will show that Michael Jackson literally put his life in the hands of Conrad Murray. Michael Jackson trusted his life t medical skills of Conrad Murray. That misplaced trust was a too high of a price to pay." DA Walgren states that Dr. Murray's actions led to Michael Jackson's death.

DA Walgren explains what Michael was doing in months before his death. Walgren mentions that Michael was getting ready for his comeback tour TII, mentions rehearsals and that Michael was living in 100 N Carolwood with his children.

Walgren mentions that Michael and Dr. Murray met in 2006 in Vegas and maintained contact. At the time Michael Jackson died, Dr. Conrad Murray was not board-certified in any medical specialty. In March 2009 Michael asked Dr. Murray to accompany him on tour. Murray agreed and requested to be paid $5 Million a year. They offered him $150,000 a month. Murray's duties included to perform general medical care, emergency medical care. He would have received $150,000, airfare to UK and housing. He would have been hired as an independent contractor. At the time Michael died the contract was not signed by Michael or AEG.

DA Walgren explains Propofol to the jurors. Walgren tells that it's not a sleep agent, it's anesthesia. Walgren goes over good and bad qualities of Propofol and tells the dangers. DA Walgren mentions Murray lied to pharmacists Tim Lopez and told him that he had a clinic and patients in California. Walgren starts listing Murray's Propofol orders and how they were sent to Murray's girlfriend Nicole Alvarez's house.

DA Walgren plays a part of an audio Murray recorded on is iPhone on May 10. Walgren mentions that Murray was recording Michael who was under influence of a unknown drug. Walgren states that this shows that the Murray knew the effect of his treatment on Michael, yet continued to order Propofol.

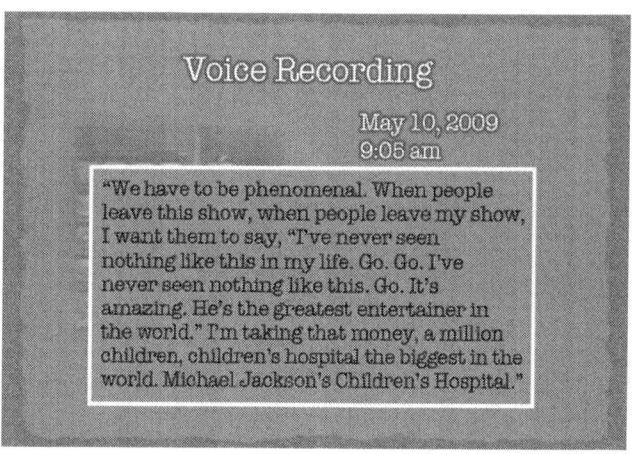

The recording said:

"We have to be phenomenal. When people leave this show, when people leave my show, I want them to say, "I've never seen anything like this in my life. "Go. Go. I've never seen nothing like this. Go. It's amazing. He's the greatest entertainer in the world. I'm taking that money, a million children, children's hospital, the biggest in the world, Michael Jackson's Children's Hospital."

Between April 6, 2009, and the time of Michael Jackson's death on June 25, Dr. Conrad Murray ordered enough propofol to give Jackson 1,937 milligrams a day, prosecutor David Walgren told jurors in his opening statement. June 19, 2009. Michael was not in good shape. He had chills, he was rambling and trembling. Kenny Ortega put a blanket on him, massaged his feet, fed him chicken and then made him go home early. June 20, 2009. There was a meeting about Michael's health. DA Walgren says that Dr. Murray scolded Kenny Ortega. " I'm the doctor not you. You direct the show leave Michael Jackson's health to me." June 23, June 24, 2009. Michael had good rehearsals. He's fine, strong and optimistic. June 25, 2009. Michael comes home around 1 AM. DA Walgren shows pictures of the house, layout, inside the rooms.

DA Walgren shows a list of Murray's phone calls and emails. Walgren mentions the 11:51 phone call with Sade Anding and tells that 5 minutes into the phone call that Sade Anding heard a commotion and

Murray stopped talking to her. DA Walgren says for 11:56 - 11:57 AM ""This is likely the time Conrad Murray first noticed Michael Jackson's lifeless body".

Walgren says that Dr. Murray called Michael Amir Williams at 12:12PM. Michael Amir Williams returned Murray's call at 12:13 PM. Dr. Murray told him to come to house, he didn't ask him to call 911. Michael Amir Williams called Alberto Alvarez and told him to go into the house. When Alberto came into the room Murray told him to collect the vials and saline bag on the IV. 911 was called at 12:20 PM. Paramedics arrived at 12:26 PM, they tried their best but Michael was gone. Paramedics asked Murray what he gave to Michael. Murray said Lorazepam and he didn't mention Propofol. Paramedics was on call with UCLA and UCLA wanted to announce Michael death on the scene. Murray wanted Michael to be transferred to UCLA. When they arrived UCLA doctors asked Murray what Michael was taking and what he gave to Michael. Murray told the doctors that Michael was taking Valium and Flomax and he gave Michael Lorazepam. Again Murray does not mention Propofol to the doctors. Michael is announced dead at 2:26 PM at UCLA. 2 days after Michael's death Los AngelesPD interviews Murray. At that time the tox results wasn't back and there was no visible trauma so the detectives did not know the reason of Michael's death. This is the first time that Murray mentions Propofol and tells his version of the events. According to Murray all the drugs he gave to Michael did not work. At 10 AM Michael tells Murray that he would cancel the rehearsal and he wouldn't need to get up at 12:00PM. After that Murray decided to give Michael Propofol. Murray claims he gave Michael 25 mg of Propofol. When Michael was lying in bed with all the drugs in his system Murray emails the insurance broker saying that Michael is fine.

11

Walgreen discusses issue of standard of care. DA Walgren explains gross negligence to the jurors and gives examples of Murray's actions that account to gross negligence. These are

- No written standard of care / risks / consent form

- Not calling 911 (especially when calling 911 is basic common sense)

- Employee / employer relationship and Murray not working for the best interest of Michael but working for $150,000. He did not use sound medical judgement.

- Deceived paramedics by not disclosing Propofol

- Deceived emergency room doctors by not disclosing Propofol

Murray had legal duty of care to do no harm to Michael Jackson. Murray with his eyes on $150K agreed to provide him massive aounts of propofol with complete disregard to all medical standards. Murray abandoned Michael on June 25. Filled with drugs, no monitoring equipment, no resuscitation equipment, left him all alone. It's clear that Murray abandoned Michael when he needed help.

Pictures shown during the Prosecution Opening Statement

Saline Bag and Propofol bottle that Murray asked Alvarez to collect

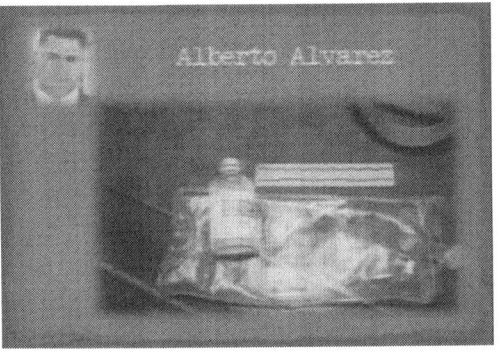

12

syringe

urine jug

IV stand

Bed

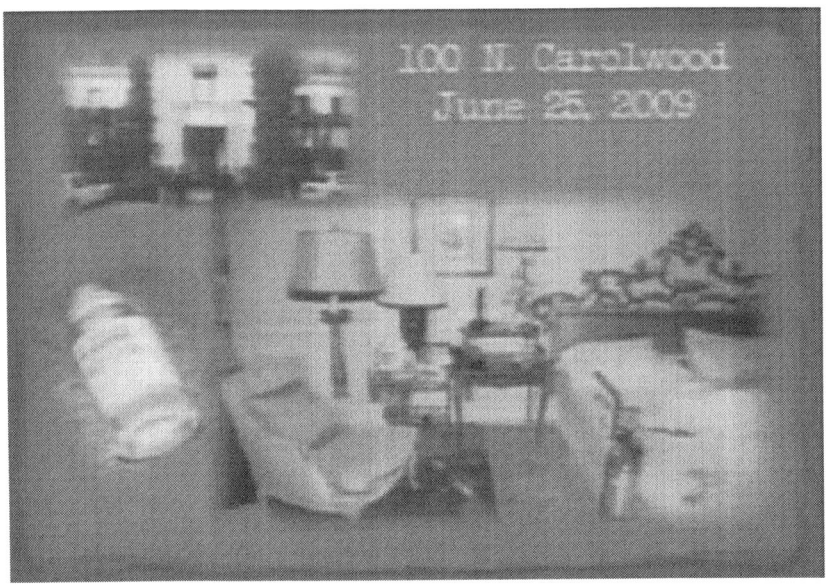

14

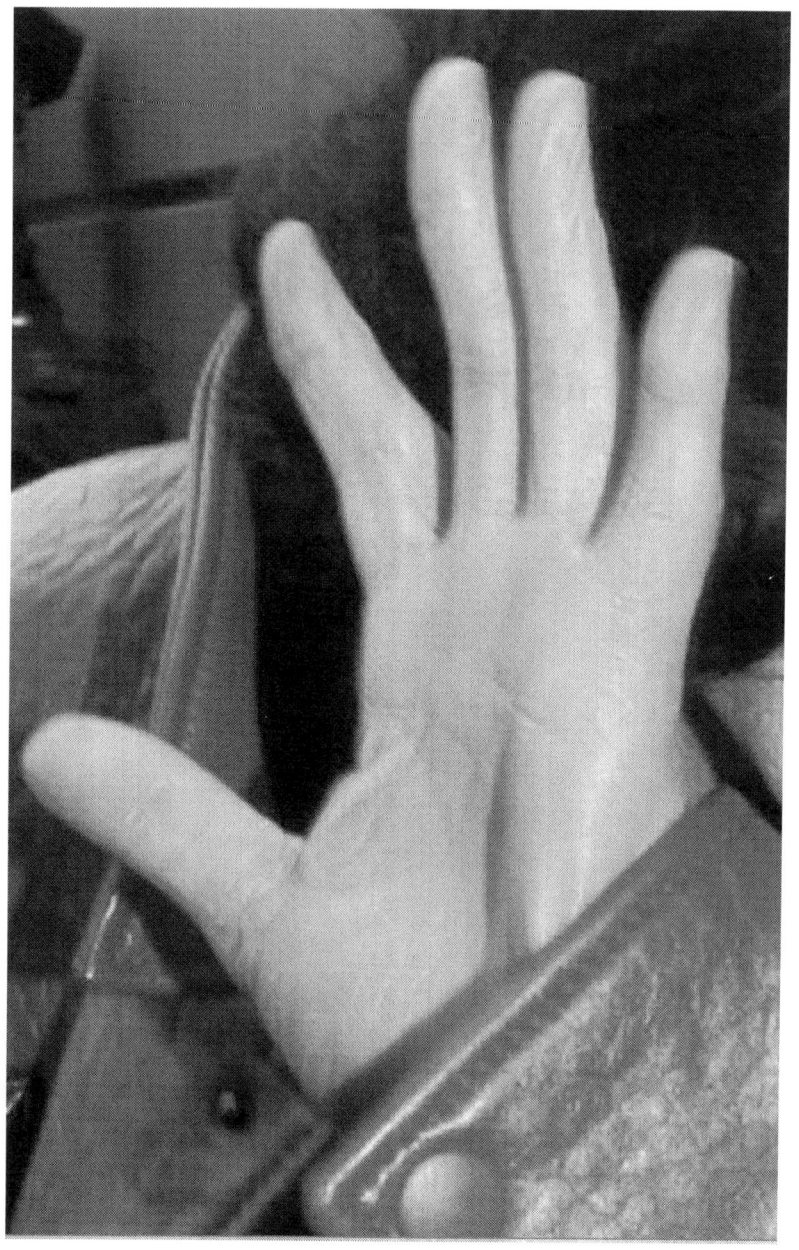

Kenny Ortega Testimony

Ortega states he has been a director since the 1980s, a choreographer since the 1970s. He first met Michael Jackson in 1990, Michael Jackson called him to work on the Dangerous tour. He was a co-creator and director of production, as well as the History tour. For HIStory tour, he supervised choreography, Michael Jackson did most of it. Ortega stated he was also responsible for costuming and lighting and the same for the This Is It tour. Michael Jackson and Ortega had been in touch for the last few years before Michael Jackson died. AEG told Ortega that Michael Jackson wanted Ortega for the This Is It tour, then Michael Jackson told Ortega himself. Ortega stressed that Michael Jackson was excited for This Is It, and that Michael Jackson said this is the time to do it.

Ortega started working in the middle of April '09 on This Is It. Michael Jackson was heavily involved. Ortega states that Michael had several reasons for wanting to tour now. First, Michael's children had taken in interest in his music and his performances, Michael felt the kids would now appreciate live performances. Second, he wanted to do a tour for his fans. Michael was allowing his fans to choose the songs which would be performed on This Is It. Third, Michael felt that his environmental songs, such as Heal the World and Earth Song, were just as important or more important now that when they were written and performed. Preparation for This is It started as Center Stages In Burbank. Ortega, Michael Jackson and Travis Payne were conceptualizing the tour. Ortega states at this point, he was meeting with Michael Jackson 3 to 4 times a week. Rehearsals began at the Forum in Los Angeles in the beginning of June, '09. Michael's children did not attend rehearsals because he wanted them to focus on school. The rehearsals lasted 5-7 hours, from late afternoon until evening. There was stating, tech work, lighting and musical rehearsals done by Michael Jackson. Ortega states he met Murray in April or May of '09. Michael Jackson introduced Ortega to Murray at his home on Carolwood Drive. Murray came to rehearsal rarely; never at Center Stages, once at the Forum and never at Staples. Michael Jackson was not showing up for rehearsals in the middle of June, the last week at the Forum. Ortega was told it was a scheduling problem, and that there was a "continued absence". Friday, June 19, while still at the Forum, Ortega says Michael Jackson "wasn't right, wasn't well". He was chilled, appeared "lost and a little incoherent". Ortega states he gave Michael Jackson some food, wrapped him in blankets and gave him a heater. Michael, according to Ortega, asked him if he could sit and watch the performance, with Travis Payne filling in for Michael Jackson. Ortega agreed. Ortega emphasizes that he'd never seen Michael Jackson like that, and that he suggested Michael go home. Ortega is asked about an email that was sent to Randy Randy Phillips at AEG Live on June 21, 09. In the email, Ortega reiterates that Michael was ill, chilled and was sent home. Ortega also states that Michael Jackson will need psychological help and lots of nurturing.

Text of the email Randy

"I will do whatever I can to be of help with this situation. If you need me to come to the house, just give me a call in the morning. My concern is now that we've brought the doctor into the fold and have played the tough love, now or never card is that the artist may be

unable to rise to the occasion due to real emotional stuff. He appeared quite weak and fatigued this evening. He had a terrible case of the chills, was trembling, rambling and obsessing. Everything in me says he should be psychologically evaluated. If we have any chance at all to get him back in the light. It's going to take a strong therapist to help him through this as well as immediate physical nurturing. I was told by our chereographer that during the artists costume fitting with his designer tonight they noticed he's lost more weight. As far as i can tell there is no one taking care responsibility (caring for) for him on a daily basis. Where was his assistant tonight? Tonight I was feeding him, wrapping him in blankets to warm his chills, massaging his feet to calm him and calling his doctor. There were four security guards outside his door, but no one offering him a cup of hot tea. Finally it's important for everyone to know , I believe that he really wants this. I twould shatter him, Break his heart if we pulled the plug. He's terribly frightened it's all going to go away. He asked me repeatedly tonight if i was going to leave him. H e was practically begging for my confidence. It broke my heart. H e was like a lost boy. There still may be a chance he can rise to the occasion if we get him the help he needs"

Sincerely, Kenny

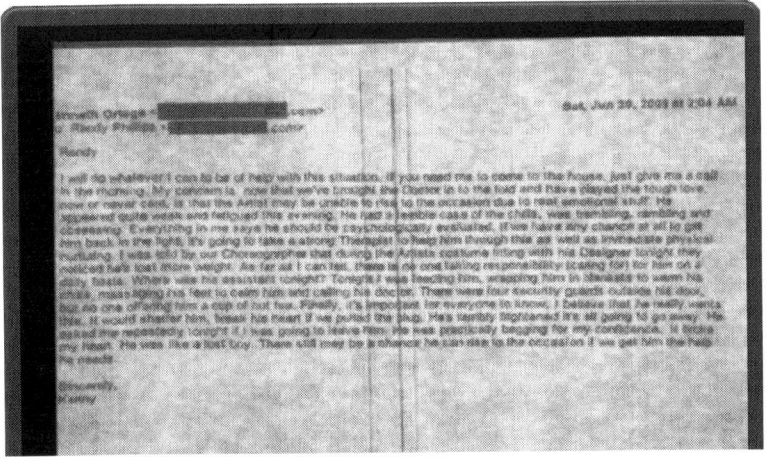

Ortega states that there was a meeting on 6/19, with the heads of AEG, Randy Phillips and Gongaware. Ortega heard that Randy Phillips and Gongaware told Michael Jackson that if he didn't start showing up to rehearsals, the This Is It tour would be cancelled.

On 6/20/09, Ortega is asked to go to Michael Jackson's house for a meeting with Randy Phillips, Frank Dileo, Conrad Murray and Michael Jackson. The topic is that Murray is upset that Ortega home. Murray tells Ortega that he should stop being an amateur doctor, and leave that to Murray. Ortega clarifies that he did not make the decision to send Michael home on the rehearsal date 6/19, it was a mutual decision between Ortega and Michael Jackson. Ortega states that Murray's demeanor is stern. Ortega states there were no rehearsals on 6/21 or 6/22. On 6/23, This Is It performance is shown, The Way You Make Me Feel, Michael Jackson wearing a red and a blue shirt. On 6/24, Michael Jackson is fully involved, a full participant. Earth Song on This Is It was done on 6/24, the very last rehearsal that Michael did before he died. Michael Jackson is wearing a black jacket and black sweats. Ortega states that the last time he saw Michael Jackson, he told him he loved him, and Michael Jackson said I love you more. Ortega tells the prosecutor that Michael Jackson had plans for This Is It beyond the London tour. He planned on touring to the US. He also planned on making movies; a full length Thriller and the Legs Diamond story, which Smooth Criminal is based on. Ortega states on 6/25 that the illusion part of This is It was supposed to happen that day. Michael Jackson was supposed to stand on a bed, flames were supposed to shoot up and Michael Jackson was disappear. He would reappear on a cherry picker above the crowd. On cross examination, Ortega denies that he told Karen Faye that he "read Michael the riot act" or "don't placate him".

Paul Gongaware Testimony

Gongaware is the co-CEO of AEG. AEG was the producer and promoter of This Is It.

Gongaware states that he was also involved with Michael's Dangerous and HIStory tours. They contracted 31 shows because Michael wanted to do 10 more shows than Prince. They put 10 show tickets on sale just to engage how strong the sales are going to be. It was sold out instantly. Then they put the rest of the shows on sale and increased the concert number to 50. Michael said that he would do 50 shows. All 50 shows were sold out and even after that there were 250,000 people still in que for tickets. They could have sold out another 50 shows.

DA Brazil asks Paul Gongaware to go over Michael's performance schedule for the upcoming weeks. July 5 rehearsals / 8 shows, August 10 shows / no rehearsal, September 9 shows/no rehearsal, October / November/ December no show / no rehearsal, January 3 rehearsals/10 shows, February 10 shows/no rehearsals, March 3 shows/no rehearsals.

DA Brazil asks Gongaware about a production meeting at Carolwood house. Gongaware says Michael came a little late because he was at Dr. Klein. He seemed little off and little slow than usual. His speech was slurred. Yet he participated to the meeting.

Deborah Brazil

Gongaware said that in May Michael told him to hire a personal physician, Dr. Murray, in May. Gongaware called Murray. Murray told him that he had 4 practices that he needed to close and lay off people and asked $5 Million a year to do it. Gongaware told him it would never happen and ended the negotiations. Gongaware believed they could get a more reasonable priced doctor in London. Michael said they needed to look after "the machine" (his body) and wanted Murray. Gongaware received a call from Michael Amir Williams who said that Michael wanted him to hire Dr. Murray. Gongaware heard on the background Michael saying "offer him 150". He called Dr. Murray again and said that he was authorized to offer him $150,000 a month. Murray accepted. Gongaware asked Murray how will this work as he wasn't licensed in UK. Murray told him not to worry and he'll take care of the license. Employment contract was being drafted.

21

Another early June meeting in Carolwood with Ortega, Dileo, Randy Phillips, Gongaware, Murray and Michael. The meeting happened because Kenny Ortega believed that Michael wasn't at the stage he needed to be and they might not be ready for the show. Gongaware said that the tone in the meeting was great and that Michael wasn't defensive on the contrary he was engaged. They discussed what they can do to give Michael everything he needs to get to where he needs to be such as health and eating habits.

Murray Trial Summaries Day 2 / September 28 -2011

Resuming with Paul Gongaware on the stand. Ms. Brazil is continuing cross examination.

The recapped schedule for tours. From Jul to Sept there were 27 shows then a break from Oct-Dec. Then there were 23 shows between Jan-Mar. (8 shows in July, 10 in August, 9 in Sept, 10 in Jan, 10 in Feb., and 3 in Mar.) After the tour ended in March there were plans to add additional shows but Paul Gongaware stressed these were only plans. Early June there was a meeting to discuss Michael Jackson's health and stamina attended byMichael Jackson,Conrad Murray, Paul Gongaware, Frank Dileo, Randy Randy Phillips. It was a positive meeting. Paul Gongaware was also aware of the June 20 meeting but did not attend. Paul Gongaware saw Conrad Murray at rehearsals at Forum rehearsal after the early June meeting. Paul Gongaware did not see Murray at other meetings. Paul Gongaware saw Michael Jackson rehearse on June 24th and 25th and thought Michael Jackson was strong, excited, full of energy, and engaged.

Defense cross examination

Defense go over Paul Gongaware's history with Michael Jackson. Paul Gongaware says he was tour manager of Dangerous and did not see Michael Jackson very much. In HIStory tour for the first leg he worked with the promoter and in the second leg he was tour executive. Paul Gongaware talked and interacted with Michael Jackson in the second half of HIStory. Paul Gongaware worked on This Is It from the start. Defense brings back the day Michael came from Dr. Klein. Paul Gongaware says he saw a slower speech pattern and a little slur in his speech. Paul Gongaware says he was on the look out for any drug usage by Michael. Paul Gongaware says his relationship with Michael was business relationship but friendly. If Paul Gongaware needed to get in touch with Michael Jackson, he would see him at rehearsals if Michael Jackson was there. Or, if needed, he would go through Michael Amir.

Meeting in early June was pushed by Kenny Ortega who was concerned that Michael Jackson was missing rehearsals. Paul Gongaware did not know how many practices Conrad Murray had, the value of his practices, or what kind of doctor Conrad Murray was. When he turned down $5 mil, Conrad Murray did not try to negotiate another price. That was the end oof their correspondence until Michael Jackson prompted Paul Gongaware to contact Murray and offer Conrad Murray $150,000/mo. Paul Gongaware did not know Murray was a cardiologist. He did not read the final contract and did not know how long Murray was to receive $150,000. He did not see the completed contract between Murray and AEG. Paul Gongaware was not involved and did not know about the contract between AEG and Murray.

Defense tried to bring up lawsuit against Paul Gongaware and AEG that is by Katherine and he was shot down.

Brazil recross

Paul Gongaware did not know Conrad Murray gave Michael Jackson nightly doses of propofol. Conrad Murray did not seem surprised that Paul Gongaware was contacting him about his services. He didn't have to explain in depth why he was calling. Paul Gongaware says a personal doctor for tour is normal but the $5 million was high in his opinion.

Defense recross

Paul Gongaware made a phone call to another doctor to get an idea about acceptable payment. Michael Jackson said "they needed to take care of the machine." There were no further conversations about any medical needs of Michael Jackson.

Kathy Jorrie Testimony

Examination of Kathy Jorrie is a lawyer with Luce, Forward, Hamilton, Scripps and is in charge of their Los Angeles office.

She was contracted by AEG to draft a contract for services involving Conrad Murray and Michael Jackson. She began drafting contract in May-June timeframe after being contacted by Tim Wooley of AEG. Tim Wooley sent her basic information. Kathy Jorrie sent first draft of the contract to Tim Wooley on June 15th. Tim Wooley forwarded the contract to Conrad Murray and Kathy Jorrie received phone call from Conrad Murray about the contract draft. The start date of Murray's contract was when all three parties signed the contract. The contract was not valid until this was done. Initally Conrad Murray contract had a end date of September 2009. Conrad Murray called Kathy Jorrie asking to change the end date to March 2010. Kathy queried Conrad Murray as to whether he asked Michael Jackson about getting paid during the hiatus of Oct-Dec and all of the way til Mar 2010. Conrad Murray said he did and Michael Jackson was willing to pay for his services during hiatus and till March 2010.

Kathy Jorrie spoke to Conrad Murray twice about changes to contract. Conrad Murray requested certain changes, one was for the start of his payment to be retroactive to May, 2009. Kathy Jorrie said Conrad Murray did not want his name on the contract but instead wanted the name of his company, Sade Anding Holdings. Kathy Jorrie said she could add the company to the contract but needed to have his name on it as well. Another change was for a medical professional to be available in London. Kathy Jorrie asked Conrad Murray why this was needed. Conrad Murray said it was for if Murray was unavailable or needed to rest, that someone would be there. There was a right to terminate the contract immediately if Michael Jackson no longer wanted Conrad Murray. Also, if the tour was cancelled. Murray wanted a provision that said if a termination for any of those reasons occurred past the payment date of the 15th of the month, Conrad Murray would not have to return the payment for that month. Kathy Jorrie had a conversation on Jun 18th with Conrad Murray about medical equipment needed to be included as a provision in the contract. Kathy Jorrie wanted to know why he needed this equipment including a CPR machine. Conrad Murray said when Michael Jackson was performing at the O2 arena he was going to be performing extraordinary things. Also considering his age, Conrad Murray wanted the machine. Kathy Jorrie asked wouldn't this be at the arena? Conrad Murray told her he didn't want to take any chances. Kathy Jorrie was worried Michael Jackson might have a heart problem or was unhealthy. Conrad Murray assured her he was healthy. Conrad Murray told Kathy Jorrie three times that Michael Jackson was in perfect health. They also discussed where Conrad Murray was licensed to practice medicine. Murray told Kathy he was licensed to practice in CA, TX, NV, Hawaii. June 23 conversation: Conrad Murray had some revisions he wanted. He asked the term to be changed from September 2009 to March 2010. Start date was changed to May 1. Contract said "services requested by the producer" Conrad Murray asked it to be changed to "artist". Kathy Jorrie asked Conrad Murray to help with medical records of Michael Jackson to submit to insurer for concert cancellation insurance. Insurer company asked for 5 year of medical history. Conrad Murray asked Kathy Jorrie to send what is required to Michael Jackson's house. He said that he had only been the physician of Michael Jackson for 3 years and since Michael Jackson was in such good health, the file would be very tiny. Kathy Jorrie later provided Conrad Murray insurer company's information so that he can contact directly. Conrad Murray repeatedly told her Michael Jackson was healthy, in excellent condition, he was great. Prosecution presented contract that Murray sent to Kathy Jorrie on June 24th. The only signature on it was Conrad Murray.

Above where Michael Jackson was supposed to sign reads: "The undersigned hereby confirms that he has requested Producer to engage Dr. Murray on the terms set forth herein on behalf of and at the expense of the undersigned."

The contract was between Murray, AEG Live, GCA Holdings with the consent of Michael.

Defense cross examination

Contract was not signed and no payment was made to Conrad Murray - at least by AEG. Conrad Murray had to provide liability insurance and medical malpractice insurance. Conrad Murray told Kathy Jorrie he would need the equipment in London. First time Kathy Jorrie talked to Conrad Murray was on the 18th. When she received the information from Tim Wooley, the CPR machine was already on the list of machines Conrad Murray needed. Kathy: "Murray said he needed the CPR machine for Michael Jackson at the venue. He did not indicate home use." Kathy Jorrie was not aware of the hours Conrad Murray would be providing services to Michael Jackson. She assumed they would be during the day. She had no hint that the services would be at night. Records were not provided to Kathy Jorrie . But she requested that medical reords be sent to the broker trying to secure the insurance (Bob Taylor). According to the contract Conrad Murray was not prohibited from doing other things at all. Contract was terminable at the discretion of Michael Jackson. Conrad Murray was not guarateed the next month of employment.

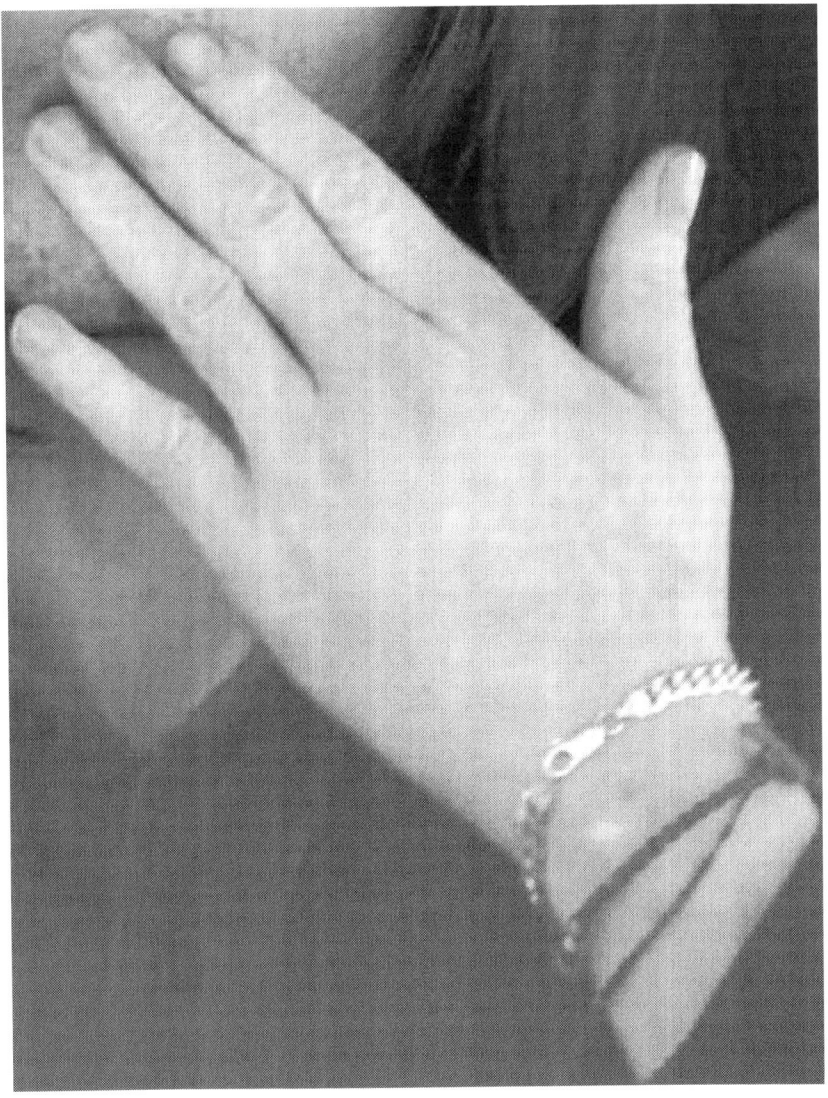

Michael Amir Williams Testimony

Personal assistant of Michael Jackson. Had been employed by Michael Jackson in mid 2007. Before this he had been brought on to archive and organize Michael Jackson's films and DVD's.

Michael Amir Williams did anything Michael Jackson needed and considered himself a friend of Michael Jackson's. Michael Amir Williams was a liason between Michael Jackson and security and major staff. Michael Amir Williams would come to Carolwood and call to make sure Michael Jackson didn't need anything. If not, he would go to the security trailer. According to Michael Amir Williams only Michael Jackson and his three children lived at Carolwood on a continuous basis. Walgren then shows several pictures depicting the layout and some interior/ exterior photos of Carolwood. Security routine: An advance vehicle, Michael Jackson in principal vehicle with driver and Michael Amir Williams and a security detail following them. Fans outside the house. If any security ever did anything against his fans, they would be gone according to Michael Amir Williams. Michael Amir Williams mentions Michael Jackson stopping, talking to fans, getting gifts, pictures to sign.

Michael Amir Williams said he was a fan first so tried to sneak to see of Michael Jackson performing. But Michael Jackson usually had him doing things for him/ running errands. It was a rule across the board that no one would go upstairs unless they were asked specifically which was very rare. Michael Amir Williams said that Michael Jackson liked his privacy. Michael Amir Williams met Murray for the first time in 2008 in Las Vegas. He saw Murray visiting Michael Jackson's house in Las Vegas in 2007. Michael Amir Williams would call Murray in 2008 at Michael's request to treat the children and him. Amir said that in Apr/May/Jun it was common to see Murray's BMW parked there after rehearsals and still there in the morning. During this time Michael Jackson asked Michael Amir Williams to sometimes call Conrad Murray even though he had a cell phone. Michael Amir Williams said they left for rehearsals late afternoon and did not return after it was dark although the time varied Michael Amir Williams said that it was not uncommon for him to call Murray ahead of time to make sure he was at home. Michael Amir Williams said they were late on the 24th going to the Staples Center. They left around 5 or 6pm give or take an hour or two. Michael Jackson was in good spirits ans was adamant about getting there on time. Amir said that he thought the rehearsal on the 24th was great. "Michael Jackson told me he only gave 30/40% at rehearsals. But I thought it was great." Michael Amir Williams lived in downtown Los Angeles and left Carolwood to go home after making sure that Michael Jackson was in the home. Security was 24 hrs around home. They would either be checking gates, doing perimeter checks but were stationed in the trailer. At 12:13pm, Michael Amir Williams received a phonecall from Conrad Murray. Michael Amir Williams was not able to answer this since he was in the shower trying to get dressed. When he came out and saw the phone, he had a message. The message said to call Conrad Murray right away. He then called Conrad Murray back. Conrad Murray didn't ask him to call 911. Conrad Murray told him to "Get here right away and send someone up" and that Michael had a bad reaction. A still photo of the phone (Michael Amir Williams's phone) was labeled People's 12 and the video of the voicemail was marked as People's 13. A transcript of the video message was labeled as People's 14.

"Call me right away. Please call me right away. Thank you."

Walgren goes over Michael Amir Williams's phone calls on the 25th.

At 12:15 Michael Amir Williams calls Conrad Murray back and Conrad Murray tells him that Michael Jackson had had a bad reaction and asks him to get someone up to the room. Amir said Murray did not ask me to call 911 initially. After he got off of the phone with Conrad Murray, Michael Amir Williams called Faheem Muhammad at 12:16 and told him to go upstairs. Faheem Muhammad told Michael Amir Williams that he was not on the property to run an errand to go to the bank. Michael Amir Williams told him to hurry and get back home. There were then 3 calls between Amir and Alvarez that were not being connected so he then contacted Derrick Cleveland (another security). He did not get him. Later he was able to talk with Alvarez. He told Alvarez to go to the house and told him to run. Nanny opened the door. Alvarez asked Michael Amir Williams for permission to go into the house and go upstairs. Alvarez hanged up the phone after a little while. Michael Amir Williams made multiple phonecalls.

Amir: "It took maybe 30/40 minutes to get from my home to Carrolwood. When he got there medics were bringing gurney down."

Michael Jackson's kids were in the car to follow the ambulance to the hospital. Michael Amir Williams thinks Conrad Murray looked frantic. Conrad Murray ride with the ambulance. People were following them to the hospital. Michael Amir Williams shielded the children with their jackets and took them inside the hospital to a private room with their nanny. They placed a security on the door. Michael Amir Williams waited outside the room they were working on Michael. Slowly people such as his manager and family came to the hospital. Later they learned that Michael Jackson dead.

After Michael was announced dead, Murray asked him if he or someone else could take him back to the house so he could get some cream of Michael Jackson's that he was sure Michael Jackson would not want the world to see. Michael Amir Williams said "let me check". He spoke about this with Faheem Muhammed. He told Faheem Muhammad he was goig to tell Conrad Murray that the police had his keys. He then spoke to Conrad Murray again who asked to be taken to go get something to eat. Michael Amir Williams refused. Michael Amir Williams went to Faheem Muhammad and told them to call the security and tell them to lock down the house and do not let anyone go in or out. Michael Amir Williams did not see Conrad Murray after that talk about food. Michael Amir Williams gave Conrad Murray's contact information to the police. After Michael Jackson 'was announced dead Michael Amir Williams and the other bodyguards loaded the cars and drove to fool the media so that the Jackson family can leave without being followed. On the ride Michael Amir Williams received a phone call asking them to come back to Carolwood. They spoke to the police at Carolwood. Oxygen tanks was normal. Security would pick oxygen tanks and bring to the house.

Defense cross examination

Defense asks if the first time Michael Amir Williams mentioned the cream to the detectives was in August 2009. Michael Amir Williams says yes.

Michael Amir Williams denies planning a lie with Faheem Muhammad. He says he just told Faheem Muhammad what he would say to Conrad Murray and Faheem Muhammad said "do whatever you need to do". Michael Amir Williams says there was a lot of police officers both at UCLA and Carolwood. Police asked him about the timeline of the day. Michael Amir Williams says that his initial talk with police wasn't in detail. Michael Amir Williams says he spoke to Michael several times a day. Defense goes back Michael Amir Williams first seeing Murray in 2007. Michael Amir Williams says that he just saw Murray to go to the house. Michael Amir Williams says he never learned or know how Michael Jackson and Murray met. Defense mentions the phone calls between Michael Amir Williams and Conrad Murray. Defense asks if sounded like an emergency. Michael Amir Williams: "When I hear someone has a bad reaction, I don't think anything fatal - me personally. I wasn't asked to call 911. He told me what to do and I did it what doctor told me to do - get someone up there quickly" 2 security on the property 24/7. House has gates and those gates are monitored. Family only allowed by Michael's request.

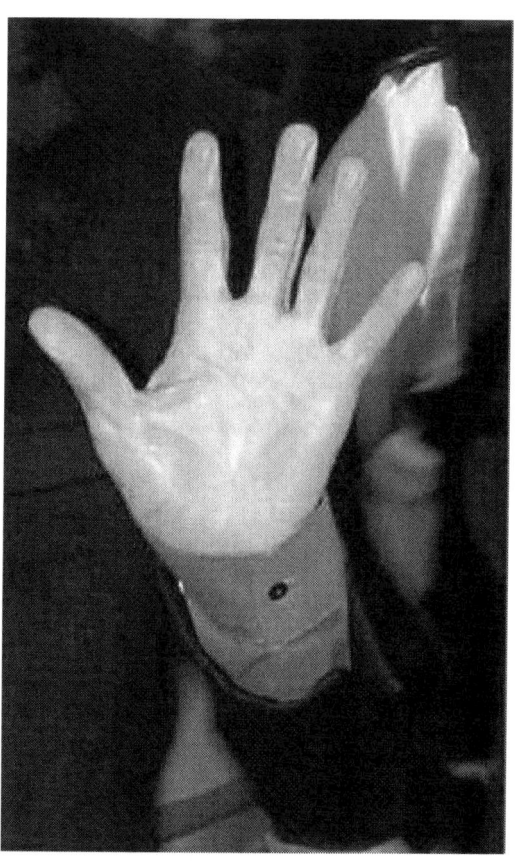

Faheem Muhammad Testimony

Prosecutor Walgren Direct

In June 2009, Faheem Muhammad states he worked as a security chief for Michael Jackson, for approximately 10 months. As chief of security, he made sure Michael Jackson's house and children were protected, and daily routine was safe and planned out. Faheem Muhammad states he was stationed in the trailer outside of the Carolwood home. Faheem Muhammad states that he would deal with Michael Amir Williams, not Michael Jackson directly. Faheem Muhammad states that he initially was hired as a driver, but then promoted to chief of security.

Faheem Muhammad states that he saw Murray daily and stayed overnight every day at the Carolwood home. Faheem Muhammad states he did not know the details as to why Murray was staying the night. Faheem Muhammad states that he saw oxygen tanks in the trailer, Murray brought the tanks to the back door, and security would bring them inside the trailer. On 6/24, Faheem Muhammad drove Michael Jackson to Staples to his last rehearsal, leaving at approximately 7 p.m. Michael Amir Williams accompanied both Faheem Muhammad and Michael Jackson to Staples. Faheem

Muhammad states that there was an underground parking lot, and that Alberto Alvarez would meet them, and take them on a golf cart to Michael Jackson's dressing room. Faheem Muhammad states that his duty was to set up security at specific doors, but that he was also able to observe some of the rehearsal. Faheem Muhammad stated that Michael Jackson's rehearsal was excellent and high energy. Faheem Muhammad states that he, Michael Jackson and Michael Amir Williams left at approximately midnight. Faheem Muhammad states that Michael Jackson stopped outside Staples to greet fans, and in front of the Carolwood home. Faheem Muhammad states that they arrive approximately 1 a.m. Faheem Muhammad states that security would normally take gifts that fans gave Michael Jackson and leave them at the bottom of the stairs. Michael Jackson would then say goodnight and go upstairs. Faheem Muhammad stated they had a security meeting, and then went home. On 6/25 Faheem Muhammad states that he arrives at Carolwood at approximately 11:45 a.m. Faheem Muhammad states that he left the property to go to the bank. Faheem Muhammad states that he then got a phone call from Michael Amir Williams, stating that Michael Jackson had a bad reaction and to go upstairs. Faheem Muhammad stated he was not at home, but that he would go back and he did. Faheem Muhammad states that he arrived back at the house, types in the PIN for the gate, and enters the house. Faheem Muhammad called Michael Amir Williams, asks if he can enter the house and go upstairs. Faheem Muhammad states the he did go upstairs. Faheem Muhammad entered the room that Michael Jackson was in, he states. Walgren asks Faheem Muhammad when he came into the room Michael Jackson was in, what did he see? Faheem Muhammad states that he saw Alberto Alvarez pacing the floor, he saw Michael Jackson's feet on the side of the bed, as Faheem Muhammad moved closer, he could see Michael Jackson's body and Murray to the side of Michael Jackson. Faheem Muhammad states that he saw Michael Jackson at the far side of the bed, his feet were on the floor. Faheem Muhammad states that Dr. Murray was to the right of Michael Jackson on the far side of the bed. Faheem Muhammad states that he asked Alberto Alvarez how it was going, Alvarez states it's not looking good. Faheem Muhammad states that he moved closer to the far side of the bed, Murray appeared to administering CPR, Murray was nervous, sweaty. Faheem Muhammad states that he then saw Michael Jackson's face and his full body. Faheem Muhammad states that Michael Jackson's eyes were open, mouth slightly open, and when asked, Faheem Muhammad states that Michael Jackson appeared to be dead. Faheem Muhammad states that he saw no medical equipment attached to Michael Jackson. Faheem Muhammad states he then realized that both Paris and Prince were inside the room slightly. Faheem Muhammad states that Prince was "slowly crying" and Paris was "balled up on the floor, crying". Faheem Muhammad got nanny and moved them to downstairs. Then Faheem Muhammad went back upstairs. Conrad Murray asked if they knew CPR, Alvarez went to help Conrad Murray with CPR. After Faheem Muhammad went back upstairs asked Alvaraz if 911 was called. Alvarez said yes. Faheem Muhammad went down again to get the cars ready. Paramedics arrived, Faheem Muhammad escorted them up to the room. Faheem Muhammad was mainly in the room while paramedics working. Faheem Muhammad left the room twice to put the children in the car and talk to the security saying that they'll be leaving soon and get ready for paparazzi. Faheem Muhammad said he saw an IV stand in the room, he did not realize any other medical equipment. They followed paramedics to UCLA. When they arrived paparazzi was at UCLA. They took their jackets to shield Michael Jackson's body so that paparazzi cannot take pictures. They also escorted the children inside. Faheem Muhammad talked to UCLA security about family arriving and not let in people trying to sneak in. Faheem Muhammad helped UCLA security to let Jackson family in and keep other people out.

Michael Amir Williams talked to Faheem Muhammad about Conrad Murray wanting to go home to get a cream. Faheem Muhammad says that they agreed that Conrad Murray should not be let into the house. Faheem Muhammad states that Michael Amir Williams came up with the story to say that police took their keys. Faheem Muhammad states that at UCLA Murray wanted to leave because he was hungry. Faheem Muhammad stated that there was a cafeteria at the hospital. Faheem Muhammad states he remembers seeing an IV stand in the room where Michael Jackson died. Faheem Muhammad states he does not remember if there is tubing attached to the IV, but he clearly remembers the IV stand in the room. Faheem Muhammad states that after he spoke to Dr. Murray, Faheem Muhammad went to the room where his children were. Faheem Muhammad believes that at that time, the children were getting ready to see Michael Jackson's body. Faheem Muhammad eventually left UCLA with Michael Amir Williams, Alberto Alvarez, and he's not sure, but maybe Isaac, a guard from Carolwood. Faheem Muhammad says he was not sure where they were going, but that the police called and asked all of the security to come to Carolwood. Faheem Muhammad states that they did talk to the police at Carolwood on 6/25. Faheem Muhammad states that he talked to the police again in August, 2009.

Defense Cross Examination - by Chernoff

Faheem Muhammad states his wife picked him up from the Carolwood home. Faheem Muhammad states that Murray asked if he would take him to Carolwood and to get him something to eat, Faheem Muhammad states he said no. When Faheem Muhammad left Carolwood, Murray's car was still at the residence. Faheem Muhammad states he watched Murray walk away from UCLA. Faheem Muhammad states he does not know what time he left the hospital. Faheem Muhammad states that the first time that he mentioned that Murray wanted to get something to eat and leave UCLA, was in August, 2009. Faheem Muhammad states that he made his statement to the police in his attorney's office. Chernoff repeated asks if Alberto Alvarez or Michael Amir Williams were there, or if Faheem Muhammad saw them before or after he talked to detectives. Faheem Muhammad states he did see Alberto Alvarez at the attorney's office. Faheem Muhammad states he knew Michael Amir Williams for 10 years, in a social capacity. Faheem Muhammad states his normal shift approximately at 11 a.m.

and leave at 7 p.m., but if Michael Jackson was leaving, he would stay and accompany him. Faheem Muhammad states he took Michael Jackson to see Dr. Klein. Faheem Muhammad states that Michael Jackson often left Klein's office tipsy, and at times, Klein's staff would have to accompany Michael Jackson downstairs and to the car. Faheem Muhammad states that Michael Jackson once said to him, "You must think I'm crazy for going to Dr. Klein's office so much." Faheem Muhammad states that he didn't see Michael Jackson one way or the other, and Michael Jackson states that he was going to Klein's office because his doctors told him that he had to go to a doctor for a skin disease. Faheem Muhammad states that at Carolwood in the month prior to Michael Jackson's death, he never saw another doctor come there. Faheem Muhammad states that he knows who Cherilyn Lee, and that she was hired for the kids. Faheem Muhammad states that he knew Lee professionally and that she was hired. Faheem Muhammad states that he called Cherilyn Lee for Michael Jackson. Michael Amir Williams told Faheem Muhammad that one of Michael Jackson's hands was hot, and one of his feet was cold, and to call Cherilyn Lee. Faheem Muhammad states that he thinks he left a voicemail, but ultimately talked to her, but cannot recall the conversation. Chernoff asks if Faheem Muhammad told the police that Conrad Murray was helping Michael Jackson to sleep. Faheem Muhammad said yes it was rumored. Chernoff asked if everyone knew, Faheem Muhammad says he can't say what other people knew. Faheem Muhammad says the security didn't discuss it among themselves. Faheem Muhammad says the house didn't have any land line phones. On 25th Faheem Muhammad came to Carolwood around 11 AM and left to go the bank after 12PM. Faheem Muhammad said that he can come and go and do tasks. Faheem Muhammad says there was a security camera recording the gate. Faheem Muhammad is not sure about a security camera recording the door of the house. June 27, Los AngelesPD asked Faheem Muhammad to help them to take surveillance tapes from the gates. Faheem Muhammad helped a technician from Los Angeles PD. Faheem Muhammad cannot remember what was downloaded. Defense again asks how many times Faheem Muhammad went up and down the stairs. Faheem Muhammad repeats 4 times going up and down the stairs again. Faheem Muhammad calls the scene shocking, seeing Michael. Faheem Muhammad says he doesn't recall what was on IV and does not recall any other medical equipment. Defense again asks about the security leaving the hospital. Faheem Muhammad said they received a call asking them to come back to Carolwood to talk to police officers. They were outside the front door talking to the detectives. Chernoff looks for pictures to show, and shows pictures of the bodyguards talking to the detectives. Faheem Muhammad yawns and nods to the jury while waiting the defense to find the picture. Chernoff spends several minutes asking Faheem Muhammad identify the people on the pictures. Faheem Muhammad said that after Carolwood he took the detective Abdul to Hayvenhurst so that he can talk to the nanny.

Prosecution Walgren redirect

Faheem Muhammad when talked to detectives on August 31, 2009 he was alone in the room with the detectives and his lawyer. Alvarez and Michael Amir Williams was not with her.

Nurse Lee is a nutritionist and that's all she does.

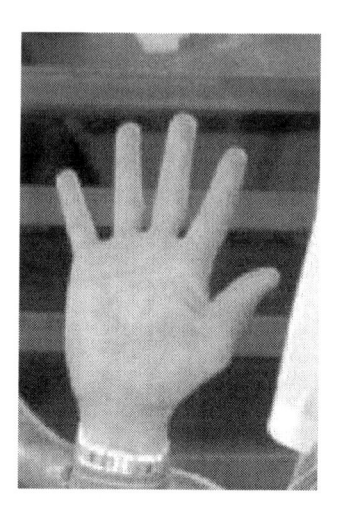

Murray Trial Summaries Day 3 /September 29-2011
Alberto Alvarez Testimony

Prosecutor Walgren direct examination

Month of June. Alberto Alvarez says that he worked for Michael Jackson in Carolwood. Alberto Alvarez was director of logistics, he was part of the advance team. He made sure everything was okay before Michael Jackson arrived to a venue.

Alberto Alvarez worked for Michael Jackson on/off since 2004. Alberto Alvarez was called to work for Michael Jackson December 2008/ January 2009. Alberto Alvarez said it was a good full time job with a good salary. Security would be in the trailer outside he house, they will only go inside when requested. Two different security: Property security and personal security. Personal security were Michael Amir Williams, Faheem Muhammad, Alberto Alvarez, Isaac and Derek. Alberto Alvarez saw Conrad Murray first after January 2009 in Carolwood. April/ May/ June Alberto Alvarez saw Conrad Murray 5-6 times a week. Alberto Alvarez knew that Conrad Murray was staying the night. Alberto Alvarez was aware about the oxygen tanks. Alberto

Alvarez from time to time saw Conrad Murray bringing empty oxygen tanks and take full ones. June 24th. After 5 PM they took Michael Jackson to rehearsals. Alberto Alvarez made sure everything was in order in Michael Jackson green room (dressing room) such as arranging the room temperature, checked the venue for security. Michael Jackson came around 6:30 - 7:00PM. Alberto Alvarez met Michael Jackson with golf cart and took him to his dressing room. Michael Jackson was very happy and in good spirits. Alberto Alvarez was behind the stage. Alberto Alvarez sometimes peeked to see his performance. Alberto Alvarez believed his performance was good. After the rehearsal they did the same routine. Michael Jackson was still happy and in good spirits. They came to Carolwood. Conrad Murray's car was already parked. Michael Jackson came home, they helped with the gifts. Michael Jackson said "goodnight". After they unloaded the gifts, they secured the front door and went to the security trailer for debriefing. After they went to home and house security stayed. June 25th Alberto Alvarez came to Carolwood at 10:15AM. He sat down in the trailer and waited for any specific instructions. He was in the security trailer around 12:15 PM. Phone records. 4 phone calls between Michael Amir Williams and Alberto Alvarez, those were attempts to reach each another. Another call from Michael Amir Williams to Alberto Alvarez, they finally spoke. Michael Amir Williams asked where was Alberto Alvarez, told him to get up and go to the front of the house without much commotion. Michael Amir Williams asked him if he was walking Alberto Alvarez said yes, Michael Amir Williams told him to run. Alberto Alvarez came to the front door and tried to open it but it was locked. Nanny came and unlocked the door. From the glass door Alberto Alvarez saw nanny Rosalind, Paris, Kai Chase and Conrad Murray on the second floor. Conrad Murray had both hands on the rail and was looking down. Alberto Alvarez told Michael Amir Williams he was in the house. Michael Amir Williams told him to run up the stairs. Prince was upstairs walking opposite direction of Alberto Alvarez. Walgren shows pictures and layout of the house and asks Alberto Alvarez to identify where Conrad Murray was and identify the rooms.

Alberto Alvarez said he only went upstairs 2 times in 6 months he worked for Michael Jackson to let Michael Jackson's hairdresser. Conrad Murray said to him "Alberto come quick", Alberto Alvarez realized the situation was serious. Alberto Alvarez hung up the phone call to Michael Amir Williams. Alberto Alvarez followed Conrad Murray into the room. Alberto Alvarez saw Conrad Murray giving chest comprehensions to Michael Jackson. Michael Jackson was in the bed. Alberto Alvarez saw Michael Jackson lying on his back, his hands extended out to his sides with palms up, his eyes and mouth was open. His face was slightly towards the left. Conrad Murray was using one hand (his left hand) giving Michael Jackson chest comprehensions. Conrad Murray said to him they need to get him to a hospital. Alberto Alvarez was walking towards the bed and reaching for his phone in his pocket. Prince and Paris followed him into the room, they were behind him. Paris screamed out "Daddy". Paris was crying. Conrad Murray said "don't let them see their dad like this". Alberto Alvarez ushered the children out the door and told them that everything will be okay and not to worry. When returned Alberto Alvarez asked Conrad Murray what happened. Conrad Murray said "he had a bad reaction". Alberto Alvarez was at the foot of the bed. Alberto Alvarez saw some sort of a plastic device on his penis to collect urine. Alberto Alvarez now knows that it was a condom catheter. Alberto Alvarez did not see any monitoring equipment, no ventilation equipment. Alberto Alvarez only saw a clear plastic tubing for Oxygen attached to Michael Jackson's nose. Alberto Alvarez saw an IV stand. Conrad Murray got some vials from the night stand and asked Alberto Alvarez to put them in a bag. Alberto Alvarez held out the bag and Conrad Murray dropped the vials. Conrad Murray told Alberto Alvarez to place that plastic grocery bag to the brown bag. Then Conrad Murray told Alberto Alvarez to get the bag in the IV stand and put it in the blue bag. Alberto Alvarez says there was a bottle in the saline bag. Walgren: "Why were you following these instructions?" Alberto Alvarez " I believed Conrad Murray had Michael Jackson's best intentions at mind, I didn't question his authority. I thought we were getting ready to go to the hospital". IV stand has 2

42

hooks. One hook had a saline bag, Conrad Murray didn't ask Alberto Alvarez to remove that one. Alberto Alvarez was only asked to remove the saline bag with the bottle. Alberto Alvarez saw milky white substance at the bottom of the saline bag.

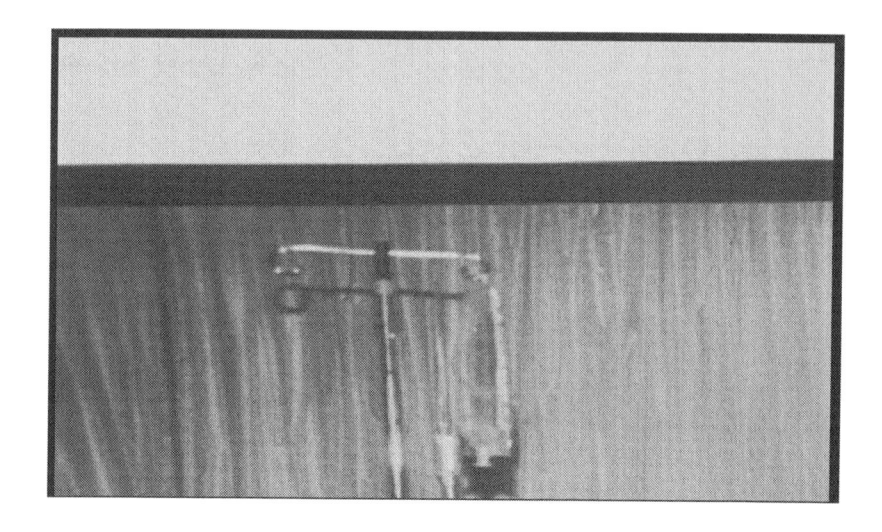

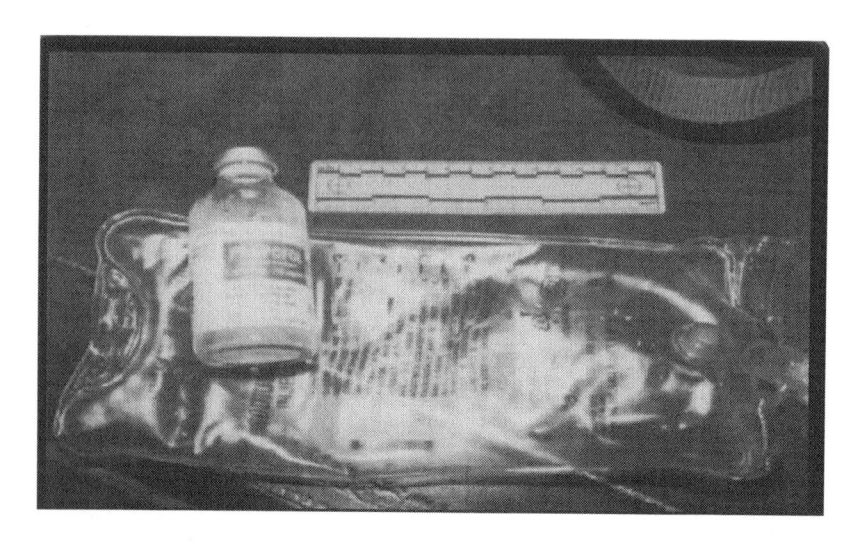

43

Walgren shows the saline bag pictures to Alberto Alvarez. The bad has a cut, Alberto Alvarez says he didn't see the cut on june 25th. Walgren shows the cut to the jurors. Walgren then shows empty 100ml Propofol bottle. Walgren replaces the bottle in the saline bag through the slit shows it to Alberto Alvarez and the jurors.

Alberto Alvarez says all these events happened very quickly. Alberto Alvarez says he was obeying Conrad Murray 's instructions.

911 call is played in court. Alberto visibly upset and looks like about to cry when listening to the call. Alberto Alvarez and Conrad Murray moved Michael Jackson from bed to the floor. Alberto Alvarez saw a clear plastic tube coming from the bag on the IV coming to Michael Jackson's leg. Conrad Murray removed it when they moved Michael Jackson. Conrad Murray took pulse oximeter from a bag and clipped it to Michael Jackson's finger. Alberto Alvarez says a few days to a week before June 25th, Conrad Murray asked the securities for Alberto Alvarez batteries. Alberto Alvarez saw Conrad Murray holding the device, Alberto Alvarez had asked him what it was and Conrad Murray said it was like a heart monitor. Faheem Muhammad arrived to the room. Alberto Alvarez said "It's not looking good". Conrad Murray asked if anyone knew CPR. Alberto Alvarez and Faheem Muhammad

looked to each other. Alberto Alvarez went to assist Conrad Murray doing CPR. Alberto Alvarez started doing chest comprehensions with two hands. Alberto Alvarez knew CPR before that day, he learned it when he was a swimmer. Conrad Murray was giving mouth to mouth. Conrad Murray said "this is the first time I do mouth to mouth. but I have to because he's my friend". Alberto Alvarez continued chest comprehensions. Paramedics arrived soon after and took over. Alberto Alvarez says there was no indication that Michael Jackson was alive. Paramedics moved Michael Jackson from the side of the bed to the foot of the bed. Alberto Alvarez went downstars twice; to check on the childern and to meet Michael Amir Williams. When paramedics were bringing Michael Jackson down, Alberto Alvarez was trying to distract Michael Jackson's kids so they wouldn't see their father like that. At UCLA Alberto Alvarez begged to paparrazzi to leave them alone saying it was a private moment, shielded Michael Jackson when going in, waited in the hospital. Conrad Murray came to Alberto Alvarez to thank for help, Alberto Alvarez said "we did our best". At that moment Alberto Alvarez didn't suspect that Conrad Murray did anything wrong. Conrad Murray first said he was hungry and asked if someone could take him home. Alberto Alvarez didn't answer, Conrad Murray then asked it to Michael Amir Williams. Alberto Alvarez last saw Conrad Murray outside the emergency room saying "I wanted him to make it". Alberto Alvarez and other security drove off after the announcement and Michael Jackson was taken to the coroners. They went to Carolwood, police was there. They stayed outside of the house while talking to the detectives. Alberto Alvarez was asked to bring children's dog Kenya to Hayvenhurst. 20-30 times media approached to Alberto Alvarez to give interviews and was offered money. Media have offerred him $200,000 to $500,000, Alberto Alvarez said no. Alberto Alvarez says this event was negative for his life. He went from a full time great wage job to bad financial position. Alberto Alvarez says he's totally wiped financially. Alberto Alvarez said he had been honest with the police to best of his ability.

Defense cross examination by Chernoff

Alberto Alvarez draw the IV bad picture after the preliminary hearing. Defense shows another drawing done for the police. Alberto Alvarez doesn't remember drawing it. Defense questions Alberto Alvarez never mentioned the pointy nub before. Chernoff says that the IV bag doesn't have any white substance in it today.

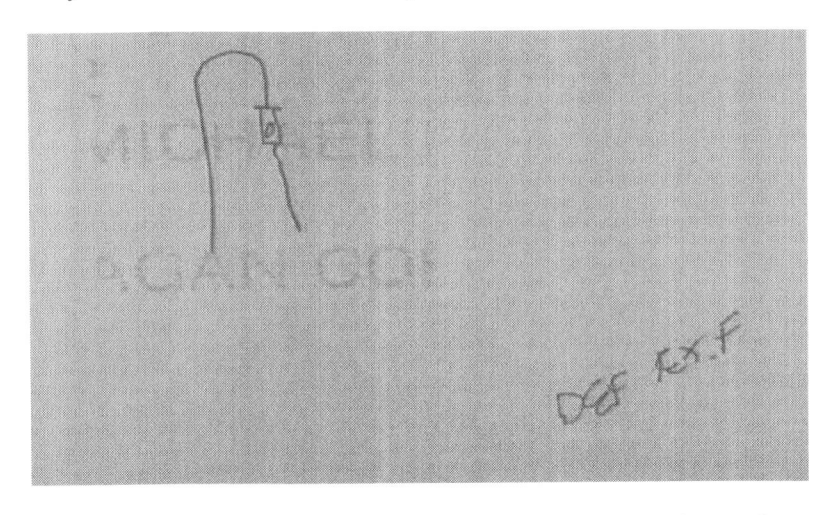

Chernoff asks if he could be confused about the timeline of events. Alberto Alvarez says no. Chernoff asks if it was possible if Conrad Murray asked Alberto Alvarez to collect the vials after the 911 call after the paramedics came and before they went to hospital. Alberto Alvarez says no. Defense going over Alberto Alvarez's phonecalls and how Alberto Alvarez went into the house. Alberto Alvarez understood something was wrong by that time but he didn't knew if it was related to Michael Jackson . Defense goes over what Alberto Alvarez did when he entered to the house. Alberto Alvarez basically repeats his previous testimony. Alberto Alvarez says he was shocked when he entered the room. Chernoff is writing Alberto Alvarez's timeline on a easel. Jurors has a problem with reading it. Defense continues with the events, at one moment they refer back to Alberto Alvarez's testimony from preliminary hearing. Chernoff is asking about the 911 call and putting the vials in a bag. Most of the questions are about if he yet called the 911 and how Conrad Murray put the vials in the bag. Basically defense is going over Alberto Alvarez's timeline of events. Walgren shows the saline bag pictures to Alberto Alvarez. The bad has a cut, Alberto Alvarez says he didn't see the cut on june 25th. Walgren shows the cut to the jurors. Walgren then shows empty 100ml Propofol bottle. Walgren replaces the bottle in the saline bag through the slit shows it to Alberto Alvarez and the jurors. Alberto Alvarez says all these events happened very quickly. Alberto Alvarez says he was obeying Conrad Murray 's instructions. 911 call is played in court. Alberto visibly upset and looks like about to cry when listening to the call. Alberto Alvarez and Conrad Murray moved Michael Jackson from bed to the floor. Alberto Alvarez saw a clear plastic tube coming from the bag on the IV coming to Michael Jackson's leg. Conrad Murray removed it when they moved Michael Jackson. Conrad Murray took pulse oximeter from a bag and clipped it to Michael Jackson's finger. Alberto Alvarez says a few days to a week before June 25th, Conrad Murray asked the securities for Alberto AlvarezA batteries. Alberto Alvarez saw Conrad Murray holding the device, Alberto Alvarez had asked him what it was and Conrad Murray Csaid it was like a heart monitor. Faheem Muhammad arrived to the room. Alberto Alvarez said "It's not looking good". Conrad Murray asked if anyone knew CPR. Alberto Alvarez and Faheem Muhammad looked to each other. Alberto Alvarez went to assist Conrad Murray doing CPR. Alberto Alvarez started doing chest comprehensions with two hands. Alberto Alvarez knew CPR before that day, he learned it when he was a swimmer. Conrad Murray was giving mouth to mouth. Conrad Murray said "this is the first time I do mouth to mouth. but I have to because he's my friend". Alberto Alvarez continued chest comprehensions. Paramedics arrived soon after and took over. Alberto Alvarez says there was no indication that Michael Jackson was alive. Paramedics moved Michael Jackson from the side of the bed to the foot of the bed. Alberto Alvarez went downstars twice; to check on the childern and to meet Michael Amir Williams. When paramedics were bringing Michael Jackson down, Alberto Alvarez was trying to distract Michael Jackson's kids so they wouldn't see their father like that.

At UCLA Alberto Alvarez begged to paparrazzi to leave them alone saying it was a private moment, shielded Michael Jackson when going in, waited in the hospital. Conrad Murray came to Alberto Alvarez to thank for help, Alberto Alvarez said "we did our best". At that moment Alberto Alvarez didn't suspect that Conrad Murray did anything wrong. Conrad Murray first said he was hungry and asked if someone could take him home. Alberto Alvarez didn't answer, Conrad Murray then asked it to Michael Amir Williams. Alberto Alvarez last saw Conrad Murray outside the emergency room saying "I wanted him to make it". Alberto Alvarez and other security drove off after the announcement and Michael Jackson was taken to the coroners. They went to Carolwood, police was there. They stayed outside of the house while talking to the detectives. Alberto Alvarez was asked to bring children's dog Kenya to Hayvenhurst.

Defense cross examination continued

Still discussing Alberto Alvarez's version of events and timeline. Chernoff writing the timeline on a piece of paper. Chernoff questions how Alberto Alvarez held the IV bag and got it from the stand. Alberto Alvarez says he got it bu holding it from the top of it. Alberto Alvarez first mentioned taking off the IV bag in August, 2009 at his second meeting with the police. He was also fingerprinted at that time. Chernoff again asks if Alberto Alvarez could be mistaken about his timeline. Alberto Alvarez said no. Alberto Alvarez: (looking at 911 transcript) Indicated when he placed Michael Jackson on floor according to transcript. OP says, let's get him to the floor-Alberto Alvarez acted on that order. Alberto Alvarez says that they got Michael Jackson on the floor while he was talking with 911 operator. Alberto Alvarez says he put his phone on his shoulder. Chernoff plays the 911 call and Alberto Alvarez identifies the point they got Michael Jackson on floor. Alberto Alvarez: Clarifies pic he drew. He clarified that there was a box with a wire sticking out of it, NOT a needle.

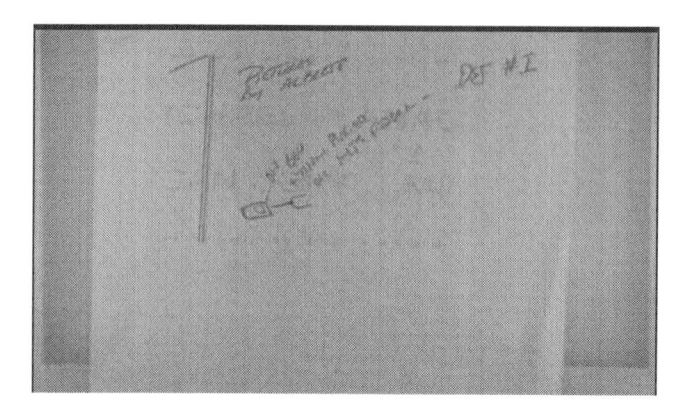

Chernoff mentions media offers. Alberto Alvarez says there have been media offers before he talked to the police August, 2009. Chernoff says Alberto Alvarez didn't mention most of the things he said in August interview in June interview. Chernoff plays a video of Alberto Alvarez at hospital. Alberto Alvarez was waiting outside the room where Michael Jackson's body was placed after he was announced dead. Chernoff mentions there was a lot of police around and asks Alberto Alvarez if he mentioned them about collecting the vials. Alberto Alvarez says no. Alberto Alvarez was interviewed by the police in the hospital.

sidebar

Bodyguards went to Carolwood, talked with the detectives. Chernoff shows pictures taken outside the house with detectives asking Alberto Alvarez to identify people in the pictures. Again Chernoff asks if Alberto Alvarez told the detectives about the vials then. Alberto Alvarez says no. Chernoff mentions saline bag and asks if that was connected to Michael Jackson. Alberto Alvarez says yes. Chernoff asks if it was connected to anything else, Alberto Alvarez says no. Alberto Alvarez sees a report on Consuelo Ng about evidence and saw detectives coming out of the house with a baby blue bag. Alberto Alvarez heard on the news about Propofol and heard it being white. Alberto Alvarez says that he realized that he handled those items and believed he needed to talk to the detectives. Alberto Alvarez believed he needed to report it to the police. Chernoff asks about Alberto Alvarez's work. Alberto Alvarez says he's unable to get a continious job. Alberto Alvarez's work history with Michael Jackson. In 2004 worked for Michael Jackson for 6 months. 2007 in Las Vegas worked for Michael Jackson for a few months. 2008 Las Vegas 2-3 months. After Michael Jackson's death Alberto Alvarez worked with Jackson family. Alberto Alvarez would call to check on the children. Katherine's assistant mentioned Alberto Alvarez could become a secruity for Jacksons. This talks happened Nov 2009. Alberto Alvarez worked for the Jacksons for a few months in 2010. Chernoff tries to ask Alberto Alvarez what other celebrities he worked for.

Objection. Sidebar.

Chernoff asks Alberto Alvarez about his relationship with Conrad Murray and if they were friends. Chernoff tries to ask questions about why would Conrad Murray would conspire with Alberto Alvarez to hide evidence.

Objection. Sustained.

Walgren redirect

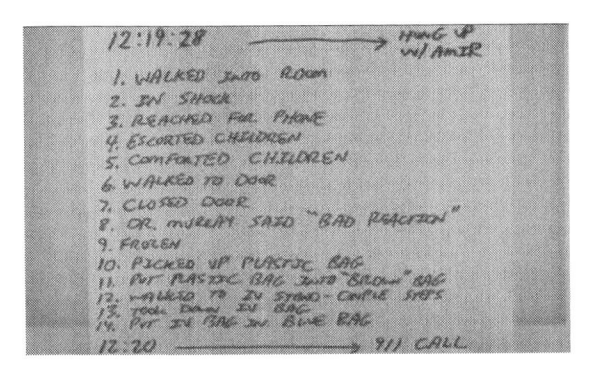

Walgren goes over the timeline Chernoff wrote, asks Alberto Alvarez if most of the events happened simultaneous continious events. Walgren asks questions very rapidly. Judge Pastor asks Walgren to slow down and jokes that "I see steam coming out"

Chernoff recross

Chernoff asks if Alberto Alvarez did these events quickly. Alberto Alvarez says he acted quickly and he's "very efficient". Laughter heard in the courtroom.

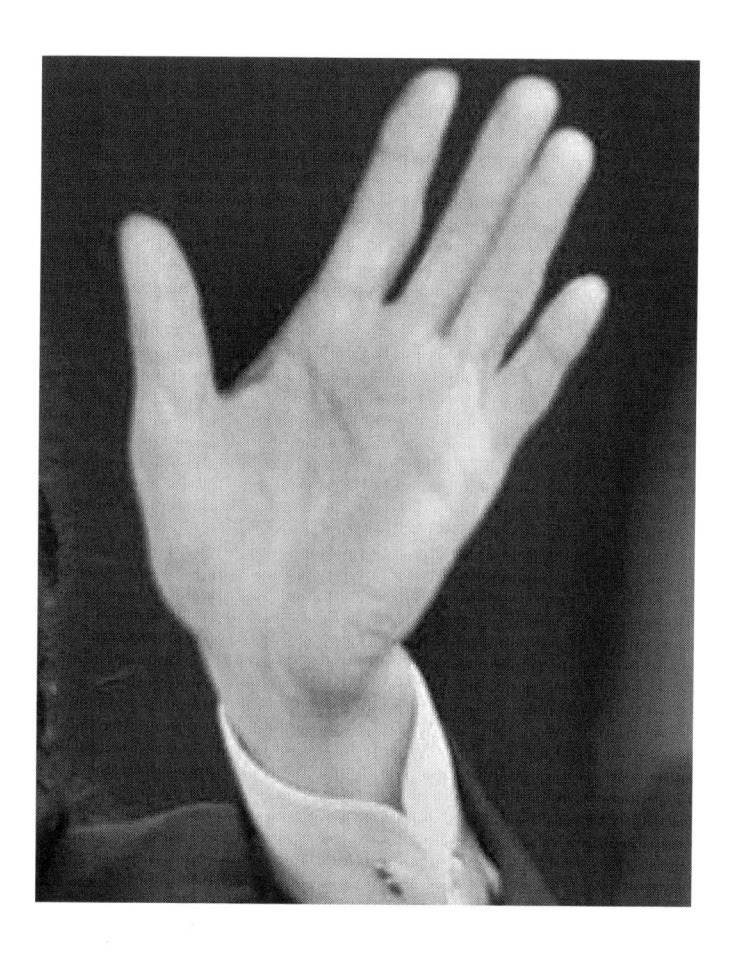

Kai Chase Testimony

Brazil direct

Kai Chase professional chef. March 2009 was working for Michael Jackson. Her duties was to prepare food for Michael Jackson and his children. Kai Chase learned what they liked and didn't like. Kai Chase did the shopping. Kai Chase says she enjoyed working for Michael Jackson and kis kids. Kai Chase wears professional chef uniform - chef jacket and bistro apron. Her apron had 2 pockets. Kai Chase said she kept track of time because she needed to follow the food cooking and had to get food on the table on time. Kai Chase says she had her cellphone in her apron pocket and kept track of time.

Kai Chase worked 6 days a week for Michael Jackson. Kai Chase came at 8 AM and prepared breakfast for the kids. Then prepared breakfast and juice for Michael Jackson for breakfast. Michael Jackson ate Granola, juices and vegetarian omelets. Healthy foods was very important for Michael Jackson and his kids. Kai Chase saw Michael Jackson eating with his kids. "It appeared to me that Michael Jackson had a close, loving relationship with his children and appeared to be happy around them." June 24. Arrived around 8:30AM. Prepared breakfast for children. Prepared Michael Jackson his beet juice which had beets, celery, apple, carrots. Kai Chase would see Conrad Murray in the mornings. He would come to the kitchen. He would sometimes come to leave or sometimes would come to get Michael Jackson's juice. Conrad Murray said Michael Jackson will be down shortly and Michael Jackson would like to have lunch with his children. Conrad Murray then went to other part of the house. Kai Chase saw Michael Jackson on June 24. They talked. Michael Jackson asked about the lunch, he smiled. Kai Chase says Michael Jackson was happy because he was going to have a lunch with his children. Kai Chase prepared the same Ahi Tuna salad so that Michael Jackson could take it to rehearsal. Kai Chase prepared Tuscan Bean soup for Michael Jackson for dinner. Kai Chase also prepared food for Conrad Murray as well. Kai Chase made dinner for children. Kai Chase left at 10 PM on June 24. June 25. Arrived between 8:00-8:30AM. Prepared breakfast for children. The soup Kai Chase prepared the previous day was still in the refrigerator. Kai Chase started to prepare Michael Jackson's breakfast. She prepared him Granola with Almond Milk. Michael Jackson's children would notify Kai Chase when Michael Jackson would eat his food. 9:45 AM Kai Chase leaves to go to market. She cames back around 10:30. Everything seemed the same as she left when she returned. Children were playing, music was playing. Kai Chase started preparing lunch. Michael Jackson always had lunch at 12:30PM. There was no difference on June 25th. Kai Chase was preparing Spinach cobb salad with organic turkey breast for lunch. Kai Chase had already prepared fresh juice for Michael Jackson. Conrad Murray didn't come to pick up the juice that day. Conrad Murray came down to the kitchen from the stairs between 12:05 and 12:10. Conrad Murray looked frantic. Kai Chase says Conrad Murray was nervous, frantic and he was shouting. Conrad Murray shouted "get help, get security, get Prince". Kai Chase stopped what she was doing and run to get Prince from the den. Kai Chase said to Prince "Hurry. Dr. Murray needs you. There might be something wrong with your father". Prince and Kai Chase went back to kitchen. Prince went to Conrad Murray. Kai Chase went back to work. Brazil asks if Conrad Murray asked her to call 911. Kai Chase says no. Brazil asks Kai Chase why she decided to get Prince. Kai Chase says Prince was in her sight and Conrad Murray seemed frantic and disturbed. Kai Chase wanted to get help as soon as possible and Prince was the closest. Security is outside. Prince was closer to her. Kai Chase returned to work. Kai Chase saw housekeeper crying at he foyer of the house. Kai Chase approached to them and asked them what was wrong, they said something might be wrong with Michael Jackson. Michael Jackson's kids were crying and screaming. They held hands and prayed in a circle. Kai Chase then saw security and paramedics running up the stairs. Kai Chase, housekeeper and the children stayed in the foyer. Soon security asked Kai Chase and the housekeeper to leave the house and Kai Chase left. Kai Chase says her heart is still broken. She is devastated. Kai Chase met with detectives a few days later. Several media contacted Kai Chase asking about what happened that day. After Kai Chase gave statements to the police, Kai Chase gave interviews to several media sources. Brazil asks if she was paid any money by US media, Kai Chase says no. Kai Chase mentions interviews she has done with the foreign media. One interview was with German media about food. She was paid $1,000 for it. Kai Chase also met with a French documentary, she was paid $1,000. She took part in 5 more interviews. She was paid in total $7,000 for all the interviews. Brazil asked if Kai Chase ever planned to get rich from her experiences with Michael Jackson. Kai Chase says no.

Defense cross Flanagan

Defense asks if Kai Chase was at house Sunday May 10th. Kai Chase says no. Kai Chase says Michael Jackson will come down for breakfast 2 times a week around 8:30 - 9:00 AM. Other days breakfast was taken up to his room. When Kai Chase come in the morning the gate was closed. She press a buzzer, tells who she is and one of the security guys will come to meet her. She can't recall which security let her in on the

25th. When she comes to the house, she had to knock the kitchen door to be let in. Children or housekeeper would let her in. On June 25th Michael Jackson's kids let her in. Kai Chase says she only had Michael Amir Williams's phone numbers. Kai Chase says there was no land line in the house and she didn't have any phone numbers for Alberto Alvarez, Faheem Muhammad, Nanny or Michael Jackson. Defense asks Kai Chase how far it was from the kitchen to the security trailer. Kai Chase explains the distance. Conrad Murray came down frantic. Conrad Murray yelled "go get help, go get security, go get Prince". Kai Chase thought it was emergency but did not know what kind of emergency it was. Kai Chase went into the den to get Prince. Kai Chase said " Prince Dr. Murray needs you. There might be something wrong with your father." Prince went with Conrad Murray. Kai Chase went back to work. Flanagan asks how old was Prince. Kai Chase says 12 years old at that time. Flanagan asks why she did not get the security. She said Prince was right in front of her. She thought there was a human being she can get immediately. She says she didn't want to take the time to go out and go to the security and get them. She didn't know if the security was there or left. She didn't want to take the chance. Flanagan goes over says that Kai Chase saw a frantic Conrad Murray and thought there was something wrong with Michael Jackson. Kai Chase says yes. Flanagan asks "He was asking for help, he was asking for security. Did you think a 12 year old child is going to be able to assist this doctor with a problem with Michael?". Kai Chase "I did what I was told and I went to get Prince". Flanagan asks if she ever saw Conrad Murray again, Kai Chase says no. Flanagan asks if Kai Chase ever told Conrad Murray that she would not get the security, Kai Chase says no.

Murray Trial Summaries Day 4/ September 30- 2011
Bob Johnson Testimony

Walgren Direct

Employed by Nonin Medical, designs noninvasive medical equipment such as pulse oximeters. Johnson states he is the Director of Regulatory Affairs Clinical Research and Quality Assurance. Johnson states his responsibilities are to get product approval with the FDA and Worldwide Health Ministries. Johnson states that the clinical research entails both animal and human research. Johnson states again that Nonin Medical designs pulse oximeters.

When prompted, Johnson states that pulse oximeters detects both pulse rate and red blood cells that have oxygen attached to them, basically determined oxygen saturation and a pulse rate, called SPO2. Johnson states that Nonin probably makes ten or models of pulse oximeters. Walgren asks if Johnson if familiar with model 9500, Johnson states yes. Johnson describes the "onyx 9500" is a fingertip oximeter, which displays both heart rate and SPO2. Johnson is asked to identify a pulse oximeter that was in Michael Jackson's bedroom at the time of death, he does. Johnson is asked to identify two numbers on the oximeter, Johnson explains that the "92" is the heart rate, and the top number is the percentage of red blood cells that have oxygen attached. Walgren then asks if the Nonin 9500 oximeter has an audible alarm, Johnson states no. Johnson also states that this particular model is used for spot checking. A doctor would use this if a patient were to come into their office to have their heart rate and pulse checked. Johnson then states that this model is not used for continual monitoring and that it is specifically label not to be used continually. Walgren then asks Johnson if Nonin makes oximeters that have an audible alarm, Johnson states yes. Walgren asks how much this particular model of oximeter costs, Johnson states $275 retail value. Walgren asks if Nonin makes a model of oximeter 2500A, Johnson states yes. Johnson states that the 2500A displays the same functions as the 9500, but also has visual and audible alarms. Johnson states that the alarm at its loudest, can be heard outside. Johnson states that the retail value of the 2500A model is $750. Walgren asks if Nonin makes a 9600 tabletop pulse oximeter, Johnson states yes. Johnson states that the readings are the same, heart rate, then moves to retail value, $1250 in 2009. Johnson also states that Nonin makes pulse oximeters that display capnography, which is the Co2 coming from a person's breath. Walgren asks Johnson if all of these models are available to lease, Johnson states that yes they are. When asked how much one of the most expensive models costs to lease, Johnson states about $40 a month.

Defense Cross

When asked if the model 9500 (the one found in the room Michael Jackson died in) is accurate, Johnson states yes. Johnson is asked if someone to monitor a patient for 15 minutes, would that model of oximeter be adequate, Johnsons states perhaps. Johnson is then asked if the pulse oximeter detects change, Johnson states yes. Johnson is asked if someone were there with a patient, under the influence of propofol for five or ten minutes, would there be a constant change in the pulse oximeter, Johnson states no. Johnson states that it is very difficult to constantly monitor the numbers, so it is not recommended for continuous monitoring. When asked what Johnson means by continuous monitoring, he states something other than a spot check or to take vital signs. Defense asks if it would be safe in monitoring every five minutes, Johnson states yes. Defense asks if it would be safe continuously for fifteen minutes, Johnson says only if the doctor is constantly monitoring the screen. Johnson states that it takes about five or ten seconds to get an accurate reading on the oximeter. Defense states that after the five to ten seconds, does the reading change, Johnson states yes. Defense then states that it can be used for constant monitoring, Johnson once again states that it cannot.

Walgren Redirect

Walgren asks if the difference between the audible versus the nonaudible pulse oximeter models is a big difference, Johnson states that it is a huge difference. Walgren states that it's the difference between life and death, Johnson states yes. Walgren states that if in another room, the inaudible oximeter is useless, Johnson states yes.

Flanagan (Defense) Recross

Defense once again asks if a doctor is constantly monitoring, is the pulse oximeter useless, Johnson states no.

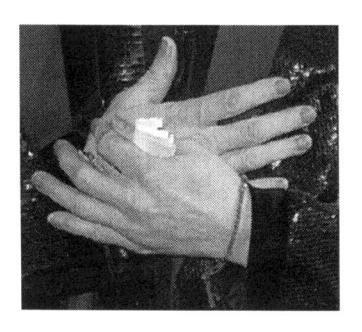

Robert Russell Testimony

Deborah Brazil, Prosecution Direct

Russell states that he had a heart attack in 2009 in Las Vegas. Russell stated that he met Dr. Murray in the emergency room in the hospital. Russell, Murray reviewed what had happened, and ultimately inserted stents to the heart to repair it. Russell states that this was the first time he had ever met Murray.

Russell states he went into the emergency room, and then went into a surgical room, where Murray and an anesthesiologist performed heart surgery. Russell states that he was awakened during the surgery, because he had been give too much medicine for his blood pressure, by the hospital staff. Russell states that after he was awakened, Murray said "here's your heart (on a screen), stay awake", and that Russell did not want to see it. Russell states that Murray installed three stents in his heart. Russell states that he wanted to leave the hospital that night, but that Murray was stern with him, told him he was minutes from death, and that if Russell left the hospital, he was a dead man. Russell was released from the hospital on approximately March 12, 2009. Russell states that he went to a follow-up visit on March 16, 2009, and that Murray advised him that he needed to have a second procedure to insert more stents into his heart. Russell states that Murray told him that because of the problems with the first surgery, Murray told Russell that he was unable to put all the stents in his heart, therefore Russell needed another surgery to finish inserting the stents. Russell states that he felt Murray treated him very well. Russell states that Murray told him that he had an opportunity to go to the UK, and take care of one person as a physician, but did not tell him who the one person was. Russell states that he made an appointment for the second surgery, and that he had the surgery in April of 2009. Russell states that the procedure was the same as the first, but that it was an outpatient surgery. Russell states that an anesthesiologist was present in addition to Murray and other medical personnel. Russell states that he went home the same day and had scheduled meetings for follow up care. Russell states that he went to the follow up visit, Murray told Russell that he had made a decision to take care of the one patient and that patient was Michael Jackson. Russell states that he has not told his staff, and that he was going to tell them after Russell and his wife. Russell states that Murray inferred that he had had an ongoing professional relationship with Michael Jackson. Russell states that he was very happy for Murray, and that Murray seemed highly excited and pleased that he would be working for Michael Jackson. Russell states that Murray advised that Russell needed further therapy for his heart and that it was important to his recovery. Russell states that the therapy for his heart began mid-April 2009 on a daily basis. Russell states that Murray is only there occasionally. Russell states that Murray advised him that he would not be there. Russell states that he asked the staff, and Murray called him at home to answer them. Russell states that he completed the therapy in early June, and had a follow-up visit on June 15 to get the results of therapy to see how Russell's heart was doing. Russell states that this visit was very important to him, but Murray did not keep the appointment. Russell states that he was notified by mail that Murray after June 15, mailed out to all patients, that Murray would be leaving his practices temporarily in order to take "a once in a lifetime opportunity". The letter stated that Murray would manage the practice, and would find a suitable replacement. Russell states that he was not surprised. Russell states he had a second follow-up visit on June 22, because Murray cancelled the appointment. Russell states that the June 22 appointment was also cancelled and was frustrated. Russell states that he felt he was dependent on Murray, because he had no referral, rescheduling and that Murray had all his medical records. On June 25, 2009, Russell calls Murray's office early in the morning. Russell states that he had formed a relationship with Murray's staff members because during the therapy, he had seen the staff members more than he saw Murray. Russell stated that he expressed his frustration to the staff members, he felt desperate, he threatened legal action, and that he felt abandoned. Russell received a voicemail later that morning from Murray on June 25, 2009. The voicemail played is Conrad Murray stating that Russell's therapy went very well. Russell states that he felt grateful that he took the time to call him. Russell felt that the statement was odd, because Murray stated that the heart was repaired, when months earlier Murray said it could never be fully repaired. Russell also stated it was odd that Murray had stated he was going on sabbatical, when all along Russell knew that Murray was going to take care of Michael Jackson. Russell stated that although at first he felt Murray's care was excellent, he also felt that he was abandoned.

Chernoff Defense Cross

Chernoff establishes that Russell and Chernoff have never met. Russell states that the medical care he received was unlike any he had never had before. Russell stated that Murray was adamant about how serious Russell's condition had been, and that Murray saved his life.

Russell states that Murray knew his wife. Russell states that his heart attack was on March 9, 2009, and that now, his heart is in good shape, according to his new cardiologist. Russell stated that his new cardiologist stated that the stents had been inserted properly.

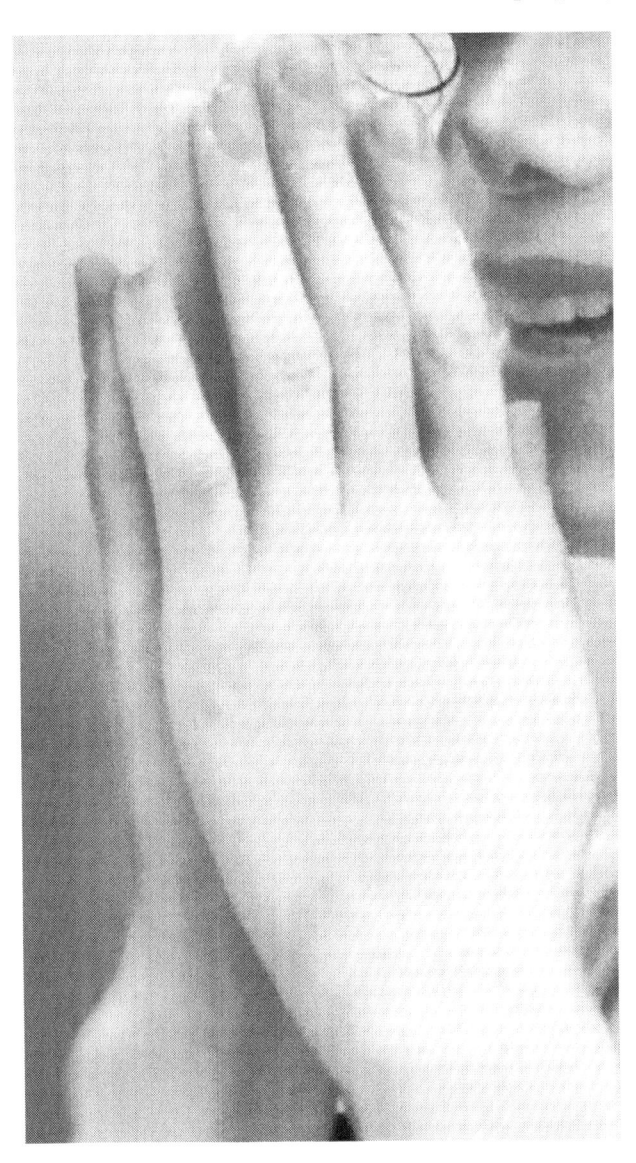

Paramedic Richard Senneff Testimony

Brazil Direct

Richard Senneff is a paramedic at Los Angeles Fire Department. Richard Senneff explains his training and experience and certification.

June 25th, Richard Senneff was working at fire station 71. They received a call to go to Carolwood. "Cardiac arrest. CPR in progress. 50 year old male. Patient not breathing" They went to Carolwood. Richard Senneff was the team leader and the radio man and he gather information and write records. Senneff rode in Ambulance 71 with Paramedic Blount. Fire Engine 71 followed them with engineer, fire fighter, fire captain and additional paramedic.

Brazil goes over People's Exhibit 43 and what's written on it.

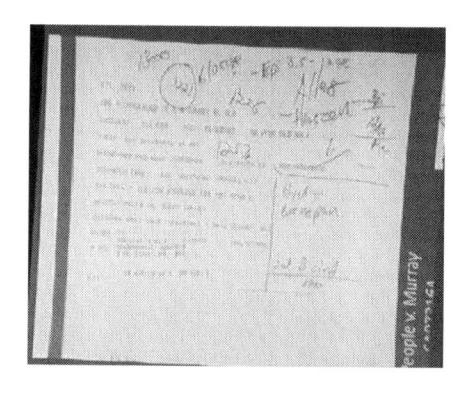

Print out information

Line 1 : Engine 71 Rescue Ambulance 71

Line 2: Address 100 Carolwood

Line 3: Incident number 5-12 Cardiac Arrest 12:21 call time 50 year old man

Line 4 : code cardiac arrest not breathing at all

Line 5: the phone number call came from

Line 6 : dispatch time the time they got the call at station 12:22

Line 7 : 911 call from a cell phone , caller is still on the phone with the dispatcher

Line 8 : Where the call is originated and transferred

At the end there's a patient identification sticker at the UCLA assigned to Michael Jackson when he was brought in.

They arrived at 12:26. Rescue ambulance entered the residence, fire truck stayed on the street. Richard Senneff got his equipment the starter kit and followed the security guards up the stairs and in the bedroom. Richard Senneff saw Conrad Murray, Michael Jackson and a security guard in the room. Richard Senneff describes the patient. Michael Jackson was wearing pajama bottoms and a top. The top was open. Surgical cap on his head. He appeared to be thin. Richard Senneff describes Conrad Murray. Conrad Murray was leaned over Michael Jackson and was holding his torso and was moving Michael Jackson from bed to the floor. Richard Senneff also saw a security person helping to move Michael Jackson to the floor.

According to Richard Senneff, Conrad Murray was frantic. When entered the room Richard Senneff asked if there was an advanced DNR (Do Not Resuscitate) order. No one answered initially. Richard Senneff repeated the question Conrad Murray said no. Richard Senneff saw an IV stand with a saline bag hanging and saw an oxygen tank. Richard Senneff was trying to gather information to understand what was happening. Richard Senneff asked three times if there was an underlying health problem. Conrad Murray finally said nothing. According to Richard Senneff this didn't make sense as there was a physician at the house and a IV stand. Richard Senneff asked how long the patient been down. Conrad Murray said "just happened right I called you". Richard Senneff says that ambulance got there very quickly and if they were called right when the event happened, they had a good chance of reviving Michael Jackson and starting his heart. 12:26 is the time Richard Senneff was in the room and making observations. Richard Senneff states that they were in the room within 5 minutes. Richard Senneff says that a firefighter and himself moved Michael Jackson from side of the bed to the foot of the bed because there was not enough space to work on the side of the bed. Richard Senneff was still trying to gather information from Conrad Murray. Firefighter Herron was doing CPR. Paramedic Blount was starting ventilation. Paramedic Goodwin was hooking up the EKG. Fire Captain was helping with anything needed. Richard Senneff was busy and didn't look to see the patient was Michael Jackson. He later learned that it was Michael Jackson.

EKG showed flatline/ asystole.

Michael Jackson had an IV on his leg. Richard Senneff checked to see if it was working and then gave Michael Jackson atropine and epinephrine - those are drugs used to start the heart. Richard Senneff saw no change in Michael Jackson's condition after administering the started drugs. Richard Senneff asked Conrad Murray if Michael Jackson was taking any medicines and was he given any medicines. Richard Senneff had to ask that question multiple times. Richard Senneff told Conrad Murray that he's seeing an underweight patient, with an IV stand and medication vials on the nightstand. At that point Conrad Murray said Michael Jackson wasn't taking anything and

Conrad Murray only gave Michael Jackson a little bit of Lorazepam for sleep. Conrad Murray said he was treating Michael Jackson for dehydration and exhaustion. By this time Michael Jackson was hooked on the machines and had received one round of starter drugs. Blount incubated Michael Jackson quickly to give air directly to his lungs. Richard Senneff was monitoring Michael Jackson's situation. Richard Senneff was also communicating with UCLA Base Situation reporting to them. Richard Senneff told the age, the situation, how long he was down, what they did. Richard Senneff was talking to the radio nurse and radio nurse was communicating with the doctors. When Richard Senneff looked to the Michael Jackson, he didn't believe that Michael Jackson was "just down". Richard Senneff observed that Michael Jackson's skin was cool to the touch; Michael Jackson 's eyes were open, dilated and dry; EKG was flatline, and capnography reading was low. They gave Michael Jackson a second round of starter drugs through left jugular vein (left neck). Paramedic Goodwin tried to find a vein in Michael Jackson's arms to locate a vein 5 times to start an IV but he was unsuccessful. Richard Senneff says it's significantly difficult to locate a vein when the blood is not circulating for a while.

After Richard Senneff first contacted UCLA and told them what they administered the first round of starter drugs, UCLA asked them if they wanted to continue or stop. Richard Senneff said they wanted to continue. After the second round, Richard Senneff talked to UCLA again. UCLA was ready to announce Michael Jackson dead. Brazil asked what happened to the IV on Michael Jackson's leg. Richard Senneff says Conrad Murray pulled the IV from Michael Jackson's leg and that's why paramedics needed to find another vein and finally found jugular vein. Conrad Murray says he felt a pulse at right femoral (right groin). Richard Senneff looked to heart monitor and he saw a flat line with CPR (lines were only moving due to CPR). Richard Senneff told his crew to stop CPR to check for pulse. The heart monitor was a clear flat-line, it means that the heart wasn't functional and there could not be a pulse. Richard Senneff and another paramedic checked for pulse, they did not felt a pulse.

People's 43 exhibit again. They are going over handwritten notes.

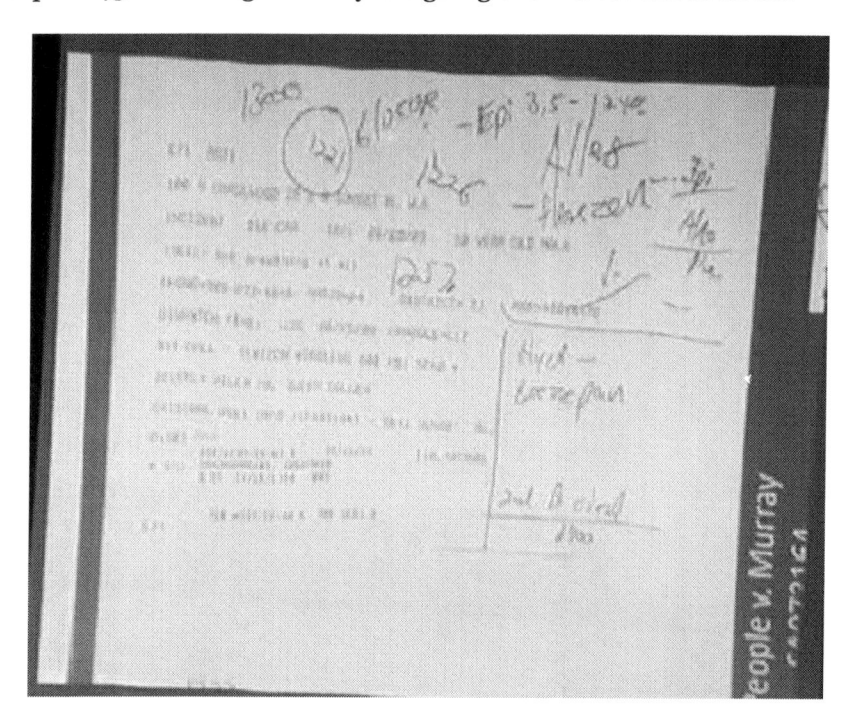

call time 12:21, glucose levels, EPI 3.5 mg at 12:40, Allergy : florazen, another EPI and atropine. 12:57 the time UCLA wanted to call Michael Jackson death. Box on the right hand side: Hydration and Lorazepam what Conrad Murray told Richard Senneff . Second bicarb - another starter drug given to Michael Jackson. Richard Senneff says the time is wrong. He wrote 14:00 but it was actually at 13:00 PM

Richard Senneff's call to UCLA is played. Conrad Murray assumes control. Conrad Murray asked paramedics to do a central line. Richard Senneff says they don't have any training or equipment to perform it. Conrad Murray asked paramedics to administer magnesium, Richard Senneff says they didn't have it. Brazil asks if Conrad Murray provided them the materials to perform these tasks. Richard Senneff says no.

People's exhibit 46

902-M. The document contains comprehensive information about the care provided. Starter drugs provided from 12:27 to 12:50. Readings are also written in the document. Medication information and Richard Senneff's own notes are written.

They gave Michael Jackson sodium bicarb before transportation. All of the paramedics and firefighters took Michael Jackson downstairs on a backboard. Some of them were carrying the backboard and the others were still performing resuscitation efforts. When downstairs Michael Jackson was put on a gurney with wheels. Richard Senneff turned back to go upstairs to get their equipment. Richard Senneff sees Conrad Murray with a bag in his hand picking up items from the floor near the nightstand.

Blue ambu bag on the floor. Richard Senneff says it's not paramedics.

Richard Senneff collects the items, go down the stairs and go to the ambulance. Conrad Murray was still inside the room. Conrad Murray joined them later. Richard Senneff was sitting close to Michael Jackson's head in the ambulance and was observing Michael Jackson. There was no changes. Michael Jackson was given another round of starter drugs on the ambulance. No change. Richard Senneff saw Conrad Murray on his cell phone. Richard Senneff says he never saw any sign of life at Michael Jackson and there was no change in Michael Jackson's situation for the 42 minutes he was with him. They arrived UCLA at 13:13 PM.

Brazil lists monitoring equipment and asks Richard Senneff if he saw them in the bedroom. Richard Senneff says "No" to them all. Brazil asks if Conrad Murray ever mention Propofol to Richard Senneff, Richard Senneff says No. Richard Senneff says Conrad Murray was alone in the bedroom for a while after he left the room with their equipment.

Defense cross by Nareg Gourjian

Richard Senneff says they got the call 12:22 and left at 12:22. Gourjian mentions the call was placed at 12:20 and transferred from Beverly Hills. Richard Senneff was not aware of it. Gourjian reminds of Richard Senneff's preliminary hearing description of Michael Jackson: pale, underweight, so thin that you can see his ribs. Gourjian asks if Michael Jackson looked real sick to him. Richard Senneff says he looked like he had a chronic health problem. Gourjian asks if it was the physical characteristics of someone that has been a drug addict for a long time. Richard Senneff says he cannot say that and he has seen drug addicts that are overweight and underweight. Richard Senneff says he just thought it was a chronic illness. Gourjian asks about Michael Jackson being on the bed. Richard Senneff says Michael Jackson was in the process of being moved, his feet on the ground and his upper torso still on the bed. IV tubing on his left calf. Defense asks if Richard Senneff asked Conrad Murray if Michael Jackson was on recreational drugs. Richard Senneff says it's a common question that he asks but he doesn't remember if he asked it or not. Defense asks Richard Senneff about Lorazepam. Richard Senneff says he's not that knowledgeable about it. Defense asks about Conrad Murray not answering the questions right away could be because he was busy. Richard Senneff says there was a lot of things going on and he was busy. Defense is going over what each paramedic doing. Richard Senneff repeats what he previously said. Gourjian mentions Paramedic Herron doing CPR and Paramedic Blount managing ventilation. And if Conrad Murray asking for help as well it acceptable. Richard Senneff answers yes you wouldn't want to do it alone. Defense reminds American Health Association (AHA) guidelines which says people should work collaboratively.

Defense asks if the CPR should be performed where the patient is found. Richard Senneff says that's wrong. Defense reads from American Heart Association (AHA) guidelines. Richard Senneff agrees with it. Defense asks if Michael Jackson had IV connected to him. Richard Senneff says yes. Richard Senneff says he didn't see anything else connected to him. Defense asks if things connected will be a factor when moving a patient, Richard Senneff answers yes. Defense asks if the chest comprehensions are adequate, would be irrelevant if the patient was on a bed or floor. Richard Senneff says correct. Defense asks questions the pulse Conrad Murray felt at Michael Jackson's femoral artery. Richard Senneff says he didn't suspect what Conrad Murray said. Defense reminds of Richard Senneff's preliminary hearing in which he said that it's common to get femoral pulse from CPR. Defense asked would it be likely that Conrad Murray actually felt that pulse. Richard Senneff answers yes. Defense asked why Richard Senneff didn't pronounce Michael Jackson dead as UCLA said. Richard Senneff said he preferred to go to the hospital as it was a VIP patient and as he was told it was a recent arrest. Conrad Murray took the control and he needed to ride in the ambulance with them. After getting Michael Jackson down to the ambulance, Richard Senneff went back to the room to pick the medical equipment left behind. Conrad Murray was also picking up items in plain sight. Defense asks if it's normal practice to pick up medical items, Richard Senneff says yes. Defense asks if Conrad Murray could have been picking up his glasses and wallet. Richard Senneff says he didn't see anything and the bed was blocking his view. Richard Senneff goes back to the ambulance. Conrad Murray came to the ambulance in a minute or so. Defense asks about the phone call Conrad Murray did at ambulance, asks Richard Senneff if he heard anything. Richard Senneff said he didn't hear anything. Defense asks if Conrad Murray was trying to help the paramedics with anything they needed when they were at Carolwood. Richard Senneff says correct. Defense asks is fractured ribs is a show of good CPR. Richard Senneff says it is common occurrence. Richard Senneff wasn't aware that Michael Jackson sustained fractured ribs. Defense asks if Richard Senneff is familiar with Propofol, Richard Senneff says no. Michael Jackson was a combination of P.E.A (Pulseless Electrical Activity) and asystole (flat lined). Defense asks if there are certain protocols to follow if someone is P.E.A. They wouldn't shock (defibrillate) a person with P.E.A. They would give CPR and give atropine and EPI and sodium bicarbonate. Defense asks if they knew Michael Jackson was given Propofol, they wouldn't be able to anything different. Objection. Sustained.

Brazil redirect

Brazil asks if there was any confusion and chaos when Richard Senneff's team attempted to save Michael Jackson's life like the defense claimed. Richard Senneff says it was not the case. Brazil asks if Richard Senneff knows the IV tubing had been replaced, removed or placed again prior to his arrival. Richard Senneff says no. Richard Senneff says that it's accurate that they believed the femoral pulse that Conrad Murray felt to be due to comprehensions and not a real pulse. Richard Senneff says by the look of Conrad Murray's face he was surprised to see him come back in the room. Richard Senneff says it was "deer in the headlight" kinda look. Richard Senneff says Conrad Murray had a trash bag in his hand.

Defense recross

Defense asks Richard Senneff 's time of estimate for the cardiac arrest. Richard Senneff says it is hard to speculate. Gourjian reminds of Richard Senneff's preliminary testimony which said "at least 20-25 minutes before we arrived there". Gourjian asks if the time of arrest could have been 12:01 -12:05PM. Defense again asks if Conrad Murray could have been getting his wallet.

Objection. Sustained.

Defense asks if Conrad Murray asked Richard Senneff to close his eyes or step outside the room. Richard Senneff says no.

Brazil re re direct

Brazil reminds of the preliminary hearing and asks if it's correct that Richard Senneff said the arrest could be anywhere from 20 minutes to 1 hour ago. Richard Senneff says correct.

Defense re re cross

Defense asks if Conrad Murray stopped doing what he was doing when Richard Senneff walked into the room. Richard Senneff says no Conrad Murray continued to do what he was doing.

Martin Blount Testimony

Brazil direct

Los Angeles Firefighter paramedic. Worked for 20 years. Became a paramedic in 1999. Trained by UCLA doctors and nurses. Every 2 years they are required to take 48 hours of trainment. Works at firestation 71.

Martin Blount drived the rescue ambulance. Richard Senneff was sitting next to him. He came to Carolwood and parked the ambulance and went into the house. Fire truck accompanied them and parked outside the street. Fire Captain Mills, Paramedic Goodwin and Herron was on the fire truck. Martin Blount saw a man lying on bed. He was on the bed fully. Martin Blount saw 2 rescue personnel getting Michael Jackson to the floor. Conrad Murray was sweating profusely, he was aggitated. Conrad Murray said "He needs help could you help him please". Martin Blount has the designated role as a driver. His job is initial treatment and assessment of the patient. Richard Senneff is responsible for communications and obtain information. Martin Blount immediately recognized it was Michael Jackson when he came in the room. Martin Blount went to the head of the patient and started basic life support. Martin Blount 's job was to provide air to Michael Jackson.

Steps:

Tongue suppressor so the tongue would not go back of the throat and wouldn't block the airway.

Head tilt back - to make airway open and unconstrusted

Ambu bag - artificial air. More efficient than mouth to mouth. Tied it to an oxgyen tank that he brought.

It took him a minute or so do these all.

Then he did advance life support which is endotracheal tube - 100% of the air is going into the lungs. It's better than ambu bag. He did did it in 45 seconds. According to Blount, Michael Jackson wasn't breathing, he wasn't moving, his eyes was fixed and dilated. Martin Blount felt that Michael Jackson was dead. Martin Blount observed an an oxygen tank and saw a long tube and nasal cannula attached to it. Nasal Cannula was on Michael Jackson. Martin Blount also saw an IV on Michael Jackson's leg and saw an IV bag on IV stand. He did not see any monitoring equipment in the room or on Michael. While Martin Blount was doing his tasks, Martin Blount was able to see the heart monitor. He saw no movement. He believed Michael Jackson was flat lined. Richard Senneff's duty was to gather medical information. Martin Blount heard Richard Senneff asked about the medications Michael Jackson took. Martin Blount heard Conrad Murray said no. For previous medical condition Conrad Murray said no. Conrad Murray said he was a healty 50 year old man. Conrad Murray said he was providing normal saline. Conrad Murray said Michael Jackson was rehearsing for 16 hours and was dehydrated. Martin Blount heard Richard Senneff asking if Michael Jackson was taking recreational drugs. Conrad Murray said no.

Brazil asks about stater drugs. Atropine and EPI. Paramedic Goodwin made multiple attempts to find a vein in the arms but he was unsuccessful. Richard Senneff found a jugular vein on the neck to administer another round of starter drugs. Martin Blount saw 3 open vials of lidocaine on the floor when he was helping Michael Jackson. Lidocaine is a heart drug. Paramedics do not carry lidocaine and did not administer it. Conrad Murray did not mention of giving Michael Jackson any lidocaine. Martin Blount did not hear Conrad Murray mentioning Propofol. Martin Blount says he did not hear anyone saying they felt a pulse. Brazil reminds him of his preliminary testimony. Martin Blount then remembers that Conrad Murray said he felt a pulse on Michael Jackson's groin area. They stopped the comprehensions to check it (comprehensions can create artificial pulse). When they checked, no one else felt any pulse. Richard Senneff was communicating with UCLA base center. Martin Blount heard UCLA was ready to announce him dead. Martin Blount never saw any signs of life and did not believe Michael Jackson was alive. Conrad Murray took over the control of the patient. Michael Jackson was put on a backboard and paramedics took him down to transfer him to UCLA. Before they were taking Michael Jackson down, Martin Blount saw Conrad Murray taking Lidocaine vials from the floor and put them in a black bag. Martin Blount never saw those lidocaine bottles again. Martin Blount rode with Michael Jackson to UCLA. He was sitting towards his head. They administered another started drugs to Michael Jackson on the ride. There was no change to Michael Jackson's situation on the ride. Martin Blount saw and heard Conrad Murray on the phone. Martin Blount heard Conrad Murray say "It's about Michael and it doesn't look good" on the phone. Martin Blount doesn't know who Conrad Murray was speaking to on the phone. Martin Blount saw Michael Jackson had condom catheter. It allows urine to be collected in a bag. It's typically used when someone not able to get up and go to the restroom. Richard Senneff asked how long the patient was down. Martin Blount heard Conrad Murray say "he's been down about 1 minute". Martin Blount felt Michael Jackson's skin,when he was on the bed he was warm. On the floor Michael Jackson felt cold to the touch. Martin Blount looking at Michael Jackson's condition believed he was longer than one minute.

Defense cross by Gourjian

Martin Blount parked the ambulance, got his equipment went upstairs to the bedroom. Martin Blount says Michael Jackson was still on the bed. Michael Jackson looked pale and thin. Gourjian shows Martin Blount a picture and asks what the black thing on the bed is.

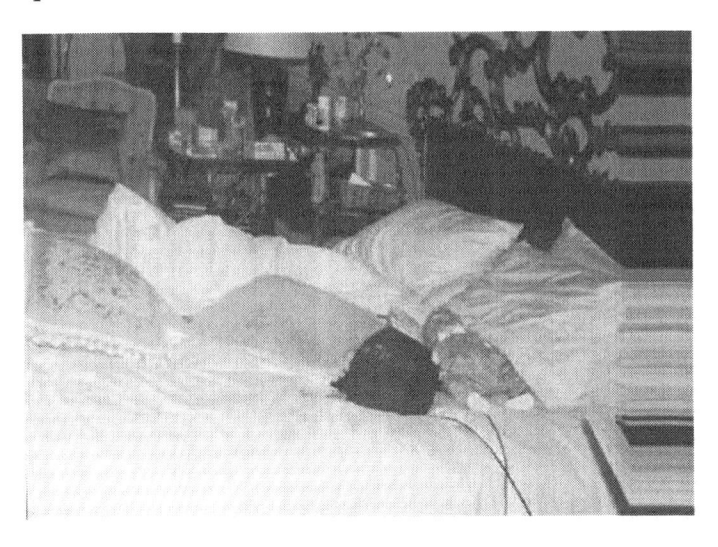

Martin Blount doesn't know what it is. Gourjian asks what are recreational drugs? Martin Blount gives examples such as heroin, cocaine. Conrad Murray answered that question as no. Martin Blount says he didn't hear Conrad Murray mentioning Lorazepam to Richard Senneff. Defense asks if Martin Blount heard Conrad Murray said "he has been down about a minute prior calling for help". Martin Blount says he didn't hear that, he only heard "about 1 minute". Gourjian goes over the AHA guidelines: comprehension first, airway next, breathing last. Martin Blount mentions in 2009 the rules was airway first but now the rules have changed. Gourjian asks is asking for assistance during CPR is normal, Martin Blount says yes. Gourjian asks about Lidocaine bottles. Lidocaine wasn't hidden, they were out in the open and in plain sight. Defense asks if Michael Jackson was P.E.A. Martin Blount says Michael Jackson was never P.E.A., he was flat-line the whole time.

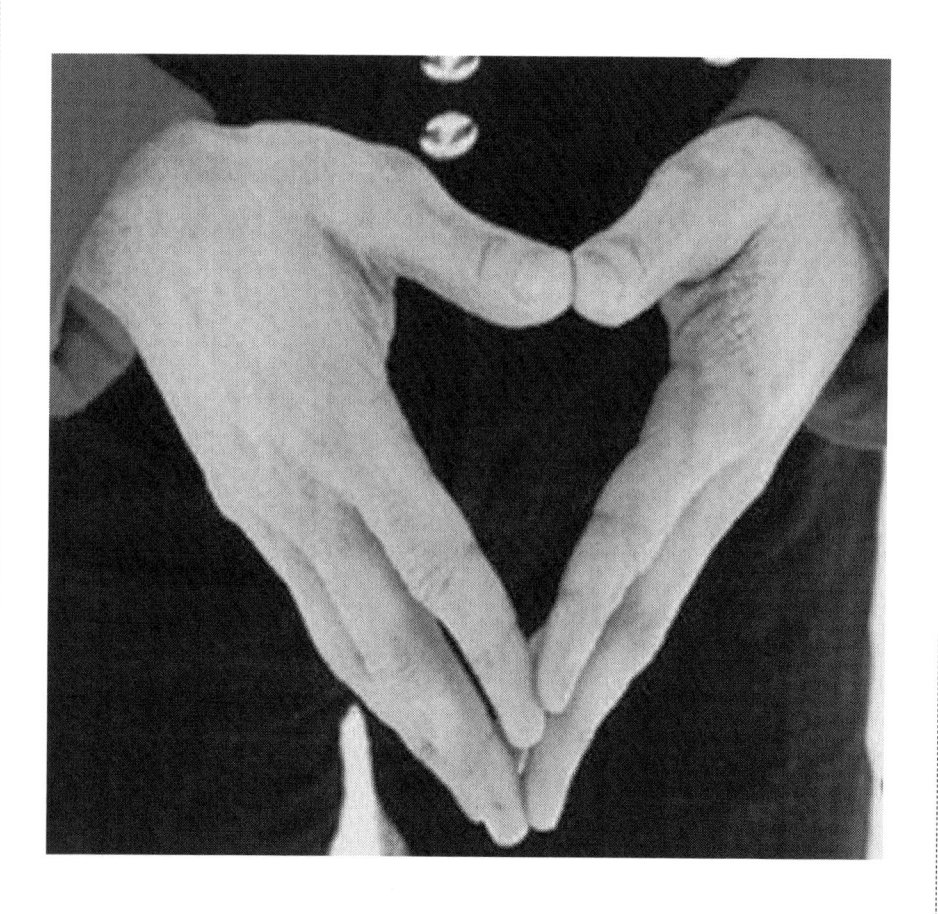

Dr. Richelle Cooper Testimony

Walgren direct

UCLA Board Certified Emergency Physician. Explains her medical background, training, education in detail.

Richelle Cooper explains what is a base station: Nurses with specialized training. They answer radio calls from paramedics, help paramedics, consult with doctors to provide further information to the paramedics. June 25th Richelle Cooper was consulting with the paramedics through base station nurse. Nurse called Richelle Cooper after receiving the call from the paramedics after the resuciation effort were unsuccessful. Richelle Cooper knew the patient was incubated and received starter drugs but still asystole for 40 minutes. Los Angeles protocol say if rescuaiation efforts are unsuccessful for 20 min person can be announced dead. After receiving the information Richelle Cooper authorized paramedics pronounce Michael Jackson dead at 12:57. Nurse called Richelle Cooper back said there was a physician on scene requesting paramedics provide another medication. It was sodium bicarbonate. Richelle Cooper said if that was a physician with an active licence they can administer it but the physician need to take over the control and the patient needs to be transported to the local hospital. When Michael Jackson came to the hospital, the care became Richelle Cooper 's responsibility. Richelle Cooper knew patient was on the way so she was waiting for the ambulance.

She assigned a team of 14 people. It included :

- Richelle Cooper and 4 residents

- at least 2 emergency technicians,

- a respitory therapist,

- a scribe nurse to record information and make calls to get consult,

- 2 circulating nurses,

- a pharmacist,

- a social worker to contact/assist family members, gather information from physicians,

- a charge nurse who assigns other staff as it's needed.

Additional doctors were consulted and came as needed. Administrative people came down after a while as it was Michael Jackson.

Richelle Cooper's main goal is to manage Michael Jackson's care. While paramedics was transferring Michael Jackson to the trauma bay. Richelle Cooper was speaking Conrad Murray and asked what happened. Conrad Murray told Michael Jackson was working very long hours, Conrad Murray believed Michael Jackson was dehyrated, Conrad Murray gave him IV and gave Michael Jackson 2mg Lorazepam, later gave another 2 mg Lorazepam and saw Michael Jackson go into cardiac arrest. Conrad Murray reported Michael Jackson had not been ill. Richelle Cooper asked about medications Michael Jackson has been given. Richelle Cooper was told Michael Jackson was given 2 doses of 2 mg Lorazepam through IV.

Walgren asks "Did Conrad Murray tell any other medicines other than Lorazepam?" Richelle Cooper says "No".

Conrad Murray said witnessed the arrest. What does it mean? Richelle Cooper says it's an observed arrest and the critical event happens when you are with the patient. It's when the patients heart and breathing stops. It means you are on site and saw it happen. Richelle Cooper asked for Michael Jackson's routine regular medications. She was told Valium and Flomax. Valium - anti anxiety medicine. Flomax is given for prostate or kidney stone. Conrad Murray did not mention any other medicines. Richelle Cooper asked past medical history , if he had a heart problem, blood clot or drug use. Conrad Murray said no to all. Richelle Cooper asked if he saw any seizures and if Michael Jackson had complained about chest pain, Conrad Murray said no. Richelle Cooper did not see any physical trauma. Richelle Cooper says Michael Jackson was clinically dead, he didn't have a pulse. There was signs of a dying heart (heart might still send some signals), pupils were dilated. Despite this they made attempts to revive Michael Jackson. They confirmed the breathing tube was in correct place and they were breathing for the patient. They checked for pulse, there was no pulse. They started CPR and tried to resuscitate Michael Jackson. They used an ultasound to examine the heart. Walgren shows pictures of trauma bay and asks Richelle Cooper to go over all of the medical items in the trauma bay. Richelle Cooper identifies items one by one.

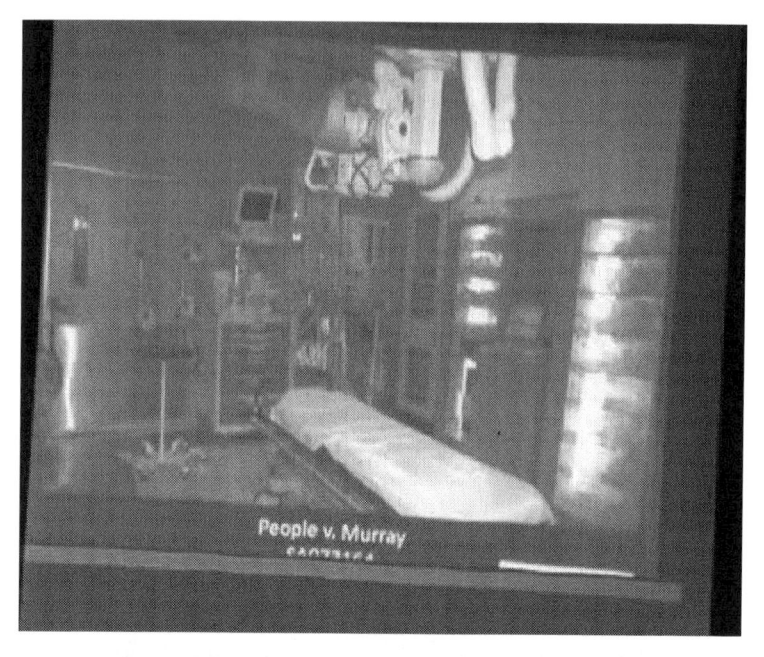

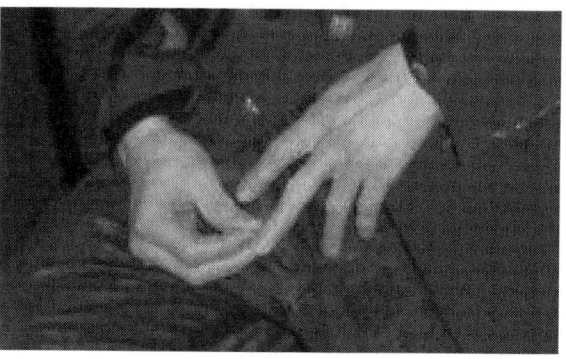

Murray Trial Summaries Day 5/ October 3-2011

Dr. Richelle Cooper Resumption of Direct by David Walgren

Cooper states that Conrad Murray indicated he had given Michael Jackson 4 miligrams of Lorazepam, with no mention of propofol. Cooper states that there were over 14 people in the room where Michael Jackson was at UCLA, but that she had the final say over everything that happened in the room. Cooper states that she was aware that paramedics have given "starter drugs" at the Carolwood home and also during transport to UCLA. Cooper states that at UCLA, epinephrine, sodium bicarbonate, vasopressin were all given to try to restart Michael Jackson's heart. Dopamine was given in a drip. Cooper states that chest compressions were given from time of arrival. Cooper states Michael Jackson arrived at 1:13 pm and was death was called 2:26, chest compressions were given continuously throughout. Cooper states Michael Jackson had an endotracheal tube, and a respiratory therapist was squeezing an ambu- bag to pump oxygen into Michael Jackson's lungs throughout. Cooper also states that Michael Jackson was hooked to monitors throughout. Cooper states that during this hour and thirteen minutes, from the time Michael Jackson arrived at UCLA, until the time of death was called, she never felt a pulse. Cooper states that when compressions were going on, they could feel a pulse. But, that a spontaneous pulse (when there are no chest compressions going on) was not found by her. Cooper states at 13:21 (military time for 1:21) one of the staff reported a pulse, but when Cooper consulted the monitor it was not consistent with a pulse. Cooper states that she made the decision at 2:26 pm to call the time of death, even though she called time of death at the Carolwood home at 12:57 pm. Cooper states that from 12:57 pm to 2:26 pm there had been no notable change in Michael Jackson 's condition. Cooper states that she noticed a condom catheter on Michael Jackson's body. Cooper states that condom catheters are used to collect urine when unconscious. Cooper states that the condom catheter was unusual for a 50 year old male who was reportedly healthy. Cooper states that she did not request Murray to sign a death certificate, because Michael Jackson was her patient. Cooper states she did not have a reason for Michael Jackson's death and therefore Michael Jackson's case would be a coroner's case. Cooper states that there was a social work team to help with the family even before the time of Michael Jackson's death was called. Cooper states that the social work team is standard care for UCLA, not initiated by Conrad Murray. Cooper states that she was notified that Michael Jackson's children were aware that their father was dead. Cooper states that she saw the children, that they were scared and that they were fairly hysterical, and taken care of by someone referred to as their nurse.

Defense Cross

Cooper states she does not know exactly time of death for Michael Jackson, she bases it on what the paramedics told her, and called time of death at 12:57 pm. Cooper states based on the information she had, she believed Michael Jackson to be dead at 12:57 pm. Cooper states that she could override Murray's request to continue to try to revive Murray, but she allowed Murray to make that call. Cooper states that her assessment when Michael Jackson arrived, he was clinically dead and that any revival would be futile. Cooper stated that Murray claimed there was a pulse, so she continued efforts to save Michael Jackson. Cooper states she was never an anesthesiologist, but she has used propofol, at UCLA you need to have privileges. Cooper states she always practices medicine in a hospital emergency room setting. Cooper states that in her use of propofol, she uses amounts that are based by case. Cooper states that she chooses a dose that will make a patient comfortable, so that the patient does not feel pain. Cooper states she never used propofol as a pre-med student. Cooper states that if 25 mg of propofol was slowly infused in 3-5 minutes, on a patient at 135 pounds, and he received no other medications, she believes if she achieved sedation, he would wake up in seven to ten minutes. Cooper does not believe that the propofol would be completely metabolized in seven minutes. Cooper states that 25 mg is very small, and would not be sufficient to sedate a patient. Cooper states that Murray stated he witnessed Michael Jackson's cardiac arrest. Cooper states that she never asked what time the Lorazepam was given to Michael Jackson. Cooper states that she previously testified that Murray stated he witnessed Michael Jackson's cardiac arrest. Cooper states that the half life of benzodiazepines varies greatly. Cooper has been to courses in procedural sedation, she has administered procedural sedation, and reviews articles on procedural sedation. Cooper states that on a healthy patient, she would start sedation at a mg per kg dose, and in Michael Jackson's case that would be 60 mg, it would keep them asleep for about 10 minutes. Cooper states that if Murray had told her that he had given 25 mg of propofol at 10:40, it would have not changed how she treated Michael Jackson as a patient. Cooper states that Michael Jackson died long before he became her patient. Cooper states that Murray stated that he thought Michael Jackson was dehydrated, had given him Lorazepam, and had witnessed Michael Jackson's cardiac arrest. Cooper states that Murray told her Michael Jackson took Flomax which is typically taken for a urinary problem. Cooper states that while it is normal to take a rectal temperature, but Cooper cannot recall if it was done. Cooper states that rectal temperature would not tell her time of death. Cooper states that there is a protocol for Los Angeles county paramedics, with 20 minutes of revival procedures, after 20 minutes with no change, it's time to call time of death. Cooper states that this is the first time that paramedics have ever asked her to continue revival procedure after she tells them to call the time of death. Cooper states that she does not recall Murray being frantic, but to be honest, she does not pay that much attention to someone other than the patient. Cooper does not recall much about Murray's demeanor, except that Murray was respectful in that he was not allowed to do procedures in the emergency room. Cooper states that Murray and a Dr. Cruz had a conversation, which she did not hear, but then the aortic pump was inserted. Cooper states that there was no urine present in the condom catheter or the collection bag. Cooper states that had there been urine, Cooper would have sent it to the lab to be analyzed.

Walgren Redirect

Cooper states that she assumed that Conrad Murray was not lying to her. Cooper states that Murray told her that Michael Jackson was working hard, was dehydrated and he had given him Lorazepam. Cooper states that all physicians do not have propofol privileges. Cooper states that they have equipment set up within a room and outside a room for issues arising in a patient who has received propofol. Cooper states that there is always an attending physician present, plus other physicians when administering propofol or another anesthetic agent.

Defense Cross

Cooper states that when administering propofol, it should go in as a slow infusion through a bolus. Cooper states that a direct injection of propofol would cause apnea, although she has never seen a direct injection done. Cooper states that continual propofol usage is rare.

Walgren Redirect

Cooper states that she is prepared as a an emergency physician to intubate patients or attend to patient's airway during procedural sedation.

Defense Recross

Cooper states she has never had a patient stop breathing during a procedural sedation. Cooper states that if there is a problem, the first thing to do is to stimulate the patient, meaning wake the patient up and that that is almost always sufficient. Cooper states that if a doctor was to administer 60 mgs to 60 kg patient, the doctor would be able to see insufficient breathing right away, that it could be determined by seeing, but that capnography would be able to detect a breathing problem first.

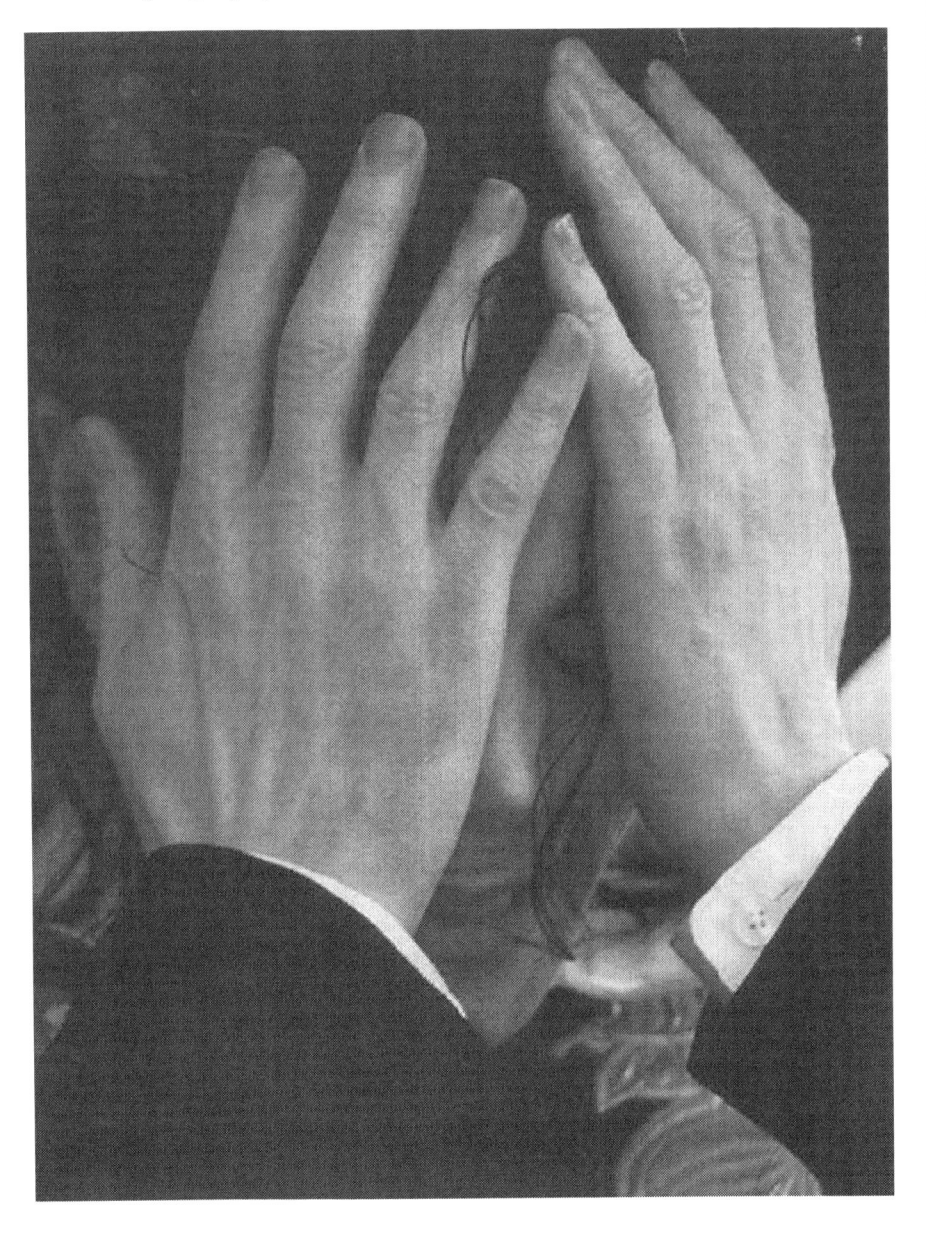

Edward Dixon Testimony

Brazil Direct

Dixon states he works for AT & T as a senior support engineer since 1997. Dixon states that he is familiar with preparations of cell phone records and has testified previously in cases regarding cell phone records. Dixon states he has reviewed Murray's cell phone records. Dixon states that Murray's cell phone account status was active in June, 2009.

Dixon states that on June 25, 2009, calls were made:

- 9:23 am Call placed to Murray's phone lasting 22 minutes

-10:14 am Call placed to Murray's phone lasting 2 minutes

-11:07 am Call placed to Murray's phone lasting 1 minute

-11:18 am Call placed from Murray's phone lasting 32 minutes

-11:49 am Call placed to Murray's phone lasting 3 minutes

- 11:51 am Call placed from Murray's phone lasting 11 minutes

- 12:12 pm Call placed from Murray's phone lasting 1 minute

-12:15 pm Call placed to Murray's phone lasting 1 minute

- 3:38 pm Call placed from Murray's phone lasting 2 minutes

- 4:31 pm Call placed from Murray's phone lasting 1 minute

-4:32 pm Same as above

-5:02 pm Same as above

Dixon states that cell phone contains data as well as calls. Dixon states that data activity occurred on Murray's cell phone on June 25, 2009:

- 1:04 am, 2:04 am, 3:04 am, 4:04 am, 5:04 am and 6:04 am, Dixon states that this is pull notification, and that information is pulled to the phone.

-8:54 am - 5:02 pm Data activity

Gourjian Defense cross

Dixon states the records do not identify who is using the phone. Dixon states that there is no way to identify what is said in a text message sent from any AT&T phone (referring to data activity). Dixon states that he does not know, as of today, who own the cell phones that Murray called on June 25, 2009. Essentially, Dixon states that he can tell if calls went to voicemail or they were answered only if they made from or to AT&T phones. Dixon states that regarding data usage, the data is set automatically, in this case, it was set at 1:04 am, 2:04 am, 3:04 am, 4:04 am, 5:04 am and 6:04 am.

11:07 am, phone call to Murray's call, Dixon states that he cannot tell whether the call was answered or it went to voicemail. Dixon then looks to his records, looking specifically at the duration of the call, and states it is identified as an incoming call, length is 1 minute, but he still cannot tell if it went to voicemail or answered.

Brazil Redirect

Brazil corrects that 3:38 pm call is wrong, it is 3:58 pm.

Jeff Strohom Testimony

Brazil Direct

Strohm states that he is a custodian of records for Sprint/Nextel, and is responsible testifying for courts who require it. Strohm states that the subscriber for the number that Brazil asks, is Conrad Murray. Strohm states that calls were made from or to Murray's phone on 6/25/09:

- 7:01 am Call made to Murray lasting 25 seconds

- 8:25 am Call made from Murray lasting 0 seconds (text message)

- 8:39 am Call made from Murray lasting 53 seconds

- 10:20 am Call made to Murray lasting 111 seconds

- 10:34 am Call made from Murray lasting 8 1/2 minutes

- 11:26 am Call made to Murray lasting 7 seconds

- 1:08 pm Call made from Murray lasting 2 minutes

Gourjian Defense Cross

Strohm states that the 11:26 am call cannot tell whether the phone was answered or not, but that the call is not a voicemail.

Dr. Thao Nyguen Testimony

Walgren Direct

Dr. Nguyen states she works at UCLA as a cardiologist/scientist. Nguyen 20% of her time spent as a cardiologist, 80% of her time she researches. Nguyen states that in June, 2009, she was a cardiology fellow. Cooper states her responsibilities included taking care of patients that were critically ill in CCU at UCLA, managing patients and supervising her was Dr. Daniel Cruz.

Cooper states she was called into the emergency room at UCLA to help with the patient Michael Jackson. Cooper states she received a page that the ER needed help with a VIP patient, named Michael Jackson. Nguyen states that Dr. Cooper was treating Michael Jackson when she arrived at the emergency room. Nguyen states that Murray introduced himself to her as Michael Jackson's private physician. Nguyen asked Murray what happened, and Murray replied that Michael Jackson was very tired, he was preparing for a concert tour. Nguyen states that she asked Murray if there were any drugs given, Murray stated 4 mg of Ativan (another name for Lorazepam). Nguyen asked if any other medications were given, Murray stated no other medications given.

Nguyen states that she asked what time the Ativan was given, Murray stated he did not know. Nguyen states that Murray told him he found

Michael Jackson not breathing, Nguyen asked what time was that, Murray stated he did not know. Nguyen states that she then asked Murray what time was 911 called, Murray stated he did not know, he had no concept of time because he did not have a watch. Nguyen states she asked for an estimate from Murray from the time he found him not breathing to the time he called 911, Murray was not able. Nguyen states that Murray never mentioned propofol to her. Nguyen states that after receiving from Murray, she consulted Dr. Cruz. Murray told them that he found a pulse, but Dr. Nguyen nor Dr. Cruz found a pulse. Murray asked both Nguyen and Cruz to continue to try to revive, Michael Jackson to not give up easily. Nguyen states that the next thing to do to try to revive Michael Jackson is to use a balloon pump for Michael Jackson's heart. Nguyen states that she feared they were running too late, that time was not on Michael Jackson's side.

Walgren Direct continued

What is a balloon pump? It is inserted into aorta to help heart. She was doubtful that it would help. It looked like time wasn't on Michael Jackson's side and he looked lifeless. She went forward with the balloon pump to show good faith. Thao Nguyen and Dr. Cruz (attenting cardiologist) could not felt a pulse but Conrad Murray told them he felt a pulse and asked them not to give up easily on Michael Jackson and try to save his life. Thao Nguyen and Dr. Cruz moved forward with balloon pump even though they thought it was futile. Dr. Cruz decided and authorizated the ballon pump. It was quite smoothly placed but the attempt was futile. Before they did the balloon pump placement, they made an agreement with Conrad Murray that this would be the last attempt to save Michael Jackson and if it didn't work they would stop the efforts. Dr. Nguyen: "We wanted Mr. Jackson to depart with dignity and respect, so we decided to end our efforts."

Shortly after the balloon pump Michael Jackson was pronounced dead. Conrad Murray did not mention propofol during all these balloon pump efforts.

Defense Flanagan cross

Thao Nguyen was called a minute before 1:35. Thao Nguyen remembers the time because she looked to her pager. Thao Nguyen was on the 7th floor in the rounding room of cardiac care. She talked to Dr. Cooper when she came into the trauma bay and Dr. Cooper pointed and introduced her to Conrad Murray saying that Conrad Murray is the physican for Michael Jackson. Thao Nguyen knew the patient was Michael Jackson because page she received was a code for "VIP named Michael Jackson". Thao Nguyen talked and asked Conrad Murray first because he was the primary source . She always goes to the source and then talks to ucla attending doctor (Dr. Cooper). Conrad Murray said to Thao Nguyen that Michael Jackson was having hard time sleeping, Michael Jackson was tired because of preparation/ rehearsal for the concert tour and Michael Jackson asked for sleeping aid. Conrad Murray told Thao Nguyen that he gave Michael Jackson "Ativan 4 mg IV". Conrad Murray didn't tell her that he gave it in 2 seperate doses. Conrad Murray didn't mention Valium or Flomax and said no when she asked if there was any other sedatives and narcotics involved. Conrad Murray did not recall the time when gave Ativan to Michael Jackson. Conrad Murray didnot remember the time of the arrest. Conrad Murray did not recall when he called EMS. Thao Nguyen had some concerns: 1)time was not on their side 2) IV for insomnia for outpatient setting is quite uncommon. The dosage wasn't too high but there was a lifeless patient. 4mg of Ativan by IV would put a person to sleep. Thao Nguyen would start with 1 mg by a mouth. IV would be stronger than by mouth usage. She wouldn't use Ativan in outpatient setting and even inpatient setting because they are better drugs that are non-sedatives and non-narcotics. Recommended dosage for Ativan is 2 -4 mg by mouth for an adult. 2 mg Ativan by IV would put a patient to sleep pretty quick in 5-7 minutes depending on the patient. If a person is used the drug before it can take them longer to sleep. Ativan half time is 12 +- 5 hours. Thao Nguyen says the amount of sleep would depend on the patient and the conditions. She says that normally people would be able to sleep through the night with that dose. Defense asks about the second dose of 2mg Ativan and if it would put the person to sleep. Thao Nguyen says yes if the person has not developed higher tolerance, if they had a high tolerance they would need higher dosage. Thao Nguyen also mentions that the even though a person's tolerance to drug could increase, their body's tolereance level to toxicty wouldn't increase. Defense asks 20 mg Ativan IV, Thao Nguyen says that it's a really high dose. Defense asks if it would kill a person. Thao Nguyen says that Ativan affects the brain and will make the brain sleepy (depress the consciousness) and it would not tell the diaphragm to breath. Defense talks about half life of Ativan. Defense asks if Ativan would be expected in to be present in blood at 12:00PM if 2mg is given at 2 AM and 5 AM. Defense asks if they would watch the patient if they gave them Ativan. Thao Nguyen says that multiple people watch them until they would gain total consciousness. Slurry speech is mentioned and Thao Nguyen says that it would be an affect of Ativan. Thao Nguyen has used Propofol. She says that they don't hear slurred speech in Propofol. Conrad Murray sounded desperate and looked devastated. Conrad Murray said "Do not give up easily, please save his life". There was no pulse but Thao Nguyen didn't know how long he didn't have pulse. Thao Nguyen believed when she was called to come down, CPR was partially successful. All Thao Nguyen knows when she came down Michael Jackson appeared lifeless and Thao Nguyen and Dr. Cruz could not find a pulse. There was typically no reason to use a balloon pump. Thao Nguyen says as Conrad Murray was there and he was trained and knew how to take pulse so Thao Nguyen gave Conrad Murray the benefit of the doubt and believed when he said he felt a pulse. Defense asks when they did the balloon pump. She says that they got the equipment in 5-7 minutes and did the balloon pump immediately after they got the equipment. Defense again goes over the agreement they did with Conrad Murray to do balloon pump and stop if it doesn't work. Thao Nguyen repeats multiple times of her previous explanations. Thao Nguyen says she asked Conrad Murray if he gave anthing to reverse the effect of atrivan. Later Thao Nguyen explains the drug

Flumazenil. 0.2 mg to prevent the further depression of the brain. To reverse the effect of Ativan it should be given immediately like in seconds. Defense questions about window of opportunity. Thao Nguyen says seconds to minutes (2-3 minutes). Thao Nguyen says you can 100% reverse Ativan but if you wait too long then you would zero chance to reverse it. It must be given as soon as you find the patient. Thao Nguyen says that antidote should be to be at hand when giving Ativan to a patient. Thao Nguyen says the next step will be to incubate the patient and to be put on a ventilator to breathe. Defense asks is she would expect 4 mg Ativan need Flumazenil. Thao Nguyen says she would not typically expect any complications in a person that is accustomed to the drug and tolerant to it. Thao Nguyen adds that anything can happen and they always use it at a monitored environment with oxygen on board.

Walgren redirect

Thao Nguyen use propofol at the hospital but uses an anesthesiologist in procedures. Thao Nguyen says at least 3 people will be in the room - cardiologist, anesthesiologist and a nurse. Thao Nguyen says Propofol will be administered in a hospital setting and furthermore only in an ICU or procedure room. Thao Nguyen also mentions that it would be administered in a designated place, with designated personnel and necessary equipment. Thao Nguyen says that crash cart should be available. Thao Nguyen says she wouldn't administer Propofol without the necessary equipment. Thao Nguyen mentions Propofol can cause negative effects and that it doesn't have an antidote so that they should be prepared for the worst when giving Propofol before they even start administering it. Thao Nguyen mentions it's a must.

Flanagan recross

Defense asks if Propofol can be used for other reasons than procedures. Defense asks if Thao Nguyen knows conscious sedation. Defense mentions that Thao Nguyen only used Propofol during a procedure so divided the responsibility with anesthesiologist and asks if there's no procedure could she give it alone (be in charge of giving Propofol). Thao Nguyen replies " I don't use Propofol when there's no procedure being done". Flanagan says that's because she never practiced outside a hospital. Thao Nguyen says she does work outside a hospital setting and she would never use Propofol in an outpatient setting. Defense asks how much Propofol she would give to someone Michael Jackson's size. Thao Nguyen says that it would depend the conditions and if other sedatives were used. Flanagan states Propofol being commonly used outside hospital setting. Thao Nguyen disagrees , Flanagan asks if Thao Nguyen knows Propofol being given at a dentist offices and gastroenterologist, Thao Nguyen says she was not aware of it and never asked what they gave and wasn't interested. Thao Nguyen says that she was only concerned with what is given to her.

Walgren redirect

Walgren asks Thao Nguyen if she has ever heard Propofol being used in someone's home in a private residence, she says that's a first.

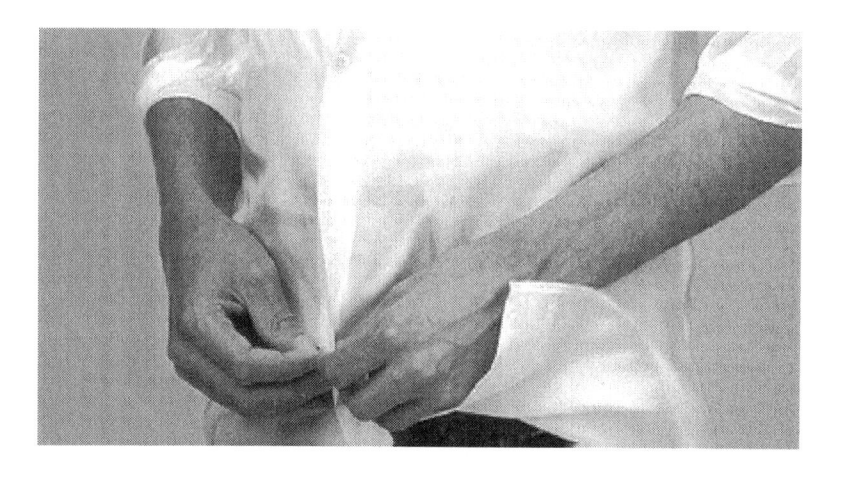

Dr. Joanne Prashad Testimony

Brazil Direct

Joanne Prashad Internal medicine physician for 9 years at a Houston Hospital.

Joanne Prashad was called to evaluate a patient for a surgery to see if the patient can undergo surgery. Joanne Prashad generally sees the patient, takes their medical history, does a physical exam and she would review medical charts. The patient had a recent surgery done by Conrad Murray, Conrad Murray had placed a stent to an artery on his leg to keep a blood vessel open. Patient was taking medications (Plavix) which was a concern for the surgeon and the anesthologist. Patient had an open wound on the leg that went to the bone. If they do the surgery the wound would additional bleed. The concern was that if the patient could continue to take Plavix or not. The stent was put into 4.5 months ago. Joanne Prashad saw that he was taking plavix medicine , generally it's taken for 6 months. She needed to learn if the medicine could be stopped. Joanne Prashad wanted to ask Conrad Murray what was his opinion about this patient and if she can tell the patient to stop the plavix and have the surgery. Brazil questions about medical chart and asks if they are important. Joanne Prashad says they are important because they can get the accurate medical information from them. Patient generally don't know the details of the medications and previous procedures. Shee called Conrad Murray's office and was given a phone number it was a answering service. She called the office again and was given a second phone number. Joanne Prashad called the second number and explains her reason for calling and she asked if this patient needs to continue to take Plavix or if they can stop it and the patient can have the surgery. Conrad Murray was clear, he said the patient need to continue the medicine for 6 months and postpone the surgery until that the time period was over. Conrad Murray properly told the medicine dosage and his treatment plan. She was surpised that she called out of the blue and he was able to give an answer. Generally doctors would say they need to review the chart and call back. Conrad Murray was clear about the treatment and about the need for the medication. 10:20 AM . It was a brief call. Conrad Murray provided the information she needed. She decided to postpone the procedure based on the information she got from Conrad Murray.

Defense Chernoff cross

Defense mentions that a lot of the times doctors doens't remember the patient but Conrad Murray did, he knew the treatment, he knew the medication. Chernoff asks if she was impressed with Conrad Murray, she says she was impressed.

Antoinette Gill Testimony

She's from Las Vegas, Nevada. She has known Murray for over 10 years. She was referred to him by a client of hers. She is a patient of Conrad Murray.

Mid June she received a letter from Conrad Murray's office. It said that Conrad Murray was going on to a sabbatical. She called Conrad Murray's cell phone on June 25th at 8:45AM. She had a short normal conversation. She was seeking referral for another physician she didn't receive it.

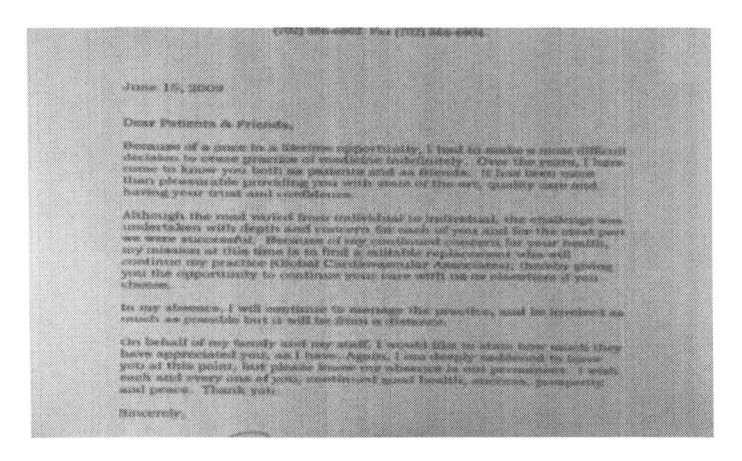

No Defense Cross

Consuelo Ng Testimony

Consuelo Ng met Conrad Murray 2003 -2004 when Conrad Murray was treating her grandmother. Consuelo Ng says Conrad Murray helped to cure her grandmother. She volunteered to work at Conrad Murray's Las Vegas office and she was working as a caregiver at a group home. She's not a nurse. She consistently volunteered in Conrad Murray's Las Vegas office 5 days a week. She worked at the front and back of the office. She did filing, answered phones and took vitals of the patients. She knows Robert Russell who used the ECP room. 3 other girls Carol, Sarah, Leah worked at Conrad Murray's office. Carol mostly handles the front office - checking in patient, scheduling appointments, answering the phones, authorizations from insurance and verification and filing of insurances. Leah works at back of the office also answer calls and help the front if needed. Sarah does the same. None of them are registered nurse. They are not licensed vocational nurses. All of them did whatever needd in the office. Conrad Murray also has an assistant administrator Stacy who worked from San Diego. Stacy order supplies, process payroll. Conrad Murray will be in Houston for a week and next week he will be in Las Vegas. Las Vegas office will be open when Conrad Murray was in Houston. When Conrad Murray is in Houston they would provide ECP threaphy and an Echo tech would come and do echocardiogram (echo).

ECP threaphy : They would wrap lower extremities, they put the patient on a Blood Pressure cuff, check oxygen level, hook up the patient on machine. They would check the oxygen level with a machine that they put it on the finger. When Conrad Murray was not in office he would call the office daily to check. When Conrad Murray was in Houston they would see patients in a partial day basis. Conrad Murray did not perform procedures in his office. His procedures will be on Friday at the hospital.

June 2009 - she did not know Conrad Murray was in California. Conrad Murray would call in to say to rechedule some patients. Brazil mentions the June 15 letter sent to Conrad Murray's patients telling that the Conrad Murray would leave his practice for a period of time. Conrad Murray told his staff that he was the personal physician of Michael Jackson before the June 15 letter. They would continue working for Conrad Murray, another physician would come and would take over but it wasn't set up. June 25, she was working in the office with Carol, Leah and Sarah. Conrad Murray called the office, she did not speak to him. 11:18 AM 32 minute call. She did not speak to him, someone else from the office could have talked to Conrad Murray. It was his normal habit to call the office when he was away. They went to lunch, they weren't seeing patients that day. When they got back from lunch, they got a call from their biller. That how they found up something happened to Michael Jackson .

Defence cross Chernoff

Defense asks if she was supbeonad to testify. She says yes. Defense goes over Conrad Murray's schedule. Mondays and wednesdays he sees patients in the afternoon, mornings makes rounds in the hospital. Tuesdays see patients mornings, make rounds in the afternoons. Fridays he does procedures at the hospital. Defense again goes over if Conrad Murray would call the office and what they would do in the office when Conrad Murray was away. She repeats the previous answers. Defense asked why she volunteered to work in Conrad

Murray's office. She says because she wanted to learn and experience how it is working as a medical assistant was. she saw how Conrad Murray treated her grandmother. Chernoff question: Did Conrad Murray had a tendency to become friends with his patients? Yes. Patients had an attachment to Conrad Murray? Yes they did. She stopped working Conrad Murray because of what happened, Conrad Murray shut down his practice due to what happened with Michael Jackson

Objection.

Sustained.

Conrad Murray talked everyone at the same time and told that he was going on sabbatical to go on tour with Michael Jackson. They were excited "because it was Michael Jackson and everyone knows Michael Jackson ". Conrad Murray told them he would be back by the end of year.

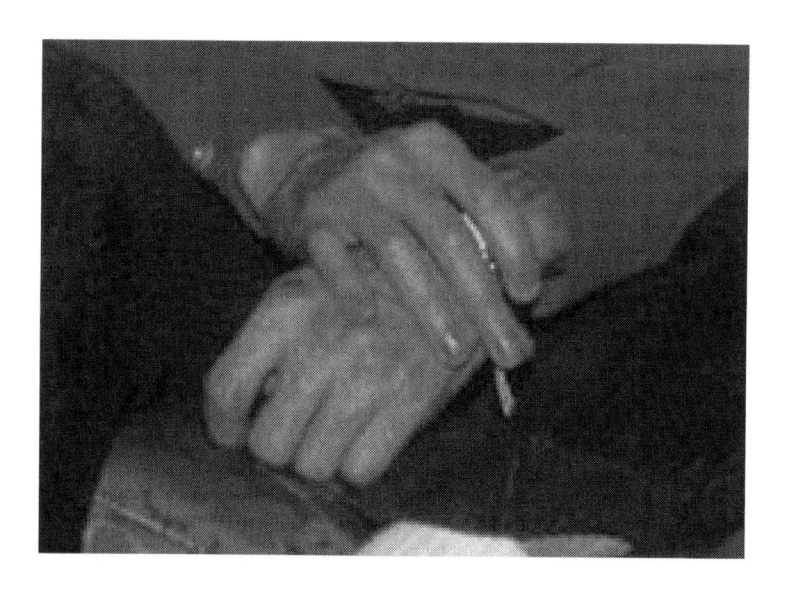

Bridgette Morgan testimony

Brazil Direct

She met Conrad Murray in 2003 in a social setting. She maintained a relationship / friendship with Conrad Murray. Conrad Murray told her that he was Michael Jackson's personal physician.

She called Conrad Murray on June 25th. 11:26 AM. Conrad Murray didn't answer the phone.

Defense cross

She lives in Los Angeles since 1998.

Brazil redirect

She met Conrad Murray in Las Vegas.

Murray Trial Summaries Day 6/October 4 -2011
Stacey Ruggels Testimony

Brazil Direct

Stacey Ruggels has worked for Conrad Murray since 1997. June 25. 10:34 AM phone call. She talked to Conrad Murray for 8.5 minutes. 11:07AM she called Conrad Murray back. She spoke to him again.

Chernoff Cross

Defense asks what the conversation was about. Stacey Ruggels says she called Conrad Murray to let Conrad Murray know that she had sent the email. It was brief call. Defense asks if she helped Conrad Murray to open an office in Houston in 2005. Conrad Murray wanted to open an office for his father's memory. Her duty was to look for places to open office. They opened the office in July 10, 2006. After the Houston office opened he would go every other week - one week Houston one week in Las Vegas. Type of patients in Houston office are people that are on fixed income and cannot afford to see physicians. Houston was a high volume office, Conrad Murray saw a lot of patients. Conrad Murray did not profit from the Houston office, there was very minimal income coming from that office.

Stacey Ruggels learned Conrad Murray was going to work for Michael Jackson April 2009. She was involved with trying get another cardiologist for Conrad Murray's place.

Brazil Redirect

Brazil asks how many offices Murray had as of June 2009. Conrad Murray only had 2 offices in Las Vegas and Houston.

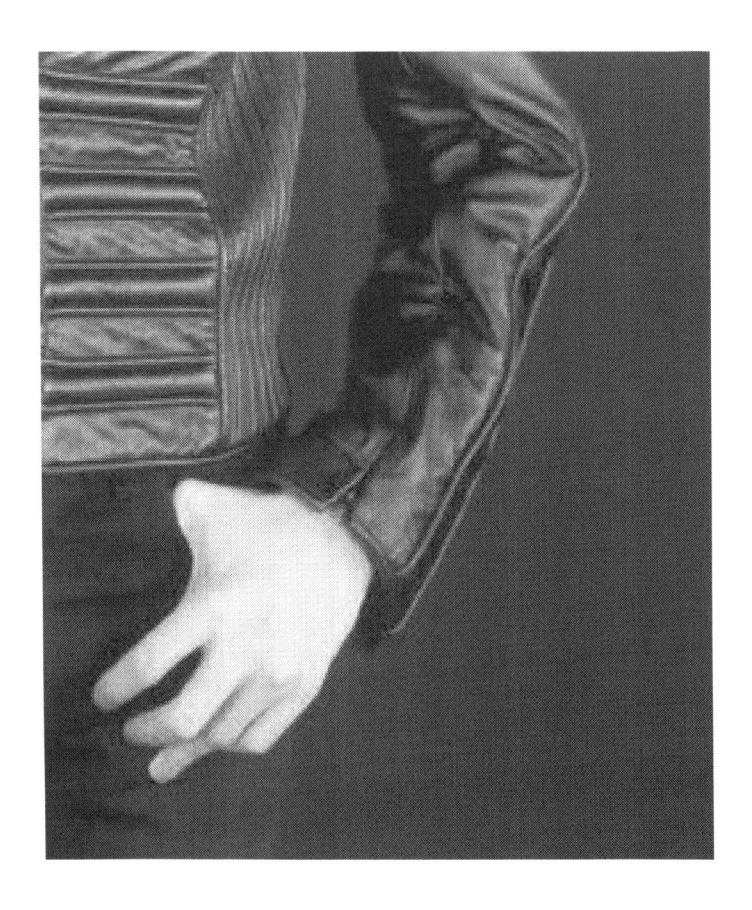

Michelle Bella Testimony

Brazil Direct

Bella met Conrad Murray in February 2008. She met Conrad Murray in a Las Vegas club that she was working. Conrad Murray gave her his phone number. She called Conrad Murray. Conrad Murray called her as well. Conrad Murray sent her text messages and she had sent him text messages.

June 25th Conrad Murray sent her a text message. June 16th she received a voice mail from Conrad Murray. Brazil wants to play the June 16 voice mail.

Objection.

Sidebar.

Brazil asks if Conrad Murray told her if he was Michael Jackson's doctor. She says yes. Conrad Murray also mentioned working for Michael Jackson on the voice mail. On the voice mail did Conrad Murray said he hoped to meet with her in the club? She says yes but the answer is stricken.

No defense recross

Sade Anding Testimony

Brazil Direct

She lives in Houston Texas and worked as a waitress. Conrad Murray gave her his phone number when they met Feb 2009. After that first meeting and phonecall they spent time together and communicted by calling each other. They exchanged text messages as well. They maintained regular contact and got to know each other better.

June 25. Conrad Murray called her. She was in Houston. The call was 11:51 AM. Conrad Murray said "Hello it's Conrad Murray. How are you doing?" She asked "how he was doing?" and said "I haven't talked to you in a while". Sade Anding had seen Conrad Murray in May in Houston and went to dinner. Conrad Murray said "Well.." and paused. Sade Anding said "let me tell you about my day". Conrad Murray didn't respond. She realized that Conrad Murray was no longer saying anything on the phone. Sade Anding says she realized 5 to 6 minutes into the phone call Conrad Murray wasn't saying anything back to her. Sade Anding said "Hello Hello" she didn't hear anything. Sade Anding pressed the phone to her ear and heard mumbling of voices. It was like the phone was in Conrad Murray's pocket. She also heard coughing. She did not recognize who the mumling voice was. She said "hello hello are you there hello" several times. She didn't receive any response from

Conrad Murray. Sade Anding hang up the phone can tried to call back and text multiple times but there was no replies. Sade Anding later learned that Michael Jackson was dead.

Brazil tries to ask about the next phonecall she had with Conrad Murray after Michael Jackson was dead.

Objection. Sidebar.

July 23, 2009. Sade Anding's father told her that Los AngelesPD detectives was in Houston and wanted to speak with her. Sade Anding called Conrad Murray and talked to him. She told that Los AngelesPD detectives wanted to talk to her. Conrad Murray said "why they are calling you? I'm sorry they are contacting you. I'm going to give you my lawyer's number. Make sure that when you speak to Los AngelesPD to have my lawyer present".

Defense Chernoff Cross

Chernoff goes over June 25th phonecall. Chernoff asks if the voices she heard could be Conrad Murray. Sade Anding answers yes. Defense asks how long she was on the phone before she hang up after she realized Conrad Murray wasn't responding. Sade Anding says 3 to 4 minutes.

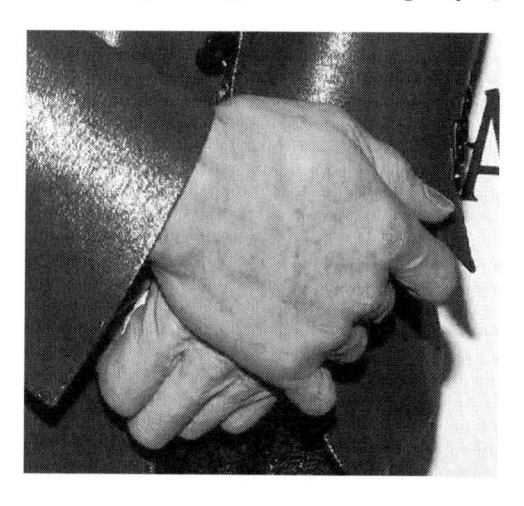

Nicole Alvarez Testimony

Brazil Direct

Nicole Alvarez met Conrad Murray at 2005 in a club at Las Vegas. They exchanged phone numbers and kept in contact. A few months later their relationship became something beyond friendship. She was in a relationship with Conrad Murray in 2009 and gave birth to a son in March 2009. She had been living in her apartment for 3-4 years.

Conrad Murray told her that he was Michael Jackson's personal physician in 2008. Nicole Alvarez says that she was interested and excited about hearing that Conrad Murray was Michael Jackson's doctor. Nicole Alvarez says that she didn't ask questions as she respected Conrad Murray's profession. Nicole Alvarez says that she met Michael Jackson around 2008. She was introduced by Conrad Murray. Conrad Murray arranged the meeting as a surprise to Nicole Alvarez. She was speechless when she met Michael Jackson. She met Michael Jackson at his home. At the time she met Michael Jackson, he was the only patient of Conrad Murray 's that she met. Nicole Alvarez says after Michael Jackson 's death she met some of Conrad Murray's patient in Houston. Nicole Alvarez says she accompanied Conrad Murray to Michael Jackson's residence 2-3 times. Michael Jackson wanted to see her son. She went to Michael Jackson's residence after

March 2009. Nicole Alvarez knew that Conrad Murray had practices Las Vegas and Houston. Nicole Alvarez says Conrad Murray didn't mention having a medical practice in California. Nicole Alvarez says that she still lives with Conrad Murray. Conrad Murray in 2009 was living in her residence and was paying her rent of $2500 and provided financial support. Nicole Alvarez says she's an actress. Brazil asks where Nicole Alvarez was working in May and June 2009. Nicole Alvarez says she was maintaining her instrument (herself), going on casting calls, auditioning and refining her craft. April 2009. Conrad Murray was living with Nicole Alvarez but not on full time basis. Conrad Murray was maintaining his practices and knew that Conrad Murray was Michael Jackson's personal physician. Conrad Murray would leave at night time to go to Michael Jackson. Nicole Alvarez knew that Conrad Murray was working for Michael Jackson, she didn't know at what capacity. Conrad Murray's routine. Conrad Murray would leave around 9 PM and return in the morning sometimes it would be early morning (6-7 AM) and later he started to come around 8-9-10 AM. Conrad Murray would go very frequently with a few off days. May 2009. Conrad Murray's activities would be similar to the April 2009. Nicole Alvarez at times called Conrad Murray while he was working Michael Jackson, she says the calls were brief. June 2009 Conrad Murray's schedule was similar. Nicole Alvarez knew that Michael Jackson getting ready for his concert tour. Nicole Alvarez didn't ask Conrad Murray about the show and rehearsals because she thought she would see the show as she would be accompanying Conrad Murray to London. She learned they would be going to London in March 2009. Nicole Alvarez wasn't aware of the negotiation details but she knew that they were arranging places for them to live. Nicole Alvarez says that she don't recall reveiving Conrad Murray 's contract through fax. Brazil reminds her about her preliminary hearing in which she said she saw the AEG contract. Nicole Alvarez says she never read the details. Brazil goes over the preliminary hearing testimony and readsthat Nicole Alvarez received a fax and looked to the contract and she looked and knew that Conrad Murray would be paid $150,000. Nicole Alvarez says as of now she doesn't recall that moment. Nicole Alvarez says that if she said that's what happened then it's true. Nicole Alvarez didn't know when they were going to London. Nicole Alvarez knew that they would be gone until November.

Direct continued

April, May, June Conrad Murray was living with Nicole Alvarez's apartment and was providing care to Michael Jackson. At the same time packages addressed to Conrad Murray were being delivering to her house. Conrad Murray would tell her that he's expecting packages. Conrad Murray didn't tell her what was in the packages. Nicole Alvarez says she didn't know what the packages contained. Nicole Alvarez says she didn't open the packages. Nicole Alvarez signed for the packages. Conrad Murray also received mail at her address. Some packages was left at her door and sometimes they were left in the common area. Nicole Alvarez would make sure that Conrad Murray knew that he had a package.

Brazil enters Fedex receipts into evidence dated April 8th, April 29th, May 1st, May 13th, May 15th, June 11 and June 16th.

June 25th. 1:08 PM. Conrad Murray called Nicole Alvarez's home number. Conrad Murray told her he was on the way to the hospital with Michael Jackson. Conrad Murray didn't want her to be alarmed. She received phonecalls from Conrad Murray in the late afternoon. Conrad Murray came to her house in the late afternoon.

No defense cross

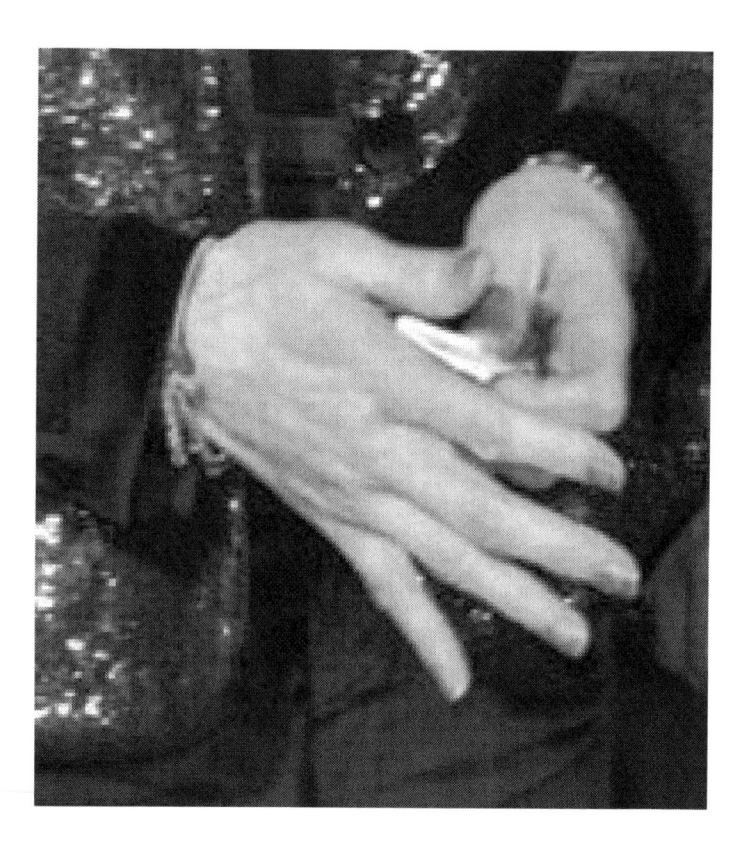

Tim Lopez Testimony

Brazil Direct

Tim Lopez owner and pharmacist of Applied Pharmacy. Applied pharmacy is a specialized pharmacy that made compounds.

Tim Lopez received a phone call from Conrad Murray at November 2008. Conrad Murray told that he had patient having Vitiligo and needed Benoquine. Tim Lopez needed to look to the raw materials to see if he can make the Benoquine. Tim Lopez told Conrad Murray he would look into it and let him know. During their office move Tim Lopez lost Conrad Murray's information and didn't call him back. March 2009. Tim Lopez received a phonecall from Conrad Murray. Conrad Murray asked why Tim Lopez didn't call him back. Tim Lopez told him that they were in the middle of the move and lost his Conrad Murray. Tim Lopez got his contact information and promised that he would keep in touch. Tim Lopez looked for the compounds to create Benoquine. Conrad Murray asked what strentgh Tim Lopez could make the cream, he said he can make the standard 20% strength. Tim Lopez said they can make 40 of 30gr tubes. Conrad Murray placed an order. Conrad Murray was also told about preordering and he needed to pay up front. Conrad Murray said he had many African American patients that suffer from Vitiligo and this was a trial basis to see how the medicine worked. Conrad Murray told he had multiple clinics and would use the cream overseas as well. Conrad Murray would have come to Tim Lopez's office to pick it up and pay with a company check for $1,200

Conrad Murray provided Tim Lopez with his medical office in Las Vegas and he told him his DEA licence number and his medical license number. Tim Lopez verified Conrad Murray's medical license and DEA number. Tim Lopez says as the cream was asked for a "trial basis" and under doctor control he didn't need to know the patient's name. Tim Lopez says he would need to know the name of the patient once they are prescribed the cream for home use. When Conrad Murray came to pick up the cream, he discussed if the cream could be delievered to his office. Tim Lopez said they could. Tim Lopez also said they needed to have credit card on account for future orders. Conrad Murray gave him his credit card number. April 2009. Conrad Murray called Tim Lopez and said he was happy with the cream. Conrad Murray asked if the pharmacy was able to order other stuff for his offices. Conrad Murray asked him to find pricing and availability of normal saline IV bags and Propofol. Tim Lopez says he didn't sell Propofol before Conrad Murray asked him about him. Conrad Murray wanted 100ml and 20ml sizes. Tim Lopez found out the pricing information for Propofol. Conrad Murray placed an order on April 6th on the phone. 10 bottles of 100ml Propofol and 25 bottles of 20ml Propofol. The first shipment was sent to Conrad Murray's Vegas office. Conrad Murray removed some items and asked if the rest can be shipped to his office in Los Angeles. April 28 order. 40 bottles of 100ml Propofol and 25 bottles of 20ml Propofol.

Brazil Direct Continued

April 30. Conrad Murray inquired about availability of Lorazepam and Midazolam in injectible form. Lorazepam is also available in a pill format. 10 vials of 10ml Lorazepam, 20 vials of 2ml Midazolam. First 2 weeks of May. Tim Lopez discussed several items with Conrad Murray. had a concern with the base of Benoquin, wanted it to be less greasy. Tim Lopez said he could do several formulas. Conrad Murray also asked if it could be done in a larger packaging size. Conrad Murray wanted packaging to look better. Conrad Murray wanted energy formulations for boost. Conrad Murray didn't want any narcotics or prescription drugs, he wanted natural products. Conrad Murray said this was for wakefulness and energy. Tim Lopez said he would look into it. Conrad Murray said his patients were complaining about injection site pain. Conrad Murray wanted a topical anesthetic that only had lidocaine cream in it. Tim Lopez did a mix for him that had 2% Lidocaine. Such creams are rub onto the skin before injecting a needle. May 12 receipt. 40 vials of 100ml Propofol. 25 vials of 20ml Propofol. 20 vials of 2ml Midazolam. 10 vials of 0.5 ml Flumazenil . Lidocaine cream 30 gr. May 14. Tim Lopez talked with Conrad Murray about Lidocaine cream. Conrad Murray wasn't getting the desired responde with thr 4% cream and wanted him to increase the strenght to 4 %. Conrad Murray asked about the energy formulation. Tim Lopez suggested several items to Conrad Murray and agreed to do more research on it. Tim Lopez also said that he would change the base of the Benoquin cream and would send Conrad Murray 3 samples and Conrad Murray would determine which one he liked better. Conrad

Murray asked Tim Lopez about Hydroquinone cream (used for Vitiligo) and Conrad Murray was interested in receiving a sample. Tim Lopez was driving to Los Angeles airport that weekend. Rather than charging Conrad Murray delivery fees, Tim Lopez offered to drive the items to Conrad Murray's office in Los Angeles. Conrad Murray said there was no need for it and he can just ship them as he always does. May 14 order. Lidocaine cream 4%. June 1. Tim Lopez had another talk about energy formulations. Conrad Murray requested Tim Lopez send some samples so that he can try them. Tim Lopez shipped these items with June 10 order. June 10. 25 vials 30ml Lidocaine. 40 vials of 100ml Propofol. 50 vials of 20ml Propofol. Hydroquinone 60 gr 20 tubes. Benoquin 60 gr 20 tubes. June 15. Conrad Murray said he was happy with the energy formulation. 10 vials 10ml Lorazepam, 20 vials 2 ml Midazolam. Saline IV 1000ml 12 bags. Conrad Murray never told him tha he was the doctor for Michael Jackson. Conrad Murray never mentioned any name of his patients. June 23 -24. Tim Lopez talked with Conrad Murray on the phone. There was a lot of background noise and he couldn't understand what Conrad Murray said. Tim Lopez said he would call him back. Tim Lopez didn't call Conrad Murray. On June 25 he learned that Michael Jackson died.

Brazil asks total number of Propofol bottles. 255 bottles of Propofol. 20 vials of Lorazepam. 60 vials of Midazolam.

Gourjian cross

Tim Lopez put in the DEA number in their system. There was no red flags. Conrad Murray was authorized to make these orders. Benoquin is not controlled substance. Propofol is not controlled substance.

Gourjian asks if there's a regulation that says he could only ship to clinics and/or hospitals. Tim Lopez says he doesn't know any regulations. Gourjian tries to ask what Tim Lopez's delivery person said about Conrad Murray (all positive and nice things). It's is sustained as it's hearsay. Gourjian asks if the medicines are for an office use, they

117

won't disclose the patient names when ordering. Tim Lopez says yes as they wouldn't know who the patient will be. Gourjian asks if this will also apply to high profile patients.

Brazil redirect

Talks about confidentiality. Asks if a physican tells the patient's identity if Tim Lopez would keep it private. Tim Lopez says yes.

Court ends early due to some scheduling issues.

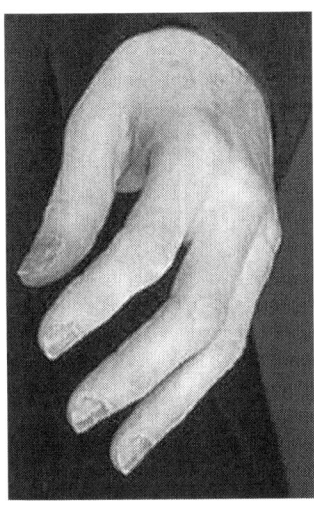

Murray Trial Summaries Day 7/ October 5- 2011
Sally Hirschberg Testimony

Prosecutor Walgren Direct

Sally Hirschberg states that she is employed with SeaCoast Medical, a medical and pharmaceutical distributor and they sell medical supplies. Sally Hirschberg states she is an account rep and she has been employed there for 10 years. Sally Hirschberg states that they have an account record of medical order records held by Conrad Murray.

Sally Hirschberg states that she holds records for a Conrad Murray on Flamingo Road in Las Vegas. Sally Hirschberg states that records reflect a Consuelo Ng, was the account rep that Sally Hirschberg worked with who represented Murray. Sally Hirschberg states that Murray's account was created in December 2006, and that the address was always the address in Las Vegas. Sally Hirschberg states that an order was placed 12/16/08, and then there is a lull in activity until 4/14/09. Sally Hirschberg states that prior to 4/09, even though there was no activity, there were phone conversations between she and

Consuelo Ng, with Murray requesting an infusion IV set. Sally Hirschberg states that 3/25/09, Murray via Ng requested a case of Safe Site infusion IV sets. Sally Hirschberg states that on 3/26/09, the account had a credit card declined, so the infusion set was not shipped. Sally Hirschberg states that on 3/31/09, nothing yet had been resolved as far as payment. Sally Hirschberg states that with regard to the infusion sets, 24 come in a case. Sally Hirschberg states that on 4/13/09, she spoke to Ng, Ng asked her to send the infusion sets to a residential address in CA, but Sally Hirschberg did not agree, it brought up a red flag in her opinion. Sally Hirschberg states that on 4/14/09, the invoice shows that the products ordered were a case of sodium chloride solution, a blood pressure cuff, some parts for the blood pressure cuff, components for infusion sets, a tubing device, 20 gauge 1 inch 3 cc syringe needles, IV catheters 25 gauge (50 in a box), transparent dressing a type of bandage, set of syringes 30 cc (40 in pkg), IV catheters, ultrasound equipment, electrode gauze (would attach to EKG machine), alcohol prep pads, gauze sponge, drape sheet (fabric cover that would drape over patient), saline bags (48), sodium chloride bags, and that the order was processed to a credit card belonging to Conrad Murray. Sally Hirschberg states that latex gloves, IV components for infusion sets, XL administration sets, exam paper for the bed, exam gloves were also ordered. Sally Hirschberg states that on 4/16/09, lidocaine 1% 25 of them were shipped. Sally Hirschberg states that on 4/21/09, blood pressure cuff and components, medex injection adapters, IV catheters were ordered and shipped on 4/24/09 as well the pump IV set. Sally Hirschberg states that on 5/12/09, her records reflect that 25 1% 30 lidocaine, more medex T connectors, a child's blood pressure cuff, tape, tourniquets, more medex catheters, blood pressure cuff for adult, shipped on 5/12/09. Sally Hirschberg states that the blood pressure cuff is packaged inside a plastic bag and then in a white box, manufactured by Starline. Sally Hirschberg states that alcohol pads, 10 cc syringes (100 in a box), saline bags, 10 cc syringes 22 gauge (100 in a box), hypodermic needles (50 in a box) were ordered. Sally Hirschberg states that on 5/19/09, Murray's order is more infusion connectors, blood pressure device for a child, IV catheters (50 in a box), urine pads, external catheter medium for urine collection, urine collection bags were ordered. Sally Hirschberg states that on June 1, 2009, an ambu-bag, and an airway kit was ordered. Sally Hirschberg states that this is the first time an ambu-bag was ever ordered, and that the airway kit price is $2.02 per kit. When asked Sally Hirschberg states that the airway kit has six in a package. Sally Hirschberg states that on 6/15/09, she talked to Ng about urine bags, that Ng wanted a small urine bag, and Sally Hirschberg told her she was not aware that small urine bags were made. Sally Hirschberg states that she later talked to Ng, who had contacted the manufacturer directly, and that small urine collection bags were not made. Sally Hirschberg states that on 6/22/09, Murray's invoice order includes catheters external wide band (small) was backordered and not shipped, urine bags, which were shipped, leg bags for catheters (medium) were ordered but not shipped. Sally Hirschberg states that she told Ng that there would be increased cost, as Ng requested the order was shipped overnight. Sally Hirschberg states that she spoke to Ng on 6/26/09 at 9:26 am PST, and that Sally Hirschberg cancelled the order per Ng's request.

Chernoff Cross

Sally Hirschberg states that Murray's company, Global CardioVascular has been doing business with SeaCoast since 2006. Sally Hirschberg states that it is not unusual for Murray's practice to order lidocaine or infusion pump sets, but often. Sally Hirschberg states that her records go back to July, 2007. Sally Hirschberg states that 7/20/07, a horizon pump set was ordered, and it was the same set that was ordered in April 24, 2009. Sally Hirschberg states that on October 5, 2007 a horizon pump set, the same set that was ordered on 6/24/08. Sally Hirschberg states that just by looking at certain items, she is able to identify them, others she cannot. Sally Hirschberg reaffirms that on April 25, and May 12 a set of IV administrations were ordered, and that there are 50 per case.

Stephen Marx Testimony

Walgren begins by offering a stipulation regarding the iPhone about to be discussed in Marx' testimony. The stipulation is the iPhone which is about to be discussed is the iPhone taken from Murray on July 28th, 2009, with a phone number of (702) ***-0973. This is the same iPhone Murray had with him on June 25th, 2009. The stipulation is granted.

Prosecutor Walgren Direct

Marx states he was a computer forensics examiner in July of 2009. He has since retired. He was employed by the DEA (Drug Enforcement Agency)in Norton, Virginia for 7 years. Marx states his job was to extract evidence from digital devices and then organize it for use by investigators. Marx confirms he has testified previously in such regard, testifying as an expert in the field of computer forensic examination. Marx confirms he conducted an analysis for Murray's iPhone mentioned above. Walgren begins asking Marx about screenshots and how such pertains to an iPhone.

Marx: As it relates to an I-Phone, the operating system of an I-Phone will save what's displayed on the screen into memory for reasons of possibly recalling it. It's a temporary saving of an image of what's on the screen. Walgren clarifies that "an image" pertains to what someone physically sees when looking at their iPhone, and this image is saved to the memory of the phone. Marx confirms this image in typically saved in a .jpeg format, as many photos are in this same format.

Walgren: Ok. And is it placed somewhere specifically on the I-Phone, or is it just floating around in an open memory space? Or where is it?

Marx: Both. It depends upon whether the operating system is making it available foe recall or whether it's an image which has been saved previously but is no longer in use.

Marx is asked about "allocated space" and states he is familiar with the term.

Marx: yes. Allocated space is space on a digital device which the operating system is actively using. In other words, if you have a storage area, the operating system will keep track of what's stored in particular areas within that. And it will recall that data. Unallocated space is space where the operating system has determined that it no longer needs the data which is saved there and in it's index marks it as no longer being necessary. And it will be overriden in time.

Walgren asks Marx if once a screenshot is placed into an unallocated space, would it be overridden eventually? Marx states it is dependent upon the storage on the device, but yes, it would. It will be set up to eventually be overridden if in unallocated space. Marx states the larger the storage area for unallocated space on the phone, the less chance of being overridden.

Marx confirms he conducted an analysis of Murray's iPhone, including an analysis of the unallocated space on the phone. Marx confirms he was able to locate some screenshots.

Marx confirms that some screenshots contain a date. Marx states some may actually contain a graphic depiction of the date on the screenshot itself. He states for others, if the screenshot coincides with data, sometimes a date can be attached to it that way as well.

Marx confirms there were a large number of screenshots available on Murray's iPhone, but there was a limited number for which he could assign dates.

Walgren shows several exhibits to the defense for which there is no objection.

The first exhibit (People's 46) is a screenshot that was recovered from the allocated space of the iPhone. The screenshot was most recently updated on June 25th, 2009 at 7:03 a.m. This particular screenshot contains the actual date.

Walgren: Okay. And based on your testimony then, does this reflect that at 7:03 or sometime thereafter thr person in possessio of this iphone was viewing this scrennshot that we see here in people's 46?

Marx confirms this to be accurate.

Walgren moves onto the next exhibit which is People's 47. Marx confirms it is a screenshot with a date of June 25th, 2009 at 9:45 a.m., signifying the phone was viewed at that time or later.

Marx states he was able to recover an email during that time. Marx states the email was located in the email database on the phone.

Walgren: Okay. And did that e-mail also reflect an exchange of e-mails all dated or the revelant ones dated june 25, 2009?

Marx: Yes. That e-mail was reffered to as a thread which would be a series of linked communications.

Marx is asked to focus his attention upon an email (People's 48) with a date of June 25th, with the greeting "Hi, Conrad" and a an electronic signature from Bob Taylor of Robertson Taylor Insurance Brokers in London. Marx confirms the email was sent from London. Marx confirms the email was sent at 5:54 a.m. Los Angeles time. Marx confirms he was able to retrieve the contents of the email.

Walgren: Okay. And it appears to be from an insurance broker regarding the upcoming tour?

Marx: I don't know if he is an insurance broker. I know that the subject matter is the insurance for the cancellation policy, yes.

Marx confirms the email appears to have included "specific inquires" regarding the health of Michael Jackson. Marx and Walgren discuss how the contents may have been displayed. Marx states the email being discussed would be visible to the reader, the actual verbiage, though a user may use differing applications to view the actual words.

Walgren: And that includes the sentence, "you confirm that as far as you are aware you are the only doctor consulted during the three-year period".

Marx confirms he sees the line reference above.

Walgren: And proceeding that sentence was, "I have advised the insurers that your records go back from the present time to 2006 when you first met with Michael Jackson in Nevada", is that right?

Marx confirms this to be true. Marx confirms there to be a series of questions pertaining to press reports regarding Michael's health. Marx confirms he was able to detect the email was read. The screenshot of the email being read is labeled as People's 50.

Marx states he does see in People's 50 the line, "From Bob Taylor and the to Conrad" as well as the time of 5:54 a.m. Marx confirms the date of June 25th and he can see the greeting "Hi, Conrad".

Marx again confirms the email was read and there was a response to the email.

Walgren: Directing your attention what was marked people's 49 for identification, was this the response of e-mail that you he obtained from your forensic analysis of the i-phone?

Marx concurs and agrees the email contains the same subject line which was "Artist Insurance".

Marx confirms the email was from Conrad Murray ("from Conrad Murray being doctor dot Murray at G.C.A. at SBC global dot net") to Bob Taylor. Marx confirms the reply sent by Murray was sent at 11:17 a.m. Los Angeles time as of June 25th, 2009.

Marx confirms the email begins with "Dear Bob" and is signed with "Sincerely, Conrad Murrray".

Walgren: "That authorization for release of his medical records in order to assist you to procure cancellation insurance policy for his show. However, authorization was denied." Goes on to say, "in regarding to he statements of his health published by the press, let me say they're all falicous to the best of my knowledge. Sincerily, Conrad Murray."

Marx is able to confirm the email sent apparently by Murray was sent at 11:17 a.m. and was created by and sent from the iPhone per a screenshot.

Marx confirms that People's 50 (this is later found to be a mistake, it should be marked as People's 51) is a screenshot for the screen one would use to enter information for an email.

Walgren: And yhe text, you can see what appears to be the bottom half of the greeting, "dear Bob?"

Marx states "yes".

Walgren: Starting with "I'm in receipt of your e-mail?"

Marx confirms this to be true. He also confirms the information in the screenshot matches up to the full-email that was recovered.

Walgren: And this keyboard visible here, is that the keyboard that pops up on an I-phone when you want to use your fingers to send an e-mail?

Marx confirms this to be accurate. He continues...

Marx: I should also add to my previous statemeny that I found a reply to this. So it does appear that it was sent.

Walgren again confirms they are discussing the email that was sent at 11:17 a.m. Walgren concludes his direct examination.

Cross-Examination: Chernoff

Chernoff asks Marx if there were forwarded emails attached to the email from the insurance broker. Marx confirms this to be true.

Chernoff: And the e-mails that will were attached that were forwarded, did you observe that they were, they seemed to be sent back and forth to accompany New York individuals regarding Michael Jackson's insurance issues?

Marx concurs.

Chernoff asks if these individuals were with AEG but Marx is not able to specifically recall. Marx is asked if he recalls someone by the name of Sean Trell in any of the emails but states he cannot recall the name and would need to review the emails to be able to answer. Chernoff asks Marx if the emails are available to him to which he states they are available to him. Chernoff concludes his cross-examination.

Upon re-direct examination Walgren clarifies misstating an evidence item.

He clarifies the following:

People's 46 was the timestamp of 7:03 a.m.

People's 47 was the timestamp of 9:45 a.m.

People's 48 was the email from Bob Taylor sent at 5:54 a.m.

People's 49 is the response by Conrad Murray at 11:17 a.m.

People's 50 is the screenshot reflecting the reading of the email mentioned above.

Walgren states he may have called People's 51 People's 50 by mistake earlier. People's 51 is a screenshot showing the keyboard and the responsive email being sent from Murray to Taylor.

Walgren has nothing further. Chernoff declines to re-cross Marx. Marx is excused.

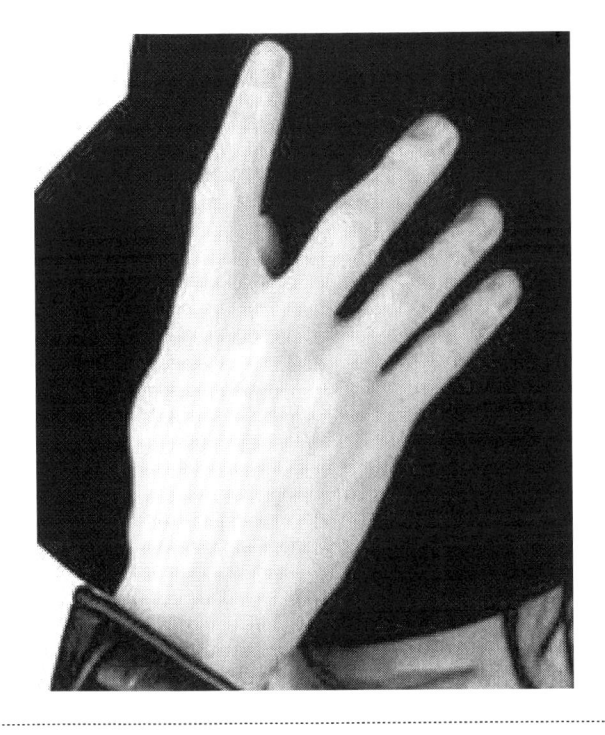

Elissa Fleak Testimony

Walgren Direct

Elissa Fleak states she has worked for the Los Angeles County Coroner for 8 years. Elissa Fleak states she went to UCLA to examine Michael Jackson and the circumstances of his death at 5:20 pm on June 25, 2009. Elissa Fleak states she examined Michael Jackson and documented his physical condition in a private room at UCLA.

Elissa Fleak states that she took the picture of Michael Jackson on the gurney, deceased. Elissa Fleak states that there were other pictures taken of Michael Jackson, but this was the first picture she took (the one that was shown on the first day of testimony). Elissa Fleak states that initially there were no obvious causes of death. Elissa Fleak states she took four bottles of blood from Michael Jackson and turned them into the coroner's lab for further toxicology testing. Elissa Fleak states that at 7:10 pm on 6/25, she went to Michael Jackson's Carolwood home. Elissa Fleak states that in the bedroom where Michael Jackson died, she located a 20 ml bottle of propofol on the floor next to the left side of the bed. Elissa Fleak states that she found the propofol bottles under a glass/metal table to the left of the nightstand, which is directly left of the bed.

Elissa Fleak is asked to identify items she found in the bedroom:

- A propofol bottle with few drops of fluid, Elissa Fleaks affirms it is the same bottle.

- An empty bottle of flumanezil nearly emptyfound near propofol bottle, Elissa Fleak affirms

- Prescription bottles: Diazepam, Lorazepam and Flomax, Elissa Fleak affirms

-Diazepam- prescribed to Michael Jackson , Murray prescribed to Michael Jackson on 6/20, 10 mg tablet

-Flomax - prescribed to Michael Jackson, Murray prescribed to Michael Jackson on 6/23

-Lorazepam - Murray prescribed on 4/28/09, 2 mg Elissa Fleak affirms all prescriptions

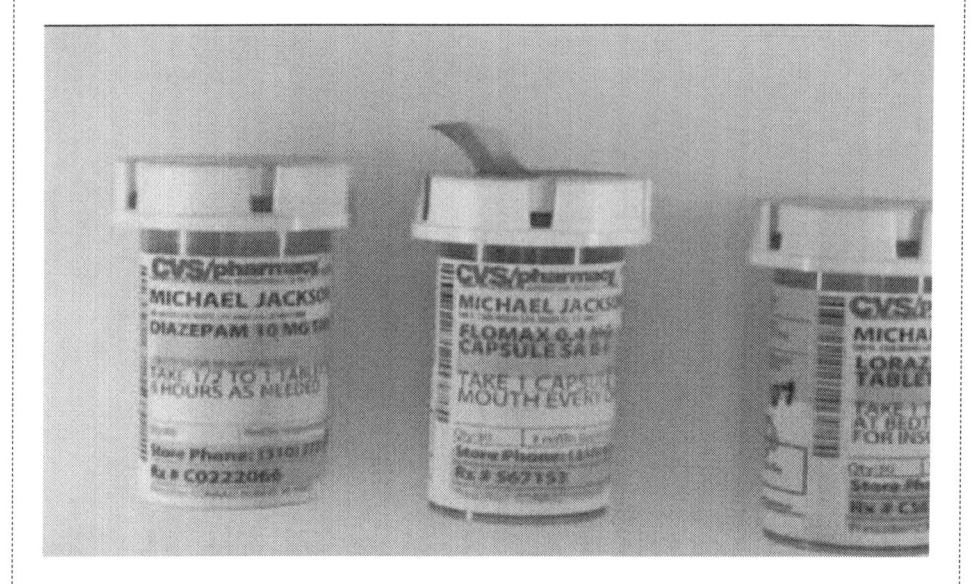

Elissa Fleak states additional prescriptions were found on the lower shelf of the table. Elissa Fleak states she found Trazadone, Flomazepam, and another drug.

Tizanadine - to Omar Arnold by Arnold Klein, 6/7/09

Flomazepam -to Mick Jackson, 1 mg tablet, Dr. Alan Dr. Allan Metzger, 4/18/09

Trazadone -to Mick Jackson, 50 mg tablet, Dr. Alan Dr. Allan Metzger 4/18/09

Temazapam -to Michael Jackson by Murray, filled 12/22/08

Hydroquinone - Applied Pharmacy name on it

Benoquin - Applied Pharmacy name on it

Lidocaine 4% - Applied Pharmacy, Conrad Murray's name on it

Elissa Fleak affirms that all of the above medications were found on the nightstand in the bedroom where Michael Jackson died. Elissa Fleak states that an ambu bag was found on the floor and an oxygen tanks, one on a rolling dolly, were all found in the room. Elissa Fleak states that alcohol prep pads, IV catheters, latex gloves, a 10 cc syringe with no needle attached to it, were also found on a nightstand in the room.

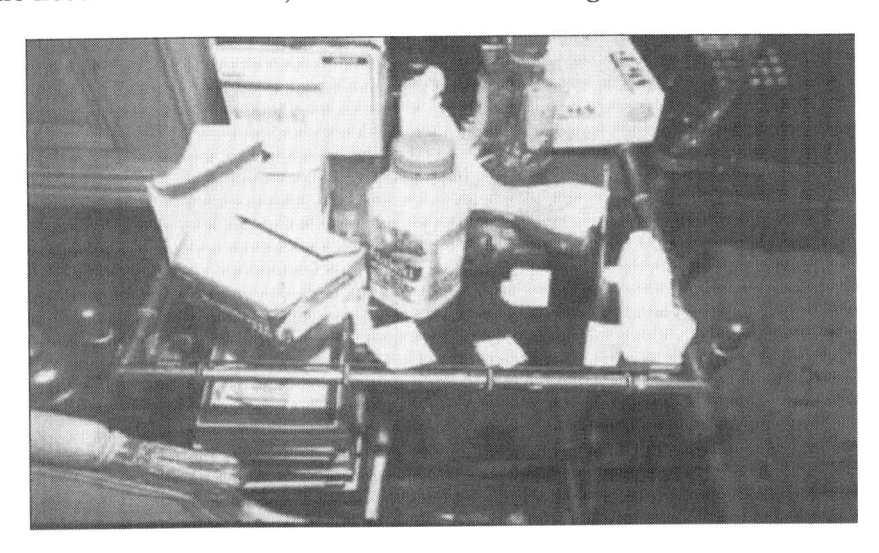

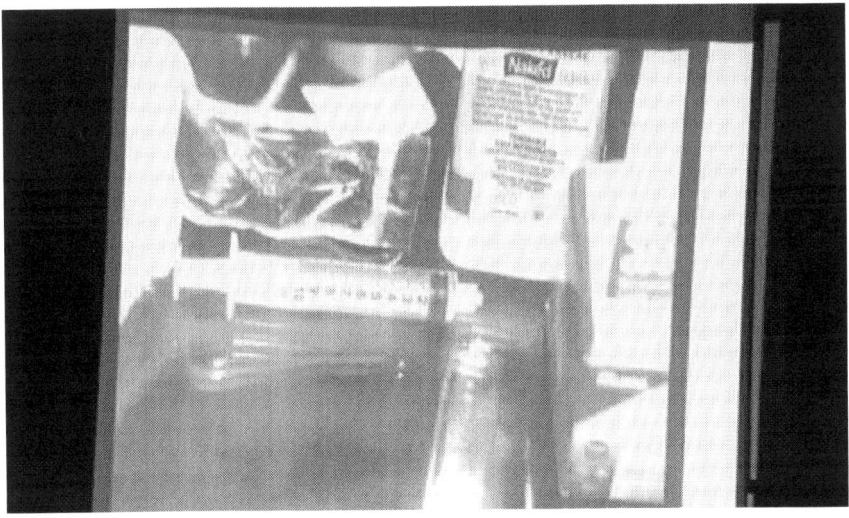

Elissa Fleak states that there was an IV catheter underneath the ambu-bag, to the left. Elissa Fleak states that she recovered a bottle of Bayer aspirin and other medical items, such as needles and supplies. Elissa Fleak states that there was a wooden chair with a jug of urine sitting on it with medical pads sitting next to it. Elissa Fleak states that all of the items were recovered on 6/25, except for the IV tubing and bag. Elissa Fleak states that she left Carolwood at 8:20 pm on 6/25, and returned on 6/29/09, to search for further medical evidence.

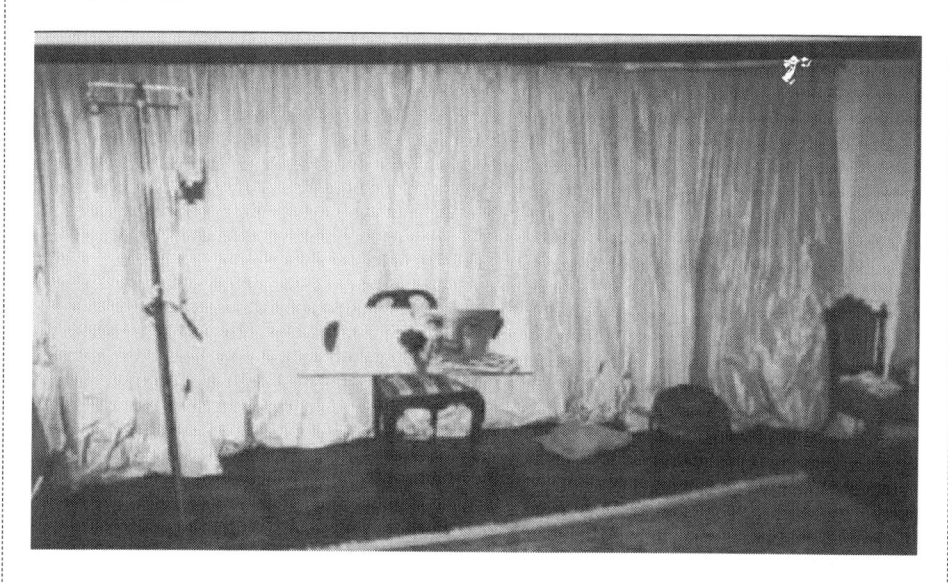

Elissa Fleak identifies that there is a large closet which adjoins the bedroom that Michael Jackson died in. Elissa Fleak states that she recovered items from the top of the closet area, including various bags, gloves and items. Elissa Fleak states a small black bag, a blue Costco bag, light/blue bag, a box of gloves and tubes of various lotion were recovered. Elissa Fleak states that the black bag had contents of a blood pressure cuff inside of a manufacturer Starline box. Elissa Fleak states that 3 bottles of lidocaine were found, 2 were essentially empty, 1 was half full and found inside the same black bag as the pressure cuff. Elissa Fleak states that the Costco bag contained a plastic grocery bag, a pulse oximeter, various items and a cut open saline bag with a 100 ml propofol inside the saline bag, Elissa Fleak states that she removed the propofol bottle from the saline bag to photograph them. Elissa Fleak states that the empty propofol bottle found within the saline bag was a 20 ml bottle.

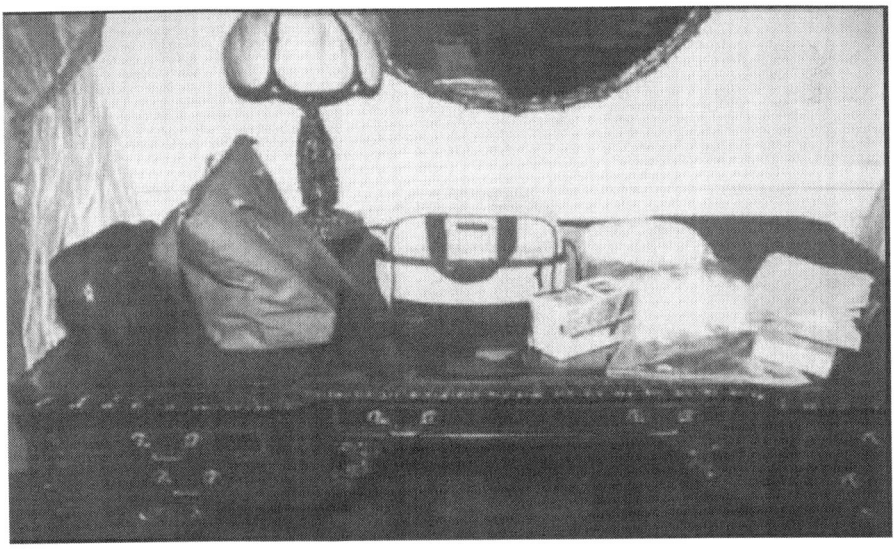

Elissa Fleak states a 10 vial of bottle of Lorazepam was found inside the Costco bag. Elissa Fleak states that 2 individual bottles, each 10 ml in size, of Midazolam were found inside the Costco bag. Elissa Fleak states that a small bloody cotton gauze pad was in the Costco bag. Elissa Fleak states that a pulse oximeter was inside the Costco bag as well as a plastic bag with various medical items in it. Elissa Fleak states that inside the plastic bag, an IV administration was found, a urinary bag was found, a wide band bag was found, Tegaderm transparent dressing was found, IV catheter empty packaging was found, various alcohol prep pads were found, Tegaderm dressing backings were found, 10 ml disposable syringe with needle packaging was found, 2 individual straps were found, a dark blue and light blue vinyl top were found, a needle or IV catheter top were found, as well as miscellaneous plastic debris were found inside the Costco bag. Elissa Fleak states that the light blue baby essentials bag contained 2 100 ml propofol bottles which were full, 7 20 ml propofol bottles, 3 were opened with various levels of liquid in them, 3 lidocaine bottle unopened, 2 unopened, 3 10 ml vials Midazolam, 2 unopened, 4 bottles of Flumanezil 5 ml in size, 2 bottles of Lorazepam, 1 unopened, 1 half full, 1 bottle from Applied Pharmacy combination of ephedrine, aspirin and caffeine, Bausch and Lomb eye drops, Medex bag containing IV tubing and syringes, a blue tourniquet, Murray's business cards were all found inside the Costco bag. Elissa Fleak states that on 6/29 she recovered the IV bag and tubing from the Carolwood home. Elissa Fleak states that 18 tubes of Benoquin cream were recovered from the cabinet next to the bags already mentioned. Elissa Fleak states that she recovered a saline bag on 6/29 that she had observed on 6/25. Elissa Fleak states that she recovered IV tubing with a spike at one end, with a roller clamp on 6/29, as well as a Y connector with attached tubing, s capped syringe inside a sharpie container.

(during this time Walgren places all the items on the table for the jury to see)

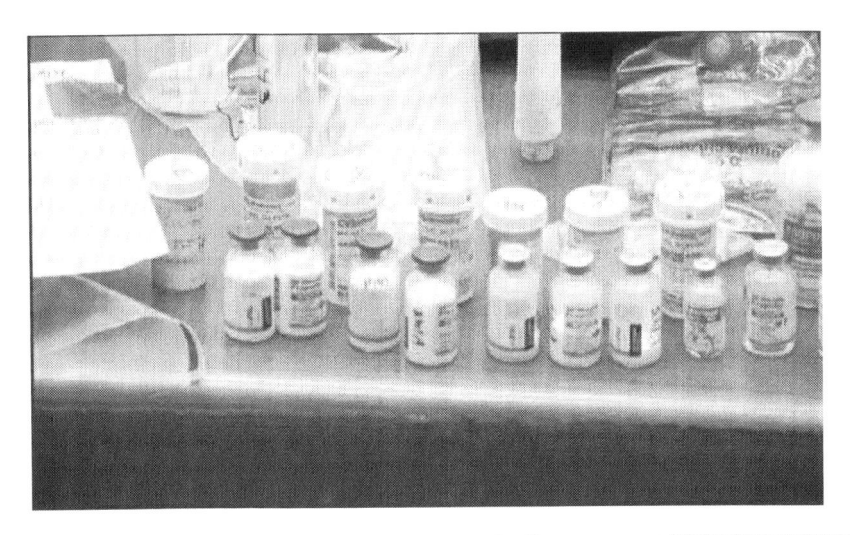

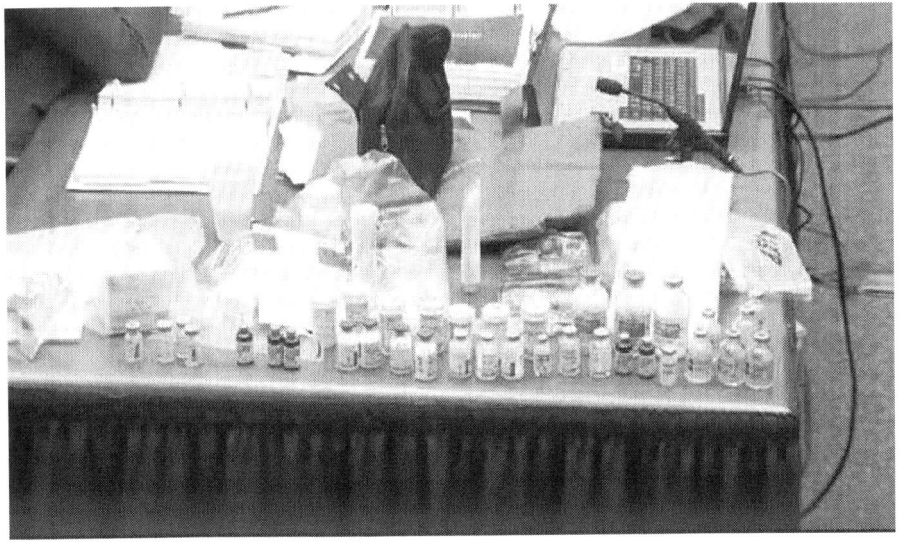

Elissa Fleak states that on July 1, 2009, she sent a subpoena seeking all relevant medical records of Michael Jackson to Ed Chernoff, Murray's attorney. Walgren wants to ask questions about the records Elissa Fleak received from Murray via Chernoff.

Objection. Sidebar.

Murray Trial Summaries Day 8/ October 6 -2011
Elissa Fleak Testimony continued

Walgren direct

Walgren enters more photographs into evidence.

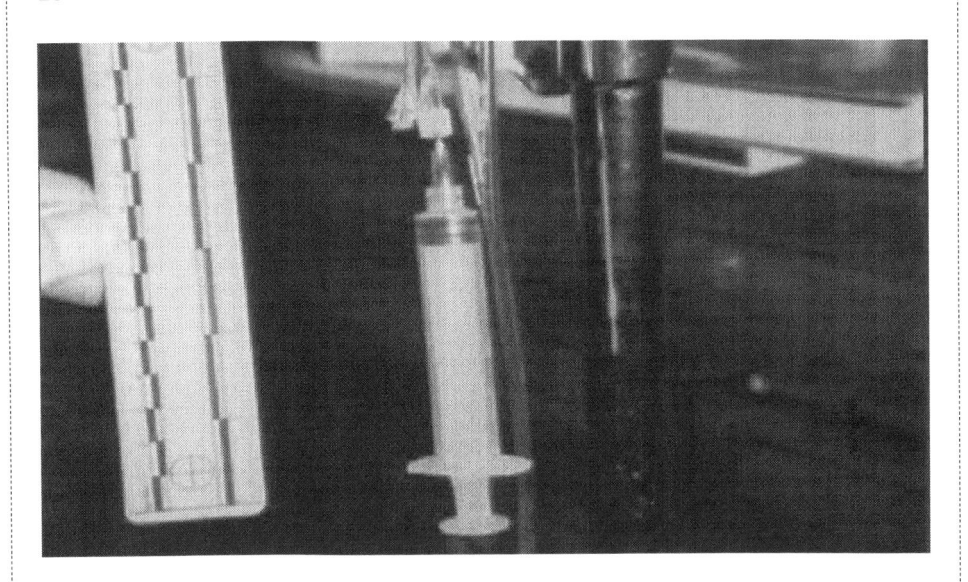

Walgren talks about "broken syringe". Elissa Fleak says she shouldn't have described it at broken syringe. She says she misdescribed the item, she should have written them seperately. She made an assumption that it was the pieces of the same syringe but she was wrong. Elissa Fleak says that she later realized that they have different tips (one square, one circle) and they don't fit together. Elissa Fleak's thumb print was found on the syringe. She doesn't know when that happened. Elissa Fleak says it might have happenned when she was moving the tables to take photos or repackaging the items. Elissa Fleak subpeonad Conrad Murray through his counsel Chernoff. Elissa Fleak wanted any and all medical records of Michael Jackson on July 1. Chernoff provided records to her. Walgren asks if the records covered April, May, June 2009. Elissa Fleak says they were all dated before that date. Walgren goes over the medical records they are from 2006, 2007, 2008 and use the names of Michael Jackson, Omar Arnold and Paul Farance (also Mike Smythe but letter crossed out).

Chernoff Cross

Chernoff asks if Elissa Fleak took more photos then it was shown to the jury. Elissa Fleak says yes. Chernoff talks about Elissa Fleak's role in this case. Chernoff talks about being a coroner investigator and the importance of her job. Elissa Fleak's job is to collect as much as information about the cause of the death and the motive for death. Chernoff mentions the importance of being accurate and being through with the investigation. Chernoff is asking who was there on June 25th. Detective Scott Smith from Los AngelesPD, her supervisor coroner Ed Winters and Los AngelesPD Crime Scene photographer. Elissa Fleak took notes, took photos and collected evidence. June 29. She went to the residence based on the information she got from Detective Scott Smith. Scott Smith told her that there would be additional medical evidence to be collected from the room next to the bedroom. Elissa Fleak didn't ask any more questions and she said that she would meet him at Carolwood. In Carolwood Scott Smith told her where the bags he was told to would be. Elissa Fleak , Scott Smith , another detective (possibly Myers) and Los AngelesPD crime scene photographer was at the house collecting evidence. They got the items out of the closet and placed it on a table. They took pictures. Elissa Fleak doesn't remember if she or Los AngelesPD took the pictures. She laid items out on the table. Defense shows a picture of items on the table. She and Scott Smith was taking notes and observing. IV bag with slit and Propofol bottle. Chernoff asks if there were more photos taken of it. Elissa Fleak doesn't remember. 3A form- evidence log form to record medical evidence in coroner's office. She did 3 3A forms on June 25, June 29 and July 8th. Elissa Fleak goes over her June 29 record. In her handwritten notes she list the cut IV bag and the propofol bottle. Chernoff asks if any of her reports that she mentioned the propofol bottle was in the IV bag. She says no. Chernoff says that "propofol in IV bag" was added to her notes in March 2011. Chernoff tries to ask question about her revised notes. A lot of objection and sustained. A week before she revised her notes , Elissa Fleak met with Chernoff at Coroner's office with other coroners and lawyers. Chernoff says he asked her about the IV bag and what was in it. Elissa Fleak says she doesn't remember. Chernoff asks when was the first time she told prosecution about the propofol bottle in the IV bag. Chernoff asks if she heard about Alberto Alvarez and his testimony. Elissa Fleak says that he didn't know him or didn't hear about his testimony saying that he saw a bottle in an IV bag. Chernoff asks about her handwritten notes from June 25th. She says after she copies her notes to her reports, she destroys her handwritten notes intentionally in all her cases. Chernoff asks if she would agree that she made substantial mistakes. She doesn't agree. Chernoff asks if not keeping her notes was a mistake, she says no. Elissa Fleak says she has her report and put everything from her notes to the written report. Flumanezil bottle found on the floor but she moved to the table. Syringe Chernoff asks if she moved the syringe from the floor to the table. Elissa Fleak says no, she found it on the table. Chernoff again mentions the "Broken syringe" - Elissa Fleak says she should have described it as two pieces and not broken. Chernoff asks about her scene report and how she wrote there was gloves on the floor and asks her to show it in the picture. She says it was closer to the urine bottle chair and cannot be seen in the current picture. Chernoff shows a picture of gloves on a chair and asks if she wrote about them in her notes. She says no. Chernoff asks if that's a mistake, Elissa Fleak says no. Chernoff asks about the droplets in the IV bag and argues that they are clear and it's not a milky liquid. Chernoff asks if the IV bag was tested. Yes it was. June 25 . She was primarily working on the bedroom. Chernoff asks if she went into other rooms. Chernoff asks if she went into the far left bedroom or not. Elissa Fleak says she did not go to that bedroom. That bedroom also has a bathroom attached to that bedroom. Coroner collected some items from that bathroom on June 26.

Several photos of urine on the chair from different angles marked by the defense. Pictures of Elissa Fleak shown. Chernoff asks when those pictures was taken. Elissa Fleak doesn't know the exact dates whether it was June 25th or 29th.

Chernoff asks how far was the table from the bed. Elissa Fleak says a couple feet.

Syringe on IV. Chernoff asks when that picture was taken. Chenoff shows 2 different pictures one taken on June 25th and another taken on June 29. One of the pictures showing the tubing around the IV pole and one does not. Chernoff says that someone was moving evidence.

Chernoff asks who's decision was to not the secure the house. Elissa Fleak says such decisions are up to Los AngelesPD. Elissa Fleak also doesn't know if the house was open for access of not.

Detective Scott Smith informed her about the additional medical items Conrad Murray mentioned there. Elissa Fleak went to the house on 29th. Elissa Fleak says she doesn't know if Los AngelesPD went to the house between June 27 and June29. Chernoff mentioning some items such as the IV stand and IV bag being collected on June 29. Elissa Fleak also did not mention the IV stand, saline bag or the syringe in her June 25 record. Elissa Fleak mentioned those in the case notes in June 27 case notes. She wrote she had additional items to write that she did not mention in the first narrative. After June 29, Elissa Fleak did not go to Carolwood. Elissa Fleak collected medical records from other doctors as well. Elissa Fleak collect those to get a better understanding of Michael Jackson's medical history. She requested medical notes from Murray, Klein, Dr. Allan Metzger, Adams, Tadrissi, Slavit, Rosen, Cherilyn Lee, UCLA medical center, Kopplen, Hoefflin. Objection. Sidebar. She collected extensive records. There were other doctors that said there wasn't any records or did not treat Michael Jackson. Chernoff asks about the juice bottle on the stand. Elissa Fleak says that she did not collect the juice bottle.

Walgren redirect

Walgren goes over the documents Elissa Fleak prepared. Investigator's narrative : Overall description of the scene. Evidence log : things are itemized and logged into evidence. Case notes : additional information for a case is listed here. 3A form medical evidence form that will detail the medical evidence versus the physical evidence or trace evidence.

Handwritten notes from June 25 was put into these documents.

Walgren asks she observed the IV stand on June 25 and have it photographed. Yes she did. On June 27 she mentioned IV stand in her notes. June 29 she picked up the IV stand and the bags from residence as evidence. Walgren mentions her preliminary hearing testimony and how she mentioned Propofol bottle inside IV bag in January 2011. Elissa Fleak removed the propofol bottle from the IV bag to see what it was. She put propofol bottle on the IV bag to photograph it. Walgren asks if there was a reason if she photographed them together. She says she intentionally photographed them together because they were found together inside one another. March 2011. Walgren, Elissa Fleak, Dr. Christopher Rogers examined some evidence. At that time Dr. Christopher Rogers mentioned that it was an IV catheter and Elissa Fleak found out that they don't go together. Walgren asks if this was a perfect investigation, she says no. Walgren asks if she ever conducted a perfect investigation , Elissa Fleak says no. Walgren asks if she in other investigations she thought she could do a better job. Elissa Fleak says yes and she did her best.

Chernoff cross

Chernoff again goes over to say Elissa Fleak didn't take the picture of the Propofol bottle in the IV bag. Chernoff shows a bunch of photos asking if Elissa Fleak took them.

Fingerprints information is stipulated

Murray's fingerprint was found on 100ml Propofol bottle found inside the IV bag. Elissa Fleak's fingerprint was found on the syringe on the table. IV bag with the slit had 4 fingerprints on it. 2 fingerprints was found on saline bag and 20ml Propofol . 1 fingerprint was found on 20 ml propofol bottle. but no identification was made about these fingerprints. The following people were eliminated by manual comparison: Michael Jackson, Conrad Murray, Alberto Alvarez, Michael Amir Williams, Faheem Muhammed, Scott Scott Smith , Mark Goodwin, Martin Blount, Jimmy Nicholas, Blanca Nicholas, Elissa Elissa Fleak, Kai Chase. No useable fingerprints on : 2 midozolam vials, 1 Lorazepam vial, 2 lidocaine vials, 1 lidacaine vial, eyedrops, tube marked bq, a bottle labelled ephedrine/caffeine/asprine , 2 100ml propofol vials, 7 20 ml propofol vials, 2 lidocaine vials, 1 lidocaine vial, 2 Lorazepam vials, 4 flumanezil vials, 3 midazolam vials, IV tubing, IV y connector tubing, syringe with needle.

In short Michael Jackson's fingerprints was not on any of the items. Murray's fingerprints was only found on a 100ml Propofol bottle.

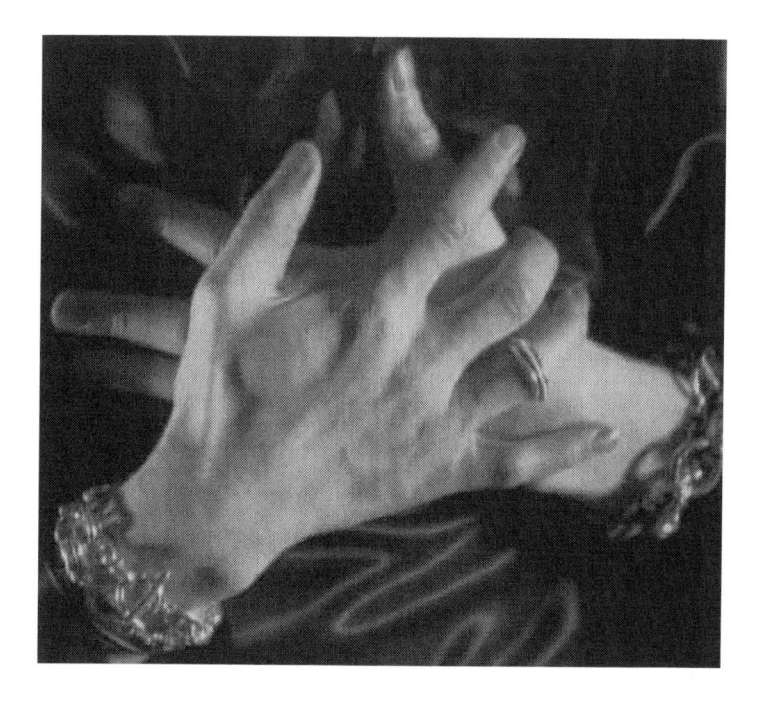

Dan Anderson Testimony

Walgren direct

Dan Anderson is employed by Los Angeles Coroner as a toxiologists for 21 years. His current position is the supervisor. He's responsible for the people and the results. Dan Anderson mentions his education, work history and certifications.

Dan Anderson talks in detail about toxicology, the type of tests they do the terms used and how they do the tests and the equipment they use. Walgren starts talking about this case. Dan Anderson received 4 samples of blood taken at the hospital and hand delivered to him by Elissa Fleak. June 26. Dan Anderson attended to the beginning of autopsy to tell what he wanted as samples. June 26 afternoon they started testing. Tests take several hour and days. They started evaluating them by Monday. They generated a 8 page report about all the samples tested. ng/ml - nanogram ug/ml - micrograms. micrograms are 1000 times bigger than nanograms.

Walgren direct continued

Dan Anderson goes over each of the findings in the report. Most majority of the test is done is using heart blood. It's the starting point.

-Femoral blood is taken from leg.

-Heart blood is taken from heart.

- Hospital blood is taken at hospital.

- Vitreous fluid is taken from behind the eyeballs.

- Liver they took a portion.

- Gastric contents are stomach contents.

- Urine samples : Urine from scene brought in a plastic urine bottle also they collected urine from the bladder during autopsy

Dan Anderson lists all the findings. You can see some of them in the following pictures. For full details check the the autopsy report.

Important findings: Michael Jackson had no alcohol, no Demerol (Meperadine), no metabolized Demerol (normeperidine) and no Cocaine, Marijuana and such. Michael Jackson had Valium, Lorezepam and Midazolam, Propofol in his system. They tested femerol blood, heart blood and hospital blood. They did 2 tests on liver for lidocaine and propofol - both was detected in liver. Stomach contents showed Lidocaine and Propofol. Urine from autopsy shows lidocaine, Midazolam, Ephedrine and Propofol. Jug of urine was tested and it showed Lidocaine, Midazolam, Ephedrine and Propofol. Vitreous (clear fluid behind the eye) showed Propofol.

Dan Anderson made a summary about positive toxicology findings.

Walgren again clearly states that there was no Demerol in Michael Jackson's system. Dan Anderson says correct. Walgren mentions Propofol in Michael Jackson's stomach. Dan Anderson compares amount of propofol in Michael Jackson's stomach is equivalent to 'specks of sugar granules'. So they are basically saying that it's too small. Syringe on the nightstand was tested. They found 4 drops of liquid in it. They detected propofol and lidocaine in it. Saline bag, tubing, Y connector and syringe on the IV was tested. They draw a diagram and determined how to test it. Walgren identifies each of the items.

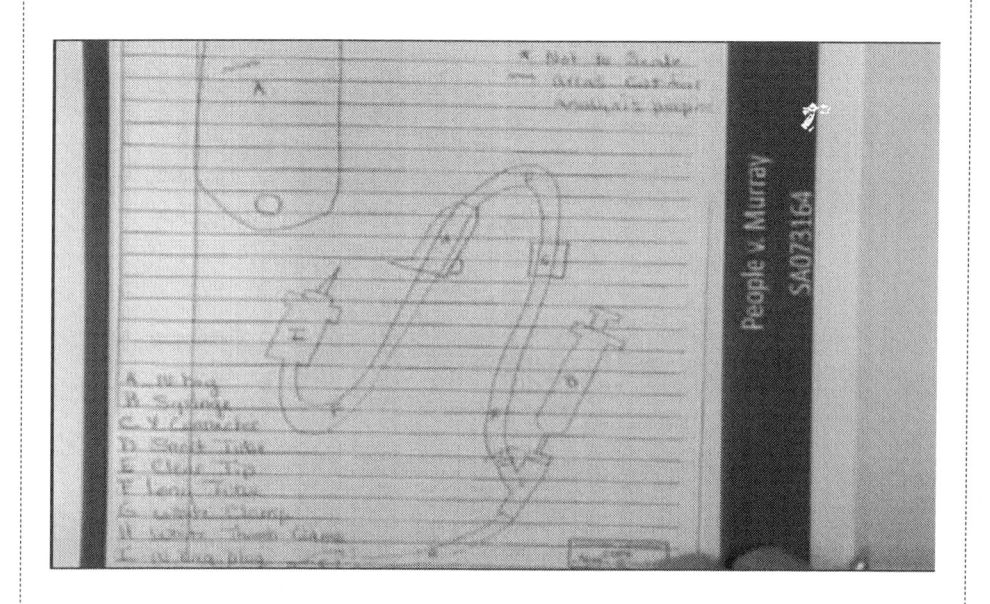

Propofol, lidocaine and flumazenil was found on the IV on the syringe and the short side of the tubing. Saline bag and long section of IV tubing had no drugs detected.

Medical Evidence #1 (collected by Coroner Investigator E. Fleak on 6/26/09)
- Propofol and Lidocaine were detected in approximately 0.19g of white fluid from a 10cc syringe barrel with plunger.

Medical Evidence #2 (collected by Coroner Investigator E. Fleak on 6/29/09)
- 4 components of an IV system tested.
    - Propofol, Lidocaine, and Flumazenil were detected in approximately 0.17g of white tinted fluid from a 10cc syringe.
    - Propofol, Lidocaine, and Flumazenil were detected in approximately 0.47g of yellow tinted fluid from a short section of IV tubing attached to a Y connector.
    - No drugs were detected in approximately 17g of clear liquid from a long section of IV tubing attached to an IV bag plug.
    - No drugs were detected in approximately 0.38g of clear fluid from a 1000cc IV bag.

Flanagan Cross

Flanagan is going over the summary report about positive toxicology findings.

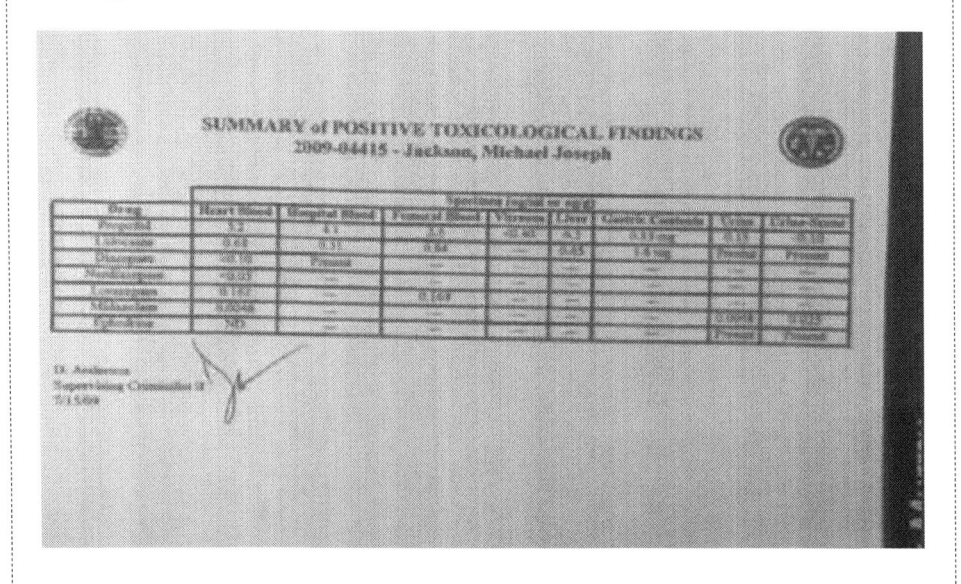

Flanagan asks why Propofol was tested on 3 different blood samples. Dan Anderson says they generally make tests on 2 samples: general blood and peripheral blood (such as from the leg femoral blood) due to postportem distribution. Dan Anderson explains that the body tissue releases the drugs back into the circulation after death and moving the body will also distribute the drugs. On this instance they also got hospital admittance blood. Flanagan asks if the reason for hospital blood result be higher is due to the drugs not having chance to be redistributed. Objection. Judge finds the question vague. Flanagan " Do you know why the hospital blood results are higher?" Answer: No. Flanagan "why is the femoral blood results are the lowest?" Answer: Postportem distribution. Flanagan confuses the witness to the point that he can't understand what is being asked. Flanagan "Why is femoral blood has the lowest results?" Answer: That's typical because tissues release drugs to the central cavity artifically raising the heart blood. Lidocaine higher in femoral blood then the heart blood. Dan Anderson says it's drug dependent. Some drugs might have different distribution pattern. Flanagan asks why the eye fluid was analyzed. They analyzed it for Propofol because Propofol was the real issue. Dan Anderson says that they didn't have enough fluid to make a full analysis. It tells him that Propofol doesn't distrubute very well to the eyeball fluid. They didn't give an exact number amount for Propofol in the eye fluid because they didn't have enough sample. Protocol tells that they can't give exact numbers in such instances as they can't gurantee the accuracy. Urine from the scene. Flanagan asks why they couldn't get the exact number amount for Propofol amount. Again It was below their lowest caliber. It was almost negligible. Ephedrine was present in the urine but wasn't in blood. It's because bladder can store things for a long time. Flanaggan asks how long ago it was used. Dan Anderson says it can't be recent as it's not in the blood and it could be used anywhere between 24 to 72 hours ago. Propofol was found in the urine from the scene. Flanagan asks if it could be from a few days ago as well. Dan Anderson agrees and says that it could also be recent. Flanagan asks if the urine from the scene was accumulated before urine from autopsy.

Dan Anderson says he has no idea when it was collected or even it's from Michael Jackson. Flanagan gives a scenario that the urine from the scene was in 7 AM and the time of death being around 12:00 and 2:26 and says that not much urine is collected after death. Dan Anderson corrects him that they actually had over 500 ml of autopsy urine which he says to be alot. Flanagan is trying to say that Michael Jackson got/given propofol after the urine in the scene was deposited in the plastic bottle because the propofol level was higher in the autopsy urine. Flanagan again confuses the witness and no one can understand what he's asking. Lorazepam. Flanagan asks if it's high. Dan Anderson says it's normal high therapeutic range. Flanagan asks how much Lorazepam Michael Jackson was given in mg. Dan Anderson says that calculation could be done but it would not be a perfect calculation as there has to be several assumptions made. Dan Anderson says it shouldn't be done. Dan Anderson mentions assumptions that needed for such calculation :drug fully distributed, redistrubution didn't happen after death and the heart blood level is not falsely elevated. Flanagan shows a book saying that Lorazepam is not subject to redistribution after death. Dan Anderson doesn't agree with it and says there have been only 2 cases stating that but he wouldn't be comfortable with generalizating it to the whole population. Flanagan still asks Dan Anderson to give a mg number. Dan Anderson goes over his records saying that based on several assumptions, it's approximately 11 mg. Dan Anderson says that they can't determine how Lorazepam was given (orally or IV) from a blood level and he doesn't know when it was given. Flanagan asks if the results indicate that Lorazepam has been in the system for a while. Dan Anderson says yes. Propofol levels was not equilibrium. Flanagan asks if a person was on a drip , would he expect the propofol levels to be in equilibrium. Dan Anderson says he doesn't know how Propofol metabolizes. Flanagan mentions that the summary Dan Anderson did has no information about Lorazepam in the stomach contents. Dan Anderson says that they only analyze stomach contents for overdose cases. Their blood test results showed Lorazepam to be in the acceptable range so they didn't test it in the stomach. Defense has tested the stomach for Lorazepam, it was .634 micrograms/ml. Flanagan says Lorazepam is 4 times concentrated in the stomach then the blood. Dan Anderson disagrees saying that it's not significant in it's opinion. Flanagan asks if it's consistent with oral digestion. Dan Anderson says no and explains that drugs will be in stomach in small levels due to "ion trapping" and doesn't necessarily mean that it's taken orally. Dan Anderson converts it to mg: 0.046 mg, that means 1/40th of a normal 2 mg pill. Dan Anderson says that it could come from the blood. Flanagan asks questions about Midazolam. Dan Anderson has not made calculations about it because the amounts are really small. Flanagan by looking to urine level of Midazolam trying to establish blood levels for it. Dan Anderson says it's not a comparison that could be done. Flanagan talks about urine and whether it would be representative of the metabolization of the drugs such as if a person urinated at 1 AM and then at 7 AM, Flanagan asks if the 7 AM urine would be representative of the 1 AM - 7AM period. Dan Anderson says there will be some contamination. Flanagan asks if the autopsy urine would be an average level of 12:30 - 7:30 AM time period. Dan Anderson is having trouble with understanding the question. Judge and Walgren also doesn't understand the questions. Flanagan asks if urine would be in equilibrium with the blood, it's beyond Dan Anderson's level of expertise. Dan Anderson says just from the urine results he cannot tell when the person would have higher levels of Midazolam in his system. Dan Anderson says he can't do it for Propofol as well. Back to stomach contents and not analyzing it for Midazolam and Lorazepam. Switching to IV set testing. Saline bag and the tubing that goes down to the y port had no propofol or lidocaine. Propofol, lidocaine and flumazenil was found in the syringe and short tubing. Flanagan asks about the amounts of those drugs. Dan Anderson says that they didn't quantify them because they didn't think it was relevant and they didn't have a standard procedure to quantify fluids from medical evidence. Flanagan asks if they can tell the proportions of lidocaine and propofol and flumazenil. Dan Anderson says they can't. Dan Anderson says they also had a very small amounts of liquids that complicated the testing as well.

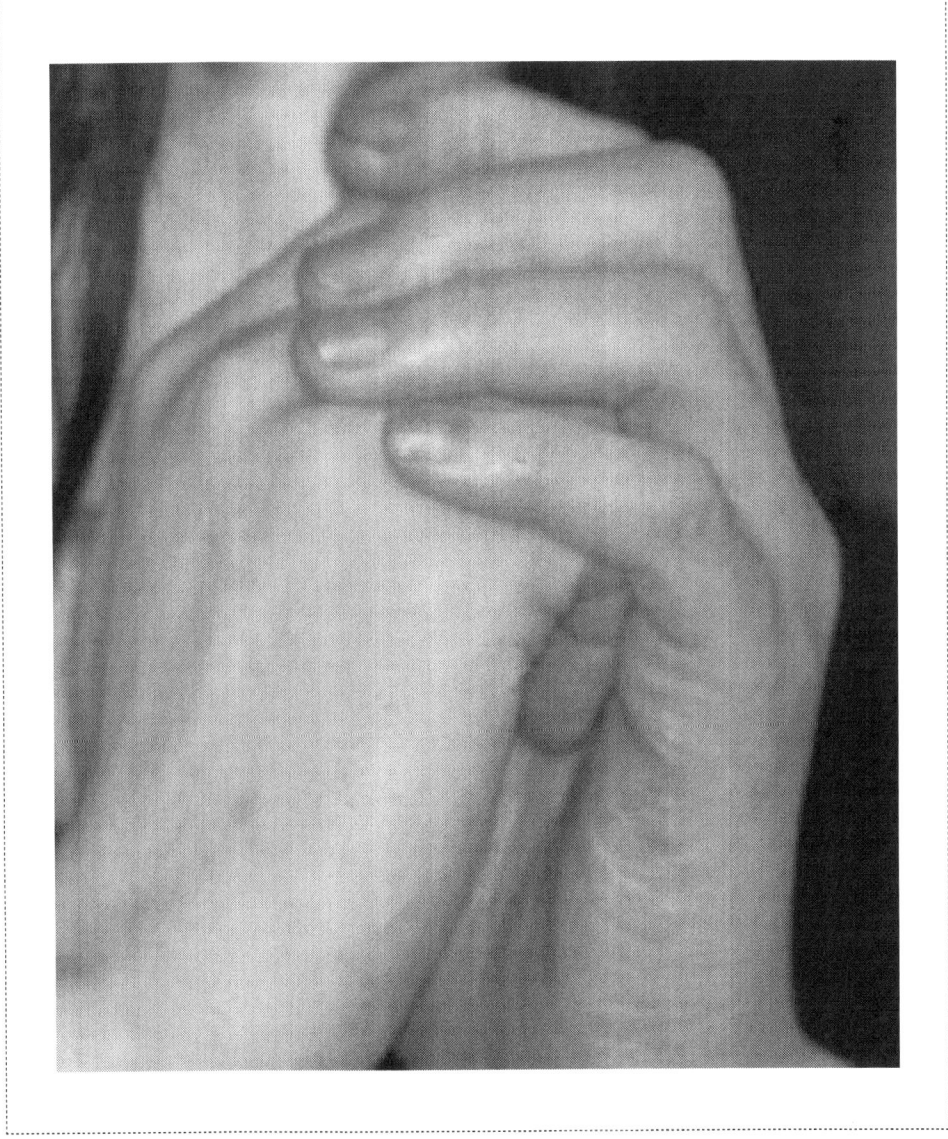

Murray Trial Summaries Day 9/ October 7-2011

Dan Anderson Testimony continued

Flanagan Cross continued

Flanagan starts off by asking about the IV bag on the stand in Michael Jackson's room where he died. Flanagan asks if the bag was analyzed for all chemicals and the only thing was saline solution, Dan Anderson states they do not analyze for solution, but there were no drugs found in it. Flanagan asks about the tubing (hanging from the IV stand), and Dan Anderson states that it was not found to have any drugs in it. Flanagan asks repeatedly whether the tubing and the IV bag were attached, Dan Anderson repeatedly states that they were not attached when received into medical evidence, according to notes. Flanagan asks if Dan Anderson tested two syringe barrels, Dan Anderson states yes and when asked, states that both barrels tested positive for propofol and lidocaine. Flanagan asks if Dan Anderson tested any apparatus that had only propofol in it, Dan Anderson states no. Dan Anderson states that the only medical equipment that had propofol and lidocaine in them were the Y tubing (connector) and the syringe barrels. Dan Anderson states that each of the syringes and the Y tubing each had Flumanezil. Flanagan asks if the proportion of propofol and lidocaine were the same in both the Y tubing and the 2 syringe barrels, Dan Anderson states that proportionality testing was not performed. Flanagan asks for Dan Anderson to define equilibrium as it relates to bodily fluids, Dan Anderson states he believes it is when the samples of the drug or their concentrations are equal. Flanagan asks how long it takes for the blood system to come to an equilibrium, Dan Anderson states its beyond his scope of expertise. Flanagan asks Dan Anderson to define therapeutic range (of a drug), Dan Anderson states that a concentration of the drug that achieves the desired effect, generally it is a safety concern because they are not safe at all concentrations. Flanagan asks what determines therapeutic range, Dan Anderson states clinical trials from the FDA, as well as the literature provided with each drug. Flanagan asks if there is a therapeutic range for propofol, Dan Anderson states no. Flanagan asks about therapeutic range for Lorazepam, Dan Anderson states that it averages 100-200 micrograms per mililiter. Dan Anderson clarifies that the average can be 180, but that everybody tolerates medications differently, and he cannot give specific ranges. Flanagan shows a Lorazepam bottle, prescription for Michael Jackson , asks Dan Anderson to read the bottle, Dan Anderson reads Lorazepam 2 mgs, 1 tablet by mouth. Flanagan asks about Michael Jackson 's blood concentration of .16% and asks if that would equal about five Lorazepam tablets, Dan Anderson states yes, regardless of the route, whether it was in tablet or IV form. Flanagan asks if Michael Jackson had the equivalent of 11 mg of Lorazepam, Dan Anderson states yes, approximately. Flanagan asks how many pills would Michael Jackson have to take to get to that level (11 mg), Dan Anderson states that it could be an accumulation over several days, and that he does not feel comfortable with assumptions of routing of medications or form of medications. Flanagan asks about ion trapping with respect Lorazepam, Dan Anderson states that he knows little about Lorazepam and postmortem redistribution. Dan Anderson states that the only way to get propofol in the stomach is through oral ingestion or ion trapping, it's not postmortem redistribution. Flanagan asks Dan Anderson to define the term ion trapping. Dan Anderson states that an acidic environment traps the ions of the drug in that environment, beyond that, is beyond his area of expertise. Dan Anderson states that other than ingestion, the only way propofol can get into the stomach by diffusion of the surrounding specimens. When Flanagan asks about the surrounding specimens, Dan Anderson answers that the liver is close, blood samples and blood itself are close to the stomach. Flanagan states that Dan Anderson is saying that Lorazepam can get into the stomach through redistribution, Dan Anderson states that it can get into the stomach by ion trapping. Dan Anderson states time and time again that this information is beyond the scope of his expertise. Dan Anderson states that he has seen many different decendents who had stomach contents with drugs in them, and that the drugs were not given orally. Dan Anderson states he does not have personal experience with a decendent that had Lorazepam in their stomach. Flanagan asks Dan Anderson about ephedrine. Flanagan asks if Dan Anderson came to understand that propofol was the most important drug in the case, Dan Anderson states yes he did. Flanagan asks if Lorazepam was important, Dan Anderson he thinks it has its importance, but that it does notraise a flag. Dan Anderson states that propofol in any case is important, Lorazepam was in therapeutic range, and that he previously testified that propofol was within range only a proper setting. When Flanagan asks what does a setting have to do with therapeutic range, Dan Anderson states that it's very important. Flanagan states that therapeutic range is desired effect, Dan Anderson states yes. Flanagan states that the literature does not take into consideration the setting, Dan Anderson states that every drug literature takes setting into consideration. Flanagan asks if Dan Anderson did the calculations with regard to Lorazepam last weekend, Dan Anderson states it was two weekends ago, Dan Anderson states that he did them because of the Lorazepam in the gastric sample, and the two urine samples done by the defense. Dan Anderson states that the urine is a historical perspective, and could be an accumulation from several days. Dan Anderson states that the Midazolam testing was done in the urine because the concentration is much higher, which helps to confirm the blood level of Midazolam. Dan Anderson states that Lorazepam levels were much more elevated in the urine than the Midazolam. Dan Anderson states Lorazepam 12,974 nanograms/ml (13 micrograms/ml) Midazolam 0.025 nanograms/ml. Dan Anderson states that the Lorazepam concentration goes up in the autopsy urine, and with Midzolam much less than Lorazepam. Dan Anderson states that the half life of Lorazepam is 9-16 hours, and that he looked it up in a medical reference book to gain that information. Dan Anderson states he doesn't know what the absorption time and/or the peak time of Lorazepam, that it is in the book, but he doesn't remember what it said.

Walgren Redirect

Dan Anderson clarifies that he never went to 100 North Carolwood. Dan Anderson states that he received vials of blood, a broken syringe with plunger, an IV catheter from Investigator Elissa Fleak. Dan Anderson states that the IV bag and IV tubing was brought to him at the lab, simply marked medical evidence #2. Dan Anderson states that the difference between blood sample and urine sample, is that the blood is what is usually happening in the body, and in the urine represents everything that the body is metabolizing out, and that the urine concentration expectation is that it would be much higher. Dan Anderson states that the urine is historical in nature and what is being expelled from the body over a certain amount of time. Dan Anderson states that the PACTOX gastric contents analysis, shows 634 nanograms/ml of Lorazepam. Dan Anderson states that the lab measured in concentration, he was provided 73.5 mls of gastric contents, in which he would multiply the two numbers to get the nanograms of stomach contents which would be 46,599 nanograms of Lorazepam left in the stomach. But the numbers Dan Anderson should have used for calculation (micrograms not nanograms) he needed to divide by a thousand, so 46,599 divided by a thousand equals 46.599 divided by another 1000 to get a mg amount, equals 0.04599 of Lorazepam in the stomach. Dan Anderson states that he went further and got a more exact amount and arrived at 0.046599. Dan Anderson states that with a 2 mg Lorazepam pill, the gastric contents are equal to 1/43rd of a single 2 mg tablet, which is a very small amount

Flanagan Recross

Flanagan asks if there is a high concentration of ephedrine in the urine, but a low concentration in the bladder, would it be fair to say it was recently taken, Dan Anderson says it's a fair assumption. Flanagan asks if it's the same with propofol, Dan Anderson states that he is not familiar with the excretion patterns of propofol.

Flanagan asks if a person were to take 7 or 8 Lorazepam tablets, and he found 14 miligrams in the stomach, would Dan Anderson state that the person had taken it recently, Dan Anderson states yes. There are numerous questions asked after this by Flanagan, but prosecutor Walgren objects and judge Pastor sustains them.

Elissa Fleak recall Testimony

Walgren Direct

Walgren goes over evidence collection and when Elissa Fleak recovered multiple evidence items. Walgren asks if there are a lot of photographs taken on multiple days. Elissa Fleak looked over the photos to identify which photograph was taken which day (June 25th or June 29th). Elissa Fleak says she went into the master bedroom briefly, looked around but did not search it. Walgren talks about IV stand and the photographs about it. 2 photos of IV tubing taken on June 25th. Tubing is draped over the handle. June 29 photos of IV stand /tubing. June 29 it's still draped over as it was on June 25. Later photos taken same day, it's no longer draped over the handle. One June 29, the investigators freed the tube (undraped it) so that the syringe can be photographed.

Chernoff Cross

Chernoff again questions about whether she went into Michael Jackson's master bedroom or not. And again brings the subject of master bathroom and photographs taken in it. In Michael Jackson's master bedroom fire place is on , TV is on as well. Chernoff shows pictures inside the master bathroom and asks if Elissa Fleak remembers the pill bottles. Elissa Fleak says she wasn't there in June 26 and those bottles were collected on June 26. Elissa Fleak says she doesn't know who collected them and who took those pictures. Chernoff shows a picture where there's no pill bottles. Chernoff asks about the briefcase in the pictures.

Detective Scott Smith Testimony

Walgren Direct

Los Angeles PD Detective for 20 years. He was assigned to robbery-homicide division in June 25, 2009. He learned about the death of Michael Jackson 3:30PM from his supervisor. He arrived at UCLA at 4:25 PM. Scott Smith went to the emergency area. He stayed there till 7:00PM. Scott Smith did not see Murray at UCLA. Scott Smith obtained security footage from UCLA showing Murray. They got footage of Murray leaving at 4:38PM.

Walgren plays the video and then shows an aerial photo of UCLA and asks Detective Scott Smith to mark the way Murray let the hospital. Scott Smith talked with Faheem Muhammed, Alberto Alvarez at UCLA very briefly. Faheem Muhammad just told he was employed by Michael Jackson and gave his contact information. Alberto Alvarez said the same things and also mentioned he went into the room to help Michael

Jackson and called 911. Detective Scott Smith didn't do any more interviews at that day. He arrived to Carolwood around 7:30PM. Scott Smith didn't know the cause of death at that point of time. At that time this was a death investigation and not a homicide information. Death investigation could be natural causes and detectives may or may not be involved. If it is homicide investigation the police department takes full responsibility. It becomes a homicide investigation if there's an obvious cause of death such as gunshot etc. This was a death investigation and coroner was leading the investigation not the police department. Detectives was on the scene to assist and support coroner's office as needed. Walgren asks if this had been an homicide investigation would Los AngelesPD be leading the investigation and collect evidence. Scott Smith says yes. On June 25th evidence was collected by coroner's office. Det. Scott Smith was assisting and overseeing the Los AngelesPD photographer. Scott Smith says they left the residence around 9:30 PM. They released the house at the request of Jackson family to private security. June 26, Detective Scott Smith attended the entire autopsy of Michael Jackson. He didn't have cause of death by the end of autopsy. They had no information to assist with the investigation. It was deferred pending toxicology results. At this time it was still a death investigation and not a homicide investigation. On June 26th Scott Smith went to Carolwood again. Coroner Ed Winters called him and said some items were given to him by family. Scott Smith went to take those items. They initially thought it was tar heroin which turned out to be old rotten marijuana. It was found in a shaving kit. Those items had no relevance to Michael Jackson's death and determining the reason of his death. In the shaving kit there was also temazepam bottle prescribed by Murray. Scott Smith had also found some empty pill bottles on June 26 in Michael Jackson's master bathroom. Walgren goes over the pictures of Michael Jackson's master bathroom taken over several days. June 25th pictures. Bathroom appears to be messy, drawer doors open, a few notes taped on the bathroom mirror. Pictures from June 26. There was no empty pill bottles or briefcase on June 25th pictures. On June 26th there's a briefcase, Scott Smith doesn't know whose suitcase it is. June 26 pictures show empty pill bottles on a ledge. Scott Smith says that he placed them on the ledge to photograph them. On June 27 Murray's attorney Michael Pena spoke with Detective Martinez. They made arrangements to meet at Ritz Carlton at 4 PM. Murray's attorneys had chosen the place. Detective Martinez and Scott Smith met with Murray and his lawyers in a room at the hotel. They conducted and recorded the interview.

Audio of Murray's interview with the police is played

June 27th Ritz Carlton. Murray is at the interview with his lawyers Chernoff and Pena. Detective Scott Smith and Martinez is doing the interview. First part of the interview: Officer is going through and asks Murray basic information as his address, phone number, weight, when he was born, how tall he is etc. Detective says the detectives at the hospital was from another division and was not handling the case. They took some notes but didn't do a formal interview. Murray seems surprised to hear that other detectives took notes after he left. Murray talks about how he met Michael. They met in 2006 and saw Michael Jackson on and off since 2006. The first time Murray saw Michael Jackson was because Michael Jackson and his kids had the flu, a bodyguard of Michael Jackson whose parents were patients of Murray referred him. Murray says he had been caring for Michael Jackson for the last 2 months. Murray tells that he received a phone call from Michael Amir Williams. Michael Amir Williams said Michael Jackson was going to do a concert-tour in London and Michael Jackson wanted Murray with him. Murray said he needed more details before accepting. He then say Michael Jackson called and said he was happy Murray was going to join him – although he had not yet committed to join Michael Jackson's team. Detectives ask about who is Murray is working for AEG or Michael Jackson. Murray says he's an employee of Michael Jackson but paid through AEG.

Murray says he had no idea that AEG were going to pay him. Detectives ask about Michael Jackson's general health. Murray says generally speaking Michael Jackson did not eat well and was very thin. He did not find any major physical change in Michael Jackson's condition except for something called subluxation of his right hip (Michael Jackson's right hip would slip out and slide back to the joint). Michael Jackson had fungal disease on his toes which was treated. Nothing more that Murray noticed. On June 24th – Murray got a called from Michael Amir Williams around 12:10 am that Michael Jackson was done with rehearsals. Michael Jackson had attended meetings and did a partial performance (not a full rehearsal). Michael Jackson wasn't complaining about anything but wanted Murray to be at Carolwood by the time he came home. Murray spent every night at Carolwood except nights he where off, which were Sundays. He spent the night there per Michael Jackson's request. Murray arrived to Michael Jackson's home at 12:50am before Michael Jackson and waited at Michael Jackson's room. Michael Jackson arrived shortly after, around 1am. Once Michael Jackson arrived, they greeted each other and talked about their days. Michael Jackson told Murray he was tired and fatigued and was treated like a machine. Michael Jackson took a quick shower and changed and came back to the room. When Michael Jackson came back to the room, Murray put on some cream/lotion on his body and back for Vitiligo. Detectives ask Murray about the bedroom. Murray tells that Michael Jackson had 2 bedrooms. No one not even cleaners would be allowed to go into the master bedroom and it would be in a bad state. Murray would see Michael Jackson in the second bedroom, the one that had IV stand and oxygen tanks. After cream, Michael Jackson wants to sleep. Murray says Michael Jackson is not able to sleep naturally. Murray says he would put an IV for hydration on Michael Jackson's right or left leg below the knee. They then talked a bit and he gave Michael Jackson Valium 1 pill 10 mg orally. As Valium's effect was delayed so around 2 AM Murray gave Michael Jackson 2 mg of Lorazepam which it was IV pushed slowly. Murray says he observed Michael Jackson but he continued to be awake for 1 hour, he says he watched him because he wanted to be cautious. So Murray decided to give him Midazolam (2 mg injected slowly) around 3 AM. Murray waited again but Michael Jackson was wide awake. Michael Jackson said he couldn't sleep. Murray suggested to lower the music Michael Jackson likes to sleep with and dim the lights and told Michael Jackson to meditate while he rubbed his feet. Michael Jackson did that reluctantly and Michael Jackson's eyes closed. Murray estimates that Michael Jackson closed his eyes around 3:15-3:20; he doesn't know it for certain because he wasn't looking at his watch at that time. 10-15 minutes later Michael Jackson was again awake. Michael Jackson was surprised that he managed to sleep after he had meditated. And they tried mediating again but by 4:30 AM Michael Jackson was sill wide awake. Michael Jackson starts to complain saying that says he has rehearsals he needs to perform and tomorrow he will need to cancel his rehearsals because he can't function if he can't sleep. Murray says then he gave Michael Jackson another 2mg of Lorazepam at 4:30 – 5:00 AM because a safe time had passed. That didn't put Michael Jackson to sleep as well. Michael Jackson complained that if he can't perform he would have to cancel the rehearsals and it would put the show behind and cannot satisfy fans if he's not rested well. Murray says that it put a lot of pressure on him. Murray tells Michael Jackson he isn't normal and the medications that he gave would make a normal person sleep for 1-2 days. (due to wanting the medications/can't sleep)…

By 7:30 Michael Jackson was still awake. At that time he gave another 2 mg Midazolam. There was still no effect. Murray says he cautiously checked the IV site to make sure the fluid and medicines was going to Michael Jackson because he wondered why Michael Jackson wasn't responding to medications.

At this time Murray says Michael also urinated.

10 AM in the morning. Nothing has worked. Murray was watching and trying to get Michael Jackson to sleep. Michael Jackson is complaining he can't sleep, he has to cancel the dates and everything has to be pushed back. Michael Jackson at that time asks "Please give me some milk so that I can sleep, because I know this is all that really works for

me". Detectives think that they are talking about actual milk and asks if Michael Jackson wanted hot or warm milk. Murray tells them it's a medicine Propofol which is "a sedative that could also be used for anesthesia". Murray gave Michael Jackson propofol through IV around 10:40. Murray had asked him how long he would sleep if he gave him Propofol because Michael Jackson needed to get up at a certain time. Michael Jackson told him it doesn't matter when he wakes up, told him to just make him sleep. Murray say he gave him small amounts to get him to sleep, he administered 25 mg of Propofol together with Lidocaine, he pushed it slowly. This time it must have been 10:50, effect is quick and Michael was sleeping now. Detectives ask if Murray had any monitoring equipment. Murray says he took all the precautions that were available to him such as oxygen and pulse oximeter. Detectives questions Murray about the dosage. Murray says 50 mg propofol was the highest amount propofol he had given Michael Jackson ever. That night he gave less due to the other medications he had given to Michael Jackson. Murray says he roughly gave Michael Jackson Propofol every day, there were rarely exceptions. Murray also says that three days leading up to Michael Jackson's death, he tried to wean Michael Jackson off propofol. He was not aware that Michael Jackson was taking this on a daily basis before he was hired. Murray was surprised by Michael Jackson's pharmacological knowledge and his mention of "milk" and "antiburn". Michael Jackson said he had taken propofol before. Michael Jackson said he used it in Germany but never disclosed other doctors' names. Michael Jackson never told him he administered it himself but other doctors let him infuse it by himself. Murray told him no he wouldn't let him to that. Murray says Michael Jackson knew that propofol was the only thing that worked for him. Murray says he often warned him about it. Michael Jackson told him he was seeing a Dr. Cherilyn Lee that she was giving him a cocktail for energy. Murray says there were a lot of IV sites on Michael Jackson's body and his veins were sclerotic. Murray asks Michael Jackson what is in the cocktail and wants to review it. Michael Jackson says he doesn't know. Later they got of Cherilyn Lee because Michael

Jackson felt she was unprofessional and cancelled an appointment. Michael Jackson felt she wasn't telling him the truth. Once in Las Vegas Murray got a call from Michael Amir Williams . Michael Jackson was in Vegas with his children for a show and he was staying at Wynn Hotel. Michael Jackson says he having difficulties to sleep. Murray tells Michael Jackson to use sleep medications (Lorazepam or restoril) that he gava to him. Michael Jackson tells Murray nothing that he or Klein or Dr. Allan Metzger gave to him works. Murray says he doesn't have any other alternatives. Michael Jackson then asks about Diprivan / Propofol and says that he knows that it works. Murray says he doesn't have it. Michael Jackson mentions Dr. Adams and that he gave him Propofol. Murray doesn't know Adams. Michael Jackson gives Murray Adams phone number. Murray calls Adams. The plastic surgeon's office Adams used doesn't allow them in the office so Murray lets them into his office on a Sunday. Adams puts Michael Jackson on a Propofol drip for 6 hours. Murray says he had monitoring equipment. Murray comes back to his office after 6 hours and Michael Jackson says he's feeling wonderful because he has slept. Michael Jackson tells Murray that this is divine guidance and other doctors helped Michael Jackson sleep for 15 10 18 hours. Michael Jackson mentioned of having another doctor – Adams- on tour with them. Adams was willing on to go on tour with them and wanted $1.2 - $1.3 million a year. Murray told it to Michael Jackson but there was no follow up and Adams didn't end up joining the team. Murray mentions that Michael Jackson wanted him to be around forever, after the tour. Murray mentions Michael Jackson's plans for a children's hospital and wanted Murray to be medical director. Detectives go back to the night of June 25. Murray gave Michael Jackson 25 mg Propofol. Michael Jackson falls to sleep but he's not snoring. Generally when he's in deep sleep he snores so he's not in deep sleep. Murray monitors him. Everything looked stable and he was comfortable. Murray needed to go to the bathroom to pee and empty Michael Jackson's urine jar.

When he came back after 2 minutes he sensed Michael Jackson wasn't breathing because he usually looked at his chest to see if he was breathing. He immediately checked Michael Jackson's pulse and got a thread pulse from the femoral area and Michael Jackson's body was warm and he assumed everything happened quickly and immediately started CPR and mouth-to-mouth. He wanted to apply medicine as well but not first because he wanted to ventilate and compression first. He saw Michael Jackson 's chest rise. Murray says he couldn't move him from the bed to the floor by himself. He then got his left hand under Michael Jackson's body and then gave him CPR and also ventilating him and made sure his chest was rising completely. He looked for the phones but phones do not work in the house. He doesn't know the address zip-code; only know its North Carolwood. The house is closed during nights and only Michael Jackson, he and the children would be there. Murray tells that security doesn't come to the house. Murray thinks it's inhumane that the security are not allowed into the house to pee. He says to talk to 911 would be to abandon him and he didn't wanted abandon him. He reached his cell phone and called Michael Amir Williams. Murray tells Michael Amir Williams to send up security. Murray says he didn't ask Michael Amir Williams to call for 911 because then Michael Amir William would have asked why and Murray was trying to assist Michael Jackson. Murray realizes that Michael Jackson doesn't have a pulse now so he lifts Michael Jackson's legs for a brief moment for auto transfusion and continue to do CPR etc. No one came to the door, no one knocked on the door. So he gave Michael 0.2 mg Flumazenil because he wanted to reverse the affects of the other drugs but Michael Jackson would not still breathing and no help was coming. He then opened the door and ran down to the kitchen and saw the chef (Kai Chase) to have the security immediately and security (Alvarez) comes upstairs. Murray tells Alvarez to call 911 and want help to move Michael Jackson's body to the floor and still helps with chest compression. Alberto talked to 911 but Murray told him to just tell the paramedics to hurry up because he wanted help to move Michael Jackson to the floor. Paramedics came and called UCLA, Michael Jackson was not breathing. They were doing chest compressions. Murray says Michael was PEA –pulseless electrical activity – which means you don't shock a patient. Michael Jackson was given starter drugs. Murray says that he felt the communication and the orders coming from UCLA was kind of slow. After 20 minutes of effort – which Murray thinks was limited – he knew Michael Jackson hadn't been gone too long and he had felt a femoral pulse. So Murray asked UCLA instead to calling Michael Jackson dead to transfer the patient to him. Murray took over the care and they took Michael Jackson to UCLA. Emergency personnel met them. They worked on Michael Jackson for an hour. Murray says probably they would have stopped sooner if Murray wasn't insisting. They don't know why Michael Jackson died but thinking pulmonary embolism could be a reason (a clot in the lungs that would shut the circulation in the lungs). Michael Jackson is pronounced dead. Murray doesn't want to sign the death certificate as he doesn't know the cause of death.

Chernoff jumps in and changes the topic to Murray trying to wean off Michael Jackson 3 days before leading up to Michael Jackson's death. Murray says he didn't know Michael Jackson used propofol before and that it was kind of a habit. Murray says he wanted to Michael Jackson to sleep naturally and tried to wean him off. Murray asks what Michael Jackson would do once the tour was over; Michael Jackson tells him he thinks he can be able to sleep then. Murray switches to lesser drugs (such as Lorazepam) to wean Michael Jackson off. Murray says Michael Jackson knew it but he was reluctant. Murray says he never told Michael Jackson that he believed he had drug dependency. He was trying a strategy and was trying Michael to transfer his confidence in Propofol to something lesser. First night Murray reduces Propofol and starts Lorazepam and Versed. Second night he removed Propofol and only gave Lorazepam and Versed. Michael told him he felt a little hangover in the day. The night Michael Jackson died Murray started with Lorazepam and Versed but nothing was working. Murray doesn't know if it was withdrawal from Propofol or if it was psychological. Murray says after trying all night with those 2 drugs he finally gave Michael Jackson Propofol so that he can sleep and so that he can produce the next day. Murray says he didn't want Michael Jackson to fail and he cared about him.

Judge stops the tape... Rest will be continued on Tuesday.

Court ends early due to Yom Kippur (Jewish Holiday)

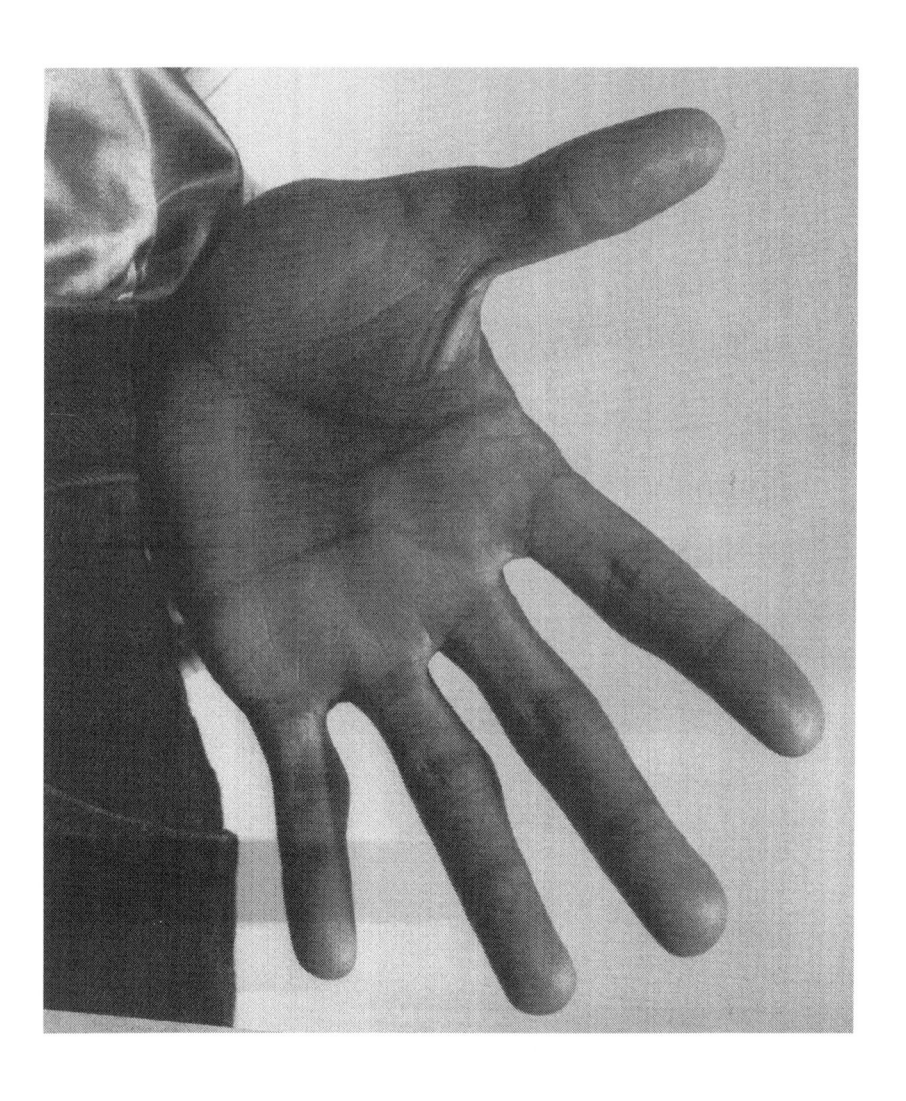

Murray Trial Summaries Day 10/ October 11- 2011

Detective Scott Smith Testimony continued

Walgren Resumption Direct

They finish playing the Murray interview tape.

Scott Smith states that the first time propofol was mentioned was in his interview with Los AngelesPD two days after Michael Jackson died, and that prior to that Murray had only mentioned he administered a sedative. Scott Smith states that he responded to UCLA and also attended the autopsy but that his knowledge was limited. Scott Smith states that very little of the questioning of Murray was limited, but that they allowed Murray to speak freely. Scott Smith states that Murray did not mention the phone calls he placed or received on June 25, and was unaware of Sade Anding at that time. Scott Smith states that Murray was surprised by the fact that Los AngelesPD had not recovered Murray's medical bags at the time of the interview, dated June 27, 2009. Scott Smith states that on June 26, 2009, there were some business cards belonging to Conrad Murray and David J. Adams found in the Carolwood home. Scott Smith states that the business cards were recovered from Michael Jackson's master bathroom by a Los AngelesPD detective. Scott Smith states that also recovered were Latanoprost, a skin cream, and three vials of eye medication from the master bedroom, prescribed by Arnold Klein. Scott Smith states that a large plastic bag with Applied Pharmacy on it, inside with benoquine to Dr. Murray was recovered the bathroom area of Michael Jackson's bedroom. Scott Smith states that there were a series of search warrants issued, the first being on June 29, 2009, to 100 North Carolwood Drive and the tow yard where Murray's BMW was. Scott Smith states that a contract recovered from the pocket of the door, and a few business cards. Scott Smith states no propofol bottles were recovered from the card. Scott Smith states the next search warrant issued on July 22, 2009 to Murray's cardiology practice and a storage unit in Houston, but that no propofol bottles were found. Scott Smith states that next search warrant issues on July 28, to Murray's Las Vegas office, home or storage unit were done, no propofol bottles found. Scott Smith states that the next search warrant was issued on August 11 to Applied Pharmacy at Las Vegas, owner Tim Lopez. Scott Smith states that this is when Los AngelesPD discovered that propofol was being sent to an apartment in Santa Monica, CA belonging to Nicole Alvarez. Scott Smith states that then a search warrant was issued for Alvarez Santa Monica home, on August 13, 2009. Scott Smith states that there were no propofol bottles recovered from Alvarez' home.

Chernoff Cross Examination

Scott Smith states that attempts had been made to contact Murray by the Los AngelesPD by phone, but that he did not personally make those calls, and that the detective who had made those calls, states that the calls went to voicemail. Scott Smith states he was aware that the press release for Michael Jackson's death was done by Jermaine Jackson, but not aware whether the press conference was actually done. Scott Smith states that he and Detective Orlando Martinez were initially assigned to Michael Jackson's death case, but that Detective Porsche was the original detective who tried to contact Conrad Murray. Scott Smith states that on June 27, 2009, the initial meeting between Murray and Los AngelesPD was set up for 2 pm, but it was rescheduled for 4 pm by Los AngelesPD. Scott Smith states the he spoke with Michael Amir, Faheem Muhammad, Alberto Alvarez, Larry Tolbert, Nanny Roslyn Muhammad, Kai Chase, Michael Jackson's family members, some housekeepers, Larry Muhammad had all spoken to Los AngelesPD on June 25, 2009. Scott Smith states that Chernoff/Murray never made any limitations as to what he did not want to talk about or time limits, during the initial meeting with Los AngelesPD. Scott Smith states that he did meet with Michael Amir Williams on August 31, 2009 and that he vaguely remembers that Williams had to leave the room briefly at one point to speak to his attorney. Scott Smith states that Murray did not leave the room, nor did he put time limitations on the interview with Los AngelesPD on 6/27/09. Scott Smith states that he had been with robbery/homicide for 1 and half years, before that he worked in another division for 10 years, 24 years as a police department, 14 in homicide. Scott Smith states that he is an avid note taker, and that he took notes for various individuals and evidence collected regarding Michael Jackson's death, because he understands the importance of those notes. Scott Smith states that he was in and out of the room while Elyssa Elissa Fleak was investigating on June 29, 2009. Scott Smith states that while Elissa Fleak was removing items, he did not make notes about what she was removing them, but after that when all items had been laid out for display purposes for photographs. Scott Smith states that on June 29, 2009, he never mentioned that he never mentioned that a propofol bottle was found in an IV bag. Scott Smith states that he was very specific with miligrams, lot numbers, etc., empty IV bags, empty pill bottles. Scott Smith states that on June 29, in the search, he found Murray's medical bags exactly where Murray said they were. Scott Smith states that there were Lorazepam bottles found in the master bathroom of Michael Jackson's bedroom, but that he was not the person who found them. Scott Smith states that the business cards were found in the vanity of the master bathroom, and that Detective Sanchez told him where they were found. Scott Smith states that he interviewed Dr. David Adams in Las Vegas. Scott Smith states that while he was at UCLA, he spoke to Alberto Alvarez. Scott Smith states that Alvarez said he was called into the bedroom, and that Alvarez was told that Michael Jackson was having a bad reaction. Scott Smith states that Alvarez never mentioned CPR, or that the propofol bottle was inside the IV bag was on August 31, 2009. Scott Smith states that Faheem Muhammad made a statement on June 25, but that he said nothing about Murray wanting to go back to the Carolwood home on that date, nor did Michael Amir Williams until 8/31/09. Scott Smith states that there was another interview with Alberto Alvarez after August 31, 2009, and but he can't remember when. Scott Smith states that he requested fingerprints from Alvarez, and he did turn them in, and they were analyzed. Scott Smith states that SID came in and downloaded surveillance video, that there were video cameras were not pointed toward the front door of the home door, but there was one on the front gate, on the keypad at the front gate, and one in the back of the house. Scott Smith states that the video that was selected to download was made collectively, but Detective Martinez did the actual downloading. Scott Smith states that they never requested any more video surveillance after June 25, 2009. Scott Smith states that although the Carolwood home was locked and guards were there, that there were people allowed in the home for the 26th, 27th, 28th of June, 2009. Scott Smith states that he does not know if a log had been kept regarding visitors at Carolwood after Michael Jackson died through June 29, 2009. Scott Smith states that he never talked to the new security at Carolwood to get a list of the people who had been in the house on the 27th, 28th, 29th. Scott Smith states that marijuana was found by family members in Michael Jackson's closet in a suitcase. Scott Smith states that he asked upon leaving Carolwood if he the home would be sealed, he stated that he was told no. Scott Smith states that Conrad Murray told Detective Porsche that he would not sign a death certificate because an autopsy needed to be performed. Scott Smith states that he interviewed other doctors besides Dr. Adams and Dr. Murray. Scott Smith states that Murray gave him the keys to his car in order to search it. Scott Smith states that he did not go personally to search Murray's property in Houston. Scott Smith states that in Las Vegas, Scott Smith recovered Murray's cell phone from his home, computer hard drives from his office, paperwork involving his practice from his offices in Las Vegas. Scott Smith states that he can't recall if he interviewed a Patrick Muhammad was interviewed, Isaac Muhammad was interviewed, and a Derek Cleveland was interviewed by Scott Smith , all of whom were security at Carolwood. Scott Smith states that Michael Jackson's death was deemed a homicide case on August 27, 2009. Scott Smith states that there was some discussion and that the lieutenant from Los AngelesPD told Ed Winter from the coroner's office to stop looking into other doctors besides Murray.

Walgren Redirect

Scott Smith states that a lieutenant from Los AngelesPD contacted Ed Winter, who had already contacted Arnold Klein, which caused some friction between the two. Scott Smith states that the DEA was assigned to look into specific doctors ultimately and that Los AngelesPD was to focus on the homicide investigation. Scott Smith states that when Conrad Murray stated he gave Michael Jackson milk, Scott Smith asked whether the milk was hot or cold. Scott Smith stated he had no idea that milk meant propofol. Scott Smith states that only one IV bag was recovered on June 25, 2009. Scott Smith states he was not present when the propofol bottle inside the IV bag was discovered, but was present when it was all laid out on a table. Scott Smith states regarding video cameras, first pointed at gate area on the outside of gates, second on an entrance underneath the residence but inoperative, third and fourth were on either side of the back side of the entrance facing pool and backyard, fifth pointed at right portion on exterior of house, one pointed facing at the inside of the gate. Scott Smith states no camera showed any door entrances, primarily for exterior perimeter video surveillance.

Chernoff Recross

Scott Smith states that when he found an empty Lorazepam bottle inside an empty IV bag, he starred it and underlined it, marking the lot number. Scott Smith states that he did not note that the propofol bottle was inside an IV bag in his notes, as he did with the Lorazepam bottle.

Re-redirect Walgren

Scott Smith again states he did not see the propofol bottle inside the IV bag, and that is why he did not document it.

Re-recross Chernoff

Scott Smith states that the DEA was going to investigate Mickey Fine Pharmacy, and that Arnold Klein was linked to the pharmacy.

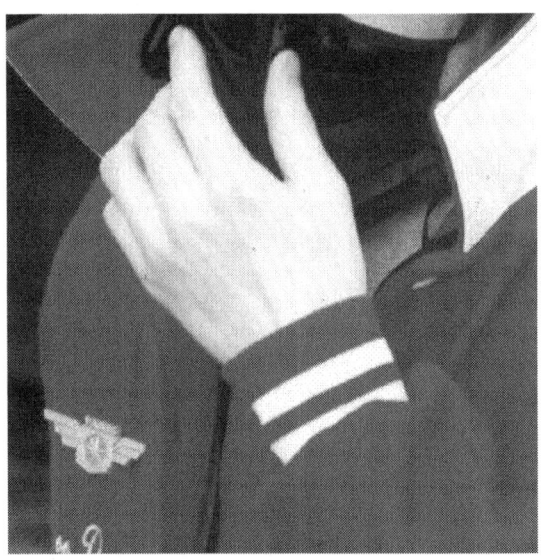

Dr. Christopher Rogers - Los Angeles County Coroner's Office Testimony

Walgren Direct

Christopher Rogers states that he is a deputy medical examiner for Los Angeles county, and that he does autopsies to find cause of death, and that he has done this since 1988. Christopher Rogers' current position the Chief of Forensic Medicine.

Christopher Rogers states he has been present for several thousand autopsies over his career. Christopher Rogers states that he did the autopsy report for Michael Jackson on June 26, 2009. On that specific day, Christopher Rogers states he was not able to specify a cause of death, there was nothing anatomically obvious to state cause of death. Christopher Rogers states that Michael Jackson was healthier than the average person of his age. Christopher Rogers states that there were incidental findings, that Michael Jackson had an enlargement of the prostate gland which meant that it was difficult to urinate so he was retaining urine, he had vitiligo, and he also had a polyp in the colon.

Christopher Rogers states that the nervous system showed mild diffuse swelling, lung exam showed chronic inflammation and scarring, radiology showed an extra rib and also some arthritis. The dental examination showed root canals and implants were done. Christopher Rogers states that an anesthesiology consultation was also done. Christopher Rogers states that a previous scalp injury caused an area of pigmentation at the top of the scalp which was scarred, Christopher Rogers was aware of the scalp injury. Christopher Rogers states that Michael Jackson was 5'9" and that he weighed 136 pounds, BMI index was within the normal range, however a thin individual. Michael Jackson's autopsy photo is shown in court. Christopher Rogers states that is, indeed Michael Jackson. Christopher Rogers states that also the autopsy photo shows 8-25-09, the date is incorrect. Christopher Rogers states that Michael Jackson did not have heart disease and no abnormalities were detected in the heart. Christopher Rogers states that coronary arteries were clear, and that almost everybody has some athrosclerosis in their coronary arteries, but that Michael Jackson had none, meaning no fat or cholesterol in Michael Jackson's arteries. Christopher Rogers states that initially he felt there was no natural disease that caused his death. Christopher Rogers states that Michael Jackson's esophagus was intact, and that there was no white, milky substance in the esophagus. Christopher Rogers states that the stomach content was examined, and that Christopher Rogers found 70 grams of drug fluid but did not show pills or capsules. Christopher Rogers states that he looked for that specifically to determine cause of death. Christopher Rogers states that he checked the mouth and upper airway (meaning the entrance to the breathing passages, mouth down the throat into the windpipe or trachea) and found no foreign material. Christopher Rogers states that he requested toxicology reports to assist him to report cause of death. Christopher Rogers states that he sought out other doctors in specialties to help him with cause of death. Christopher Rogers states he read Conrad Murray's interview with Los AngelesPD to help him and asked for medical records from Murray, but was never able to obtain any records from Murray.

Christopher Rogers states that he was at some point, able to determine cause of death, and the manner was homicide. Christopher Rogers states that he based his homicide report on 1) Murray's statement to the police he administered the propofol and benzodiazepine 2) it's not appropriate to give propofol for insomnia, that the risk outweighs the benefit, and in addition, the setting in the home did not provide for the use of an EKG monitor, a precision dosing monitor, equipment available to revive Michael Jackson adequately, not an endotracheal tube, no meds to improve circulatory function and 3) and that the circumstances do not support self-administration of propofol, because Murray stated that he only gave Michael Jackson 25 mgs, went to the bathroom, returned from the bathroom to find Michael Jackson not breathing. Christopher Rogers states that you would have to assume that even though Michael Jackson was under the influence under the influence of propofol and other sedatives, injects himself with propofol, seems less reasonable than Murray giving Michael Jackson propofol from time to time. Christopher Rogers states that since they did not find a precision dosing device, and that he feels that it would be easy for the doctor to give too much propofol, rather than Michael Jackson self injecting propofol himself. Christopher Rogers states that the cause of death was acute propofol intoxication, and the contributing condition was the benzodiazepine effect. Christopher Rogers states that Lorazepam and Midazolam, both sedatives were a smaller contribution to Michael Jackson's death, and could exacerbate respiratory depression, causing someone to stop breathing. Christopher Rogers states that it could have also stopped the heart from beating. Christopher Rogers states that a diagram was made of Michael Jackson's body during the autopsy, noting various IV puncture marks during revival efforts. Christopher Rogers states that on Michael Jackson's right arm, left arm, neck, just below the left knee (where Murray had administered the IV, not revival puncture mark). Christopher Rogers states that he observed the empty propofol bottle that was found in Michael Jackson's bedroom, noting that it was unusual as the stopper had a center which had a linear opening, showing that it did not show any needle punctures. Christopher Rogers states that the linear opening is an opening from side to side in the center of the rubber stopper of the empty bottle of propofol, indicating it was not made by a syringe needle. Christopher Rogers states that the linear opening could have been made by a spike.

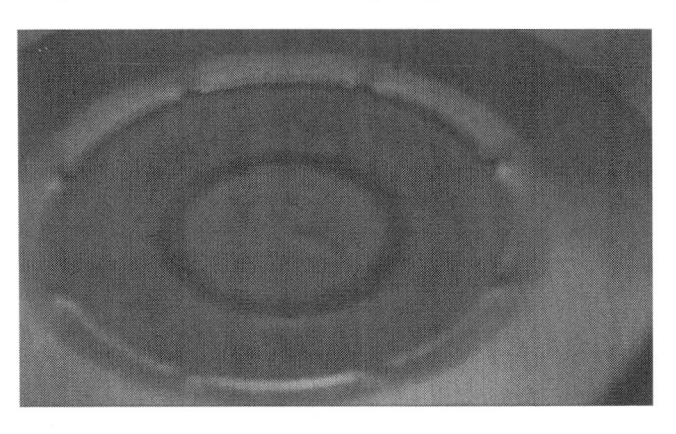

Walgren Direct continued

Walgren asks if Roger checked the autospy picture during the lunch break and if the picture was corrrectly dated as June 25th. Christopher Rogers says yes. Walgren reminds that when they went to break they were talking of a spike. Walgren shows a spike and asks Christopher Rogers to identify it.

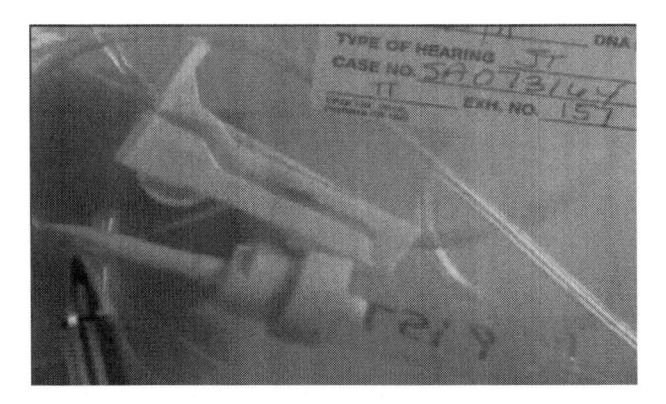

On March 2011 Christopher Rogers reviewed some evidence. Christopher Rogers identified what Elissa Fleak called a needle as IV catheter with a needle still present. It appeared unused. Christopher Rogers also examined the syringe from the nightstand. According to Christopher Rogers it did not appear to fit.

Flanagan cross

Defense asks if Christopher Rogers reviewed his preliminary testimony, the coroner's report, his notes, expert reports to refresh his memory before today's hearing. Christopher Rogers says he reviewed those items as well as another autopsy report and reviewed toxicology results. Flanagan asks if he reviewed a report from Dr. Steven Shafer who is an anesthesiologist in Columbia University. Christopher Rogers reviewd that as well. Flanagan asks if he has reviewed toxicology results from outside labs about stomach and urine. Christopher Rogers did not see those. Flanagan asks if Midazolam, Diazapem and Lidocaine toxicology results are consisted with what Murray told the cops. Christopher Rogers answers yes. Flanagan asks if it's correct that what Murray said about Lorazepam in his interview doesn't match with the toxicology results and also mentions that Propofol is hard to determine as it metabolizes fast. Christopher Rogers says it's true and they also don't know how much and how fast Murray gave Michael Jackson Propofol. Flanagan asks if they can't be sure who gave it. Christopher Rogers says yes. Flanagan asks why would IV bottle be spiked. Christopher Rogers says it's done for giving it continuosly to maintain sedation. Flanagan asks if spiking would also help to empty Propofol bottle quickly than getting it out with syringe. Flanagan asks if you wanted to mix Propofol with saline spiking it would make it faster to pour it into the saline bag. Flanagan mentions a way of doing Propofol drip by mixing with saline solution. Flanagan again mentions that emptying the Propofol bottle with a spike would be more efficient than using a syringe to get it out. Flanagan asks if propofol - saline mix was done, you would expect to see an IV bag with Propofol in it. Christopher Rogers says there was no Propofol found in the bag. Flanagan asks if any evidence of propofol was in the y connector, syringe and the tubing below the y connector. Christopher Rogers answers yes. The portion above the y connecter was negative for Propofol. Flanagan mentions Propofol's shelf life of 6 hours. If it's not used it has to be thrown out. Flanagan says that it doesn't make sense if one will only use 5ml of Propofol to get it from a 100 ml Propofol bottle as they will need to throw away the 95 ml. Flanagan asks about lidocaine and Christopher Rogers explains why it's used. Flanagan asks about if Propofol needs to be slowly infused and not rapidly. Flanagan asks what the blood levels will show if a person is given 25mg of Propofol. Christopher Rogers doesn't know. Flanagan asks how much sleep would such dose of Propofol would bring. Christopher Rogers says 5 minutes and Propofol would have no effect after 5 -10 minutes. Flanagan asks what happens if 25 mg is injected rapidly. Christopher Rogers say that you'll have a locally high concentration and it would mean a higher risk of cardiao respitory arrest. Flanagan goes over the information that Propofol needs to be slowly administered. Flanagan asks if someone is slowly administering Propofol if they would see any negative effects such as breathing stopping. Christopher Rogers answers yes. Flanagan asks if a slow injection is given and the patient is watched for 15-20 minutes and if after that time period if something goes bad if it wouldn't be due to Propofol. Walgren objects because it's not considering other benzos. Flanagan changes his hypothetical to ask if a person is sleeping more than 5 minutes that wouldn't be due to Propofol and if he could be sleeping due to being tired / fatigue. Christopher Rogers agree. Therapeutic level of Propofol. Christopher Rogers says it's dependent on intended use. Michael Jackson had 2.6 mg Propofol in his femoral blood. Flanagan asks if due to post mortem redistribution if that numbers could be problematic. Flanagan goes over articles to say that Lorazepam does not redistribute and ask Christopher Rogers about the Lorazepam amounts. Christopher Rogers say that they are very close and it might or might not show that there was no redistribution. Pills in stomach. They wouldn't distribute to the body until they are disolved. Flanagan switches to stomach contents. It was a dark liquid. Flanagan asks if there could be fruit juice in the stomach and asks if they ever identified the content of the stomach. Christopher Rogers say they didn't. Flanagan asks if they saw any tablets or capsules. Christopher Rogers says they didn't. Flanagan says they could get dissolved and they can't tell if a person has taken tablets by looking to stomach contents. Toxicology would be needed to determine it. Flanagan asks if toxicology results show that Lorazepam, would it mean consumption of Lorazepam. Flanagan shows the Lorazepam in stomach toxicology results. Flanagan mentions Lorazepam concentration being 4 times higher than the femoral blood levels. Flanagan mentions the amount equals to 1/43 of a tablet but it doesn't show how many tablets are actually taken as the pills dissolve over time. Lorazepam levels in the blood didn't cause any red flags because it wasn't too much. Flanagan shows 2 Lorazepam pill bottles found in Michael Jackson's house. Both had 30 pills (60 total), one bottle is empty the other one has 9.5 pills left in it. Flanagan mentions that Christopher Rogers thought benzodiazepines had an effect on the death. Midazolam and Diazepam found in the blood was low and insignificant. Flanagan asks what level one Lorazepam pill would cause. Christopher Rogers says it should be at therapeutic level. Flanagan brings out the Baselt book that says for 1 pill .018 in 2 hours. Flanagan tries to ask if 1.69 blood level would mean it would require 9-10 pills. Objection. By judge's order Flanagan goes into hypothetical scenarios. Christopher Rogers can't understand questions. A lot of objections and judge sustains them one after another very quickly. Flanagan mentions half life of Lorazepam (9 to 16 hours) and bioavailability. It's beyond expertise of Christopher Rogers. Flanagan asks if what level of Propofol would be lethal. Christopher Rogers says 1 to 17 mg per ml. Flanagan asks if a person with 2.6 level of Propofol would feel pain. Christopher Rogers says yes. Flanagan again asks Lorazepam levels of 1.69 and how many pills it would mean. Overruled due to improper hypothetical. After several hypotheticals Flanagan gets Christopher Rogers to say it would equal to 9 pills. Flanagan mentions that stomach and urine wasn't tested for Lorazepam. Flanagan talks about urine samples. If urine sample in autopsy has higher levels of Lorazepam then the scene urine, would the blood would have higher level of Lorazepam then the blood at 7:30 AM as well. Christopher Rogers says he can't answer because there are too many variables. Flanagan gives the scenario of 2 mg Lorazepam at 2AM and 5 AM and then 8 pills being taken around 10 AM , if the urine level of Lorazepam would be higher at autopsy urine then the scene urine. Christopher Rogers answers yes. Flanagan goes over the homicide conclusion. Christopher Rogers mention 4 factors contributed to that conclusion. 1st factor Propofol and benzodiazepines is administered by another. Flanagan again asks questions about Lorazepam which is beyond expertise of Christopher Rogers. 2nd factor non hospital setting. Flanagan asks if chronic insomnia cannot be treated by Propofol. Christopher Rogers says that it's not general way to treat it. Flanagan mentions insomnia has different levels and if Propofol might be used. It's beyond Christopher Rogers expertise. 3rd factor standard of care. Christopher Rogers made that determination with the help of the anesthologist. 4th factor Circumstances do not support self administeration. Christopher Rogers says that he thought what was reasonable. To Christopher Rogers it's reasonable to believe that Murray miscalculated and gave too much Propofol. He finds it less reasonable for Michael to wake up and while still under influence of sedatives and manage give himself Propofol and it killed him and all these happened within 2 minutes. Flanagan talks about the positioning of the IV line. IV was beyond left knee and it was 6 inches long till the y connector. Flanagan asks if a person can touch an area around their knee. Christopher Rogers agree. Flanagan asks about if anyone can do a bolus injection and if it can stop the heart. Flanagan asks if someone else was giving the injection other than Michael Jackson would they see if there's a problem. Christopher Rogers say you hope that they do.

Walgren redirect

Walgren brings up what was mentioned earlier and asks is it true if a person found with eyes open it would mean they died quickly.

Christopher Rogers says it's not true. People can die slowly and still have eyes open.

Oxygen tank was analyzed at july 13, 2009. It was empty.

Walgren says that most of the defense questions pharmacology - what happens to drugs when they enter into the body. It's not Christopher Rogers area of expertise. Christopher Rogers is an expert in determining cause of death. He's not an expert in Propofol or Lorazepam. Walgren mentions the lethal levels of 1 to 17 mg Propofol and asks if smaller numbers than we have seen in Michael Jackson can cause death. Christopher Rogers answer yes. Walgren goes over Lorazepam bottles. They are both prescribed by Murray. One is filled April 28, 2009. It was for 30 pills - 9.5 remaining. Second one is filled April,2.2009. It was for 30 pills and it's now empty.

Walgren mentions the hypotheticals Flanagan asked. Tells Christopher Rogers to assume Murray was telling the truth in his interview and gave Michael Jackson Valium and then 2 injections of midozolam and Lorazepam and then Propofol. In that scenario if he left the patient alone to swallow Lorazepam pills, and there's no monitoring equipment, no airway management equipment and no resusitive equipment. Christopher Rogers says it's still homicide. Walgren gives the same sets of events but the scenario self administration of Propofol instead of Lorazepam. Christopher Rogers would still classify it as homicide.

Flanagan cross

Flanagan asks about the oxygen and asks if the valve was open or closed. Christopher Rogers doesn't know. Flanagan asks how long would it take it to become empty. Christopher Rogers say it depends on how open the valve is. Flanagan asks if it's in therapeutic levelswould it empty in 2 weeks. Christopher Rogers say probably. Flanagan mentions Christopher Rogers answers about how he's not knowledgeable about Lorazepam and asks doesn't he need to be knowlegeable about that to make determination in this case in regards to the cause of death. Christopher Rogers says he doesn't know how these levels are achieved but they are the cause of death. Flanagan talks about Lorazepam levels being close to the levels required to be unresponsive to painful stimuli and Propofol levels are half the required to be unresponsive to painful stimuli. Flanagan asks Christopher Rogers to assume that Murray was telling the truth in his interview. Flanagan mentions the midazolam and diazapam numbers match but Propofol and Lorazepam levels are a lot higher.

Walgren redirect

Walgren asks why he do an consult with an anesthologist. Christopher Rogers says because it was a comples problem. The doctor he consulted told him that the levels was consisted with general anesthesia.

Flanagan recross

Flanagan mentions rapid injection again and asks if rapid injection would have negative effects of respirtory and cardiovasculary depression.

Murray Trial Summaries Day 11/ October 12- 2011
Dr. Alon Steinberg Cardiologist Testimony

Walgren Direct

Alon Steinberg is a board certified cardiologist for 13 years. He is not an expert in anesthesia, sleep medicine, pharmacology or addiction medicine.

Alon Steinberg has reviewed Conrad Murray's resume. Conrad Murray was not board certified on June 25th 2009. Alon Steinberg tells board certification is an extensive 2 day test and 90% of the cardiologists that take it pass it. Alon Steinberg is an expert reviewer for the California Medical Board, he reviews other doctors' actions to ensure the standard of care has been respected. 3 levels are possible: no deviation, simple deviation and extreme deviation. Extreme deviation is also defined as gross negligence.

Alon Steinberg has conducted a review for this case. He had conducted 8 prior reviews. In 4 cases he found no deviation; in 4 cases he found simple deviation of care. This is the first time he's seen an extreme deviation from standard of care. Cardiologists use sedation for many procedures and sometimes they use Propofol. Cardiologists are expert in mild or moderate sedation. In conscious sedation the patient is able to talk and respond to touching. Deep sedation is when patients are only responsive to pain or repeated stimuli. General anesthesia is when patients feel no pain. Cardiologists are not trained in deep sedation. When deep sedation is needed, they call anesthesiologist and that's the only time they use Propofol. When they are giving mild or moderate sedation they use benzodiazepines. For deep sedation they are required to give Propofol with an anesthesiologist. Alon Steinberg has reviewed this case. He has focused his review based on Conrad Murray interview with police. Alon Steinberg wanted to judge Conrad Murray on his own words. Alon Steinberg found 6 separate extreme deviations from standard of care.

1- Propofol was not medically indicated. Alon Steinberg mentions Propofol is an anesthesia. Alon Steinberg tells there was no written informed consent. The patient must be informed of the risks and benefits of treatment. Alon Steinberg never heard of Propofol used for insomnia. Steinbers says that using Propofol for insomnia is gross negligence and extreme deviation.

2- Propofol was given in a home setting, without proper equipment and without proper staff.

Walgren asks what equipment needed. Alon Steinberg says that first a pulse oximeter with an alarm is needed but Murray's oximeter didn't have an alarm. Alon Steinberg says he had to stare to Michael Jackson nonstop every second. Alon Steinberg says he should have automated blood pressure cuff, to check blood pressure at least every 5 minutes. Murray had a manual cuff and did not use it. Next thing is needed is an EKG monitor to track the heart rhythm. Another thing that is needed is oxygen with a nasal cannula or mask. You need suction in case the patient regurgitates and you need to get it before it goes into patient's lungs. Another equipment needed is an Ambu bag. Murray had an

Ambu bag but did not use it, he did mouth to mouth. You also need to have a way to call for help. Backboard is needed in case CPR is needed. You also need a back up battery for the equipment in case of a black out. Other equipment needed is equipment needed for airway such as endotracheal tube. Endotracheal tube requires trained staff to place it. Also you need a defibrillator. A lot of special drugs are also needed. Those are fluamzenil, narcan, lidocaine, betablockers, atropine, dopamine, epinephrine, prednisone, dextrose. Alon Steinberg says when giving sedation you also need BLS (basic life support) and ACLS (advanced cardiac life support) trained assistant.

3- Inadequate preparation for an emergency. You need to have the drugs ready, equipment ready, have a person ready to help you. You need to be prepared to use those medicine and equipment in the case of emergency.

4- Improper care during the arrest. Michael Jackson's breathing had stopped and Conrad Murray didn't follow proper protocol.

Alon Steinberg explains cardiac arrest which is when heart stops beating. There's no blood pressure and the patient collapses. In that case you call 911, use a defibrillator, and do CPR on a hard surface. In Michael Jackson's case, it was a respiratory arrest. Michael Jackson stopped breathing and the oxygen goes down. Then heart started to beat harder while trying to distribute little oxygen in the body. According Conrad Murray's statement this is where Conrad Murray found Michael Jackson. If you do nothing, the heart weakens because of lack of oxygen, and stops contracting but there is still an electrical activity. That's PEA (Pulseless Electrical Activity). After PEA, there's asystole. Alon Steinberg says Conrad Murray should have called 911 immediately then try to arouse Michael Jackson, should have used the Ambu bag and give him Flumanezil. Alon Steinberg says it's inexcusable that Conrad Murray did chest compressions. This was a respiratory arrest not a cardiac arrest and there was blood pressure and pulse. Conrad Murray should NOT have done CPR. Conrad Murray's

CPR was poor quality because Michael Jackson was on a bed. It has to be done on a hard surface such as on the floor and should have done CPR with 2 hands. Alon Steinberg says it would have been very easy to put Michael Jackson on the floor.

5- Failing to call for help. Conrad Murray should have called 911 immediately. Conrad Murray should have known that he didn't have any of the medications and the equipment and he had to call for help. But Conrad Murray instead called Michael Amir Williams which caused a significant delay. EMS was only 4 minutes away. If Conrad Murray had called them he could have gotten help sooner.

For every minute delay in calling EMS, there are less and less chances the patient will survive and there is a risk of permanent brain damage. Walgren: "Every minute counts". Alon Steinberg also thought it was bizarre to call an assistant instead of calling 911. Conrad Murray as a medical doctor should have realized he needed help and call 911.

6- Failure to maintain proper medical records. Medical records are important because of several reasons. Insurance companies want them. Second reason is litigation. The most important reason is for better health care for the patient. Conrad Murray did not document a single thing. He didn't ask when the last time Michael Jackson ate was, he had no vital sign records, he had no physical exam. There was no informed consent. He didn't write what medication he gave and what was the reaction. Conrad Murray was confused and was not able to explain Michael Jackson's history or what he gave him to the ER doctor or EMTs. Walgren asks if he could be dishonest rather than confused.

Alon Steinberg concluded that these extreme deviations directly contributed to Michael Jackson's death. Without these deviations, Michael Jackson would still be alive.

Walgren asks based on Conrad Murray's statement if he gave benzodiazepines and only 25mg Propofol if the risk of respiratory depression is foreseeable. Alon Steinberg answers yes. Walgren assumes everything happened as Conrad Murray described and as Conrad Murray left Michael Jackson alone, Michael Jackson was able to take Lorazepam pills or Propofol. Alon Steinberg says all the things he said still apply. Alon Steinberg says you never leave the patient and always monitor patient. If Michael Jackson self administered, means that Murray was away, and that should not have happened. Alon Steinberg compares leaving a patient under the effect of Propofol to leaving a baby sleeping alone on the kitchen counter. Alon Steinberg says the baby might have woke up and fall down. Alon Steinberg also mentions that medication should not have been within Michael Jackson's reach. Steimberg explains how in hospitals every medication will be under lock and says that having medications out in the open is a foreseeable risk that the patient can self administer and take the wrong medication.

Flanagan Cross

Alon Steinberg is not currently trained in using Propofol. When Alon Steinberg was New York he had privileges to use Propofol. In his current work he does not have the privileges and he hasn't used it in 7 years. When he was in New York he felt confident in using Propofol because he was trained in protecting airways. Flanagan asks if there is a difference in the equipment needed for moderate and deep sedation. Alon Steinberg answers no, they will be the same. Flanagan asks if Alon Steinberg thought Conrad Murray's declaration to the cops was thorough and complete. Alon Steinberg says he assumed it was complete. Flanagan asks how Alon Steinberg knows Conrad Murray didn't have informed consent. Alon Steinberg says because there was none. Flanagan asks if the informed consent can be oral. Alon Steinberg says it has to be written. "If it's not written it's not done." Alon Steinberg says he has never heard an oral consent. Flanagan asks if any written document had anything to do with Michael Jackson's death. Alon Steinberg says if Michael Jackson had been informed about risk and benefits, he might not have agreed to this. Alon Steinberg says he cannot know if Michael Jackson had been informed, but assumes he was not informed that a powerful dangerous drug would be used on him without proper monitoring. Alon Steinberg assumes Michael Jackson would not have agreed to it. Flanagan asks if Alon Steinberg know anything about Michael Jackson's propensity towards drugs and mentions Demerol and Klein. Flanagan asks what if Michael Jackson was an addict; would he have agreed to it? Alon Steinberg says if he was an addict, he wouldn't give it to him in the first place. Other doctors that use Propofol could be dentists, gastroenterologist, pulmonary doctors, ER doctors. But their societies have advice on how to use it and they are trained. Their societies outline the same monitoring equipment that Alon Steinberg mentioned. Alon Steinberg says there's no difference in equipment needed for conscious sedation. Flanagan asks what killed Michael Jackson? Alon Steinberg says a respiratory arrest because he still had a pulse that means there was a heart rate and blood pressure. Conrad Murray said there was blood pressure and pulse, it was later PEA. Alon Steinberg says that according to Conrad Murray he found Michael Jackson around noon and EMS arrived at 12:26. There was a delay in calling 911 for at least 12 minutes. Flanagan mentions Conrad Murray made a lot of time estimations and it might be all precise. Flanagan asks what 2mg of Lorazepam would do to a patient. Alon Steinberg says he's not an expert, he gave it as a sedative orally before but he never used IV. Alon Steinberg says he gives it an hour before the procedure orally. Flanagan asks further questions about Lorazepam, Midazolam.

Objections. Sustained.

It's beyond his area of expertise. Flanagan turns the subject to Propofol and say that Michael Jackson and Conrad Murray had been discussing Propofol for the past 3 night and Conrad Murray told Michael Jackson it was not good for him and he was trying to wean Michael Jackson off. Alon Steinberg states that Conrad Murray said that he gave 25mg initially and started Michael Jackson on IV. Flanagan denies that there was an IV. Alon Steinberg understood that after that initial 25mg dose, there was a drip based on his police interview. Alon Steinberg cites a lot of examples in Conrad Murray interview referencing IV and says it makes sense because 25mg would not keep Michael Jackson asleep. Flanagan insists there was no drip on the 25th, Alon Steinberg insists there was a drip, they both give examples in Conrad Murray's Los AngelesPD interview. They agree it's not clear, but Alon Steinberg says it makes no sense. It's logical Conrad Murray gave a drip. Michael Jackson logically would have woken up, and there was no reason that Conrad Murray changed his methods. Flanagan says that 25mg is not a heavy dose and it would make Michael Jackson sleep 4 to 7 minutes. Alon Steinberg agrees. So Flanagan asks if Michael Jackson was still asleep he was sleeping for other reasons such as being tired. Alon Steinberg says that he would have worried that Michael Jackson was still asleep if Michael Jackson was not on a drip. Protocol says that after Propofol you should watch the patient. Alon Steinberg says just looking at Michael Jackson doesn't tell if he's in mild sedation or in deep sedation. Alon Steinberg says they need to be continuously checked for their reaction to stimuli. Alon Steinberg says Conrad Murray should have woken Michael Jackson up. Alon Steinberg says the fact that Michael Jackson was still asleep after 10 minutes, if there was no drip, is very alarming. Alon Steinberg it might mean that something was going wrong. Flanagan mentions a study that Propofol was successfully used on refractory chronic primary insomnia in Taiwan. Alon Steinberg says that the article dates back to 2010, in 2009 when Conrad Murray gave Propofol there was no medical knowledge that Propofol could be given for sleep. Conrad Murray was unethical in giving Propofol with no medical knowledge. Article mentions Propofol given for 2 hrs per night 5 nights, not 8 hours per night for 2 straight months. The article says that this test was successful, but it's still not used as a sleep medication because it's still experimental, there is not enough data about this. It needs to be extensively researched and tested. Conrad Murray is the first doctor he's heard who used Propofol for insomnia. Flanagan asks how Alon Steinberg knows Conrad Murray didn't use Ambu bag, Alon Steinberg says because Conrad Murray said he did mouth to mouth. Flanagan asks how Alon Steinberg knows Conrad

Murray didn't use the blood pressure cuff, Alon Steinberg says because it was not on Michael Jackson. Alon Steinberg says pulse oximeter was not on Michael Jackson. Alon Steinberg says he doesn't know what happened between 11 and 12 or how long Conrad Murray watched Michael Jackson or when Conrad Murray went to bathroom. Flanagan asks if he has an idea about the actual time of death. Alon Steinberg says Michael Jackson was pronounced dead at 2:26PM but he was probably clinically dead for some time. Alon Steinberg says Michael Jackson savable when Conrad Murray found him based on his interview. Alon Steinberg says Conrad Murray said he left Michael Jackson for 2 minutes. By using Ambu bag, by arousal and changing the effects of the medicines and if 911 was called Michael Jackson was savable. Flanagan tries Alon Steinberg to assume that Conrad Murray was gone longer than 2 minutes. Alon Steinberg is not comfortable making those assumptions as he based his report on Conrad Murray's statements. Flanagan mentions the phone calls; Alon Steinberg does not want to comment on them. Alon Steinberg says saying Conrad Murray was on the phone tells him that Conrad Murray shouldn't have been on the phone and if Michael Jackson would only given 25mg it would wake him up. Alon Steinberg says that it tells Michael Jackson was on a drip. Flanagan wants him to assume if Conrad Murray was gone longer than 2 minutes if Michael Jackson was savable. Alon Steinberg says he was savable because according to Conrad Murray's statement Michael Jackson had a pulse, blood pressure and heart was still beating and with proper equipment he could have been saved. He could have given Michael Jackson oxygen. Alon Steinberg says Michael Jackson wasn't PEA when Conrad Murray came back because he had a pulse. Flanagan asks how he knows know Michael Jackson had a pulse, Alon Steinberg says because Conrad Murray said so. Flanagan asks if it could PEA. Alon Steinberg says in PEA there's no pulse. Flanagan asks what Conrad Murray should have done. Alon Steinberg says he should have called 911 and it would have taken 2 seconds. Alon Steinberg says protocol says doctors are allowed 2 minutes to determine the situation. Flanagan asks if Conrad Murray went down to ask for help in 12:05 – 5 minutes after – if it would be a violation of standard of care. Alon Steinberg says he didn't have the right equipment so he should have called 911 immediately.

Sidebar

Flanagan tries to talk about Kai Chase. Alon Steinberg says Conrad Murray didn't ask Kai to call 911. Flanagan asks what if Conrad Murray called for help in 5 minutes but not in 2 minutes. Alon Steinberg says it's still a deviation from standard of care. Flanagan asks if he talked to Conrad Murray to review the case. Alon Steinberg says no and he didn't ask. Alon Steinberg used Conrad Murray's 2 hour interview. Flanagan asks what Conrad Murray should he have done in 2 minutes. Alon Steinberg says call 911, tilt the head to open airway, make him breathe with Ambu bag and give Flumazenil. Alon Steinberg says he would have called 911 first. Alon Steinberg says Conrad Murray had to increase Michael Jackson's breathing. Flanagan asks if Conrad Murray make a mistake in asking someone to call 911 Alon Steinberg says he had no one around and he had to call 911. Alon Steinberg says for the time it takes to call for security Conrad Murray could have called 911. He had a cell phone. Alon Steinberg says it would have taken him 2 seconds to say "I'm a doctor, there's an arrest, come to 100 Carolwood now" and then Conrad Murray could have put 911 on loudspeaker and continue to do what he was doing. Flanagan asks if he's aware that EMS said Michael Jackson was cool to the touch. Yes but Conrad Murray said he was warm. Alon Steinberg says you get cold in 26 minutes when you have no blood pressure. Flanagan asks if Alon Steinberg have no doubt that if 911 had been called immediately Michael Jackson would still be alive. Alon Steinberg says he have no doubt about that, they could have saved him. Conrad Murray said that he lost the pulse after calling Michael Amir Williams at 1212. So if the paramedics had been there at 1205 or 1210, they could have saved him. Flanagan says that Conrad Murray was in emergency situation and he could be mistaken in his estimations. Alon Steinberg says there is clear evidence that there was a delay in calling 911 as Conrad Murray went downstairs and called Michael Amir Williams rather than calling 911. Flanagan asks based upon these facts if Alon Steinberg thinks Conrad Murray is responsible of Michael Jackson's death. Alon Steinberg says yes. Flanagan asks if Conrad Murray should have dropped Michael Jackson on the floor, in spite of the IV line. Alon Steinberg says he should stop the Propofol drip first and then he should be careful with the line when he's putting Michael Jackson down the floor. Flanagan asks rather than suction would it be okay to turn patient his side and clean the mouth with a finger will be okay. Alon Steinberg says suction is needed. Flanagan asks if a doctor has only 1 patient, he would still need to document everything he does. Alon Steinberg says he does because obviously Conrad Murray didn't recall what he had given when he talked to UCLA or with the paramedics. Flanagan says that not having records did not kill Michael Jackson. Alon Steinberg says it wouldn't cause his death but it's still deviation.

Walgren Redirect

Alon Steinberg states that Murray did not act like he was ACLS certified. Alon Steinberg states that he used propfol in New York, but it was in hospital settings. Alon Steinberg states that gastroenterologists, dentists and ER doctors who use Propofol receive appropriate training, with a trained staff and appropriate monitoring equipment are necessary. Alon Steinberg states that an article about the Propofol study in Taiwan: published in 2010, was an experimental study. The patients were given Propofol in a hospital, with the appropriate equipment, the experiment was approved by their ethics committee. Alon Steinberg states that written, informed consents were obtained from the patients. Alon Steinberg states that 8 hours of fasting occurred prior to being given Propofol, and that the Propofol was given by an anesthesiologist. Alon Steinberg states that the patients were constantly monitored and pulse oximeters were attached to the patients. Alon Steinberg states that the Propofol was administered by an infusion pump, a drip was not used. Alon Steinberg states that no other benzos were used. Alon Steinberg states that the authors of the article specifically state that the study was experiment, and that is does not dictate a standard of care. Alon Steinberg states that what Murray was doing was essentially an experiment. Alon Steinberg states that if he had to assume that Murray gave only 25mg, that there was no drip, would he draw the same conclusions? Alon Steinberg states yes, that standard of care was deviated from in an unmonitored setting, without appropriate equipment, response was inappropriate, medical records were inappropriate and that it was be a foreseeable prediction that there would be respiratory depression (stop breathing). Alon Steinberg states that Murray played a direct, causal role in Michael Jackson's death.

Recross Flanagan

Alon Steinberg states that the sleep study showed that Propofol helped insomnia. Alon Steinberg states that in his analysis for the CA medical Board, that Murray deviated from the standard of care for Michael Jackson. Alon Steinberg states that the lack of a backup battery did not lead to the cause of Michael Jackson's death, however, 5 out of 6 deviations did lead to Michael Jackson's death. Alon Steinberg states that he did read Murray's interview with Los AngelesPD that he gave Michael Jackson Propofol for 40-50 days without incident. Flanagan asks if Alon Steinberg has made certain assumption, Alon Steinberg states no. Alon Steinberg states that he didn't assume that Murray gave Propofol, that Murray didn't have the proper equipment, the delay in calling 911, improper care during the arrest, that all of these things are facts.

Walgren re-redirect

Alon Steinberg states that even if the defense theory that Michael Jackson self-injected Propofol and therefore accidentally killed himself, according to Conrad Murray's own words, Murray would still be the causal factor in Michael Jackson's death.

Dr. Nader Kamangar/ Sleep Medicine Expert Testimony

Walgren Direct

Nader Kamangar states he is a pulmonary care/sleep medicine/critical care physician at UCLA. Nader Kamangar states he is board certified in four areas: internal medicine, pulmonary medicine, critical care, and sleep medicine.

Nader Kamangar states he is a medical reviewer for the CA Medical Board , and that he assessed Murray's care to Michael Jackson for the medical board. Nader Kamangar states that is Propofol used in critical care unit on a daily basis. Nader Kamangar states he is trained in using Propofol. Nader Kamangar states Propofol is used for placement of endotracheal tubes, and for people on breathing machines. Nader Kamangar states that Propofol is the most commonly used drug for this. Nader Kamangar states that he found multiple deviations of standard of care with regard to Conrad Murray's care of Michael Jackson: 1- Propofol was given in an unacceptable setting : using this deep sedation agent in a home setting is inconceivable and an egregious violation of standard of care.

2- ACLS certified: the person who gives Propofol must be trained in ACLS and airways management. There was a risk of hypoventilation (diminishment in rate of breathing), apnea and obstruction of the airway.

3- Need of assistance: Murray needed a second person (a nurse) to monitor, to pay complete and utter attention to Michael Jackson, especially if Murray was going to leave the room; this goes without saying. This violations Hippocratic oath, to abandon his patient.

4- Pre-procedure setup : imperative to be prepared for unforeseen circumstances. Things can change very quickly. A patient may look good, and the next minute there's a problem. Murray needed a suction catheter, because patients can regurgitate into their airway, and block the airway, this can cause death. A crash cart (medication on hand: adrenaline, ephedrine, medication to correct the heart beat, etc...) , pulse oximeter, defibrillator, automated infusion pump (precise dosing for Propofol) even with people who are intubated; Nader Kamangar states that all of these factors are extreme deviation of standard of care and are the equivalent of gross negligence. Nader Kamangar states that he has never seen someone giving Propofol at home in such settings, and would not have expected to see that.

5- Charts / medical documentation: or medical history, reactions to a medication. For example a blood pressure can look normal, but not be normal for a particular patient, and that change in blood pressure could be the indication of a problem.

6- Michael Jackson was left alone, which is not acceptable, especially since Murray didn't have the right equipment.

7- Use of benzodiazapines: using Lorazepam and midazolam on top of Propofol can have higher effects: more significant respiratory depression, decrease cardiac output (often a consequence of respiratory depression), decreased blood pressure and cardiac arrest can occur directly, or because of low levels of oxygen.

8- Dehydration: blood circulation is not good when you are dehydrated, causes low blood pressure. Benzos and Propofol would also lower blood pressure. Murray should not have used benzos or Propofol if the patient is dehydrated.

9- Failure to call 911: 911 should have been called immediately.

10- Improper CPR: Murray stated there was a pulse, therefore the heart was beating, so the problem was respiratory not cardiac. Murray should have dealt with airway management by placing an ambu-bag over Michael Jackson's mouth. Murray's administration of CPR was ineffective; it was not on a hard surface, and it was done with one hand. Correct CPR correctly allows about 20% of the normal blood circulation, so if you do it incorrectly

Nader Kamangar states that assuming Murray found Michael Jackson at noon, and calls Michael Amir Williams at 12:12 pm, the significance of the 12 minutes is that the what is the lack of blood flow to vital organs, especially to the brain. Nader Kamangar states that some individuals are more susceptible than others to a lack of oxygen. Nader Kamangar states that generally it takes 3 to 4 minutes before brain cells start to die. Nader Kamangar states that time is really important. Nader Kamangar states that because 911 was called at 12:20 pm, with the passage of 20 minutes, it reaches a point where it becomes irreversible. Nader Kamangar states that Murray deceived paramedics and ER staff because did not provide the accurate information, which is a deviation of standard of care. Nader Kamangar states that Murray did not properly evaluate insomnia. Nader Kamangar states that insomnia can have many causes, so it's important to have a detailed history. Nader Kamangar states that Murray needed to exclude secondary problems (psychological problems, substance abuse, underlying conditions, chronic anxiety, depression, etc...) Nader Kamangar states that insomnia is defined by no restful sleep for 4 weeks or more. Nader Kamangar states that once all the secondary problems are ruled out, primary insomnia is considered. Nader Kamangar states that in order to diagnose/treat insomnia. a detailed sleep history is needed. : when do they go to bed, when do they fall asleep, when do you wake up, etc.. check sleep apnea. In some cases you need a sleep study. Nader Kamangar states that a detailed pharmaceutical history was needed; both prescribed or over the counter (example migraine pills contain caffeine, that can cause insomnia), illicit drugs. Nader Kamangar states that a detailed physical examination was needed; some underlying conditions can cause insomnia, for example asthma, congestive heart failure, diabetes, bladder problems, enlargement of prostate, thyroid conditions, etc... Nader Kamangar stated blood testing was needed to rule out certain conditions : examples diabetes, kidney problem, restless legs , etc... Nader Kamangar states that a good blood workup would reveal the use of narcotics, if the doctor asks the patient for one. Nader Kamangar states that if the patient is not giving the information, a doctor can simply refuse to treat the patient. Nader Kamangar states that when all the above mentioned are done, then the doctor can treat the underlying condition that causes the insomnia. Nader Kamangar states that in this case, Murray didn't have a detailed history. In addition, Murray didn't check what the root problem for Michael Jackson's insomnia was before treating him. Nader Kamangar states that Murray did say that he saw that other doctors were treating Michael Jackson, he said he saw IV sites. Nader Kamangar states that if Murray could not get that info from Michael Jackson, Murray should have refused care, refused to give further medication. Murray didn't do that, and that was unethical. Nader Kamangar states that Murray bypassed the evaluation of insomnia, bypassed the detailed history which was a deviation of care. Nader Kamangar states it was obvious there was probably secondary causes in Michael Jackson's insomnia (substance abuse or anxiety or depression) and that these underlying causes should have been treated. Nader Kamangar explains about sleep hygiene techniques that can help in case of insomnia (using a bedroom to sleep only, among other things) Nader Kamangar explains about sleep restriction, that the doctor should tell the patient to go to bed later, and limit their time in bed. Nader Kamangar states that relaxation techniques can be used to treat insomnia. Nader Kamangar states that all these can usually work better to treat insomnia than pharmacological approach, but that the pharmacological approach can also be used. Nader Kamangar states that Murray did not use any of the above approaches on Michael Jackson, that Murray went direct to the pharmacological approach.

Nader Kamangar states that the pharmaceutical approach: 3 medications that are not benzos should be used first, because they are not addictive . Nader Kamangar states that a newer drug is melatonin something less addictive.

Nader Kamangar cites 4 different benzodiazepines that deal with insomnia. Nader Kamangar states that others are used also, but their main goal is to treat underlying conditions (anxiety). They are used in tablet form.

Midazolam: not appropriate for long term use for primary insomnia

Valium: not appropriate for long term use for primary insomnia

Lorazepam: can be used on short term basis, tablet form. Really addictive after 3 to 4 weeks. Used to treat underlying conditions, not primary innsomnia.

Nader Kamangar states that the use of midazolam and Lorazepam to treat insomnia was an extreme deviation of care, especially in IV form. Nader Kamangar states that it is inconceivable to use Propofol for the management of insomnia, regardless of the setting. Nader Kamangar states that it is "beyond comprehension, inconceivable and disturbing." Nader Kamangar states that it is beyond a departure of standard of care, especially when underlying causes for insomnia were not treated.

Nader Kamangar states that even if Michael Jackson took Lorazepam and Propofol himself, Murray was the causal factor in Michael Jackson's death, especially if Michael Jackson had substance abuse problems. Nader Kamangar states that the Lorazepam and the Propofol should not have been readily available to Michael Jackson. Nader Kamangar states that there is a risk of respiratory complications, especially if Michael Jackson was dehydrated, and that any competent doctor would have been aware of the risk.

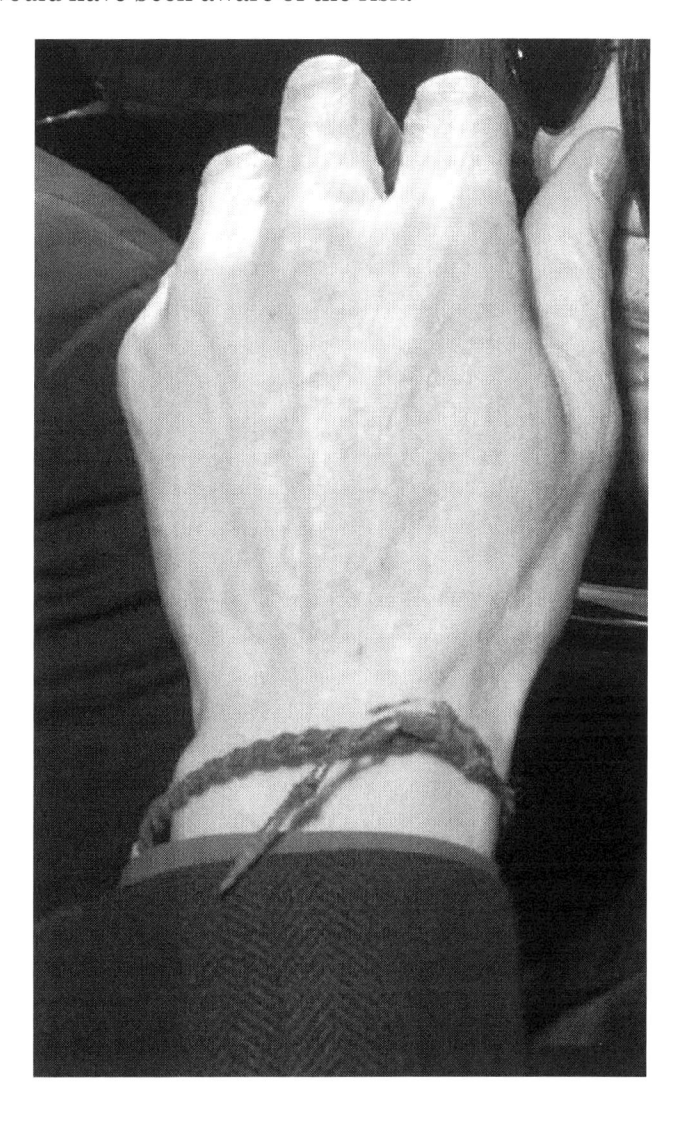

Murray Trial Summaries Day 12/ October 13-2011

Dr. Nader Kamangar Testimony continued

Flanagan cross

Conrad Murray treated Michael Jackson with Propofol with no problems for 2 months. 3 days before Michael Jackson's death Conrad Murray tried to change the treatment. Nader Kamangar says he read it in Conrad Murray's statement police. Flanagan asks if he experience any patient that was resistant to his recommendations. Nader Kamangar says he would send them to another specialist if it's not in his area of expertise such as psychological issues. Nader Kamangar says he would realize his limitations. Nader Kamangar says patients have right to refuse therapy as long as they make an informed decision. Flanagan asks what if a patient is totally resistant and wants to do it in a certain way, what he would do. Nader Kamangar says he would refuse the treatment and try to understand the problem and why the patient does want it and may refer the patient to another specialist. Flanagan asks if Conrad Murray had these conversations with Michael Jackson. Nader Kamangar doesn't know as there were no medical records. Nader Kamangar says if a patient asks for inappropriate therapy you need to get to the root of it. You should try to understand why they are refusing an appropriate therapy and try to get the appropriate care for that patient. He would make sure that they get the right care and says that he would not give the patient a care that he thinks is inappropriate. Flanagan says Conrad Murray gave Propofol for 2 months and Michael Jackson had no problems. Nader Kamangar says he can't answer because he doesn't know Michael Jackson's state of mind and his situation. Nader Kamangar says in the evaluation of the degree of deviation from standard of care, the end result doesn't matter. He didn't consider Michael Jackson's death. Flanagan says a doctor can practice bad medicine but the result might not be bad. Nader Kamangar says it doesn't make it okay. Even if a treatment doesn't cause death, it might still be gross negligence.

Flanagan asks if Nader Kamangar can tell what happened on june 25th. Nader Kamangar says Michael Jackson was receiving very inappropriate therapy in home setting, with inappropriate cocktail drugs, with inappropriate equipment, in a dehydrated patient, delay in calling 911. Nader Kamangar says it was a disaster that resulted in Michael Jackson's death. Flanagan asks what was an inappropriate cocktail: valium + mizadolam +Lorazepam+ 25 mg Propofol. Flanagan asks if this cocktail can cause Michael Jackson's death. Nader Kamangar says "absolutely", especially combination of Propofol and Lorazepam, in a dehydrated patient, whose vitals were unknown (blood pressure, heart rate etc). Nader Kamangar calls this the "perfect storm" that killed Michael Jackson. Flanagan says Nader Kamangar doesn't know if Murray had that info or not. Nader Kamangar says Conrad Murray didn't record anything, had no records; there was no way to determine the trends and changes. Flanagan says not having documents doesn't mean Conrad Murray didn't know those vitals. Nader Kamangar says not having documentation means that Conrad Murray didn't have the information. Nader Kamangar says you can't take care of a patient only from a memory. Nader Kamangar says it's a recipe for disaster. Nader Kamangar gives an example of being with a single patient for long hours. Nader Kamangar says they keep notes. Nader Kamangar says needs to refer to the charts frequently to get a better picture. It's imperative to have charts. Nader Kamangar says without them you can't see the trends and see differences. Flanagan asks if Nader Kamangar thinks there's no way Conrad Murray remembered what he was doing. Nader Kamangar says keeping records is standard care especially when you give such a powerful drug as Propofol. Flanagan says not keeping the charts, for example not writing down 2 mg Lorazepam, did not kill Michael Jackson. Nader Kamangar says he's talking about vital signs, it's not only about writing the medicines. Nader Kamangar says it's a combination of many factors that killed Michael Jackson and says the failure of chart is a contributing factor. Nader Kamangar says it's bad medicine to not keep charts.

Nader Kamangar says Michael Jackson death was directly caused by Propofol + Lorazepam. Nader Kamangar says Lorazepam increased the side effects of Propofol. Nader Kamangar says it can be a lethal combination in a patient that is not monitored. Flanagan asks questions about levels of the medicines, Nader Kamangar says he wants to defer it to a pharmacologist. Flanagan asks if Nader Kamangar reviewed the records of Arnold Klein and saw that he gave Michael Jackson 6500 mg Demerol (pain killer) with Midazolam (sedative) over 3 months. Flanagan asks if Michael Jackson had a Demerol problem. Nader Kamangar says he cannot answer that question. Flanagan asks if 200mg Demerol is a large dose. Nader Kamangar says it's a significant dose and says he avoids using Demerol because it makes someone more hyper, excitable and creates more stimulation. Flanagan asks if Demerol can cause insomnia. Nader Kamangar says it's correct. Flanagan asks if Michael Jackson had insomnia problems. Nader Kamangar says he clearly had insomnia. Flanagan asks if Nader Kamangar made a determination of what type of insomnia. Nader Kamangar says doctors made no effort to determine that. Nader Kamangar says there were suggestions about the reasons for Michael Jackson's insomnia such as performance anxiety and issues with certain medication (Demerol).

Flanagan asks if Michael Jackson had refractory insomnia. Nader Kamangar says he cannot say that. Flanagan asks if he read Conrad Murray's records from 2006 -2009 on Michael Jackson. Nader Kamangar says Conrad Murray gave Michael Jackson sleep medications as well as knew he was prescribed sleep medicines by other doctors. Flanagan says multiple doctors prescribed sleep medicines. Flanagan asks if Nader Kamangar ever had a patient that was not forthright in their medical history. Nader Kamangar says he tries to get information from patient and from other doctors and hospitals. Flanagan says patients have to sign a release; they can't get the medical records. Nader Kamangar says it's true. Nader Kamangar says if they can't get information from the patient, they would ask people that live with the patient for information and use sleep diary logs. Nader Kamangar says without getting these information we wouldn't give Ambien to a patient. Nader Kamangar says if a doctor gives Ambien without a work up it would not be a serious deviation. Nader Kamangar says the doctor still needs to determine the cause and gather information. Flanagan mentions physical examination and asks if an enlarged prostate can cause insomnia. Nader Kamangar says urination problems can keep a patient up. Flanagan asks if they would check the arms for needle marks. Nader Kamangar would be a part of a physical exam. Flanagan asks if he can determine if a person is taking intra muscular Demerol. Nader Kamangar says you can able to see it in some individuals and not by some. Nader Kamangar says Conrad Murray could have understand if Michael Jackson got Demerol from Michael Jackson's behavior, slurred speech and from people who witnessed the change of behavior such as the bodyguards. Nader Kamangar says Conrad Murray could have talked to his security, assistant and Conrad Murray could have confronted the patient. Flanagan asks if there are studies about Propofol as a treatment for insomnia. Nader Kamangar says they are just experimental and it's in no way in a standard of care. They go over the Taiwan study. It dates back to November 2010. Patients had been extensively evaluated, informed consent was obtained, and they fasted for 8 hours. The study was done in a highly monitored setting, receiving Propofol via an IV pump. 64 patients received Propofol. Patient fell asleep better and have less sleep interruptions. Patients had no complications because they were highly monitored. It's very preliminary experiment with good results. It has no clinical applicability and the doctor that conducted the study stated that there was need for further study. Flanagan asks why it is incomprehensible to use Propofol for insomnia. Nader Kamangar says it was a study, in a highly monitored setting. Nader Kamangar says it is incomprehensible and inacceptable to give Propofol, especially with no monitoring and home setting. Flanagan asks if 25 mg Propofol is a very low dose. Nader Kamangar says yes. Flanagan states you wouldn't expect problems with such a small dose. Nader Kamangar says it depends on the patient. Such as if the patient is dehydrated (low blood pressure), had other medication (such as Lorazepam) etc, there can be a problem that can lead to respiratory depression. Flanagan asks questions about Lorazepam. Nader Kamangar says it's not FDA approved for primary insomnia, especially the IV form. Lorazepam in oral form can be used if cause of insomnia is anxiety, for a very short period of time of 3 to 4 weeks. Nader Kamangar says oral form is appropriate for a short period of time as it created dependency and IV is inappropriate because monitoring is necessary. Even with monitoring, it's not FDA approved for insomnia. Flanagan asks if Lorazepam was appropriate with anxiety due to This is it. Nader Kamangar says there should have been a psychological or psychiatric help and says he would not have used it in this case and try to cure the underlying issue. Nader Kamangar states that Ativan/Lorazepam in short periods of time, can be used for secondary insomnia associated with anxiety, even though it is not FDA approved. Nader Kamangar stresses that either drug should be only used for secondary insomnia, not primary insomnia. Nader Kamangar states that Murray indicated he had a bag of saline infused, but because there was no charting of medical records, there is no way to know how much saline was being infused into Michael Jackson. Nader Kamangar states that Michael Jackson was producing urine, based on Murray's interview with Los AngelesPD. Nader Kamangar states that 25 mg of Propofol would sedate someone for 6-10 minutes with no other meds, with no residual effects. Nader Kamangar states he would expect the person to have an increasing consciousness, and that the person would wake up by the 6-10 minutes. Nader Kamangar states he would not expect a patient to sleep after that time period, even if they were extremely tired. Nader Kamangar states that it would be the doctor's obligation to determine whether the patient was sleeping (if possible) and wake them up, and determine if they are responsive to stimuli. Nader Kamangar states that even if a doctor has the lack of judgment to use Propofol like Murray did on Michael Jackson, it is incumbent on the doctor to continually monitor the patient. Nader Kamangar states that by visually monitoring, there is no way to determine if the patient is naturally asleep or still sedated. Nader Kamangar states that Propofol can be used for conscious sedation in a highly monitored setting. Nader Kamangar states that in his initial report, he stated that Michael Jackson had massive doses of Propofol. Nader Kamangar states that he believes that Michael Jackson was given an unregulated drip IV of Propofol, after the initial injection push of Propofol. Nader Kamangar states that he believes that the sequence most likely is that Michael Jackson had a respiratory arrest, causing cardiac arrest. Nader Kamangar states that Murray should have called 911 first, especially given the lack of tools Murray had available. Nader Kamangar states that he should have determined whether he was breathing, determined his pulse, manipulate the airway, and tilt the jaw back to determine if there was blockage. Nader Kamangar states that he is aware that there were no working landline phones at Carolwood. Nader Kamangar states that he is aware that the 911 call took 2:43, and that paramedics got there in less than 6 minutes. Nader Kamangar states that even if Michael Jackson self medicated with excessive Lorazepam and bolus pushed Propofol, Murray is still responsible for Michael Jackson's death.

Walgren Redirect

Nader Kamangar states that he would call 911 immediately, it's a moral/professional obligation, but it's basic common sense as well. Nader Kamangar states that Walgren provided him with Dr. Klein's medical records. Nader Kamangar states that Murray stated in his interview with police multiple times that he was aware that Michael Jackson was seeing Dr. Klein. Nader Kamangar states that the study done in China on Propofol was done in a hospital, highly monitored, using a very precise drip, was used as an experiment and would need another study done to positively state that Propofol could be used for insomnia. Nader Kamangar states that one of the fundamental tenets of the doctor/patient relationship is putting the patient first. Nader Kamangar states that this means knowing when to say no to a patient, and that if, assuming Michael Jackson asked for the Propofol, the doctor has the professional, ethical and moral obligation to say no. Nader Kamangar states that he makes the final decision as to the appropriate care of the patient, not the patient. Nader Kamangar states that Murray's interview indicates his inability to give precise information about oxygen saturation, although Murray indicated the oxygen saturation was in the high 90's and then stated 02 saturation was 90. Nader Kamangar states that a doctor could be grossly negligent and survive, however in Michael Jackson's case, Murray was grossly negligent in multiple cases and this is what caused Michael Jackson's death.

Recross Flanagan

Nader Kamangar states that Murray said he immediately performed CPR, but that Nader Kamangar should have called 911. Nader Kamangar states that he is aware Murray said he went partially down the stairs, but that nobody could do the same job as the paramedics, so that should have been done first. Nader Kamangar states that although Murray states he asked the chef to call security and she did not do so, Nader Kamangar is not sure whether he is aware of that fact.

Re-redirect Walgren

Nader Kamangar states again that Murray should have immediately called 911.

Re-recross Flanagan

Nader Kamangar states that if there was someone in a hallway, and he was in a room with a person who was medically down, he might shout to the hallway, but ultimately it is his responsibility as a doctor to call 911.

Dr. Steven Shafer -Anesthesiology Expert- Testimony

Walgren Direct

Dr. Steven Shafer states that he is a professor of anesthesiology at Columbia University, adjunct professor and Stanford and UCSF. Dr. Steven Shafer states that he has worked at Columbia since 2007, at Stanford since 1987, tenured at 2000. Dr. Steven Shafer states that he teaches a class in pharmacokinetics at UCSF.

Pharmacokinetics deals with math models that deals with drug concentrations in the body to determine what the drug actually does to the body, which helps determine dosages of meds and what is effective and what is not. Dr. Steven Shafer states that pharmacokinetics is a discipline that is growing, and that it determines labels for every med, core of pharmaceutical companies, core of FDA, and services doctors on how to use the med safely and reduce toxicity. Steven Shafer states that the three schools he hold professorships at are ranked among the top medical schools in the US. Steven Shafer states that he is editor-in-chief for the journal Anesthesiology and Analgesia, which publishes manuscripts (studies) of issues related to anesthesiology. Among the 70 board members that sit under Dr. Steven Shafer , Steven Shafer states is defense witness Dr. Paul White. Steven Shafer states that the journals' acceptance rate for manuscripts is roughly 21%, so about 4 out of 5 submitted are rejected. Dr. Steven Shafer states that due to the editor in chief position for the journal, he is exposed to unusual cases that he never thought he might read about. Steven Shafer states that in 1987 the FDA had problems determining proper dosage levels of Midazolam, therefore the FDA was very particular about dosing instructions for infusing Propofol. Steven Shafer states that he did the infusion rate analyses and the start rate of Propofol for the label AstraZeneca. Steven Shafer states that in particular, he analyzed the reduction of dosing in elderly patients, and that almost all label dosing was done by Steven Shafer in 1991. Steven Shafer states that drugs that are marketed, one drug is marketed as a chemical name, in this case Propofol. Dr. Steven Shafer states that the retail name is Diprivan, and that it differs slightly from Propofol because there is a fat solution (emulsion) added to the Propofol. Steven Shafer states that max sedated means monitored anesthesia care, the care a patient expects, with a controlled dose, and monitoring. Steven Shafer states that titration means increasing or decreasing the dose according to each patient. Steven Shafer states that pharma means drugs, kinetics means motions, so pharmacokinetics means drugs in motions. Steven Shafer explains that when meds are given, drugs go thru several processes or motions, first when meds goes into the patient it becomes more diluted. Second the bloodstream takes the drug everywhere in the body, delivers to the brain, and will move the drug to the liver and metabolized there. Steven Shafer states that the liver chews the drug up, that the pieces can go to the blood, or to the bile, then to the intestine. Steven Shafer states that they can go to the kidneys and the kidneys then remove the blood from the body. Steven Shafer states that he is an expert in pharmacokinetics, specific to Propofol. Steven Shafer states that he developed the module of the software that eventually determined Propofol dosing on labels for all Propofol bottles.

court ends early due to a scheduling issue. There's no court on Friday October 14 as well. Testimony will resume on Monday October 17.

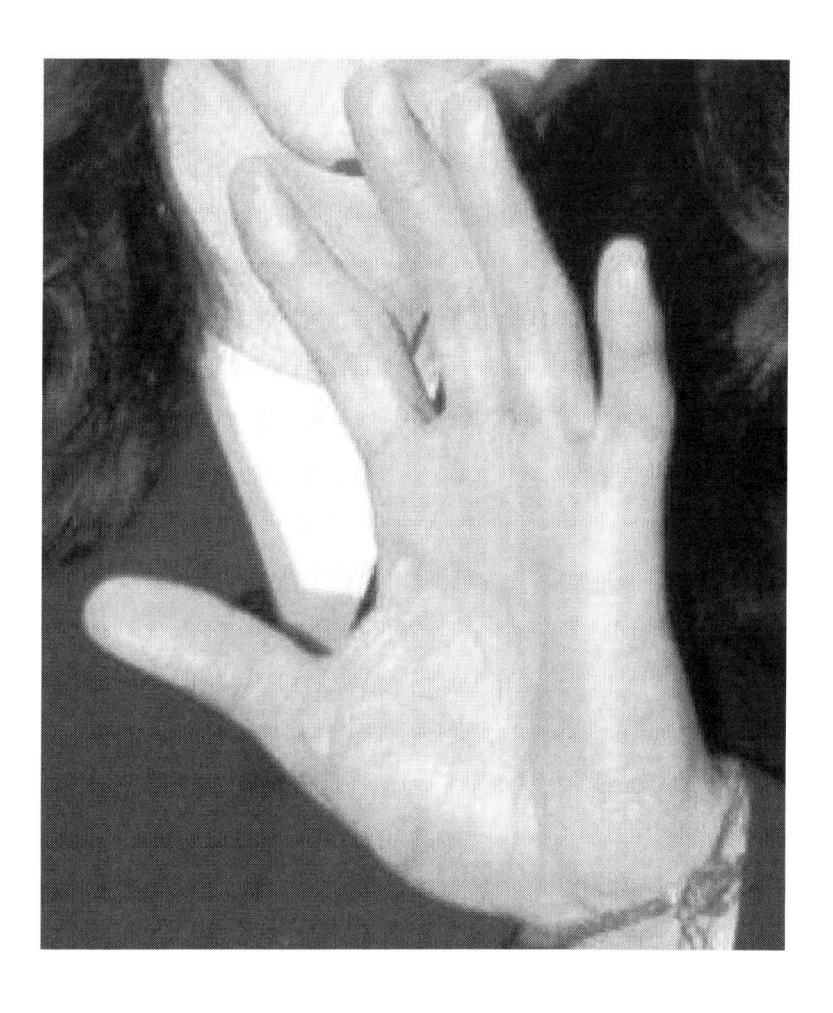

Murray Trial Summaries Day 13 , October 19, 2011
Dr. Steven Shafer Testimony continued

Walgren Direct continued

Walgren goes over again the credentials of Dr. Steven Shafer by showing the journal he's editor in chief and multiple research articles written by Dr. Steven Shafer . Research articles examine the differences in regards to gender, age. Dr. Steven Shafer also had research done on Lorazepam, Midazolam and Lidocaine. DA Walgren says that he will ask about these topics during testimony. Walgren mentions difference between intensive care sedation and procedure related sedation (MAC). Steven Shafer tells that intensive care sedation would be for longer time, MAC would be shorter. Dr. Steven Shafer says that all the work he has done on this case was for free. He says he never charged money for testimony because he feels it's inappropriate and unethical to benefit from medical misadventures. Dr. Steven Shafer says he doesn't want his integrity to be questionned as well Dr. Steven Shafer also says he wanted to get involved in this case to restore general public's confidence in anesthesia and doctors. Dr. Steven Shafer says that he's asked daily by his patients "Are you going to give me that drug that killed Michael Jackson?". He says that he hopes to alleviate this unneeded fear with his testimony. Dr. Steven Shafer has brought several medical items for demonstration. First he starts with explaining Saline bag and it's ports. Later Dr. Steven Shafer tells what and IV is. Infusion(Drip) when drug drips in slowly. Dr. Steven Shafer explains that Propofol comes in a glass vial, there's an aliminium seal and a rubber stopper on top. To get the drug out you need to go through with a slow needle or a large spike to get the drug out.

Walgren asks Dr. Steven Shafer to demonstrate to get Propofol out of the bottle. Dr. Steven Shafer demonstrates to get out Propofol with a syringe / needle. Dr. Steven Shafer tells to get Propofol out you need to replace Propofol with air so that Propofol will go into the needle.

Walgren asks Dr. Steven Shafer to examine 100 ml Propofol bottle from the scene. Shafer says that it has a spike hole and not a needle hole.

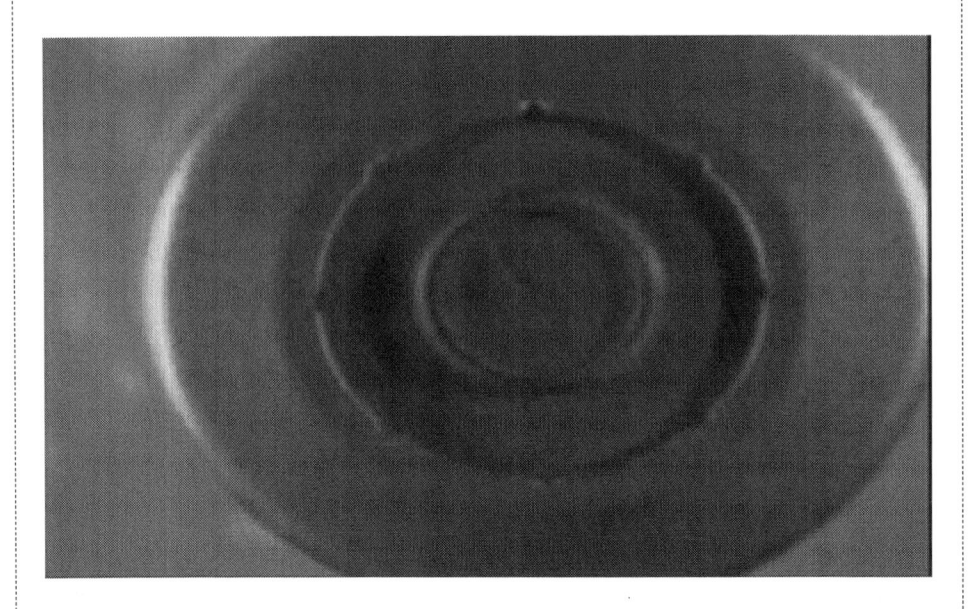

Dr. Steven Shafer has made a video for his case, to demonstrate what is necessary for sedation, even for 25mg Propofol. Playing the video : «*an over view of safe administration of sedation*» The doctor first prepares the room, checks the equipment. Video shows multiple equipment for airway management such a tube for the throat, a tube for the nose, an equipment for intibation, a throat mask for air. Organizes these items. Then the doctor checks the oxygen equipment. Doctor checks if the oxygen supply work, checks nasal cannula, checks to see if nasal cannula is measuring carbon dioxide by capnometer. Doctor tests anesthesia breathing circuit. This is the equipment used if the patient stops breathing and the doctor needs to push oxygen into the lungs. Doctor then checks the back up oxygen. This is used if for some reason the breathing circuit fails. Doctor then checks suction apparatus. This is important because if the contents of the stomach gets into the lungs or if the vomit (bile) gets into the lung, it would destroy the lungs. This is why patients are told to not to eat or drink prior to anesthesia. if the patient vomits or the contents of the stomach come to the mouth, the doctor has to be very quick to clean them with the suction equipment before it goes into the lungs and destroys the lungs. Next step is to set up the infusion pump. It takes a few minutes to set it up. In the video they use a syringe pump. Doctor first draws Propofol into the syringe. As Dr. Steven Shafer demonstrated this is not easy. You need to draw air into the syringe and do multiple draws to fill the syringe. Dr. Steven Shafer tells a narrow tubing has to be used in the infusion pump as the wide tubing could be problematic. Then the doctor programs the pump, putting the patients weight, correct drug name, infusion rate. Doctor verifies the information for a second time. Next step is to assess the patient. Anesthesiologist is repsonsible for knowing his patient. Makes a physical examination, first thing is airway, listens to the lungs, checks the heart. Always done for each procedure, for every patient. No exception. Doctor also gets the informed consent of the patient. Doctor informs the patient of risks and explains what the procedure entails, asks the patient if he has any questions, then patient signs the informed consent form. Dr. Steven Shafer says oral consent is not binding, and is not recognized. Some steps are not shown on the video. These are: patient put on table, monitoring equipment such as blood pressure cuff, pulse oximeter, ECG are put on patient. Oxygen in place, intravenous catheter is put into the patient. Afther these doctor pauses to verify again. Doctor does one last check before injecting the Propofol. Propofol infusion pump is started. Anesthesiologist is close to the patient, monitors the patient. Doctor keeps records of the vitals. Chart is a necessity to track the patient and the patterns. It's a responsibility to the patient.

In this part of the video, we are shown examples of what can go wrong.

First example is when blood pressure drops. Dr. Steven Shafer says this is very common and they see it everyday. Propofol lowers blood pressure especially if the patient is dehydrates. Doctor gives ephedrine through the IV line. Generally blood pressure comes to normal levels.

Second example is carbon dioxide. The monitor shows that carbon dioxide stopped. It means the patient is not exhaling and the airway is obstructed. Doctor immediately does chin lift and jaw thrust. Dr.

Steven Shafer this is also done very routinely. Dr. Steven Shafer says the most common reason is because the tongue is blocking the airway and by doing a chin lift and jaw thrust you can move the tongue.

Third example is apnea. This is when the patient doesn't even try to breath. In this instance you need to take over for the patient and force air into the lungs. Doctor removes the nasal cannula, places the mask on the patient's mouth and nose and squeeze the bag to push oxygen into the lungs.

Fourth example is aspiration (not shown on video). This is when the patient vomits and/or stomach contents come to the mouth. Patient is turned sideways and before the next breath you need to suction everything.

Fifth example is cardiac arrest. Heart stops beathing and the patient stops breathing. Doctor does a 2-3 second assesment to make sure that the monitor has not failed. Then the doctor calls for help. First thing is always to call for help. One person begins CPR, one person is ventilating the patient and other person gives resuscitation drugs. Alls of this is done to keep the patient alive for enough time to fix the problem that caused the arrest. These efforts are continued until the patient is revived, or is pronouced dead.

Walgren Direct continued

Dr. Steven Shafer says that the safeguards and requirements apply to all doctors who perform sedation, for any type of IV sedatives. Some nurses are also trained about sedation. These guidelines apply to them as well. Walgren asks if Conrad Murray's intent were to give 25mg would these standards still apply. Dr. Steven Shafer says yes and continues to say the patient (Michael Jackson) had other IV sedatives, profound inability to sleep, he was exhausted, dehydrated; and he had been given sedatives for some time and he could have saome elements of dependency or withdrawal. Walgren asks if it possible to go in saying I'll only give a small amount so I don't need these guidelines. Dr. Steven

Shafer says it's a trap. Even for a little sedation, it's a slippery slope, you may have to give more. You never know how the patient will react. Dr. Steven Shafer says there's no such thing as a little sedation and the worst disasters happen when people cut corners. Facts in this case suggest that virtually none of the safeguards for sedation were in place when Propofol was administered to Michael Jackson. Walgren asks Dr. Steven Shafer explain how patients reacts different to the same dose of sedatives. Dr. Steven Shafer says that some patients will need half the usual dose and some patients will need double the dose. Dr. Steven Shafer says 25 mg is the limit when a patient migh stop breathing. Dr. Steven Shafer says you can't assume that this will be an average patient. Dr. Steven Shafer says you always assume your patient is at the edge of sensitivity and prepare for the worst case scenario. Dr. Steven Shafer did a report about this case dated April 15th, 2011. In his report he used some terms.

Minor violation: not consistent with standard of care, but would not expect to cause harm for the patient unless there are several other violations

Serious violation: expected to cause harm to the patient, in combination of other violations

Egregious violation: These should never happen in the hand of comptent doctors. An egeregious violation can alone be catastrophic for the patient. Competent doctors know that bad outcome is a high possibility

Unconscionable vioation: It goes beyond the standard of care. It's an ethical and moral violation as well as a medical violation.

Walgren goes over Dr. Steven Shafer's report and 17 egregious violations he identified. Lack of basic airway equipment, egregious violation. Michael Jackson died because he stopped breathing which is expected when you give IV sedatives. It must be there without question.

Walgren asks Dr. Steven Shafer assume that Conrad Murray had left only for 2 minutes and Conrad Murray had the equipment if Michael Jackson could have been saved? Dr. Steven Shafer says yes and probably Michael Jackson had an obstructed airway and even a simple chin lift might have been required to save Michael Jackson. Dr. Steven Shafer says that Conrad Murray says he didn't use the ambu bag. Dr. Steven Shafer says mouth to mouth is less effective and gives used air. Lack of advanced airway equipment. Those are eqipment such as laryngeal mask, or laryngoscope and endotracheal tube. Dr. Steven Shafer had described it a a serious deviation originally but changed his mind to en egregious because of the setting. Conrad Murray had no help. Dr. Steven Shafer says that it's his view that Conrad Murray had anticipated to give 100 ml vials. Conrad Murray had purchased at least 130 100 ml vials, Dr. Steven Shafer believes that's at least one per night. Dr. Steven Shafer says it's an extraordinary amount for one patient; between april – to 25th june, that 80 nights, 1937 mg/night. Walgren asks how he came to this determination. Dr. Steven Shafer says Propofol is an environment for bacteria dveelopment. Once a bottle is opened with a needle, it has to be used within 6 hours. Dr. Steven Shafer says this suggests Conrad Murray planned to use 100ml, if he didn't he would purchase smaller vials.

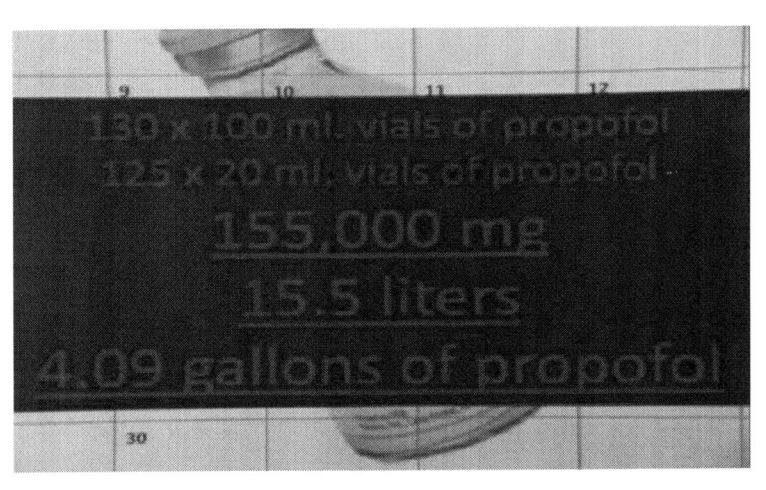

Lack of suction apparatus, egregious violation. Dr. Steven Shafer reminds the jury that any stomach content and/or vomit has to be suctioned so that it won't go into the lungs. Dr. Steven Shafer says there's no evidence that Michael Jackson was asked to fast for 8 hours prior being given Propofol. Due to this Michael Jackson was at greatly higher risk. Therefore a suction equipment was needed. Lack of infusion pump, egregious violation. There was no infusion pump. Without it the rate can not be precisely controled and the risk of overdose is very high. Dr. Steven Shafer says in his opinion this is likely contributed to Michael Jackson's death. Walgren asks without an infusion pump how can one person control the drip. Dr. Steven Shafer answers by roller clamp. It's a plastic wheel that pinches the tubing to decrease the amount. Dr. Steven Shafer says it's extremely imprecise and that was the only thing available to Conrad Murray when he gave Propofol. Lack of pulse oximetry, egregious violation . The pulse oxieter that Conrad Murray used was completely inappropriate. It's not intended to be used for continuous care as it had no alarm. Dr. Steven Shafer says that on monitors in hospital they can see it on the screen and there is a tone. Doctors will hear the tone changes which alerts them that there's a problem. In Michael Jackson's case only way to monitor was to take his hand and continoiusly look to it. If there was a proper equipment, there would be a monitor showing the vital signs from distance and there would be an alarm that could have saved Michael Jackson's life. Lack of blood pressure cuff,egregious violation. Propofol lowers everyone's blood pressure. Doctors would treat it with additional saline solution or with less Propofol. Michael Jackson was dehydrated, the risk are higher for exagerated response. If blood pressure falls the body shuts down the flow to the arms and legs and concentrates on providing blood to heart and the brain. The drug becomes more potent. Dr. Steven Shafer says the manual blood pressure cuff that Conrad Murray had in his bag in the cabinet is useless. Lack of ECG, egregious violation. ECG allows you te see he heart rate, the heart rythm. This is routine monitoring. In this case Conrad Murray couldn't know what kind of therapy to use when

Michael Jackson went into arrest. Lack of capnography, an egregious violation. Dr. Steven Shafer initially thought that it was not a violation as other specialist doesn't use it. However in Michael Jackson 's environment it was a disaster. If Conrad Murray had it he would have known immediately that Michael Jackson had stopped breathing. Lack of emergency drugs, serious violation. Dr. Steven Shafer doesn't think lack of emergency drugs contributed to Michael Jackson's death. Dr. Steven Shafer says if Michael Jackson had a low blood pressure as he wasn't going through surgery, Michael Jackson could have been woken up and hydration and stopping Propofol would have been enough. Lack of charts, egregious violation as well as unethical. Dr. Steven Shafer says a doctor needs charts to asses what's going on and the changes. Dr. Steven Shafer says the patient or if the patient doesn't survive the family has a right to know what happened and what the doctor did. Dr. Steven Shafer gives an example and Dr. Steven Shafer looks clearly upset. Dr. Steven Shafer says he knows how he would feel if his father , brother or son went to a medical facility for 80 days and died and the doctors told him they don't know what happened because they have no reports. Dr. Steven Shafer says it's unbelieveable that after 80 days of treatment there's not a single record of treatment. Dr. Steven Shafer says that not keeping records is also illegal in California. Dr. Steven Shafer says that doctors has to keep records even if the patient doesn't want them and confidentiality cannot be an excuse. Dr. Steven Shafer says that in Conrad Murray 's interview he mentioned Michael Jackson could have been dependent on Propofol and that would require a referral but he can't do that referral as he had no records. Obligation to get information about the patient. Dr. Steven Shafer says it's doctors responsability to know everything about their patient to provide care. Dr. Steven Shafer says Conrad Murray mentions IV sites but didn't follow it through and asked what's happening. Walgren asks what if the patient says it's none of your business, Dr. Steven Shafer says that then he would say "Then I can not be your doctor". Dr. Steven Shafer the only physical evidence of Michael was done months ago. Dr. Steven Shafer says Conrad Murray mentioning Michael Jackson being dehydrated but yet he do a simple blood pressure check. Dr. Steven Shafer says there's no history, not even a simple recording of the vital signs. Dr. Steven Shafer calls this serious violation and that no doctor does that. Failure to maintain a doctor patient relationship , egregious violation. In this relationship doctor would put the patient first. It doesn't meean to do what the patient asks, it's to do what's best for patient. If patient asks for something foolish or dangerous, doctor should have said no. Dr. Steven Shafer describes the relation between Conrad Murray and Michael Jackson as employer employee relationship. Patient stated what he wanted, Conrad Murray says yes. Dr. Steven Shafer compares Conrad Murray to a housekeeper that does what she's told. That's what an employee does. Dr. Steven Shafer says Conrad Murray was not exercising his medical judgement and he was not acting in Michael Jackson's best interest. Conrad Murray completely abandonned medical judgement. Dr. Steven Shafer says the very first time Michael Jackson asked for Propofol, Conrad Murray should have sent Michael Jackson to a sleep specialist. Lack of Inormed consent, egregious and unconscinable. An informed consent would have involved that Propofol is not a treatment for insomnia, It woud have explained risk of death and alternative treatments. Dr. Steven Shafer says there's no proof that Michael Jackson knew that he was putting his life at risk. Dr. Steven Shafer again mentions that the consent has to be written. Michael Jackson was denied his right o make an informed decision. Need to continuously observe the mental satus, egregious and unconscinable. Dr. Steven Shafer says that doctors need to stay with the patient and Conrad Murray abadonned his patient. Dr. Steven Shafer compares giving sedation to driving a motor home. Dr. Steven Shafer says you cannot leave the steering wheel on a highway to relieve yourself. If you do it would be an disaster. Dr. Steven Shafer says in 25 years he has been a physician he have never walked out of the room. Continious monitoring/observation, egregious violation. Conrad Murray left Michael Jackson alone and he was on the phone. Dr. Steven Shafer says youcan't multi task especially if you have no monitoring equipment. Dr. Steven Shafer a patient who is about to die, doesn't look that different from a patient that is okay. Dr. Steven Shafer says from a distance you can't tell if a person is breathing. Dr. Steven Shafer says he believes Murray may have been in the room and have not realised Michael Jackson stopped breathing. Dr. Steven Shafer says resuciation would have been easy as all needed is to stop Propofol and make Michael Jackson beathe. Dr. Steven Shafer once ahain reminds that it's common that patients would stop breathing during anesthesia and it's expected. Dr. Steven Shafer says all Conrad Murray was monitoring all he needed to do was to lift the chin and ventilate. Lack of continuous documentions, egregius and unconscionable violation. Dr. Steven Shafer says documentation is part of giving care. Dr. Steven Shafer says if Conrad Murray had the reports he would have seen that the oxygen saturation lowered or the heart rythm changed. Failure to call 911 timely, egregious violation. Dr. Steven Shafer says in that setting Michael Jackson could not have been revived without assistance. Dr. Steven Shafer says calling 911 was the highest priority given the lack of help and equipment. Dr. Steven Shafer says if calling 911 was not possible, Propofol should not been given at all. Dr. Steven Shafer says assuming Conrad Murray realised there was a problem at 12:00 he doesn't understand that Conrad Murray left a voice message to Michael Amir Williams and how it took 20 mn to call 911. Dr. Steven Shafer calls it unconceivable and completely and utterly inexcusable. Dr. Steven Shafer says if Conrad Murray left only for 2 minutes and called paramedics immediately Michael Jackson would be alive with some brain damage. If Conrad Murray realized Michael Jackson was in trouble in 2 minutes and had the airway equipment Michael Jackson would be alive and uninjured. Walgren asks how effective is a one handed CPR on a bed. Dr. Steven Shafer says the patient sinks into the bed and it's ineffective. Even if Conrad Murray had his hand behind Michael Jackson's back it's ineffective because you need your body weight to do effective CPR. Dr. Steven Shafer says you need 2 hands, one hand is not enough. Dr. Steven Shafer says Conrad Murray hould have called 911 first and then moved Michael Jackson to the floor. Dr. Steven Shafer also says based on Conrad Murray's interview the issue here was not that the heart stopped; Michael Jackson e stopped breathing. Conrad Murray said there was pulse. If there was a pulse what he needed to do was to have oxygen into his lungs. There was no need for CPR if there was a pulse. Dr. Steven Shafer says a lay person would use mouth to mouth as they have no other means. For a doctor it shows that the doctor doesn't have equipment needed. Dr. Steven Shafer says that he doesn't understand why Conrad Murray raised Michael Jackson's legs. Dr. Steven Shafer calls it a waste of time. Dr. Steven Shafer says raising the legs is done when you thing there's not enough blood in the heart but that wasn't Michael Jackson's problem. His breathing had stopped. Dr. Steven Shafer says that it shows Conrad Murray was clueless about what to do. Walgren asks what is flumazenil. Dr. Steven Shafer explains it's a frug that reverses the effects of Lorazepam and midazolam. Dr. Steven Shafer says he's curious why Conrad Murray gave it. Dr. Steven Shafer says it doesn't fit with only giving 2 doses of 2 mg several hours before. Dr. Steven Shafer says he believes that Conrad Murray knew that there was a lot more Lorazepam.Dr. Steven Shafer talks about deception of paramedics and UCLA doctors and not mentionning Propofol, egregious and unconscionable violation. Dr. Steven Shafer says a person's life was in the balance, it's inexcusable. Dr. Steven Shafer says he also mischaracterized this event as a witnessed arrest. Dr. Steven Shafer says a witnessed arrest is not an arrest for lack of breathing, it is usually something like a heart attack. So the therapy of the paramedics and ER doctors was not appropriate. In an arrest you have only seconds to choose a treatment, paramedics and ER doctors were not given the corect information. Dr. Steven Shafer says witholding information is a violation of patient's trust. Walgren asks what is polypharmacy. Dr. Steven Shafer explains it's administering many drugs at once and it's a serious violation. Dr. Steven Shafer says what Conrad Murray gave to Michael Jackson didn't make any sense. Dr. Steven Shafer says Midazolam and Lorazepam are very similar drugs and the only difference is how long they stay in the system. Dr. Steven Shafer says he doesn't understand why Conrad Murray switched from midazolam to Lorazepam and back. Dr. Steven Shafer says that he thinks that Conrad Murray did not understand the drugs he was giving. Walgren asks if 25mg Propofol is a safe dose. Dr. Steven Shafer says in this setting there was no safe dose. Midazolam an Lorazepam were given. Michael Jackson had received benzos for 80 nights, he could have been dependant or in withdrawal from the benzos or Propofol. Dr. Steven Dr. Steven Shafer says he never heard a person given Propofol for 80 nights and doesn't know what would happen. Walgren asks about the Taiwan study. Dr. Steven Shafer says there are over 13000 medical articles about Propofol, 2500 articles about Propofol and sedation and there's only one article on Propofol and insomnia. It's this study done in 2010. Dr. Steven Shafer says that he wouldn't published the Taiwan study because the dose of Propofol that was given is not mentioned. Dr. Steven Shafer also says that the conditions of the study doesn't apply here. That study was done in a hospital, by anesthesiolgists, patients had fasted for 8 hours, they were monitored, an infusion pump was used, Propofol was used for 2 hours for 5 days during two weeks. There was no other medication. The patients were treated within the standard of care. Dr. Steven Shafer says the article actually highlights Conrad Murray 's deviations from standard of care. Walgren asks even if Michael Jackson had taken Lorazepam and/or Propofol would these 17 deviations would still be relevant and if Dr. Steven Shafer would consider Conrad Murray responsible for Michael Jackson's death. Dr. Steven Shafer answers yes. Walgren asks about doctor patient relationship. Dr. Steven Shafer says it's dated back centuries ago. Dr. Steven Shafer says that doctors have power to give drugs and cut open a patient etc and this is because they are entrusted to do that because they are supposed put the patient first. Dr. Steven Shafer reads hippocratic oath. Dr. Steven Shafer says when Conrad Murray agreed to give Propofol to Michael Jackson, he put Conrad Murray first. When Conrad Murray was showing up every night with Propofol and saline bags, he was putting Conrad Murray first. When Conrad Murray withheld info from paramedics and ER doctors, he put Conrad Murray first.

Murray Trial Summaries Day 14 / October 20- 2011

Dr. Steven Shafer Testimony continued

Walgren direct

Walgren starts talking about Propofol. Walgren asked Dr. Steven Shafer if he would provide his opinion in this case around March 2011 and gave Dr. Steven Shafer Los AngelesPD and toxicology reports. Walgren also gave Dr. Steven Shafer a report from Dr. Paul White . Dr. Paul White had written that Michael Jackson could have orally digested Propofol. Dr. Steven Shafer says that he was disappointed because oral Propofol cannot get pass liver. Dr. Steven Shafer says by the first pass effect liver would almost remove all of the Propofol.

Dr. Paul White

Dr. Steven Shafer has prepared a presentation called "Propofol not orally bio-available"

Slide 1 is the title.

Slide 2 shows the digestive track of human body. Dr. Steven Shafer identifies the organs. Dr. Steven Shafer says oral Propofol would come to the stomach, it would pass into the blood and all of that blood would go into the liver and only after it passes the liver it would go back to the blood vessels.

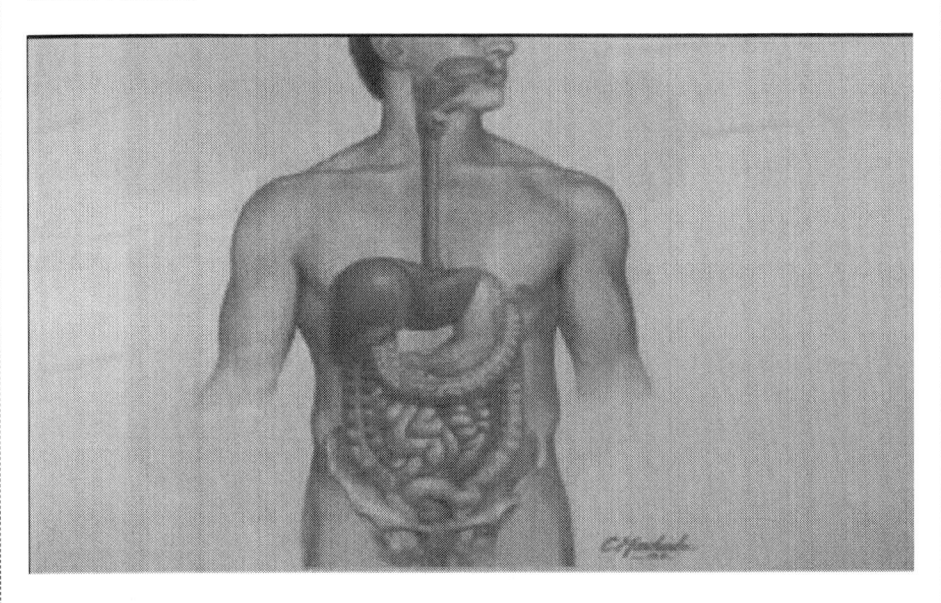

Slide 3 is a close up of the digestive track. It shows all the veins from the digestive track goes into the liver. Dr. Steven Shafer explains first pass effect of Propofol. 99% of the drug would have been removed and there's no reason to expect that oral Propofol would have any effect. Dr. Steven Shafer wrote in his report there is 0 possibility that Michael Jackson died because of oral Propofol.

Slide 4 is a 1985 article by Dr.Glen (doctor to developed Propofol - Dr. Steven Shafer says that he deserves to be called Father of Propofol)about Propofol. In this study Propofol was given to mice, they found that IV doses was effective but even 20 times the IV dose is given to animals orally would not produce general anesthesia.

Slide 5 1991 Study on piglets. This research shows that less than 1% of Propofol would be bio available in the piglets. This shows that Propofol would be cleaned out the system by the liver.

Slide 6 1996 research done on rats. In this study they found out that 10% of the Propofol was available in rats. Dr. Steven Shafer says it's because rats are a different species. It still shows that a majority of Propofol (90%) is cleaned out of the system.

Slide 7 - US Patent dated June 23,2009. The research findings in this study was done in rats and the bio availability of Propofol was less than 1%.

Slide 8 - US Patent dated Nov 17, 2009. Another research done on dogs and monkeys and the bio availability was less than 1%. All of these information was available when Dr. Paul White and Dr. Steven Shafer wrote their reports.

Rest of the slides - Dr. Steven Shafer then did a research about the oral bio availability in humans. Dr. Steven Shafer says there was nothing published as humans as subjects. Dr. Steven Shafer participated in a study done on human volunteers in Chile. 6 students volunterred. First 3 volunteers drank 20 ml/200mg of Propofol and other 3 drank twice that dose (400mg). they mesasured pulse, blood pressure and sedation was measured. They regularly took blood from the arm and measured for Propofol. None of the volunteers was sedated after orally digesting Propofol. Level of the oxygen never dropped, blood pressure never dropped. The study was presented last week in Chicago in a conference. Dr. Steven Shafer also got a lifetime achievement award in that conference.

> **Bioavailability of Oral Propofol in Humans**
> Victor Contreras, MD[1]
> Pablo O. Sepúlveda, MD[2]
> Steven L. Shafer, MD[3]
>
> 1. Departamento de Anestesiología, Escuela de Medicina, Universidad de Concepción, Chile
> 2. Departamento de Anestesiología, Facultad de Medicina, Clínica Alemana-Universidad del Desarrollo, Santiago, Chile
> 3. Professor of Anesthesiology, Columbia University, New York
>
> Measurable Sedation (OAA/S): None
> Oxygen desaturation: None
> Drop in blood pressure: None

Last slide is the conclusion of the human study, there was no effect of oral Propofol on humans.

Dr. Steven Shafer says he did the research because of this case and DEA wanting Propofol to be a controlled substance. Dr. Steven Shafer thinks DEA is trying to do this because they believe Michael Jackson could have drank it. Dr. Steven Shafer says that he wants to show that the drug cannot be abused orally. Dr. Steven Shafer says that he told Walgren on the first phone call oral effect of Propofol was not possible and he later seek out these additional surveys and even conducted a study on humans to show that there was zero possibility.

Walgren brings another presentation. This one is about Lorazepam. (long sidebar due to objection by chernoff)

Slide 1 title.

Slide 2 A study that was done by Dr. Steven Shafer. He looked to Lorazepam or Midazolam. They gave it to patients by a computer. Blood was gathered at regular interval from the patients artery to study the concentration. The study was done at Stanford, and they colected a huge amount of data.

Dr. Steven Shafer reviewed toxicology levels in Michael Jackson and he's aware that Conrad Murray said 2 doses of 2mg of Lorazepam. Dr. Steven Dr. Steven Shafer ran models to see if this dose would cause the Lorazepam levels in Michael Jackson's blood. 2 doses of 2mg of Lorazepam is not supported by the blood levels. The model shows that the concentration of 2doses of 2 mg at 2 am and 5 am is about 10% of what was found. Dr. Steven Shafer says Michael Jackson was administered more Lorazepam.

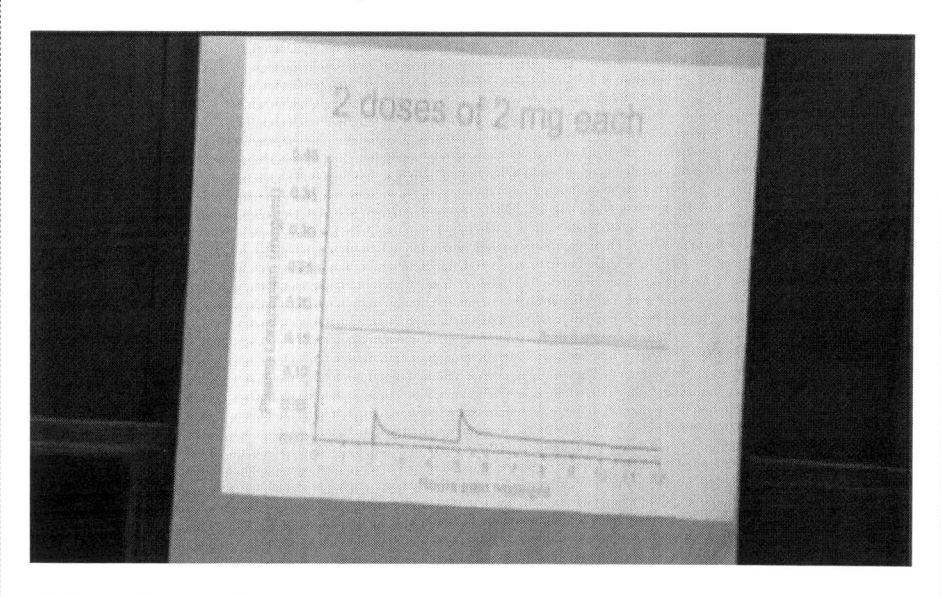

If the 2 doses of 2 mg was given at 2:00 and 5:00 AM was the only amount given to Michael Jackson , the concentration the coroner should have found is 0.025, not 0.169. Dr. Steven Shafer shows another model to reach 0.169 level at 12:00 noon. It shows 10 doses of 4 mg between midinght and 5 am. This number is consisted with the vials found at Michael Jackson 's house (10 ml bottles with 4mg per ml concentration which equals to 40mg). Dr. Steven Shafer explains metabolite of Lorazepam called Lorazepam glucoronide. The liver attaches sugar to the Lorazepam molecule so the kidneys can process the Lorazepam. This process makes the drug inactive. Lorazepam glucoronide has no effect. The Lorazepam will have an effect, but not its metabolite. The coroner looks for the levels of Lorazepam and not its metabolite. Walgren shows the defense test done for Lorazepam. Pacific Toxicology converted the metabolite back to the drug itself and after this analyzed for Lorazepam. So their results was inflated as it included both the drug and it's metabolite. Their results for Lorazepam and its metabolite was 0.634 concentration. Pacific Toxicology didn't seperate between Lorazepam and it's metabolite. Walgren asks how can Lorazepam be found in the stomach. Dr. Steven Shafer showing the digestive track explains the process. After IV injection the active drug goes to the blood. Later it goes to the liver and liver converts it to its metabolite. 25% of the metabolite goes to the bile and then the bile drains it into the intestine. At the junction between the stomach and small intestine, some of the metabolite sloshes back into the stomach. Dr. Steven Shafer says Michael Jackson had 1/43 of a pill of Lorazepam and most of it was the metabolite and the true amount of Lorazepam was much smaller. Dr. Steven Shafer says that this proves that Michael Jackson did not swallow Lorazepam for at least 4 hours prior to his death (between 8 AM and 12PM). So Flanagan's hypothetical scenario of Michael Jackson taking Lorazepam pills around 10AM is not possible. Walgren and Dr. Steven Shafer switched to discussing Propofol. Walgren goes over several studies that Dr. Steven Shafer has done about Propofol. Dr. Steven Shafer used the models that include age, weight and gender from those studies to run models about Propofol found in Michael Jackson. Dr. Steven Shafer says that Propofol acts in the brain and it's the brain makes you fall asleep or stop breathing. So it's the brain concentration that matters. Defense witness Dr. Paul White was a participant in one of the studies to show at what concentration of Propofol a person would stop breathing. At 2.3 mg/ml half of the patients would be expected to stop breathing. The range of apnea is 1.3mg to 3.3mg/ml . At 1.3mg, 5% of patients stop breathing, at 3.3mg 95 % stop breathing.

Another study was done on pigs to determine the the delay between apnea and the time when blood circulation stops. The result showed that there is 9 minutes between respiratory arrest and cardiac arrest.

Dr. Steven Shafer did simulations for this case. He assumed the time between respiratory arrest and cardiac arrest to be 10 minutes as a human being has more oxygen than a pig and Michael Jackson was on supplemental oxygen. Propofol concentration found by the coroner in Michael Jackson's in femoral blood was 2.6 , that's the concentration when blood circulation stopped. Dr. Steven Shafer is trying different scenarios to reach to that number. Concentrations of Propofol rises quickly and also falls very quickly. This is because of the liver and Propofol goes to other tissues.

Scenario 1 : Only 25 mg Propofol bolus injection

Michael Jackson would have been below the point where half of the patients would stop breathing (2.3) but above the 5% limit (1.3). He would have stopped breathing from 1minutes to 2 and half minutes after the injection. After 3 minutes everyone would be expected to breathe again. So even with a small dose there's a risk for short period of time. As Michael Jackson was given other drugs he would have a higher risk. Dr. Steven Shafer doesn't think this is what happened to Michael Jackson. Michael Jackson would be apneic for 2minutes and his blood circulation would have lasted at least 10minutes and Propofol would have been metabolised. So the femerol amount would have been much smaller than the coroner had found. Dr. Steven Shafer rules out this scenario.

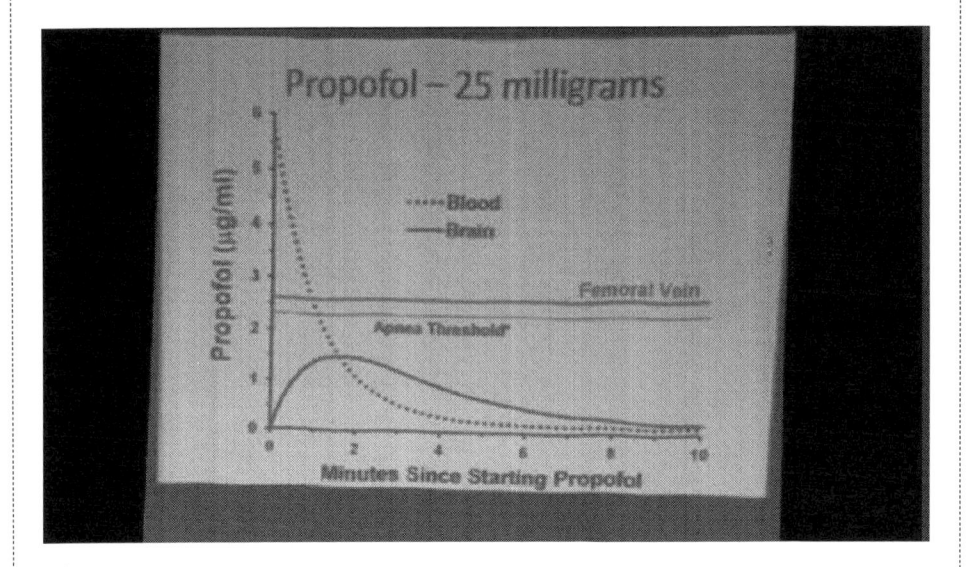

Scenario 2 : 50mg Propofol bolus (half of the needle is filled with Propofol and other half with Lidocaine)

Michael Jackson would likely have stopped breathing 1 minutes to 3 / 4minutes after he was given the dosethe dose. (not breathing for 3 minutes wouldn't cause brain damage) The heart would continue beating for 10 minutes. Again 50 mg Propofol wouldn't give the amount measured in the femoral blood. Dr. Steven Shafer rules out this scenario as well.

Scenario 3 : 100 mg Propofol bolus (All the syringe is filled with Propofol)

Patient would stop within 1 minutes and heart would have stopped after 10minutes. Femoral blood level would have been under what coroner found. Dr. Steven Shafer rules out this scenario.

Multiple Self Injection Scenarios

Scenario 4 : 6 self injections 50mg each over 90mn Self injection would involve drawing Propofol and injection through the port . It takes time and requires coordination. Based on Conrad Murray 's interverw Michael Jackson had poor veins so self injection is unlikely and would be extremely painful without lidocaine. 50mg would put Michael Jackson sleep and make him sleep about 10 minutes and it would get a little longer with each injectionas there would be a little Propofol left in the blood. Circulation would stop after 10 minutes. Femoral blood level would be well under the numbers found by coroner. Dr. Steven Shafer rules out this scenario.

Scenario 5 : 6 injections 100 mg each over 3 hours.

This is an anesthetic dose. Michael Jackson would stop breathing and the circulation would stop after 10 minutes. Again the blood level of Propofol would be well below than what was measured in femoral blood. Dr. Steven Shafer says Michael Jackson would have probably died after first or second injection ,but coroner would have found a lower femoral level of Propofol.

Walgren Direct continued

Multiple Injections by Murray Scenarios

Scenario 6: 6 injections 50mg each. In this scenario Michael Jackson would have stopped breathing multiple times and under this scenario Michael Jackson wouldn't be alive and the femoral blood level would be achieved. Dr. Steven Dr. Steven Shafer says this doesn't make sense as Conrad Murray had to reinject repeatedly and the injections needed to

234

continue after the breathing and the heart stopped. So Dr. Steven Shafer rules out this scenario.

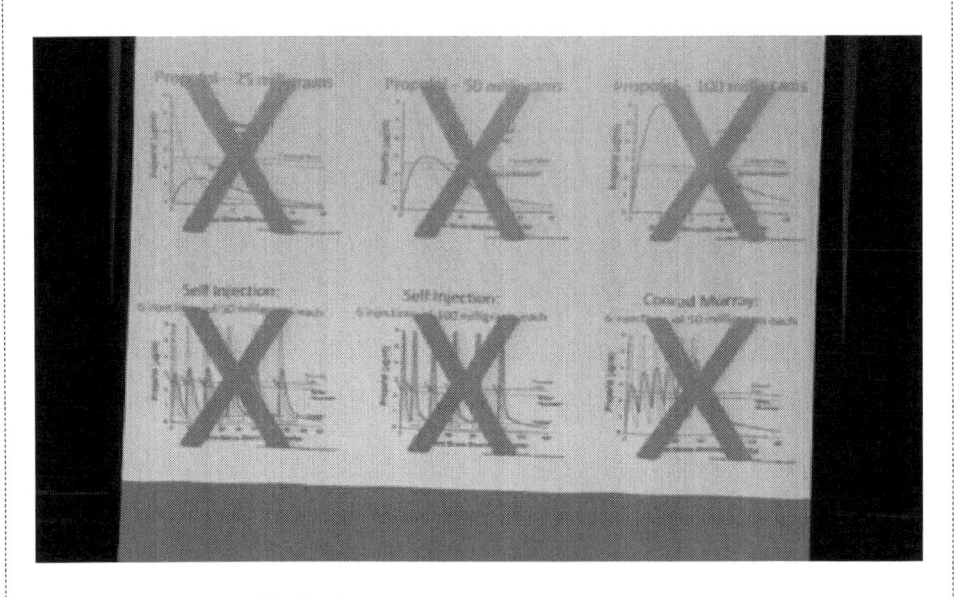

Scenario 7 : 100ml infusion, 1000 mg

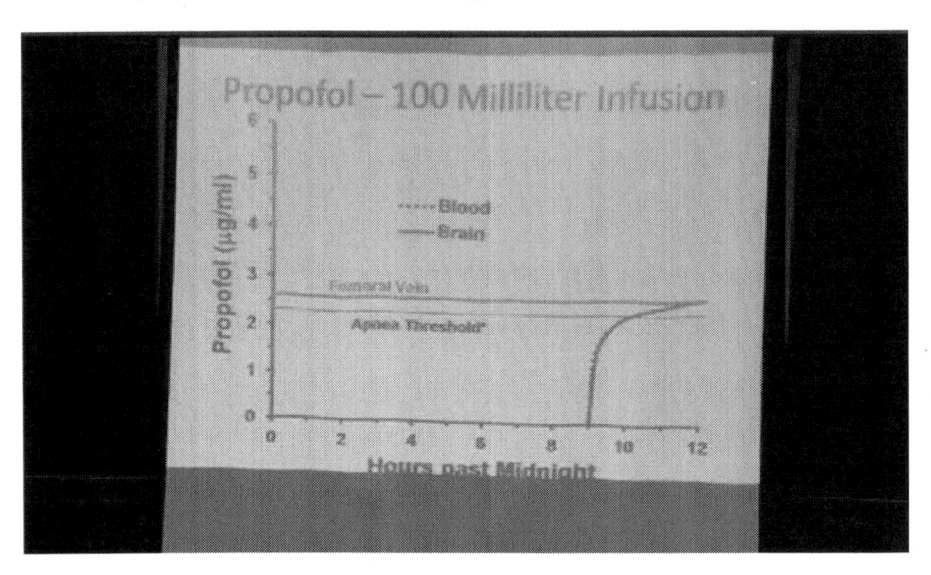

In this model an infusion is started at 9:00AM and there was a bolus before the drip. When you give a drip , there is not much difference between blood and brain concentration. Levels first raise quickly. Later the liver would start to metabolize the Propofol and the levels would slowly rise. When the patient approached to the apneic threshold breathing would have slowed down at a slow pace and carbon dioxide would have gone up. If there had been capnometry you would have seen the carbon dioxide go up.

At 10:00 am Michael Jackson continues breathing but without capnometry Conrad Murray doesn't see that there is a problem. Around 11:30 to 11:45 breathing would have stopped as there is no oxygen in the lungs. Michael Jackson died at about noon with the infusion still running. This is the only scenario Dr. Steven Dr. Steven Shafer could generate that produces the femoral level found at Michael Jackson consistent with Conrad Murray's explanations of how he gave Propofol. This scenario fits all the data in this case. This what Dr. Steven Dr. Steven Shafer thinks happened. Conrad Murray could have detected there was a problem with capnometry, pulse oximetry. If Conrad Murray was with Michael Jackson he would have seen slow breathing and could have turned off Propofol. Conrad Murray might have thought everything was okay and walked out of the room. Dr. Steven Shafer again mentions that Conrad Murray bought 130 100ml vials which Dr. Steven Shafer thinks measn 1 vial per night. Walgren and Dr. Steven Shafer starts working on a IV setup demonstration. Dr. Steven Shafer brought same/similar equipment of what Conrad Murray used or bought. Dr. Steven Shafer hangs a bag od saline on the IV pole. He attaches the infusion set tubing to the saline bag. In the infusion set there's an injection port with a rubber stopper where you can stick a needle to give mediciation. Dr. Steven Shafer shows a 22 gauge catheter (same size as what's used on Michael Jackson). Catheter remains in the vein (needle doesnt). Dr. Steven Shafer attached the catheter to the saline tubing and shows that the fluid goes through very quickly. Saline bag has a non-vented tubing as there's no need for a vented tubing with the saline (the saline bag will shrink). For Propofol you'll need a vented tubing. Conrad Murray bought vented infusion sets from Sea Coast. Dr. Steven Shafer shows the vented infusion set that Conrad Murray bought. It has a apparatus on top that allow the air to come in. This tubing is designed to be used with an infusion pump but there was no pump.

Spike from Propofol tubing woul have been stuck into the bottle and this would be consistent with the tear found at the 100ml Propofol bottle from Michael Jackson's house. Dr. Steven Shafer sticks the spike into the Propofol bottle and hangs it on the pole with the plastic handle on the bottle.

Walgren shows that the 100ml bottle found in Michael Jackson 's home also had the same handle. Objection by the defense.

After the sidebar the following stipulation is entered to the record : the handle of the bottle was lifted for demonstration by Walgren. When the bottle was found, it was still attached to the bottle and unused. Conrad Murray in his statement to the police said that he turned of the saline before giving Propofol with a syringe. Dr. Steven Shafer shows the rubber clamp and how you can stop the flow with the clamp. Dr. Steven Shafer demonstrates infusing 25mg of Propofol with syringe as Conrad Murray mentioned in his interview. Propofol doesn't come out of the tube as the saline is turned off and not coming to push Propofol out. So Conrad Murray's description of infusing it over 3 to 5 minutes is impossible if the turned off the saline. You need to unclamp the saline for Propofol to come out. Dr. Steven Shafer demonstrates the vent on the Propofol tubing. If he closes the vent Propofol stops, if he opens the vent Propofol runs through. Dr. Steven Shafer then hook the vented tubing with a needle to the y connector. Dr. Steven Shafer says that this is an extremely unsafe setup that is all based on gravity. If one bag is lifted there will be more force in that bag and it would slow the other one. If saline stops, Propofol speeds up. If the rate of the saline is changed, it would change the rate of the Propofol. This is why this system is very dangerous. The only way to control the speed is the clamps. Walgren asks about the IV bag with a slit. Dr. Steven Shafer says perhaps murray didn't know there was a hanging handle or didn't want to use it. Dr. Steven Shafer puts the Propofol bottle with the spike into the cut IV bag to demonstrate it's possible.

Dr. Steven Shafer says this system explains why the long tubing found at the house didn't test positive for Propofol, but the short tubing did. There was another long tube which was connected to the popofol bottle.

Dr. Steven Shafer empties the Propofol bottle quickly and removes the long vented tubing that had Propofol in it. It fits in his hand. Walgren asks if that tubing would fit into a pocket. Dr. Steven Dr. Steven Shafer says yes. Walgren does a recap of Dr. Steven Shafer 's testimony: 17 egregious deviations of care, 4 of them are also unetical, has shown a video about the way Propofol is safely given, has explained that oral consumption Propofol was impossible, that Michael Jackson received more than 4mg Lorazepam, that at 10 am it was impossible that Michael Jackson swalllowed Lorazepam,scenarios suggested an IV drip, demonstrated the IV set up and that the infusion line could be compacted in one hand and fit into a pocket. Walgren asks if Conrad Murray was the direct cause of Michael Jackson's death if Michael Jackson self injected/digested Propofol/Lorazepam. Dr. Steven Shafer says yes as Conrad Murray was the one that brought the Propofol, left patient with access to the drugs and started the IV line. Dr. Steven Shafer says Conrad Murray is responsible for every drop of Propofol or Lorazepam.

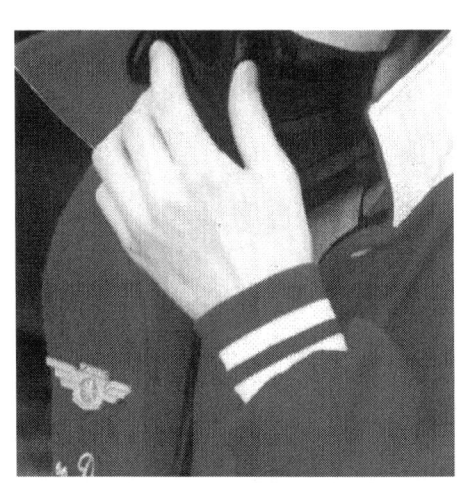

Murray Trial Summaries Day 15/October 21- 2011

Dr. Steven Shafer Testimony continued

Hearing starts with 221 - A stipulation . The term "tab handle" on Propofol bottleis defined.

Walgren direct continued

Walgren asks if Dr. Steven Shafer reviewed 8 page toxicology report by the coroner. Dr. Steven Shafer says yes and that it showed pure true level of drugs, it doesn't include the metabolites. Dr. Steven Shafer evaluated the procedures that is used by the coroner. Dr. Steven Shafer mentions that he made his simulations available to the defense and volunteered to help. Walgren asks if dying eyes open mean anything. Dr. Steven Shafer says it doesn't mean slow or quick death. After Walgren's question Dr. Steven Shafer says it's a possibility that Michael Jackson woke up and manipulated the infusion line and that would mean Conrad Murray left Michael Jackson alone. Dr. Steven Shafer also wrote this in his report. Walgren asks if this had happened would Dr. Steven Shafer 's opinion change about Conrad Murray . Dr. Steven Shafer says no and even if Michael Jackson woke up and opened the rubber clamp, it will still be Conrad Murray 's responsibility and Conrad Murray wasn't available and let this happen. It's still considered abondonment.

Chernoff cross

Chernoff goes over what Dr. Steven Shafer does and his models. Dr. Steven Shafer can determine concentration from dosage. Dr. Steven Shafer says he usually knows what dose is given. Dr. Steven Shafer says that as people are different his models are built to give ranges. The median is the representative of the half of the people's response to a particular drug. In this case Dr. Steven Shafer only had the concentration and he had the calculate the dose from the concentration.

Chernoff mentions that there was only one IV line found at the scene. Chernoff asks if Dr. Steven Shafer's theory of what happened is a bold statement. Dr. Steven Shafer responds as he believes it to be an honest statement. Chernoff asks if there's any particular reason Dr. Steven Shafer brought a different IV line for the saline bag. Dr. Steven Shafer contacted Sea Coast medical to get theexact line but the shipping would have taken 2-3 weeks so he brought the other line. Chernoff shows the exact IV line to Dr. Steven Shafer. (The IV line Chernoff shows is dirty and has brown stuff on it. Dr. Steven Shafer wonders if it's blood, Chernoff says it's not). Chernoff then asks why Dr. Steven Shafer brought a vented IV line for the Propofol. Dr. Steven Shafer says that a vented line is needed to get Propofol out. Chernoff asks why Dr. Steven Shafer assumed Conrad Murray used that IV line. Dr. Steven Shafer says that SeaCoast reports shows that Murray ordered that line and it shows he intended to use it. Chernoff asks how Dr. Steven Shafer could know if Conrad Murray used it in Michael Jackson's room. Dr. Steven Shafer says because he needed a vented IV line. Dr. Steven Shafer says the bottle had a spike tear but there was no needle hole in the Propofol bottle. If there had been a needle hole, Conrad Murray could have used another IV tubing. Dr. Steven Shafer says that as this bottle only had a spike tear, there had to be a vented IV line. Dr. Steven Shafer says that this is the only vented IV line he saw in Conrad Murray's orders and he had it shipped to California. Chernoff says perhaps there was no tubing at all. Dr. Steven Shafer responds how would you draw the Propofol then? Chernoff says that Los AngelesPD did not find a vented line. Dr. Steven Shafer says it's easy to hide and take with a person. Chernoff asks why wouldn't a person also take the bottle and the needles. Dr. Steven Shafer says that needles can hurt and bottles are bulky. Chernoff tries to emphasize that this is all Dr. Dr. Steven Shafer's opinion. They discuss back and forth about what's an opinion. Dr. Steven Shafer says what he says is based on medical knowledge and some are facts and some are his opinions. Dr. Steven Shafer says "It's my opinion that one should not lie to UCLA doctors".

Chernoff mentions that Conrad Murray said that he used a 10cc syringe but Dr. Steven Shafer used a 20cc syringe. Dr. Steven Shafer says the size of the syringe was irrelevant. Chernoff again goes over that Dr. Steven Shafer used a different IV tubing for saline bag, a different shape Propofol bottle and a larger syringe. Dr. Steven Shafer answers yes. Chernoff asks about the tear on the saline bag. Dr. Steven Shafer says it peaked his interest and he bought 3 IV bags for $150 and estimated the tear on the bag. Chernoff mentions that Walgren called Dr. Steven Shafer on March 31st and then sent him statements and reports. Chernoff goes over Dr. Dr. Steven Shafer 's report and that he used "might" to describe what happened. Dr. Steven Shafer also referenced Alberto Alvarez's statatement and that he saw a Propofol bottle in a bag. Chernoff asks if Dr. Steven Shafer ever met or talked with Alberto Alvarez and if he made the assumption that Alberto Alvarez was telling the truth. Chernoff says that the handle on the 100ml Propofol bottle found on the scene was not used. Dr. Steven Shafer says it's irrelevant and that whether the bottle was in the bag or hung on the pole it wouldn't make a difference. Chernoff asks if it's reasonable that rather than hanging the Propofol bottle by the handle, Conrad Murray would go all the steps to empty and cut the bag and put the Propofol bottle inside it. Dr. Steven Shafer says it's reasonable. Chernoff says that Conrad Murray is on trial for his life and there's a sidebar. Chernoff asks about the medical malpractice lawsuit that Dr. Steven Dr. Steven Shafer testified 10 years go and if he didn't like the doctor in that case. Dr. Steven Shafer says he didn't like the doctor. Dr. Steven Shafer says he testified once before but he consults on trials twice a year. Chernoff goes over Dr. Steven Shafer 's resume. When Dr. Steven Shafer was a medical student at Stanford University, Dr. Paul White was an assistant professor in anesthesia. Dr. Steven Shafer published papers with Dr. Paul White. Dr. Steven Shafer wrote the software and helped with mathematical models for Dr. Paul White's study in 1888. Chernoff goes over the Propofol insert and asks Dr. Steven Shafer to show which parts was his contribution. Dr. Steven Shafer circles and underlines the parts he did.

Chernoff goes over other studies / articles and books Dr. Steven Shafer worked on. Chernoff mentions the work Dr. Steven Shafer and Dr. Paul White did together. Dr. Steven Shafer and Dr. Paul White has known each other for almost 30 years and in 2009 Dr. Steven Shafer nominated Dr. Paul White for an award. Chernoff mentions Dr. Steven Shafer's statement when he said "he was disappointed" with Dr. Paul White about saying oral consumption. Dr. Steven Shafer says he was disappointed and that's how he felt. Chernoff asks if Dr. Steven Shafer knows this trial is on TV and shown internationally.

Walgren objects

Chernoff asks if Dr. Steven Shafer knows the circumstances of the letter Dr. Paul White sent to Flanagan and that it was rushed in 2 days due to threats of contempt. Objection and Sidebar. Chernoff talks about Propofol found in Michael Jackson's stomach. Dr. Steven Shafer sent the piglets study to Walgren and told Walgren there's was no human study. Dr. Steven Shafer then contacted Chilean professors for the human study but Walgren didn't ask for that study. Chernoff says that defense paid for a study on beagles and Dr. Paul White did that study.Chernoff asks who paid for the Chilean study. Dr. Steven Shafer says he paid $600 for the Propofol and the students volunteered. The study was also presented in an international conference. Chernoff asks why would he do a 2 month student, write a paper and present it at a conference if Propofol not being orally bio-available was something that 1st year student will know. Dr. Steven Shafer says it's better to have human data because it's not ambiguous and there would be no question about humans. During questioning we learn that Dr. Steven Shafer himself swallowed 20 ml Propofol before he did the study. Chernoff asks if Dr. Steven Shafer knew Dr. Paul White wouldn't say Michael Jackson swallowed Propofol. Dr. Steven Shafer says he didn't and stull doesn't know what Dr. Paul White is going to say.

Chernoff shows the 40 mg Lorazepam graph. Dr. Steven Shafer says that it shows repeated bolus injections (10 injections) for every 30 minutes frim midnight till 5 AM. Chernoff says in his model the first shot was at midnight but Michael Jackson was still at rehearsal then. Dr. Steven Shafer offers to do another simulation. Chernoff asks why he removed the "responsive to painful stimulus", "not responsive to painful stimulus" lines from his graphs. Dr. Steven Shafer says he wanted to make it as easy as possible for the jurors. Chernoff says based on his simulation Michael Jackson would be sleeping from 2:30 AM to 11:00AM. Dr. Steven Shafer says as Michael Jackson was exposed to benzos for 80 nights, it's impossible to predict Michael Jackson's reaction to Lorazepam. Chernoff asks how he knows Michael Jackson had benzos for 80 nights. Dr. Steven Shafer answers based on Murray's statement and pharmacy orders. Chernoff says that benzos being bought doesn't mean that they are used. Dr. Steven Shafer says that he stand by his statement that says "information suggests a higher dose possibly 40 mg". Chernoff asks if Dr. Steven Shafer did a simulation for oral Lorazepam. Dr. Steven Shafer didn't do a simulation for it. Chernoff asks Dr. Steven Shafer to tell what happens if a person swallow a tablet. It goes to the stomach, half of the pill absorbtion is in 22 minutes, it would then go to the liver subject to first pass, it would have 92% bioavailability and then it would go to the blood and to the tissues and brain. Metabolite would go to the bile and to intestines and stomach. The process is same for the IV Lorazepam as well. Chernoff shows a graph that combines 2 injections of 2mg Lorazepam injections and 40 mg dose graph. Chernoff and Dr. Steven Shafer goes over that Michael Jackson could not have swallowed Lorazepam in his last 4 hours. Chernoff mentions the Midazolam simulation and the numbers match to what Conrad Murray said he gave. Chernoff shows the 25mg Propofol injection graph and another graph that Dr. Steven Shafer did for Dr. Paul White . This second graph shows 25 mg being given over 5 minutes. Dr. Steven Shafer says the induction dose is given over 2 minutes because it's less painful to the patient.

Chernoff asks what's the danger of a rapid infusion. It's apnea.

Chernoff tries to go over the graph using the blood level, Dr. Steven Shafer says he need to look to brain levels. Chernoff asks what was Michael Jackson's brain concentration of Propofol. There was no measurement for that in coroner's report.

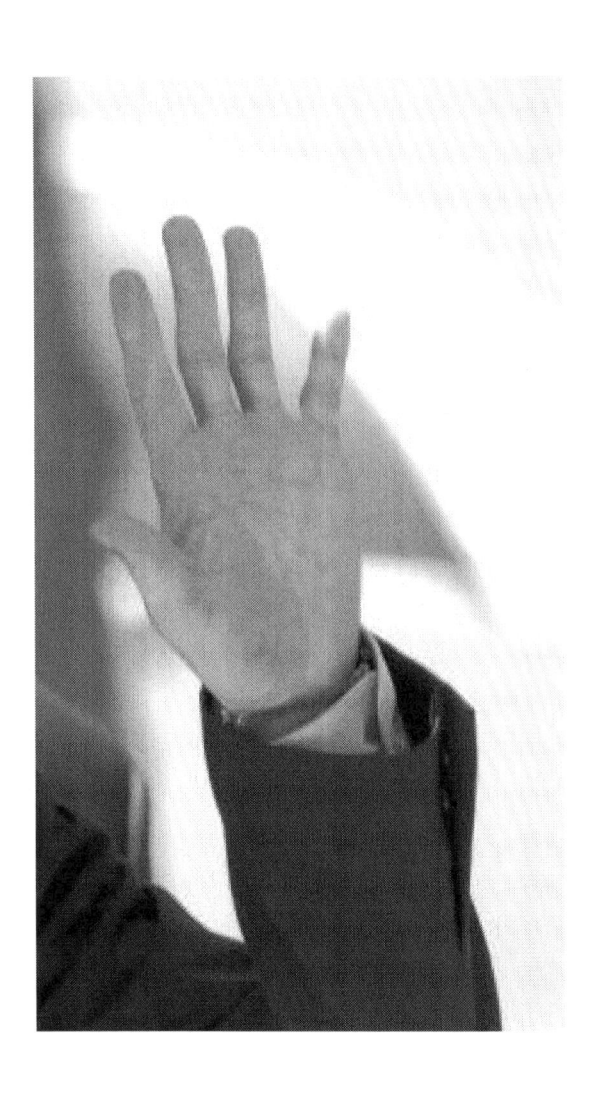

Murray Trial Summaries Day 16/ October 24- 2011

Dr. Steven Shafer Testimony continued

Chernoff Cross

Chernoff asks if one of the dangers of rapid bolus injection of Propofol is apnea. Chernoff goes over the insert of Propofol and reads that slow techniques are preferred over rapid injection to avoid apnea or hypotension. Chernoff goes over Dr. Steven Shafer's simulations. 25 mg rapid Propofol injection apnea is about 2 minutes. Defense's simulation of 25 mg pushed over 3 to 5 minutes, there's a low risk of apnea after 4 -5 minutes. Propofol would not be as risk after 10 minutes. Chernoff asks how Dr. Steven Shafer came up with 50mg Propofol dose. Dr. Steven Shafer says Conrad Murray in his interview said he mixed Propofol 1:1 with lidocaine and the syringes were 10cc. Chernoff asks if Conrad Murray gave Michael Jackson 50 mg Propofol if there would be apnea after 4-5 minutes. Dr. Steven Shafer says it's difficult to say as he doesn't know Michael Jackson's pharmaceutical state. Chernoff shows Dr. Steven Shafer's 6 self injections of 50mg Propofol injections and asks if there could be indefinite number of possibilities. Dr. Steven Shafer agrees. Dr. Steven Shafer did self injection simulations because of Dr. Paul White mentioned them as a hypothesis in his letter. Chernoff asks if Dr. Steven Shafer is aware that there are health care providers who died because of self injection of Propofol. Dr. Steven Shafer is aware about articles mentioning that. Chernoff goes back to the self injection and asks if the person is self injecting do they have to do it quick. Dr. Steven Shafer agrees and says that they can't do it over 3 minutes. Chernoff asks if Dr. Steven Shafer 's simulations were out of thin air. Dr. Steven Shafer says most are based on Dr. Paul White's letter and hypothesis of multiple injections. Chernoff switches to Lorazepam's half life in stomach. It's 22 minutes. Every 22 minutes the amount is cut in half. 8 mg swallowed 22 minutes later would be 4, another 22 minutes later it would be 2mg, another 22minutes it would be 1 mg , so in 4 hours , there would be a very low amount of free

Lorazepam in the stomach. They go over Greenblack's study. Lorazepam reaches a peak concentration in 2 hours after an oral dose. Drug goes into the stomach, and is being removed by liver and distribution in the tissues. So as long as the drugs come in the levels in blood raise, the concentration rises. When fewer drugs come in, it is removed faster than it comes in, so levels drop. Chernoff argues that even if there might be small percentage in the stomach, levels could be at peak in blood. Chernoff states that Dr. Steven Shafer cannot remove the possibility that Michael Jackson woke up and swallowed Lorazepam. Dr. Steven Shafer says he needs to know what time but it cannot be after 8AM. Chernoff asks questions about the urine levels of Lorazepam and Propofol. Dr. Steven Shafer did not do examinations / calculations based on urine levels. Chernoff asks if urine in the bladder could be evidence for or against 100ml Propofol drip. Dr. Steven Shafer says he doesn't know and he needs to research and find models. For some questions Dr. Steven Shafer says he needs information about Propofol glucoronide and it wasn't tested. Chernoff states that Dr. Steven Shafer's analysis is based on repertory arrest and he did not take into cardiac arrest. Dr. Steven Shafer says correct. Chernoff mentions the comments Dr. Steven Shafer wrote about Demerol on his report. Dr. Steven Shafer had written Michael Jackson liked Demerol but was not addicted to it. Chernoff asks if he's an expert in addiction, Dr. Steven Shafer says he's not an expert but seen examples and talked to other doctors about it. Chernoff asks about rapid detox. It's when the patient is detoxing for opiates while under sedation. Chernoff asks if Dr. Steven Shafer knows the dangers of opiates. Dr. Steven Shafer says they are dangerous for many organs.

Walgren redirect

Walgren again mentions that Dr. Steven Shafer's work is pro bono (free of charge). Dr. Steven Shafer says it's his custom in these types of cases. Dr. Steven Shafer says that he had worked for the defense and prosecution on different cases. Dr. Steven Shafer says his position on any case is based on the science.

Dr. Steven Shafer also shares his research, databases and software for free online as well. Dr. Steven Shafer wants to promote the science and even though he can earn some money for his programs he makes them available for free. Walgren goes over the IV lines and Dr. Steven Shafer says he can't say which line was used, all he knows the line had to be vented. Walgren shows People's 157 and Excel IV line and it's a vented line. Seacoast order shows that Murray bought 150 of those vented lines. Exel vented line is a lot smaller than the one used for demonstration. Walgren mentions Dr. Steven Shafer's testimony was interrupted due to a death in his family. Walgren asks if there is anything extraordinary saying than Michael Jackson received more than 25 mg Propofol. Dr. Steven Shafer says no and the defense is saying the same thing. Dr. Steven Shafer says that he couldn't find any scenario that support self injection and the only scenario he could find was Propofol was still running when Michael Jackson died. Walgren asks about Demerol. Dr. Steven Shafer says he read Klein's records and based on them he couldn't say if he was an addict or not and he's not an addiction specialist. Walgren mentions that there was no Demerol in Michael Jackson's system. Dr. Steven Shafer says he has done one scenario for the defense and if they asked he would have done more. Walgren mentions the new lab results about Lorazepam that shows 0.008mg of Lorazepam in Michael Jackson's stomach which equals to 1/250th of a tablet and mentions that this is smaller than 1/43rd of a tablet mentioned by the defense. Dr. Steven Shafer says he gave his opinion based on 30 years of expertise and says Conrad Murray should have monitored Michael Jackson. Dr. Steven Shafer says his opinion is not made out of thin air. It actually comes from published studies and established standards of care. Walgren asks if Dr. Steven Shafer believed what Conrad Murray said that Michael Jackson liked to push the drug and he was dependent on Propofol if self injection was a foreseeable risk. Dr. Steven Shafer agrees. Walgren shows another Lorazepam scenario of 9 doses of IV Lorazepam 4 mg each starting at 1:30 AM. This would also explain the levels found in Michael Jackson's blood.

248

Recross by Chernoff

Chernoff asks if the last scenario was done this weekend, because of what Chernoff said on Friday. Chernoff asks if 100ml IV drip Propofol was an extraordinary claim. Dr. Steven Shafer says it's an ordinary claim. Chernoff argues that Dr. Steven Shafer is changing his testimony about the IV line used for Propofol. Dr. Steven Shafer says that Chernoff is misstating his testimony and he only said the line had to be vented. This goes on for some time.

Prosection rests their case.

Defense case starts

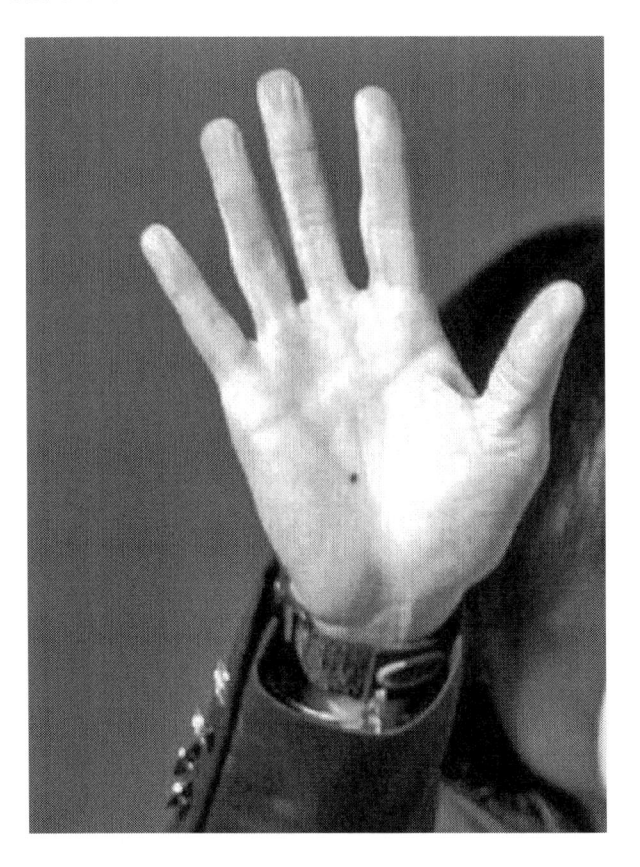

Donna Norris Testimony

Direct by Gourjian

Norris works at communications evidence unit Beverly Hills police department. She goes over the 911 call.

12:20:18 time 911 was called

12:20:21 begins to ring

12:20:26 called picked up

12:20:50 called transferred to Los AngelesFD

12:21:03 dispatcher at police dept hangs up.

12:21:04 911 system released the call

Duration of the call at the police department was 46 seconds

the call was made on June 25th 2009

Data shows which cell tower the call came from, the part of the cell tower, cell phone provider, and a number the police can call if they need to trace back the call.

No Cross by Walgren

Alexander Suppal Testimony

Gourjian Direct

Suppal is a Los Angeles PD police surveillance specialist for 11 years.

On June 25th he was asked to go to Carolwood to retrieve the videos. Suppal probably went around 7:30pm on June 25th. Detective Martinez was there. Security staff couldn't play back the videos. Suppal's first task was to find the hard drive so he had the trace the lines back to the source. Suppal finds the DVR in the basement of the house. They get a monitor and hook it up to the DVR. Suppal was with Detective Martinez and a tall African American security guard.

They rewinded the video to the time Conrad Murray and Michael Jackson came home. Gourjian plays a 7 minute video. It's a camera that looks at the gate. It shows time as 00:45AM. Multiple cars arrive at 00:47AM, 00:50AM and 00:58AM. A car leaves around 01:06 Video shows security guards and fans as well. Gourjian shows another video. This is from a camera outside on the keypad. It shows 3 cars come in and close up of the driver's face. It also show the fans waiting outside the street.Suppal did not go back to download additional footage. No one asked him to.

No cross by Walgren

Detective Dan Myers

Direct by Gourjian

Myers is a detective with Los AngelesPD since 1994. He was assigned to the case on June 29th, 2009. He interviewed Alberto Alvarez on August 31,2009. They interviewed Alberto Alvarez in an office building. Michael Amir Willliams an Faheem Muhammad was interviewed the same day at the same place as well but Myers doesn't know if Michael Amir Willliams & Faheem Muhammad was in the building when they interviewed Alberto Alvarez. On Agust 31st Alberto Alvarez made several drawings. One of the the IV bag with a bottle hanging on an IV stand. The second drawing was the pulse oximeter he saw on Michael Jackson's finger. These drawing and interviews was done 4 days after coroner's press release that identified the cause of death as Propofol. On June 25th, Alberto Alvarez never mentionned putting away medication or the bottle in the bag. Gourjian shows another drawing - an IV bag- Myers says he has never seen it before.

No cross examination

Detective Orlando Martinez

Direct by Gourjian

Martinez is an Los AngelesPD detective for 10.5 years. He went to UCLA on June 25th around 3:30PM. At UCLA the(Martinez and Scott Smith) spoke different people. Martinez was present during half of Alberto Alvarez's interview on June 25th. Alberto Alvarez didn't mention putting away any vials or mention seeing a bottle in a bag. Martinez went to Carolwood around 7:30PM and he didn't see Alberto Alvarez there. He saw Faheem Muhammad . Alex Supall , surveillance specialist for the Los AngelesPD, was at Carolwood to retrieve the security footage. Martinez made the decision to only download Michael Jackson's and Conrad Murray 's arrival. Martinez was not at August 31st 2009 interview of Alberto Alvarez but saw Alberto Alvarez in September to take his fingerprints. On April , 2011 Walgren called Martinez and asked him to bring certain evidence items to his office. Walgren also told him that Alberto Alvarez will be there. Alberto Alvarez was parked at the police building and walked to Walgren's office with Martinez. Martinez had brough a box of evidence items but only showed the saline bag, Propofol bottle and pulse oximeter to Alberto Alvarez. Gourjian shows the drawings Alberto Alvarez made on

August 2009 and the saline bag he draw on April 2011 and says that they are significantly different.

Cross by Walgren

Walgren mentions that Alberto Alvarez testified to the bottle in the saline bag and pulse oximeter in January. Walgren asks Martinez to explain the April 2011 drawing of the saline bag. Martinez says when he showed the saline bag to Alberto Alvarez, Alberto Alvarez said there was an additional chamber. Martinez asked him to draw it to explain.

Redirect by Gourjian

Gourjian says during preliminary hearing Alberto Alvarez didn't testify that the Propofol bottle was the one he saw. Walgren objects saying that at that Alberto Alvarez hadn't seen the evidence. Gourjian says Alberto Alvarez never mentioned the additional chamber on August, 2009. Martinez says he mentioned if after seeing the saline bag on April 2011. Martinez once again mentions that Alberto Alvarez was only shown 3 items, saline bag, Propofol bottle and pulse oximeter on April, 2011.

Dr. Allan Metzger

Direct by Chernoff

Dr. Allan Metzger met Michael Jackson 15 to 20 years ago. Dr. Allan Metzger's relationship with Michael Jackson began professionally and later became close as friends as well. Dr. Allan Metzger was Michael Jackson's main physician when he was in Los Angeles and he treated Michael Jackson for various things. Dr. Allan Metzger says Michael Jackson saw other specialists as well.

Dr. Allan Metzger has borugh 5 page medical records with him. Dr. Allan Metzger has seen Michael Jackson in his office on 23 June 2003. Michael had called him on 12 June 2008. At 2008 call Michael Jackson mentioned sleep issues and skin problems. Dr. Allan Metzger gave him Tylenol PM for sleep and talked about Michael Jackson's general health and back strain. Dr. Allan Metzger told Michael Jackson when he came to Los Angeles to see him and Klein. Dr. Allan Metzger says he frequently talked with Grace about the kids. Dr. Allan Metzger visited Michael Jackson at his home on April 2009. Dr. Allan Metzger thinks it was a weekend and early afternoon. On that day Michael Jackson , his kids and his security was at the house. Grace wasn't at the house. When they started talking the kids were in the room but later they went outside. Dr. Allan Metzger and Michael Jackson talked privately. Dr. Allan Metzger says the whole visit was 1 hour and 30 minutes and he talked to Michael Jackson privately around 20-30 minutes. They talked about medical issues and the stress Michael Jackson was under due to the rehearsals and upcoming tour. Michael Jackson did not mention seeing another doctor. Michael Jackson was lucid. He was excited and was talking about creative things. Dr. Allan Metzger says he showed both excitement and fear. His fear was about not doing a good job with 50 shows. Michael Jackson believed he was up to the task but he was fearful about staying healty. They talked about nutrition and hydration. Michael Jackson was doing well with chronic back issues. Dr. Allan Metzger says Michael Jackson was also under stress due to his sleep disorder. Michael Jackson was lucid, was exited, talking about creative things, he was in a state of exitement and fear. Fear was about not doing a good job with 50 shows, Michael Jackson believed he was up to the task, but he was fearful about staying healthy. They talked about nutrition, Michael Jackson had chefs for healthy food, hydration, Michael Jackson was doing well with his chronic back issues, he was also under stress due to his profound sleep disorder. Dr. Allan Metzger says sleep has been an issue for 15 -20 years for Michael Jackson especially during touring. Dr. Allan Metzger says he traveled with Michael Jackson on tour. On April 18 2009 Michael Jackson asked for "juice" intravenous sleep medication because Michael Jackson didn't believe any oral medication would be helpful. Dr. Allan Metzger says Michael Jackson didn't mention any drugs by name. Dr. Allan Metzger says from experience he knows previous oral medications doesn't work. Dr. Allan Metzger has tried Xanax, Tylenol PM before. In April 2011 he gave Michael Jackson klonapim and trazadone to try but not to be used together. He asked Michael Jackson to call him and tell him which one worked. Dr. Allan Metzger did not speak to Michael Jackson after that day.

Chernoff asks who is Randy Rosen. Dr. Allan Metzger says he works with him for pain management issues. Chernoff asks what kind of pain Michael Jackson was suffering from. Dr. Allan Metzger answers chronic back sprain due to overworking and a couple of injuries. Dr. Allan Metzger says he doesn't know Rosen's speciality and the question about what kind of medication given at Rosen's clinic is sustained. Dr. Allan Metzger says he also presumed Michael Jackson would see Klein for his vitiligo and some minor procedures. Michael Jackson mentioned Dr. Allan Metzger that he needed a doctor in London. Dr. Allan Metzger says Michael Jackson was concerned about hydration, sleep issus and injuries and wanted a doctor with him.

Cross by Walgren

Walgren asks about IV treatment. Mezger says he told Michael Jackson it was dangerous and it should not be done outside of a hospital. Walgren asks if any amount of money would make Dr. Allan Metzger to give Michael Jackson IV drugs. Dr. Allan Metzger says no.

Chernoff redirect

Chernoff asks if Dr. Allan Metzger told Michael Jackson IV sleep medication would be dangerous. Dr. Allan Metzger says he told Michael Jackson anything IV would be dangerous. Dr. Allan Metzger is not sure if Michael Jackson asked him for an anesthetic, Michael Jackson said "sleep medication".

Cherilyn Lee Testimony

Direct by Chernoff

Cherilyn Lee is a nurse practioner that focuses on holistic nutrion. As a nurse practioner she has been doing this on and off for 15 to 20 years and has worked with athletes and entertainers. As a nurse practioner she can write prescriptions but she choose not to. She says she doesn't like what medicines does to people, she prefer natural treatments. On January 2009 she received a call from Faheem Muhammad , who is the son of her friend. Faheem Muhammad told her Michael Jackson's kids had a cold and Michael Jackson wanted her to come and see the kids. While she was looking to the kids, Michael Jackson talked with her and asked her what she does. Michael Jackson told her he felt a little tired. Cherilyn Lee said that she can do some blood tests on him and try to help him with nutrition. Cherilyn Lee went the next day and did a physical test on Michael Jackson. She draw blood for lab tests and asked him questions to determine what caused his fatique. Michael Jackson didn't mention his sleep problems on that day. He just said he had difficulty to fall asleep. Cherilyn Lee says Michael Jackson was drinking "red bull" (an energy drink) and she felt red bull might be the cause. She told Michael Jackson about red bull and Michael Jackson said "whatever you tell me to do, I will stop". Chernoff asks if Michael Jackson seemed fatigued. Cherilyn Lee says no. Cherilyn Lee also says Michael Jackson told him that he thought he could be anemic. Overall Cherilyn Lee thought Michael Jackson was a healthy and loving person. Cherilyn Lee gave him nutritional smoothies with protein, B12 shots, myers coctail and vitamin C IV. Cherilyn Lee says she did blood test before she started to gove Michael Jackson IV and they were normal. Cherilyn Lee goes over the dates she saw Michael Jackson and what she gave him. She saw Michael Jackson after he came from London and he told her he was tired. At the end of March Michael Jackson asked her if she would go to London with him. On April 12 easter Sunday. Cherilyn Lee visited Michael Jackson. Michael Jackson told her he had a sleep problem and nothing she gave him was working. Cherilyn Lee offered to do a sleep study in his home and Michael Jackson said he didn't have time for that. Michael Jackson wanted her to see he couldn't sleep and asked her to stay a night and watch him to sleep. Cherilyn Lee agreed. Michael Jackson had "sleepy tea" (a herbal tea), had myers cocktail and Vitamin C IV. The catheter was on his hand because Michael Jackson had very small veins. Michael had also joked that he had "squiggly veins". Other than being small he had no problems with his veins. Cherilyn Lee watched him to sleep for 5 hours. Michael Jackson waked up around 3 AM.

Murray Trial Summaries Day 17/ October 25- 2011

Cherilyn Cherilyn Lee Testimony continued

Direct by Chernoff

Cherilyn Lee has reviewed her charts last evening. Cherilyn Lee says she's not feeling well. Judge Pastor takes a break so that she can rest. Cherilyn Lee has a PhD in nutrition and she's a certified nutritionist and believes in holistic medicines. Chernoff goes over her records. April 12 Michael wanted products for sleep but did not tell her what he wanted. April 19 she went to Michael Jackson's house in the morning to prepare a smoothie and gave Michael Jackson B12. Michael Jackson said he had trouble sleeping and asked her to watch him sleep. He told Cherilyn Lee that he had a pattern of 2 to 3 hours sleep. Michael Jackson also asked about Diprivan (Propofol), Cherilyn Lee didn't know what it is. Michael Jackson told her it's the only medication that gets him to sleep right away. Cherilyn Lee says she doesn't know if Michael Jackson had received Propofol in the past, he seemed to have familiarity with it. Cherilyn Lee talks about natural ways to sleep and sleep hygiene with Michael Jackson. Before coming back that evening Cherilyn Lee searched Diprivan and called a doctor. Doctor told Cherilyn Lee what Diprivan is and it's never used at home. Cherilyn Lee tells this to Michael Jackson. Michael Jackson says doctors had told him it was safe and he thought he would be safe he if he had someone at home to monitor him. Cherilyn Lee goes to her office and gets her PDR and shows the adverse effects to Michael Jackson. Michael Jackson tells her he had Diprivan for surgery and he had fallen asleep so easily. Michael Jackson says he needed rest to work. Cherilyn Lee checks her records and corrects that Michael Jackson actually slept 3 hours (not 5 hours) according to her records. When Michael Jackson woke only sleeping 3 hours on April 19th he wasn't happy. He said only thing that would help him sleep was Diprivan and asked Cherilyn Lee to help him find someone that would give it to him. Cherilyn Lee didn't see Michael Jackson after that.

June 21st she received a call from Faheem Muhammad . Faheem Muhammad called to say that Michael Jackson wanted to see her. Cherilyn Lee heard Michael Jackson in the background saying "tell her what's wrong with me, one half of my body is hot, one half is cold". Cherilyn Lee told Faheem Muhammad that someone needed to take Michael Jackson to hospital. Cherilyn Lee was in Florida when she got the call. Cherilyn Lee mentioned the June 21st phone call to the police and said that it could be a central nervous system problem. Cherilyn Lee says this was one of the symptoms of Propofol she had mentioned to Michael Jackson. Cherilyn Lee says on July 2009 when she talked to the police, she didn't know what medication Michael Jackson was taking. In July 09, when she talked to the police, she didn't know what medication Michael Jackson was taking.

Walgren cross

Walgren goes over medical records of Cherilyn Lee. She kept detailed reports.

January 29 Cherilyn Lee saw the kids for colds. February 1st she came back to give nutritional supplements. She did a medical checkup. Michael Jackson said he had vitiligo and lupus. Cherilyn Lee says Redbull cans were obvious. Michael Jackson went to sleep with light , music and movies on. Michael Jackson said when performing he would sweat a lot and people would have to mop the floors. Walgren shows the part that she has written Michael Jackson's vital signs. Michael Jackson wanted to start a nutritional program so she planned to do lab work. She drew blood and Michael Jackson had small veins. She told Michael Jackson to stop drinking Red Bull. February 2nd and 3rd she saw Michael Jackson . She kept documenting progress notes, her impressions, her recommendations and complaints if any. February 16th Cherilyn Lee looked to Michael Jackson's vitals and discussed lab results with Michael Jackson . The plan was Michael Jackson needed to discontinue Red Bull drinks. She took blood again to see the effects of the treatment. Cherilyn Lee says Michael Jackson had greatly improved and his results were normal. March 9 Cherilyn Lee went over the lab results with Michael Jackson and again kept documented all of her findings, impressions, recommendations and complaints. March 13 Cherilyn Lee was again documenting her findings. March 16 Michael Jackson had no complaints and felt good. Plan was to continue with vitamins, Myers cocktails and nutritional supplements. March 20th, March 24th, March 26th, March 31st Cherilyn Lee continues to see Michael and document everything. April 12th Michael Jackson's main complaint is that he needs products to sleep and he's willing to try natural products. April 19th Michael Jackson's energy is good but he's unable to sleep and the natural products don't help him to sleep. April 19 morning Michael Jackson requested Cherilyn Lee to observe him to sleep. Michael Jackson said he needed something that would "knock him out". Michael Jackson asked for Diprivan. Cherilyn Lee never heard of Propofol before. She searched and made a phone call and found out it was used in hospitals for surgery. Cherilyn Lee told Michael Jackson that it was not safe to use at home. Michael Jackson assured her that it was safe and he "only needed a doctor to monitor him while he sleeps". Cherilyn Lee brought back PDR from her office and showed it to Michael Jackson and explained him the side effects. PDR has several side effects. Some of them are dizziness, agitation, chills, trembling and memory loss. Cherilyn Lee asked Michael Jackson "what if you forget your lines?". Michael Jackson said "I would never forget my lines". Michael Jackson again told her that doctors said it would be safe. Cherilyn Lee asked "I understand you want a good night's sleep. You want to be "knocked out" but what if you don't wake up?". Michael Jackson said "I'll be okay I only need someone to monitor me with the equipment while I sleep".

Cherilyn Lee gets emotional and starts crying.

April 19 night Michael Jackson fell asleep at 12:15 AM and woke up around 3:15AM. He said he needed Dirpivan IV. Cherilyn Lee said it would be dangerous and Michael Jackson repeated he would be okay if a doctor monitored him. Cherilyn Lee says she was not willing to give

Michael Jackson IV Propofol. She says it wasn't used at home and it was not a sleep medication.

She never saw Michael Jackson again.

July 2009 Cherilyn Lee was interviewed by police. She said she told Michael Jackson "no one who cared or had your best interest at heart is going to give you this".

Chernoff redirect

Chernoff asks if she gave interviews to the media before talking to the police. She says yes. Cherilyn Lee explains that one of her patients is a PR and arranged the interviews. Chernoff asks about the June 21st call. She doesn't' remember the time she received the phone call. She was in hospital herself.

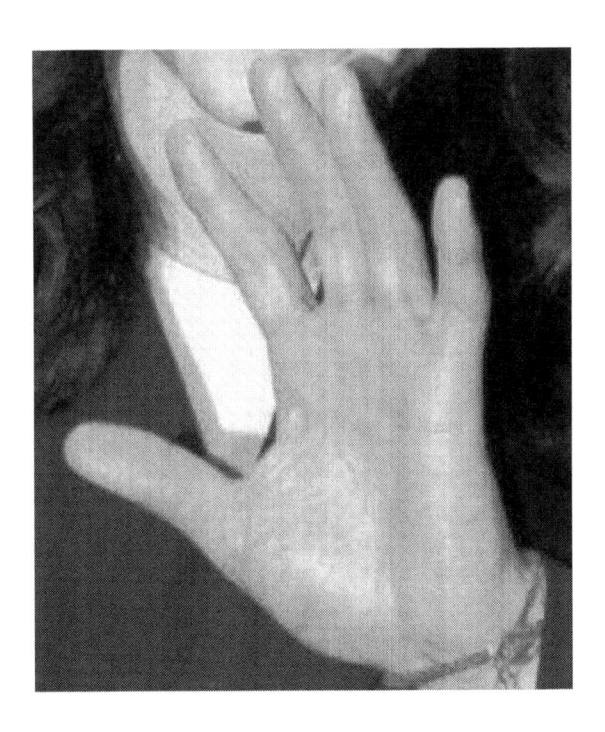

Amir Dan Rubin Testimony

Chernoff Direct

On June 25th he was chief operating executive at UCLA medical center. Rubin starts by explaining the layout of UCLA. On June 25th he got a call saying that there was a "person of interest" at the hospital, he didn't initially knew it was Michael Jackson.

Rubin was outside the ER room and tried to secure the area for privacy and security. Rubin organized 3 conference rooms: one for the family, one for the police and one for other people. The third conference room was used for a meeting about a press release. There were people from AEG and UCLA. Jermaine Jackson was in the room as well. Rubin came and went from the room. Rubin saw Conrad Murray in the conference room reading the press release and commenting that the cause of death was not known. Conrad Murray looked distressed. Press release was given in the auditorium in the basement by Jermaine Jackson.

Walgren Cross

Walgren mentions Katherine Jackson was notified about the death of Michael Jackson by Richelle Cooper. Rubin told the police that he heard the "anguish of a mom hearing about losing her child and from a personal perspective it was not a good thing to hear".

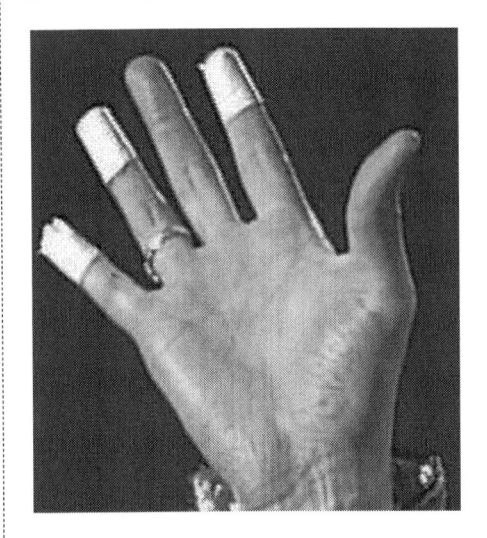

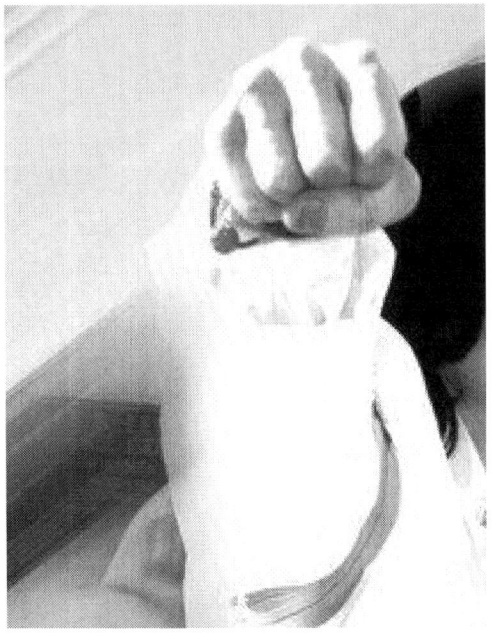

Randy Philips Testimony

Chernoff Direct

Randy Phillips is the president and CEO of AEG Live. Prior to working with AEG he ran a record company. Randy Phillips has been in the entertainment business for 30 years. He explains what AEG and AEG Live does, the venues they operate etc. Randy Phillips first met Michael Jackson in the mid 1990s. Randy Phillips had brought Los Angeles Gear endorsement deal to John Branca and Michael Jackson . Next time he saw Michael Jackson was in 2007. At the time he was CEO of AEG and Peter Lopez, Michael Jackson's attorney, had contacted AEG for a tour. A meeting in Las Vegas had been arranged with Michael Jackson, Lopez and Michael Jackson's manager.

Chernoff direct continued

AEG was contacted by Peter Lopez about Michael Jackson potentially going back on stage in 2007. RP was this would have been monumental achievement for AEG as Michael Jackson was the greatest star. The meeting happened in Las Vegas with Lopez, another lawyer named

Cross, Raymone Bain and her assistant. The meeting lasted 90 minutes. At that time Michael Jackson wasn't ready to back to stage so Randy Phillips didn't pursue it any further. August 2008 AEG got contacted by Tom Barrack fro Colony Capital who bought the note on Neverland. They met and talked about concerts. Randy Phillips met with Tohme same week. Tohme said Michael Jackson wanted to restart his career, first do live shows and then put out new music. Randy Phillips met with Michael Jackson at September 2008. The plan was to do a residency show at the O2. Randy Phillips calls only special artists can do that and it's like "bringing the mountain to Muhammad". Michael Jackson seemed motivated and receptive to the idea. Randy Phillips had other meeting with Michael Jackson to talk about creative stuff. Randy Phillips met with Michael Jackson on Halloween (October 31st). Michael Jackson mentioned Randy Phillips how he wanted to restart his career and how he was living like a vagabond. The meeting got emotional and both RP and Michael Jackson cried. AEG contract was for 31 shows. Michael Jackson came up with that number as he wanted to do 10 more shows then prince. The contract was signed at Michael Jackson's house on January 2009. Chernoff tries to ask many questions about the contract but it's sustained. Judge didn't allow that line of questioning. Press conference was on March and AEG advertised initially 10 shows. Chernoff tries to ask Michael Jackson being late to press conference etc but the judge doesn't allow it. After the announcement they did a presale and the demand was unbelieveable. Gongaware told Randy Phillips to ask if Michael Jackson would do more shows. Randy Phillips talked to Tohme and got a phone call from Michael Jackson after 20 minutes. Michael Jackson said he would do 50 shows maximum and had 2 conditions. He wanted a house outside London with 16 acres, horses, pastoral for his kids and he wanted Guinness book of world records to be present at the 50th show. In March Michael Jackson told he wanted Ortega to be the director of the concerts. Ortega was hired and then auditions were done and additional personnel were hired in April. Rehearsals started in May. Michael Jackson talked about a personal doctor in May. RP was away and heard it from Dileo, Gongaware and Whooley. They asked if Randy Phillips can talk Michael Jackson out of hiring his own doctor. Randy Phillips told Michael Jackson it would be expensive to bring a US doctor to London and asked if Michael Jackson would hire a doctor that's based in London Michael Jackson was firm and said he wanted his own physician. Gongaware negotiated with Murray. There was a meeting at the first week of June. Dileo was worried about Michael Jackson not eating enough. Conrad Murray said he'll make sure that Michael Jackson ate properly and he'll give Michael Jackson supplemental protein drinks. Conrad Murray told them Michael Jackson's health was good. Randy Phillips say it is obvious to him that Michael Jackson trusted Conrad Murray and they had close relationship. This was the first time Randy Phillips met Conrad Murray. There was a concern raised by Ortega at the second week of June. Ortega felt like Michael Jackson wasn't as engaged as he needed to be. The main concern was Michael Jackson's focus and attending rehearsals. Randy Phillips says he wasn't sure what Ortega meant by tough love and pulling the plug. Randy Phillips say no one was contemplating pulling the plug and there was no concern that the show would be cancelled, they would have been postponed. After Ortega's email Dileo called and asked Randy Phillips to arrange a meeting. Randy Phillips called Conrad Murray to arrange the meeting. During one conversation Randy Phillips mentioned Conrad Murray that Michael Jackson was seeing Klein. Randy Phillips mentioned this because at one production meeting Michael Jackson wasn't as focused as he usually was (Randy Phillips say Michael Jackson was generally laser focused). Randy Phillips asked Michael Amir Williams if Michael Jackson was okay and Michael Amir Williams had told him he just came back from Klein. June 20th meeting. Michael Jackson, Conrad Murray, Randy Phillips and Ortega were present. Ortega started by saying Michael Jackson needed to focus and show more engagement. Michael Jackson told Ortega that he was ready and "you build the house and I'll put the door and paint". Randy Phillips went to rehearsals on June 23rd and 24th.

June 25th Randy Phillips got a call from Dileo around 10:30 – 11:00AM. Dileo told him Michael Jackson was having difficulty breathing and told him to go to Carolwood. It took Randy Phillips 15 minutes to arrive to Carolwood. When he arrived paramedics were leaving the house so Randy Phillips followed them to the hospital. Dileo joined him at hospital. Randy Phillips saw Conrad Murray at the hospital. Conrad Murray was in severe distress and Randy Phillips doesn't remember what Conrad Murray said.

Walgren cross

Randy Phillips says he learned in May 2009 that Michael Jackson had a personal doctor. Randy Phillips say he had no knowledge of what Conrad Murray was doing as treatment to Michael Jackson. Randy Phillips says it never got to the point that they considered to pull the plug on This Is It concerts. Randy Phillips says he mentioned that Michael Jackson was seeing Klein in the meeting at the first week of June. Randy Phillips says Conrad Murray either knew or said that he would check into it. Randy Phillips again asked about This Is It concerts. Randy Phillips says Michael Jackson was motivated and that he's a genius. Randy Phillips again tells how the concerts were increased to 50 shows. After the presales demand Gongaware asked him to talk to Michael. Randy Phillips called Tohme and Michael Jackson called him within 20 minutes. Michael Jackson said he'll do 50 shows but wanted Guinness Book of World records to document it and he wanted an estate for his kids. Randy Phillips says that Michael Jackson was a phenomenal father. Walgren goes over the meetings. The meeting in first week of June was about Michael Jackson not eating enough and Conrad Murray said he'll take care of it. Michael Jackson had great trust in Conrad Murray. 19th June meeting was about missing rehearsals. Conrad Murray was very reassuring and told Ortega to take care of the show and Conrad Murray was the doctor and he would take care of Michael Jackson's health. After being told what time paramedics was leaving the house, Randy Phillips says he might be mistaken about the time he got the phone call about Michael

Jackson on June 25th. Randy Phillips says he attended rehearsals on June 23rd and June 24th. Last time he saw Michael Jackson was on June 24th. Randy Phillips says he had Goosebumps while watching Michael Jackson. Michael Jackson walked to his car with Randy Phillips . "He put his hands on my shoulders as we were walking out and he said to me, 'You got me here, now I'm ready. I can take it from here.' And that's the last I saw him," said Randy Phillips .

Chernoff redirect

Randy Phillips said he never felt that Michael Jackson was not able to do the shows. Randy Phillips says the reason the initial shows were pushed back had nothing to do with Michael Jackson's health. Randy Phillips says during the meeting they were always reassured by Conrad Murray. Chernoff talks about cancellation of the shows. Randy Phillips says AEG had a contractual obligation to Michael Jackson and they (Michael Jackson and AEG) would have to mutually agree on cancelling the tour. Chernoff asks if contractually Michael Jackson was responsible for the production cost, Randy Phillips says yes. Chernoff tries to ask more about the contract such as insurance but they are sustained. Chernoff asks what Ortega meant by tough love, pulling the plug. Randy Phillips says he doesn't know and that he's not in Kenny's mind. Chernoff asks why he mentioned Klein to Conrad Murray. Randy Phillips say at one meeting Michael Jackson was distracted and when he asked Michael Amir Williams if Michael Jackson was okay, Michael Amir Williams said he just came from Klein. Another time it was mentioned Michael Jackson couldn't; come to a meeting because he had been at Klein.

Michael Hansen Testimony

Flanagan Direct

Michael Hansen works at Pacific Toxicology. They got samples from the coroner's office and did tests for total Lorazepam (the drug and metabolite) for the defense.

Flanagan tries to ask questions but they can't be answered because it's beyond knowledge of Michael Hansen . There are a lot of objections. Flanagan has no further questions

Walgren Cross

Walgren asks how long Michael Hansen knew Flanagan. Michael Hansen says since 2009 and his firm worked with Flanagan's firm for decades. Walgren asks about the stomach contents test. They looked for total Lorazepam (free drug and the metabolite) because it's their standard procedure. They found it was 634ng/ml. In their analysis they did not differentiate between the drug and the metabolite. It was later sent to another lab in Pennsylvania to determine the free Lorazepam. The results were 84 ng/ml. It equals to 0.006 mg which is 1/333 of a 2mg tablet. Walgren asks if Dr. Steven Shafer contacted the lab asking about their methodology for the drug testing. They didn't respond and notified Flanagan. Ms Brazil called the lab to get the procedures and said if they don't respond she would have to get the court involved. Only after this they provided their procedures to the prosecution. Walgren says they got a corrected version of toxicology results and defense's copy didn't have correction. Walgren asks why but Michael Hansen doesn't know the reason.

Flanagan redirect

Flanagan says the quantity found by the coroner is 0.008 mg but their lab found 0.006mg and asks the reasons. Michael Hansen says it could be due to the timing of the testing and degradation or it could be due to methods used.

Murray Trial Summaries Day 18 / October 26-2011

Gerry Causey Testimony

Gerry Causey met Conrad Murray 11 years ago in Las Vegas when he had a heart attack. He was 57 years old and had high blood pressure but didn't expect to have a heart attack. Conrad Murray talked to him for a few minutes about the procedure, made sure he understood and made him sign papers. He didn't want to be sedated for the procedure.

Gerry Causey says that he received one stent and kept seeing Conrad Murray for controls after the procedure and they became friends. Gerry Causey says that Conrad Murray explains everything in simple terms and doesn't rush the patients. Once Gerry Gerry Causey spent 4 and half hours in Conrad Murray's office. Gerry Causey says Conrad Murray isn't greedy because he didn't charge his deductible. Conrad Murray told him he would be back and gave him his phone number.

Walgren cross

Gerry Causey had given 2 media interviews about Conrad Murray.

Conrad Murray had informed him he was leaving his practice around April. After Walgren's questioning Gerry Causey says he was treated for a heart condition and not for a sleep disorder or drug dependency. Walgren asks where the procedure happened. Gerry Causey says it was in a hospital, he signed papers, and there were monitor and 3 additional people in the room. Gerry Causey got put additional stents all again in a hospital with additional personnel present.

Chernoff redirect

Gerry Causey says he was not paid for media interview and gave them to help his friend Conrad Murray. Gerry Causey says he helped Conrad Murray because of love, compassion and he doesn't think he did what he's accused of.

Walgren recross

Walgren asks even if Conrad Murray acted with gross negligence would he still be here to support Conrad Murray. Gerry Causey says yes.

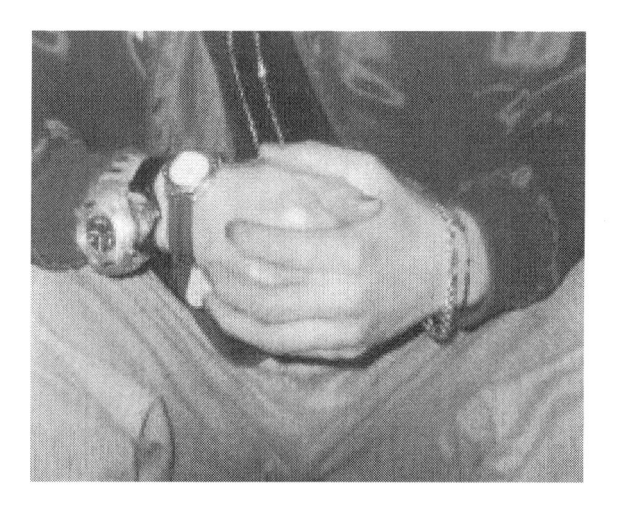

Andrew Guest Testimony

Andrew Guest met Conrad Murray in 2002. He was 39 years old and had pain in his chest, arm and had a headache. Conrad Murray put stents to him and solved his chest pain.

Andrew Guest says that Conrad Murray is the best doctor and explains everything and makes sure that you are okay.

Walgren cross

Gerry Causey did media interviews as well. Walgren asks what kind of treatments he got. It was for a heart condition and Conrad Murray had a team to help him and necessary medical equipment was available. Walgren asks if Conrad Murray gave him Propofol in his bedroom. Andrew Guest says no. Walgren asks if every patient deserves the level of care he had. Andrew Guest says yes and wants to add something but Walgren doesn't let him.

Chernoff redirect

Andrew Guest wanted to add Conrad Murray provides great care in his office too. Andrew Guest also says that he wasn't paid by the media and he talked to the media because he believes Conrad Murray needs support.

Walgren recross

Andrew Guest says that nothing would change his mind about Conrad Murray.

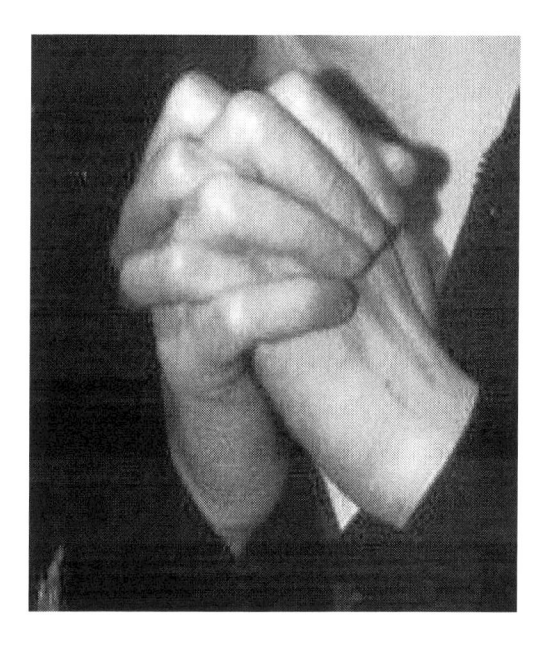

Lunette Sampson Testimony

Lunette Sampson had 3 heart attacks. In 2008 she had a heart attack while Conrad Murray was out of town. Another doctor told her that she's okay. Conrad Murray didn't agree with the doctor and wanted her to have a test done. She didn't have the test and had another heart attack.

Lunette Sampson says that Conrad Murray is very caring and takes his time with the patients (he doesn't rush). Lunette Sampson says Conrad Murray is not greedy and he takes care of people pro bono and pays for medication when patients can't pay.

Walgren cross

Walgren asks who asked her to testify. Lunette Sampson was contacted by Conrad Murray's PR people. Conrad Murray never mentioned he was going to work for Michael Jackson. He just said that he was going to London for a year and referred her to another doctor. Lunette Sampson says she was distresses because she doesn't trust other doctor because of what happened to her.

Walgren mentions a discipline letter Conrad Murray got from Sunrise Hospital. On December 24th Conrad Murray was called at 11:00AM and at 11:05AM. Conrad Murray called the hospital back around 12:00PM and asked the staff to call another doctor. Conrad Murray got to the hospital at 01:56PM. This was 3 hours after he was first called and there was a serious risk of blood clotting for the patient. Lunette Sampson was not aware of this letter. Walgren asks what kind of treatment Lunette Sampson received. She says heart condition. Walgren asks if Conrad Murray knew what the other doctor did to her is because the other doctor kept records.

Chernoff redirect

Due to hospital procedures doctors are supposed to call in within 1 hour and 20 minutes.

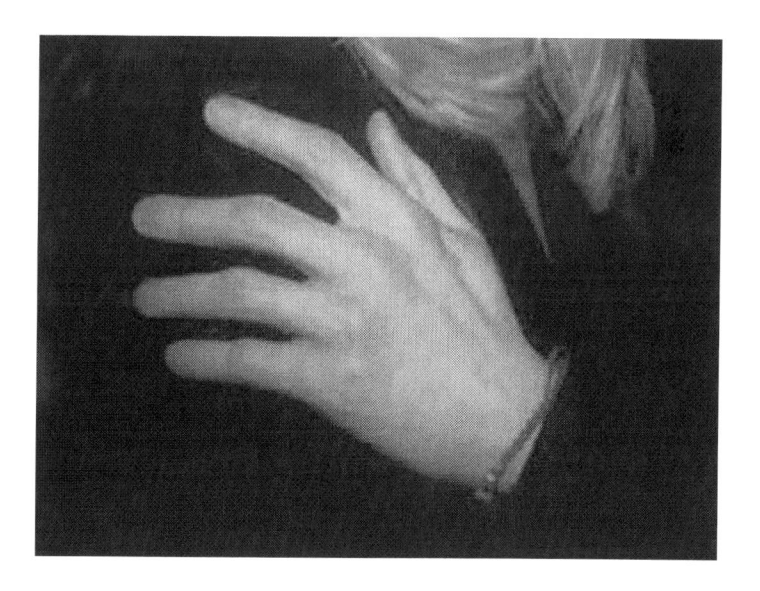

Dennis Hix Testimony

Dennis Hix lives at a house next door to Conrad Murray's children in Las Vegas and met Conrad Murray around 1999. He had heart problem. His previous doctor told that it can't be fixed but Conrad Murray fixed his problem. Conrad Murray put 6 stents in a hospital.

Dennis Hix says Conrad Murray is the best doctor and helped his brother for free when he didn't have the money to go to ER.

Walgren cross

Dennis Hix received a letter from Conrad Murray in 2009. Conrad Murray didn't say what he was going to do and never mentioned Conrad Murray. Walgren asks what Dennis Hix was treated for. It was for heart condition and several other things but it was not for sleep disorder or drug dependency. Dennis Hix says he doesn't know if kept records for his medical treatment.

Ruby Mosley Testimony

Ruby Mosley lives in Houston in Acres home community. Acres home is a senior citizen low income area. Ruby Mosley says she knew Conrad Murray's father. In 2006 Conrad Murray opened a clinic in honor of his father.

Ruby Mosley says Conrad Murray is not greedy and if he was greedy he wouldn't open a clinic in a low income area. Ruby Mosley says Conrad Murray didn't do much money in Houston and opened the clinic because Conrad Murray's father had a clinic there and Conrad Murray made a commitment to continue the medical care after his father. Ruby Mosley says she and her husband is treated by Conrad Murray. Conrad Murray put her stents.

Walgren cross

Walgrens asks if Ruby Mosley met Sade Anding. Ruby Mosley says she saw Conrad Murray at the clinic and does not know what he did in his personal life. Ruby Mosley says Conrad Murray is very knowledgeable and can recite details as it related to medical care plans.

280

Chernoff redirect

Ruby Mosley says that Conrad Murray took his time with the patients and explained everything to her. Appointments could go on for an hour. Ruby Mosley says he saw patients no matter how long it took. Ruby Mosley says she misses Conrad Murray.

Court ends early due to scheduling issues

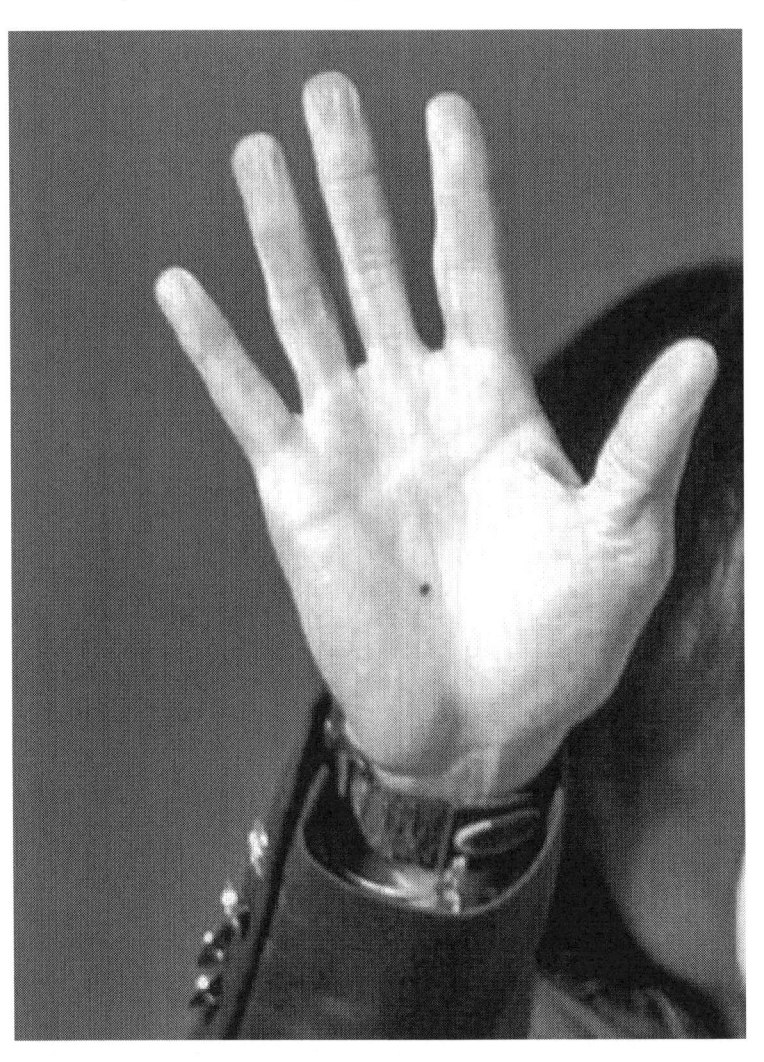

Murray Trial Summaries Day 19/October 27-2011
Dr. Robert Waldman Addiction Specialist

Chernoff Direct

Dr. Robert Waldman states that addiction specialists help patients to stop using alcohol and/or drugs. Dr. Robert Waldman states that if a person came to him looking for help, he would first do an interview and a complete history; repetitive use, age of onset, history of all substances of abuse, history of adverse consequences of use such as legal, social consequences. Dr. Robert Waldman states that a complete medical history but also to focus on the consequences.

Dr. Robert Waldman states that there are different types of treatment programs depending on the substance that a person is addicted to. Dr. Robert Waldman states he asks the person if the addiction has caused legal issues, problems in their marriage, etc. Dr. Robert Waldman states that he has treated professional athletes and celebrities with addictions to prescription pain pills. Dr. Robert Waldman states that the signs of withdrawal can be performance changes, behavior changes, use beyond the regular use can come from a dependence.

Dr. Robert Waldman states that demerol is an older drug, and since then, there have been newer drugs that have surfaced. Dr. Robert Waldman states that opioids are prescribed for pain. Dr. Robert Waldman states that people who stop using prescription pills they have been abusing, the situation is not safe, nor is it comfortable. Dr. Robert Waldman states that people in denial of their addiction, telling everyone surrounding them that they don't have a problem. Dr. Robert Waldman states that interventions are necessary at times, because addicted people don't want to give up their daily lives, or live by the rehab's rules. Dr. Robert Waldman states that addicted people hide the use, and do everything in their power to maintain their privacy and discretion, including patients who hide their addictions from a variety of doctors and pharmacies (referred to as doctor shopping) Dr. Robert Waldman states that to keep their addiction from family or friends, addicts use drugs away from them. Dr. Robert Waldman states that there are two ways to help a opioid addict, one is a opioid substitution drug such as methadone, but one has to enter withdrawal first before they can use the opioid substitution drug. The second method is given through lots of benzodiazepines for sedation through the withdrawal process. Symptoms of opioid withdrawal consist of sweating, tachycardia, muscular aches, bone pain, abdominal cramps, vomiting, severe anxiety, hot and cold chills, diarrhea. Dr. Robert Waldman states that an addict's greatest fear is that they are going to be uncomfortable going through withdrawal. Dr. Robert Waldman states that both Lorazepam and ativan can be used for opioid withdrawal. Dr. Robert Waldman states that withdrawal time is variable, and often the addict will say they do not need the rehabilitative drugs anymore because they are now comfortable. Dr. Robert Waldman states that anesthesia can be used to withdraw from opioid addiction, and while under anesthesia, other drugs can be given to alleviate drug withdrawal symptoms. Dr. Robert Waldman states that he reviewed the medical records of Michael Jackson from Dr. Arnold Klein, statements/testimony from witnesses. Dr. Robert Waldman states that Michael Jackson's medical records begin in January and end on

June 22, 2009. Dr. Robert Waldman states that on March 12, a page from the medical records shows that a patient named Omar Arnold (Michael Jackson alias) was treated with Restylne/Botox and received Demerol injections for those treatments. Dr. Robert Waldman states that Restylne and Botox are fillers for wrinkles, but he is not familiar with the drugs. Dr. Robert Waldman states that he asked his colleagues whether the REstylne or Botox would be painful enough to call for demerol, and his colleagues said no. Dr. Robert Waldman states Michael Jackson also received Midazolam on this day, and that the doses of demerol were above average, meaning it was a large dose. Dr. Robert Waldman states that on April 6, Michael Jackson's medical records reveal that at 8 pm, demerol was given at 200 mg and 1 mg midazolam, in one shot. On April 9, Michael Jackson received at 3:30 pm an injection of demerol at 200 mg, and midazolam 1 mg. On April 13, Michael Jackson received 200 mg of demerol and 1 mg of Midazolam at 11:15 along with Restylne for both the 13th and the 9th. April 5th Michael Jackson received 200 mg demerol and midazolam 1 mg injection. April 17th Michael Jackson received Botox in the armpit for perspiration, 200 mg demerol 1 mg midazolam, then another demerol 100 mg injection 1 mg midazolam for a total of 300 mg demerol. April 21, Michael Jackson received Botox to groin, demerol 200 mg midazolam 1 mg, an hour later demerol 100 mg. Dr. Robert Waldman states that the progression from 200 mg of demerol to 300 mg demerol is significant in that he believes Michael Jackson was developing a tolerance of demerol. April 22 11:30 am 200 mg demerol 1 midazolam an hour later, 100 mg of demerol, an hour later 75 mg demerol for total of 375 mg demerol along with Botox. Dr. Robert Waldman states he has never given 375 mg of demerol to a patient. April 23, Michael Jackson received 100 mg demerol, 1 mg midazolam, so the total for the 3 days (April 21,22,23) demerol injection was 775 mg. Dr. Robert Waldman states that April 27, Michael Jackson received 11:30 200 mg demerol 1 mg Midazolam an hour later 100 mg demerol and 1 mg midazolam. On April 30, Michael Jackson received 200 mg demerol 1 mg midazolam, two hours later 100 mg demerol 2 mg Midazolam. May 4, Michael Jackson received 200 mg demerol, 1 mg midazolam, an hour later 100 mg demerol 1 mg midazolam. Dr. Robert Waldman states that he believes Michael Jackson was dependent on demerol and possibly/probably addicted to opioids. Dr. Robert Waldman states that six weeks of very high opioid use would provoke a dependence for anyone. Dr. Robert Waldman states May 5, 200 mg demerol, 1 mg midazolam, then 100 mg demerol 1 mg midazolam. May 6, total 300 mg demerol in two separate doses, 2 mg midazolam in two separate doses. Dr. Robert Waldman states that there are not any notes in the medical records from Dr. Klein, because there are no signatures or initials from Klein. Dr. Robert Waldman states that total demerol given to Michael Jackson in three days (May 4,5,6) is 900 mg. Dr. Robert Waldman states that opioid withdrawal entails anxiety, restlessness, insomnia. Dr. Robert Waldman states insomnia is very common, nearly universal with opioid withdrawal. Dr. Robert Waldman states that the simplest way to end withdrawal from demerol would be to provide benzodiazepines.

Walgren Cross

Dr. Robert Waldman states that it is possible to be addicted to benzodiazepines, including Lorazepam. Dr. Robert Waldman states that he did not review Conrad Murray's statement as to what happened the night before and the morning of Michael Jackson's death. Dr. Robert Waldman states that he was unaware that Murray was shipping Lorazepam and midazolam to his girlfriend's apartment, but he was aware that Murray was giving them to Michael Jackson. Dr. Robert Waldman states that the shipping of benzodiazepines was not pertinent. Dr. Robert Waldman states that opioid and benzodiazpine withdrawal do not have the same symptoms. Dr. Robert Waldman states that he based his opinion that Michael Jackson was physically dependent on demerol on the medical record from Klein, but would be highly suspicious of diagnosing Michael Jackson as an addict based on the same record. Dr. Robert Waldman states that he is not board certified in drug addiction. Dr. Robert Waldman states that he is involved in dialysis professionally. Dr. Robert Waldman states that this involves a process by which a machine provides kidney function for those patients whose kidneys do not function properly. Dr. Robert Waldman states that he requests a urinalysis for patients who he feels have been lying to him, but not for every patient. Dr. Robert Waldman states that he works in his office and a number of facilities that are confidential. Dr. Robert Waldman states that he works at Visions Treatment Facility, Clearview Treatment Facility, Authentic Recovery Center, Cliffside Malibu and his office. Dr. Robert Waldman states that he is a consultant and he sees patients at all the above facilities, and also does dialysis but cannot pinpoint how many hours he works a week. Dr. Robert Waldman states he has determined that some of his patients have not received adequate care prior to treating those patients. Dr. Robert Waldman states that the easy part of his job is getting patients off the drugs, the hard part is keeping them off the drugs. Dr. Robert Waldman states that the Botox/Restylne injections from Dr. Klein were given in the cheekbones, chin and facial tissue. Dr. Robert Waldman states he has not used demerol in his practice for two decades, as there are much better and safer drugs to use. Dr. Robert Waldman states that with demerol, withdrawal symptoms would appear within a day. Dr. Robert Waldman states that there are significant lapses of demerol shots in June, 2009. Dr. Robert Waldman states that most common withdrawal symptoms of benzodiazepine: anxiety, insomnia, crawly skin. Dr. Robert Waldman states that he would agree with the CA State Medical Board's requirement that controlled substances should be in a locked cabinet, to prevent theft. Dr. Robert Waldman also agree with CA State Medical Board's requirement that medical records are kept by all physicians. Dr. Robert Waldman states that doctors and patients decide what kind of medical care that is best for the patient.

Chernoff Redirect

Dr. Robert Waldman states that he read the testimony of both Faheem Muhammad and Michael Amir Williams.

Dr. Robert Waldman states that although there are blocks of time that Michael Jackson did not receive demerol, it was concerning.

Walgren Recross

Dr. Robert Waldman states that a chart he created was made only for his own use representing Michael Jackson's doctor visits with Dr. Klein. Walgren and Dr. Robert Waldman go back and forth over what each area represents. Dr. Robert Waldman admits that he has made mistakes in the chart, including April 20, 2009. On April 20, Michael Jackson was not seen by Klein, but Dr. Robert Waldman entered data into his chart that reflect that date. Dr. Robert Waldman states that the chart does not reflect a June 4 entry, in which Michael Jackson did receive injections from Klein. Dr. Robert Waldman states that he was not personally aware that Conrad Murray was Michael Jackson's personal doctor during April, May and June of 2009. Dr. Robert Waldman states that he was aware that Conrad Murray was Michael Jackson's personal doctor through the media when Michael Jackson died.

Chernoff Re-redirect

Dr. Robert Waldman states that he reviewed a summary from Chernoff of Michael Jackson's medical records and the medical records themselves of Dr. Klein's. Dr. Robert Waldman states that the medical records were very difficult to read and therefore, there were charts made for Dr. Robert Waldman 's personal use.

Dr. Paul White Testimony

Flanagan Direct

Dr. Paul White is an anesthesiologist that's currently retired. He's still consulting and involved in research projects. Dr. Paul White lists his education, his board certification, his articles, books, his awards and research.

Flanagan asks about Dr. Steven Shafer and the research they did together.

Flanagan called Dr. Paul White in January 2011. Dr. Paul White heard about Conrad Murray and didn't want to be a part of this case about the death of an icon and he says he doesn't like the public attention. After his wife's encouragement Dr. Paul White agrees to review the docs.

Flanagan asks and Dr. Paul White agrees that he cannot justify the elephant in the room that Conrad Murray infused Propofol to Michael Jackson and abandoned him.

Dr. Paul White says his initial report was based on Conrad Murray's police interview and autopsy report with 13 expert opinions. Dr. Paul White was surprised and says if Conrad Murray did what he says in his interview Michael Jackson wouldn't have died. Dr. Paul White asked to meet with Conrad Murray. Flanagan tries to ask if he met Conrad Murray but sustained. Dr. Paul White flies to Los Angeles to meet with Flanagan and Chernoff and was given the transcripts of the preliminary hearing. Dr. Paul White wrote a letter that had his conclusions but he currently doesn't think the same way. In his letter he wrote oral consumption as a speculation based on other expert's testimony and says that he was not aware of the studies about oral bioavailability. Dr. Paul White says he learned about them from Dr. Steven Shafer's report. Flanagan asks about the Chilean study. Dr. Paul White says he felt bad that Dr. Steven Shafer himself drank Propofol. Dr. Paul White mentions his concerns with that study there was no blind test and one subject had similar levels to Michael Jackson. He had done a study on beagles and agrees that there was no absorption by the stomach. Dr. Paul White and Dr. Steven Shafer think that one subject might have absorption through the mouth esophagus and they thought of doing a Propofol lollipop to sedate patients non-invasively.

Dr. Paul White mentions the variations in blood levels from the same dose and he says its 5 fold. For example from the same dose of Propofol, you could get a blood level from 1mg/ ml to 5 mg/ml.

They show some examples from articles that show patients with different blood levels.

Dr. Paul White says most centrally active drugs have the same variability in the blood levels such as Lorazepam. Again example articles and graphs are shown to demonstrate variability in the levels.

Dr. Paul White mentions Propofol as sedative hypnotic. Low doses cause sleepiness, reduces anxiety. Medium dose means deeper sedation and higher dose means that patient is not responsive to pain and anesthesia. Benzos have the same variability.

Flanagan asks about off label use. Sleep in a ICU is on label and sleep at home is off label. Flanagan asks about the Chinese study about Propofol and insomnia. Dr. Paul White says that he found the study interesting and the authors should be given a chance. He says he understands Dr. Steven Shafer's concerns but those could be corrected with a review. Flanagan asks if Dr. Paul White has read the toxicology report for Michael Jackson. Dr. Paul White says he has. Flanagan asks about polypharmacy. Dr. Paul White explains that it's combining drugs. It's reducing the side effects by combining lower doses of drugs. Dr. Paul White gives the example of pain management and mixing opiates and non opiates to reduce opiates side effects. Dr. Paul White says that it's common in their area and that midazolam + Propofol is a standard technique. Flanagan shows a graph done by Dr. Steven Shafer that shows 2 doses of 2 mg Lorazepam given at 2AM and 5AM. The graph has 2 lines of responsive and non responsive to pain levels. Dr. Paul White says Lorazepam is not an analgesic, doesn't understand these line.

Flanagan tries to find the graph for midazolam but he can't. Court ends 15-20 minutes early.

Murray Trial Summaries Day 20 /October 28- 2011

Dr. Paul White Testimony continued

Flanagan Direct

They still discuss the variability between people. Propofol's effect site is the brain and the amounts in the brain are not measurable in living humans so they use alternative measures such as EEG.

Flanagan shows several papers and graphs that show that levels and effects in patients vary a lot. Dr. Paul White explain why models are not representing each and every patient and models are just an average. Flanagan switches to Dr. Dr. Steven Shafer's graph for Lorazepam (2 doses of 2 mg). Dr. Paul White says this is accurate for an average patient but not for Michael Jackson. Dr. Paul White says if Michael Jackson was taking oral Lorazepam, you would expect to see residual levels of Lorazepam from previous days. Walgren objects to the use of word "oral". Dr. Paul White says as Conrad Murray said he treated Michael Jackson with Midazolam and Lorazepam, he would expect to find residual levels but Dr. Paul White doesn't know how much Michael Jackson was given to make this determination. Flanagan shows Dr. Steven Shafer's graph for Midazolam (2 doses of 2 mg given at 3AM and 7:30AM). Actual blood concentration for midazolam in autopsy report was close to Dr. Steven Shafer's model. Flanagan shows graphs done by Dr. Steven Shafer that combines Midazolam and Lorazepam, another graph that shows 25mg Propofol given over 3 to 5 minutes and another graph combining all (25mg Propofol, 2 doses of 2 mg Lorazepam and 2 doses of 2 mg Midazolam).This combination doesn't show a dangerous situation. Flanagan and Dr. Paul White goes over a study and based on that Dr. Paul White says that 25mg of Propofol would provide minimal sedation and help with anxiety relief and bring a little sleepiness. Dr. Paul White says that Conrad Murray gave minimal sedation. Flanagan asks what is moderate / mac/ conscious/ procedural sedation. Dr. Paul White says there's verbal response, airway is unaffected and cardiovascular functions will be okay. Dr. Paul White says hospitals require doctors that use conscious sedation be trained so that if they mistakenly sedate the patient in a deep sedation they can rescue the patient. Flanagan shows that Conrad Murray has a certification from Sunrise Hospital in Las Vegas for moderate sedation. That allows Conrad Murray to evaluate the patient, administer sedation, manage a compromised airway, provide adequate ventilation in case of apnea, rescue a patient from deeper sedation, and monitor the patient to evaluate sedation. Flanagan shows Dr. Steven Shafer's graph for 40mg Lorazepam. Initially the doses started around 12:00AM but later Dr. Steven Shafer corrected the time. Dr. Paul White says the average patient would be dead at the very least comatose for several hours, receiving 40mg over 5 hours. Dr. Steven Shafer did that simulation because of the 10ml vial found at the house. For Dr. Steven Shafer's modified simulation (9 doses of 4 mg each starting at 1:30AM), Dr. Paul White says it doesn't fit with the vial found in the house. Also last doses would have been given when he was still asleep. Flanagan shows the graph with 40 mg Lorazepam with 2 doses of midazolam and Lorazepam. Dr. Paul White ays that it doesn't make sense when Michael Jackson was highly sedated with Lorazepam, Midazolam would be given to him. Flanagan shows a computer simulation: 2 doses of 2 mg Lorazepam (2AM and 5AM) and an oral dose of 20 mg (10 pills taken at the same time) at 7AM. This graph assumes there was no residual Lorazepam from previous days. Flanagan shows another graph. It's the same but assumes a residual level for 10mg for last 5 days. It would achieve the same result with 16 mg oral Lorazepam (8 pills) taken at 7AM. Flanagan says the amount of Lorazepam in Michael Jackson's stomach was very low. Dr. Paul White says the pill will dissolve in 15 minutes and the absorption halftime is 22 minutes. Dr. Paul White says that it's normal that there was a little Lorazepam found in his stomach. Dr. Paul White says that his Lorazepam simulations are more reasonable and that 40 mg simulation of Dr. Steven Shafer is irrational. Dr. Paul White says the simulation with residual level is more realistic.

Dr. Paul White says that maybe Michael Jackson didn't take 8 pills at once. Maybe he took a few at one time and then later took some more such as at 6 AM and 8 AM. Dr. Paul White says it's a speculation but it's more reasonable than 4mg boluses every 30 minutes Dr. Paul White explains the small amount of Lorazepam in the stomach by absorption half-life. Flanagan mentions another article and asks finding equivalent of 1/300th of a pill in stomach is consistent with Dr. Paul White's simulation. Dr. Paul White says you would not expect to find free Lorazepam in the stomach if it was given via IV.

Dr. Paul White says that as there was free Lorazepam in the stomach it has to be oral consumption. Dr. Paul White goes over Dr. Steven Shafer's simulations. Dr. Paul White says Dr. Steven Shafer's simulations have Propofol injections in 30 seconds to 60 seconds and say that it's inconsistent with Conrad Murray's interview. Dr. Paul White says Dr. Steven Shafer's simulation of 100mg bolus is inconsistent with lidocaine. Dr. Paul White says such injection would burn tremendously in small veins. Dr. Paul White says multiple injections of 50mg is inconsistent with lidocaine levels found at autopsy. Dr. Paul White says it would be difficult for Michael Jackson to draw Propofol himself 6 times and the defense never claimed that. Dr. Paul White says 25mg scenario is less absurd as its minimal sedation. Flanagan asks if a person could be awake to do a 25mg injection over 30 seconds and Dr. Paul White answers yes. Dr. Paul White adds that the blood concentration depends on how fast the injection is done. Slow injection would have less effect on the heart and respiratory system. Flanagan shows a graph with Lorazepam and Midazolam and a rapif 25mg bolus Propofol. Dr. Paul White says if a fast bolus was put on the Lorazepam levels, the combination could be lethal. Dr. Paul White says Dr. Steven Shafer's 100ml infusion (IV) was inconsistent with Conrad Murray's interview. Dr. Paul White says that an IV system was needed and the handle of Propofol was not used. Dr. Paul White says bottle in the bag would be too low and it would be dangerous. Also Dr. Paul White says if the patient moves or someone touches the tube the bottle could fall. Dr. Paul White says he can't think of a reason to not use the handle and go to the hassle of cutting the bag with a knife. Dr. Paul White says before the infusion pumps the practice was to empty the Propofol bottle into the saline bag. If you do that when the bag is empty you would see the Propofol residue on the bag and the chamber. There was no Propofol in the bag or in the long tube. Dr. Paul White says there's no evidence that there was an IV and says that he think there was no infusion. Dr. Paul White again mentions Dr. Steven Shafer's simulation of 100ml IV. He says it's an incredible coincidence that the patient dies when the bottle runs out. Dr. Paul White also says that Propofol in the urine doesn't support the 100ml IV over 3 hours. Dr. Paul White says according to urine levels the most consistent scenario is a self injection of 25mg Propofol between 11:30AM and 12:00PM. Dr. Paul White says that Dr. Steven Shafer 's scenarios don't reconcile with Conrad Murray 's statement, evidence at the scene, urine concentration. Dr. Paul White says his scenario with self injection fits fit everything.

Court ends early. Media reports that Prosecutor Walgren asked for time to get ready for cross.

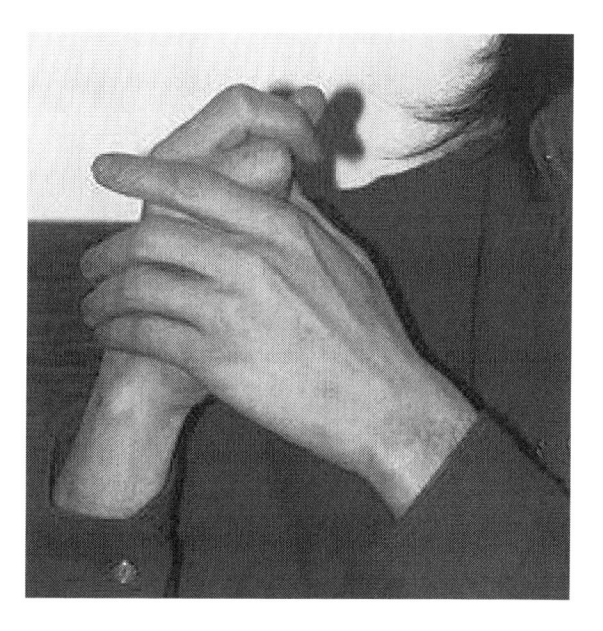

Murray Trial Summaries Day 21/ October 31- 2011

Dr. Paul White Testimony continued

Walgren cross

Dr. Paul White is retired after 30 years of clinical care, teaching and research. Dr. Paul White says he's an expert in the use of Propofol, not expert in pharmacokinetics and dynamics modeling. He asks other people to do that such as Dr. Steven Shafer.

Walgren asks if there were instances Dr. Murray deviated from standards of care on June 25th and the preceding 2 months. Dr. Paul White agrees. Walgren asks what did Dr. Paul White understood from Conrad Murray's police interview. Dr. Paul White says he understood Conrad Murray gave 25mg to 50 mg Propofol with 5 CC of lidocaine. Based on interview, could not say how Conrad Murray administered the drip. Dr. Paul White says there could be a number of possibilities about the drip and multiple IV tubes as described by Dr. Steven Shafer is one of the possibilities. Dr. Paul White agrees and says that giving Propofol without proper monitoring could be dangerous and could result in cardio-respiratory depression. Dr. Paul White says at the minimum he would want to have an ambu bag. Walgren asks Dr. Paul White if he has given Propofol in a bedroom. Dr. Paul White says he has never heard of it. Dr. Paul White says that he knows Propofol being given in medical offices and clinics. Walgren asks about the suctioning equipment. Dr. Paul White says it's desirable to have it but vomiting is fairly rare. Dr. Paul White says pulse oximeter is essential and blood pressure cuff is important. Dr. Paul White says for an infusion you measure blood pressure every 5 minutes and for minimal sedation you measure it every 5 minutes. Capnography is not utilized everywhere, Dr. Paul White finds it useful but not very precise. Walgren asks if failing to maintain medical records is egregious deviation from standard of care. Dr. Paul White says charts are needed but in this case it didn't contribute to death. Dr. Paul White also classifies it as minor to moderate deviation from standard of cares. Walgren asks about pre procedural assessment. It's when the patients overall condition is evaluated to see if there are any factors that can increase cardio respiratory depression. Respiratory depression from Propofol is mentioned to be rare and generally happens when narcotics are present. Walgren asks how much Dr. Paul White has been paid by the defense. Dr. Paul White says that he was paid $11,000 so far. Dr. Paul White says he also charges $3,500 a day for court appearances but he didn't ask that because defense doesn't have the resources. Walgren asks if Dr. Paul White ever had a patient that stopped breathing after Propofol. Dr. Paul White says he did (after general anesthesia) and he assited them with an ambu bag and mask or other ventilation techniques such as endotracheal intubation or laryngeal mask. Walgren mentions doctor's oath of "do no harm" and asks if Conrad Murray violated this by giving Propofol. Dr. Paul White says Conrad Murray did not harm. Walgren asks who makes the final decision – the doctor or the patient. Dr. Paul White says both share the responsibility but the doctor have the option to walk away. Dr. Paul White says he would never administer something he considers inappropriate, he would walk away. Walgren asks if it is easy to go from a level of sedation to the other. Dr. Paul White agrees that the monitoring is required but 25 mg dose is a very minimal dose that would wear off after 15 minutes. He says monitoring a patient for that dose for around 15-30 minutes would be enough and then it's okay to leave the patient. Walgren asks about pulse oximeter without an alarm. Dr. Paul White says it has no value when you are out of the room. Dr. Paul White also states that 25 mg Propofol wouldn't have effects after 25-30 minutes. Walgren asks if benzodiazepines would have an effect. Dr. Paul White says if they have been given hours before they would have little effect. Dr. Paul White tries to justify Conrad Murray's treatment saying that this was an unusual case with the goal being sleep and what Conrad Murray leaving Michael Jackson was acceptable.

Walgren asks what if the patient liked to push Propofol. Dr. Paul White says he would not left the room.

Dr. Paul White asks about failure to call 911. Dr. Paul White says he cannot justify it but also adds the situation was different, Conrad Murray didn't know the address and the house was not easily accessible. Walgren pushes Dr. Paul White. Dr. Paul White says Conrad Murray should have called 911 sooner but it wouldn't have made a difference in this case. Dr. Paul White says he would have started resuscitation and call 911 within 3 to 5 minutes. Dr. Paul White say he doesn't think everything Conrad Murray said to the police is true. Dr. Paul White says in emergency situations it's hard to remember the details and Conrad Murray could have overlooked to mention Propofol and didn't do it in a devious way. Walgren suggests that the other alternative is that Conrad Murray lied. Dr. Paul White reluctantly agrees. Walgren does over the letter Dr. Paul White gave to the defense. In the letter it's written that sedatives, analgesic and benzos may increase the risk of Propofol. Dr. Paul White says high concentration of Lorazepam and 25mg Propofol given too fast causes arrhythmia, and a rapid demise. Dr. Paul White mentions although Conrad Murray bought Propofol Michael Jackson had his own stocks of Propofol. Walgren asks where he saw this information. Dr. Paul White says Conrad Murray told that to Dr. Paul White. Walgren shows the IV tubing found in the scene and asks if it is easily concealable and fits in the hand or in the pocket. Dr. Paul White admits to that. Walgren mentions how Dr. Paul White speculated that Michael Jackson drank Propofol and now Dr. Paul White rejects that's the cause of death. Dr. Paul White says Dr. Dr. Steven Shafer explained why there could be Propofol in the stomach and why it would not cause death. Dr. Paul White says he did his 3 page letter in a very short time as Flanagan needed something from him. Dr. Paul White says he did not write any other report. In the letter Dr. Paul White wrote Michael Jackson self administered either by injecting or orally. Flanagan had mentioned oral Propofol before he wrote the letter and Dr. Paul White says he did a search but did not find anything about it. Walgren asks if according to Dr. Paul White the only option was to blame the victim. Dr. Paul White says if Conrad Murray only given what he said he did, there was to be something else. Walgren asks if Dr. Paul White now blames Michael Jackson for Lorazepam as well. Dr. Paul White says yes. Walgren asks if Dr. Paul White took everything Conrad Murray said to be the truth. Dr. Paul White says yes. Dr. Paul White says what Conrad Murray said in regards to drug administration is consistent with the autopsy report. Walgren goes over the report and point outs that Dr. Paul White now says Michael Jackson died of a rapid bolus but he never wrote that in his report / letter. Walgren asks if he came up with any other theory that does not attribute the drug taking to Michael Jackson. Dr. Paul White says no.

Walgren asks who Dr. Gabriella Onellis is. Dr. Paul White says she's a PhD in biomedical engineering. Dr. Paul White met her for the first time last week and asked is she could calculate the amount of free Propofol you would expect to see in the urine after a 3 hour 100mk infusion.

Walgren mentions that Dr. Dr. Steven Shafer provided software for the models to the defense and Dr. Paul White only provided computer codes on paper. Walgren goes over the 10 AM Lorazepam theory. As the peak effect will be in 2 hours it first nicely with 12 AM. Last week when Dr. Steven Shafer testified that Lorazepam had to be taken at least 4 hour prior to death that's when Dr. Paul White met with Onellis. She created several scenarios. Dr. Paul White says he was not aware of the 10 AM Lorazepam theory. Walgren asks if Michael Jackson came and asked him to work for him to give Propofol, if he would accepted the job. Dr. Paul White says absolutely not. He says no amount of money could convince him to do it because of time required, the responsibility and off label use of Propofol. Walgren asks if Dr. Paul White's 11:40AM self administration theory is based on a lot of assumptions for the lack of medical records.

Dr. Paul White agrees. Walgren asks if for his theory he used Conrad Murray leaving the room for 2 minutes. Dr. Paul White says no.

Walgren asks about the beagle Propofol study. Dr. Paul White says that Flanagan knew a veterinarian that could do the study and he had no part in it. Dr. Paul White says he only got a report from Flanagan that oral Propofol had no effect on beagles.

Walgren asks when Dr. Paul White assumes that Michael Jackson took Lorazepam was Conrad Murray out of the room as well. Dr. Paul White says Michael Jackson was walking around. Walgren objects as Dr. Paul White is telling what Conrad Murray told him. Dr. Paul White says he understood that Conrad Murray was in the another part of the room (adjacent bedroom etc) or not watching. Dr. Paul White says Conrad Murray wasn't aware that Michael Jackson took Lorazepam.

Walgren asks Dr. Paul White if he's aware that Conrad Murray left the room only once. Dr. Paul White says yes. He also says that he believes Conrad Murray was away around 7 AM. Dr. Dr. Paul White says when Conrad Murray was on the phone he was presumably away from Michael Jackson because he was sleeping.

Dr. Paul White's theory is that Conrad Murray drew 50 mg Propofol and lidocaine and gave half of it to Michael Jackson and left the half full syringe. Dr. Paul White then says Conrad Murray was in the corridor, Walgren objects as he is once again telling what Conrad Murray told Dr. Paul White. Dr. Paul White thinks after Conrad Murray gave Michael Jackson the half the syringe and observed him left him to talk on the phone and went to the bathroom. Dr. Paul White thinks Michael Jackson could have injected in that 40 minutes.

Walgren asks if Michael Jackson injected through the IV port and the syringe was originally on the chair. Walgren asks if wouldn't it raise an alarm when Conrad Murray found the syringe in the injection port. Walgren also asks if according to his theory Michael Jackson fell back to bed in the same position.

Walgren asks if it's Dr. Paul White's understanding that Michael Jackson moved around the house wheeling an IV stand with a condom catheter on him and a urine bag attached to his leg. Walgren asks if isn't it a possibility that Conrad Murray injected the additional Propofol. Dr. Paul White answers yes if he wanted to harm Michael Jackson. Walgren asks if putting Michael Jackson to sleep was mild/minimal sedation which means response to verbal stimuli. Walgren asks if it makes sense to him. Dr. Paul White says providing sleep doesn't need a higher level of sedation. Dr. Paul White says he believes that Michael Jackson didn't receive Propofol on the 23rd and 24th based on the urine levels.

Dr. Paul White says during the 6 weeks prior Conrad Murray gave Michael Jackson 1 or 2 boluses of Propofol (25 to 50 mg) and followed it with an infusion that the Propofol bottle was emptied into an IV bag. Walgren again objects as Dr. Paul White is once again telling what Conrad Murray told him. Dr. Paul White speculates that it was minimal to moderate sedation. Walgren cites several articles written by Dr. Paul White. One article says that MAC (moderate sedation) requires the same level of standard of care as general anesthesia.

Guidelines for Office based anesthesia (written by Dr. Paul White) :

1-appropriately trained personnel

2-anesthesia equipment

3-complete documentation of care provided

4-monitoring equipment

5-recovery area with appropriate staff

6-availability of emergency equipment

7-plan for emergency transport of patients to a site that provides more comprehensive care, should a complication occur

8-documention on a quality assurance program

9- continuous training of physician

10- safety standards that can't be jeopardized for patients' comfort or cost

Walgren asks if these standards should apply if Propofol is administered in a bedroom ? Dr. Paul White says that he wouldn't give it in a bedroom and Dr. Paul White eventually agrees that giving Propofol in a home requires the minimum requirements of office based anesthesia.

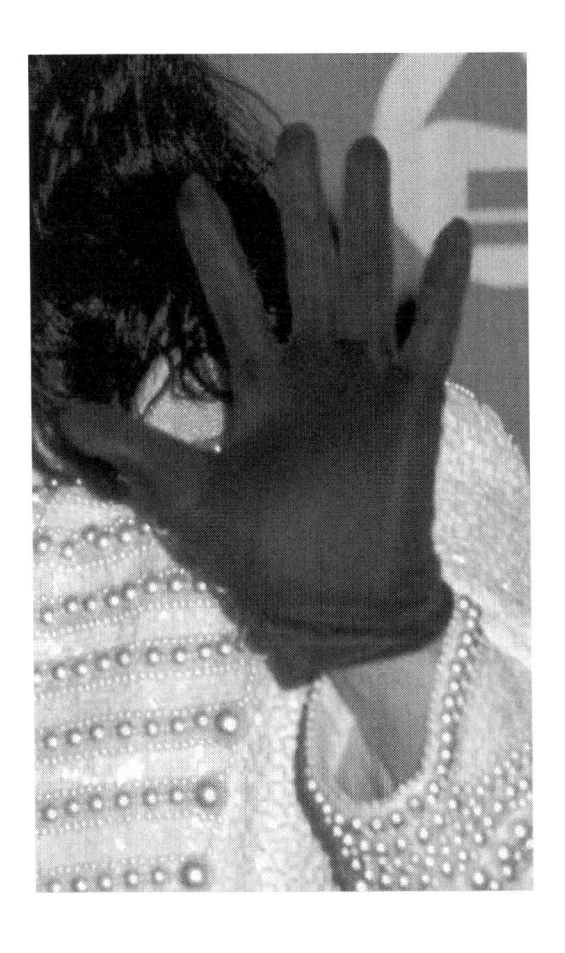

Murray Trial Summaries Day 22/ November 1- 2011

Dr. Paul White Testimony continued

Flanagan redirect

Flanagan again mentions the variability in the models. Flanagan shows the Lorazepam model that includes 16 mg oral consumption which is based on 0.0013 mg in the stomach content. If you move the oral intake to 8 AM, the amount of free Lorazepam in the stomach would equal to the 0.008mg found in the autopsy and the concentrations find in blood. Flanagan goes over the 0.3 free Propofol in the urine. In a model about 100 ml Propofol infusion over 3 hours the level of Propofol would range from 1 to 3 mg in urine. 1 mg is the 10 times the amount found at autopsy. Flanagan mentions the burn feeling of Propofol will be increased by small veins, the concentration of the drug and the speed of the injection. Lidocaine is given before the infusion, or at the beginning. Dr. Paul White says given the half life of lidocaine and with a 3 hours infusion there shouldn't be lidocaine found at autopsy, and there was 0.84 mg/ml at autopsy. Dr. Paul White says if there were 2 injections, Lidocaine would have been given twice and Dr. Paul White would expect the lidocaine to be around the levels found at autopsy. Flanagan mentions standard of care versus standard of practice. Dr. Paul White says standard of care is the ideal that they would seek for every patient but it's not always possible. Flanagan goes over minimal sedation. There would be normal response to verbal simulation. Flanagan asks if he took an ambient if Dr. Paul White would be able to wake up by talking to him. They discuss 25 mg Propofol. Dr. Paul White sys it would reduce anxiety and generally would not produce sleep. Dr. Paul White says it could create a restful state if the patient is very tired. Dr. Paul White also says that any noise in the room would wake the patient up. Dr. Paul White says with minimal sedation airway, breathing and cardiovascular functions will not be affected. Flanagan's redirect of Dr. Paul White is over. Walgren does not recross.

Off camera judge asks Dr. Murray if he will testify. Murray says that he won't testify. Judge gives a 30 minute break so that the prosecution can decide whether they would do a rebuttal.

After the break Walgren calls Dr. Steven Shafer for rebuttal.

Dr. Steven Shafer Rebuttal Testimony

Walgren direct

Walgren asks if Lorazepam is given IV would some of it go to the stomach. Dr. Steven Shafer says yes and it has nothing to do with post mortem distribution. Walgren asks and Dr. Steven Shafer agrees that there's no way to differentiate between Michael Jackson taking oral Lorazepam and Conrad Murray giving Michael Jackson oral Lorazepam. Walgren brings up Dr. Steven Shafer's 100 ml Propofol infusion over 3 hours. Dr. Steven Shafer says it doesn't show when Michael Jackson died and it was not necessarily at 12:00PM. Dr. Steven Shafer says it was basically to show that Michael Jackson died with infusion running. Walgren asks about the IV setup. Dr. Steven Shafer says controlling the rate with the clamps are commonly done with some medication that you don't need to precisely set the rate but a pump is required for Propofol. Dr. Steven Shafer says the Lidocaine levels found at autopsy is not inconsistent with 100 ml infusion over 3 hour simulation. Dr. Steven Shafer says Lidocaine could have been mixed into the Propofol bottle. Walgren asks about the main risk of Propofol and Dr. Steven Shafer says its failure to breath and the lack of oxygen in the heart kills the heart. Walgren brings up the article the defense used in their simulation about the unchanged Propofol in the urine. Dr. Steven Shafer says he researched the literature. 1988 article that the defense used says they found very little (0 to 0.3) unchanged Propofol in the urine but they didn't know if it was free Propofol or its metabolite.

Dr. Steven Shafer says there are newer articles on the subject. The most detailed one is a 2002 article. 2002 article measured the actual unchanged Propofol and the level was between 0.002% to 0.004%.

Autopsy urine Propofol was 0.15 mg/ml . 500 ml of the urine = 82.50 micrograms of Propofol .

Walgren shows a table from the 2002 article. The average Propofol found is 70.71 micrograms of Propofol in the urine; it corresponds to a dose of 2000 mg. Dr. Steven Shafer says this absolutely rules out Dr Dr. Paul White 's theory and it actually suggests that Michael Jackson received more Propofol that what even Dr. Steven Shafer thought. Walgren asks about standard of care such as for an anesthesiologist providing care in a remote location (ex: radiology suite, etc..), . Dr. Steven Shafer says you have less tolerance for error, because you have no back up. You should not take short cuts. Dr. Steven Shafer says if there was such a thing as bedroom based anesthesia, if you have an error, you have mortality. So the standards of care would actually be higher.

Flanagan cross

Flanagan argues with Dr. Steven Shafer about what he wrote in his report about lidocaine. Dr.Steven Shaferthinks Flanagan misunderstood what he wrote. Flanagan asks Dr. Steven Shafer to read a paragraph from his report.

Flanagan goes over the 2002 article and if the 25 mg Propofol dose was a sub anesthetic dose. Dr. Steven Shafer says in most patients it's a sub anesthetic dose and it depends on what other medication is on board. Flanagan is trying to say that the article didn't mention sub anesthetic doses.

Walgren redirect

Walgren tries to clear the issue about the article and the use of sub anesthetic dose, Dr. Steven Shafer says the use of a larger doses makes the result more precise, that's all.

Both sides work on a stipulation. Stipulation 52a says that Peoples 52 reflects the accurate phone numbers. Both prosecution and the defense rest their cases. Judge informs the jurors that both sides asked for a day to prepare for their closing statements. Judge excuses the jurors. In a not televised afternoon session judge and the both sides work on jury instructions. There will be no court on Wednesday November the 2nd. Closing statements and jury instructions are set for

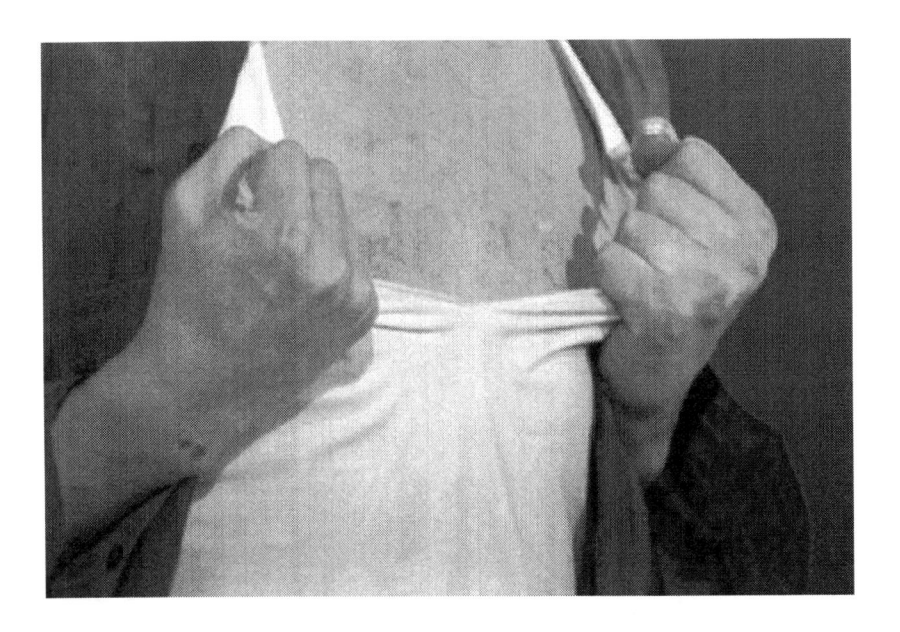

Conrad Murray guilty in Michael Jackson's death

Tuesday, 08 November 2011

Conrad Murray was convicted Monday of involuntary manslaughter in the drug-overdose death of singer

As he did throughout the trial, Jackson's personal physician showed no emotion as the verdict was read. His mother also had no visible reaction. Someone in the Jackson family row of seats shrieked.

Murray's lawyers asked for him to remain free on bail until he is sentenced Nov. 29, but Superior Court Judge Michael Pastor said no. Noting that Murray was convicted of a homicide, Pastor said his "reckless" behavior in Jackson's death showed a "significant and demonstrable" risk to the public.

Murray was handcuffed and led out a side door.

Michael Jackson rehearses for his 'This is It' tour on June 23, 2009, at the Staples Center in Los Angeles.

Leaving the courtroom, Jackson's mother, Katherine Jackson, kissed one of the prosecutors, Deborah Brazil. His sister La Toya and brother Jermaine hugged her and prosecutor David Walgren.

Michael Jackson supporters react outside the courthouse as Conrad Murray's guilty verdict is announced.

Katherine Jackson said later, "I feel better now."

La Toya Jackson said she was overjoyed.

"Michael was looking over us," she said.

Outside the courthouse, jubilant Jackson fans cheered and sang Beat It as they held signs that read "guilty" and "killer." Passing motorists honked their horns.

In Las Vegas, Donna DiGiacomo, a friend and former patient of Murray, sobbed and said she thought the jury was under "overwhelming pressure to convict."

"This man didn't deserve this," said DiGiacomo, 53, a former teacher's aide. who said she didn't believe Murray did anything to intentionally harm Jackson. "They needed a scapegoat."

The conviction means Murray will automatically have his California medical license suspended, Los Angeles County District Attorney Steve Cooley said at a news conference after the brief court session. He said he hoped the other states where Murray is licensed to practice medicine — Nevada, Texas and Hawaii — would do the same.

Pastor handed the case to the seven-man, five-woman jury Thursday after closing arguments by Walgren and lead defense lawyer Ed Chernoff. Over nearly six weeks of testimony, jurors heard from 33 prosecution witnesses and 16 defense witnesses. More than 340 exhibits were available in the jury room as the panel mulled a verdict.

Jackson, 50, died on June 25, 2009, of an overdose of the surgical anesthetic Propofol, aggravated by effects of the sedative Lorazepam. Murray, 58, was charged with a single count of involuntary manslaughter. He pleaded not guilty.

Walgren said Murray caused Jackson's death through acts of "criminal negligence" in using a hospital-grade drug for insomnia in Jackson's home without proper monitoring and resuscitation equipment. Murray also acted negligently in delaying 20 minutes before calling 911, attempting CPR incompetently and failing to tell rescue personnel he had used Propofol, Walgren said.

A negligent failure to act can be involuntary manslaughter under California law. Walgren adopted this theory, too, saying Murray had failed to fulfill a doctor's legal duty to care for a patient.

Murray's attorneys said Jackson, not Murray, administered the fatal overdose in an upstairs bedroom of his rented mansion in Murray's absence. If that was the case, Walgren argued, it was criminally negligent of Murray to be absent from the bedside — while using the bathroom or "distracted" by phone calls and e-mails — when he was supposed to be monitoring Jackson's sedation.

"No one has sought to prove that Conrad Murray sought to kill Michael Jackson," Walgren said. But Murray "acted so recklessly with the life of Michael Jackson in his hands that it amounts to indifference to the very life of Michael Jackson," he said.

At the time he died, Jackson was in final rehearsals for This Is It, a series of 50 comeback concerts to begin in London a month later. Murray, a cardiologist with practices in Las Vegas and Houston, had treated the entertainer and his three children for various ailments in Las Vegas from 2006 to 2008. Jackson, who had complained of insomnia for years, hired Murray in April 2009 on a $150,000-a-month contract to care for him exclusively through the rehearsals and shows.

Murray told police two days after Jackson died that, over the course of two months, he had given the singer Propofol intravenously to put him to sleep. Jackson told Murray and other health care providers that only Propofol worked to bring him sleep quickly, trial evidence showed. Despite Jackson's pleas for Propofol on the morning he died, Murray told police, he gave only half the usual dose — a single "push" of 25 milligrams over three to five minutes — because he was trying to "wean him off" the drug.

Prosecutors heaped doubt on Murray's story. Dr. Steven Shafer, an anesthesiologist and Propofol expert testifying for the state, said computer modeling based on Propofol concentrations in Jackson's blood at autopsy proved that Murray must have given 1,000 milligrams of Propofol — 40 times more than he told police — through a three-hour IV drip that continued running even as Jackson died.

Walgren argued that Jackson died in an "obscene experiment" by Murray, who the prosecutor said was using an unprecedented and "bizarre" mode of treatment.

More than eight days of the trial were consumed by a battle over science between Dr. Steven Shafer and Dr. Paul White of Dallas, a retired anesthesiologist noted for early studies of Propofol. Dr. Paul White, testifying for the defense, said there was no IV drip. Citing a 1988 Propofol study, he said a drip would have produced much higher Propofol levels than the coroner found in Jackson's urine.

The prosecution countered Dr. Paul White with a 2002 study that Dr. Steven Shafer said proved that Jackson's urine concentration of Propofol was consistent with a drip.

Paramedics could have been on the scene in four minutes, possibly reviving Jackson after he stopped breathing, Walgren said. Witnesses said Murray didn't ask a security guard to call 911 until after he first tried CPR unsuccessfully, asked Jackson's chef to "get help, get security" and telephoned Jackson's personal assistant to ask him to come to the house.

"What on Earth would delay a medical doctor in making that call, other than to protect himself?" Walgren said.

Then, in neglecting to tell paramedics and emergency room doctors that he had administered Propofol, Murray showed consciousness of guilt, Walgren said. "That is Conrad Murray knowing full well what caused Michael Jackson's death," the prosecutor said.

Walgren strongly suggested that Murray had concealed crucial evidence — the IV tubing he had used for Propofol — in the big pockets of cargo pants he wore that day.

In a "corrupted" doctor-patient relationship with Jackson, Walgren said, Murray acted subserviently rather than as a doctor putting the patient's interests first. Acceding to Jackson's demands for nightly Propofol, Murray "is an employee saying yes to what he is asked, instead of saying yes to what is best for Michael Jackson's health — as any ethical, competent doctor would do," Walgren said.

Murray did not take the stand.

Walgren showed the jury a photo of Jackson's two sons, ages 14 and 8, and his 13-year-old daughter, and repeatedly focused on their loss of their father. "To them, this case doesn't end today or tomorrow or the next day," Walgren said. "For Michael's children, this case will go on forever because they do not have a father."

Walgren never used the title "doctor" for Murray, always calling him "Conrad Murray" neutralizing any respect in which people hold physicians. Chernoff always called his client "Dr. Murray."

Chernoff said in his closing argument that the prosecution was blaming Murray for what Jackson and others did. Murray "was just a little fish in a big, dirty pond," Chernoff said.

He put responsibility on the pop star and on the concert-tour promoters, whom he said were pressuring Jackson. Chernoff also blamed Jackson's dermatologist, who he said had given him Demerol.

In finding Murray guilty, the jury accepted the argument that at least one grossly negligent act, or failure to act, by Murray was a "substantial factor" in causing Jackson's death.

Jackson's parents, Joe and Katherine Jackson, and a delegation of his five brothers and three sisters attended the trial regularly. Jackson fans thronged the hallway outside the courtroom daily. After Walgren's closing argument, Jackson fans cheered loudly and shouted, "Thank you!"

Murray faces a sentence that ranges from probation to a maximum of four years in prison. He also faces possible loss of his medical licenses in California, Nevada, Texas and Hawaii.

The judge, not the jury, will decide Murray's sentence. A recent change in state law means Murray could serve his time, if any, in a Los Angeles County facility rather than a state penitentiary.

Ed Chernoff Closing arguments

- Walgren's argument is exactly why we have a jury trial in America.

- Walgren gave bits and pieces of statements from witnesses regarding Propofol, rather than the whole context.

- Defense team has never stated that Conrad Murray did not make mistakes. But this case is not a medical board hearing or a civil lawsuit. For a crime to be proven, the prosecution has to show that Conrad Murray actually killed Michael Jackson. Prosecution must show criminal negligence, but also the specific act was the cause of death, otherwise this is not a crime.

- What defense believes is that Murray found Michael Jackson in distress, at 12 pm. The very first thing Murray did was try to revive Michael Jackson. At 11:51 Sade Anding received a phone call from Murray. From Anding's testimony defense believes she listened for about 2 minutes before hanging up. From 11:18 am until 12 noon, Murray was on the phone. If Murray had found Michael Jackson anywhere between 11:18 am and noon, the same thing would have happened that Sade Anding reported when she was on the phone with him (Murray would have dropped the phone and tried to revive

Michael Jackson). Defense states that from 11:18 am to 12 noon, Murray never found Michael Jackson not breathing.

- The nature of Propofol, is a 10 minute drug. The only way to keep Propofol actually working after that is through an IV drip or IV injection. The prosecution spent 6 weeks trying to prove a drip theory, because the evidence proves that Murray injected Propofol into Michael Jackson's IV prior to him leaving the room. The prosecution wants the jury to convict Conrad Murray for Michael Jackson's actions.

-Alberto Alvarez stated that he has had a hard time finding steady employment since MJ died, and that he was offered $500,000 for his story. Alvarez stated when he first talked to police, all he claimed he did was call 911. But when Alvarez spoke to police in August 2009, he then stated he comforted the children, he hid evidence for Murray and he comforted the children. The story became monumentally more compelling and valuable. Chernoff asks the jury if they honestly believe that Alberto Alvarez, after this trial is over, is not going to cash in on MJ's death story?

-Alvarez stated that he grabbed MJ's legs, Murray got MJ's shoulders and they took him and placed him on the floor. Alvarez stated that Murray asked him to take the IV bag off the stand and that there was a milky substance in the bag, but when tested there was nothing in the bag. Chernoff reminds the jury that the EMT's stated that they found MJ on the floor not the bed.

-The problem with prosecution theory starts with Alvarez inconsistencies, but moves on to Elyssa Fleak, and that she never mentioned a bottle in a bag originally. In the notes that she didn't destroy, there is no mention of a Propofol bottle inside a cut IV bag, and there are no photos of it either. Fleak only mentions it 18 months later in testimony.

-Detective Smith, who Chernoff claims is a methodical, consummate professional, took notes of a smaller bottle of Lorazepam with an IV bag inside a bag fromt eh room where Michael Jackson died but did not remember seeing a vial of Propofol inside a cut IV bag. Chernoff says that the reason Smith never saw it is because it never existed.

-April, 2011: Alvarez is interviewed by LAPD, and draws a picture of the IV bag. Chernoff states that the tubing, the IV bag, insinuating that LAPD coached Alvarez into drawing a bag that was similar to the bags the LAPD had at the interview. Chernoff states that the prosecution's theory was solidified then.

-Chernoff questions Dr. Shafer's testimony: stating that the IV tubing was hung to prove the prosecution's theory that Murray used an IV drip. Chernoff states that the short tubing used for testimony is used for an IV drip, the short tubing that Murray claims he used would be for IV injection. Chernoff states that Shafer testified he was wrong the next day, even though Murray's life is on the line. Chernoff states that the short tubing is proven to be used by Murray from medical records that show Murray ordered the short tubing only, and no long tubing, therefore showing that Murray did in fact, use an injection IV rather than a drip IV.

-Chernoff states that Dr. Shafer is a pharmacokineticist first and an anesthesiologist second. Chernoff stated that the prosecution turned Shafer into a cop, and that Shafer stated what he believed he happened as if it were true, but it's merely opinion.

-Chernoff on Dr. White: White is completely honest and said when needed, I don't have those qualifications to comment on certain testimony, but Shafer never said that. Chernoff states that White knows more about Propofol than Shafer will ever, ever know. White just tried to tell the jury the truth, for $11,000. Chernoff states that Shafer gave simulations, one right after another, and none of them have anything to do with the case except for one, and that one is because the defense asked him to do it. Shafer showed a rapid bolus demonstration, when nobody from the defense ever asked him to do that. Shafer worked backwards on his theory (from concentration to dose), and when someone does that, there are a million different outcomes.

-Michael Jackson could not have died from what Murray admitted he did (25 mg injection to IV) and Shafer admitted that. Chernoff questions whether Shafer is a scientist or a prosecution advocate.

-Chernoff states that prosecution cannot prove a crime. When Chernoff asked Shafer about oral Lorazepam ingestion, Shafer stated that Michael Jackson's stomach held 1/300th of a tablet. Chernoff states that defense knows Michael Jackson orally ingested Lorazepam, and that's Shafer's exhibits are nothing representative of any proof, it represents nothing.

-Chernoff states that there are two reasonable scenarios about Lorazepam. First is Michael Jackson went into his bathroom and swallowed Lorazepam and Murray didn't know. Chernoff states that if this case were about anyone else, Murray wouldn't be on trial.

-Chernoff states that Murray's patients were willing to come to court and testify in front of cameras for him. People that know Murray believe that he could never have a disregard for human life as prosecution has claimed.

-Chernoff states that if Murray is such a liar, why did he tell LAPD he had been giving Michael Jackson Propofol for 60 days straight?

-Definition of criminal negligence: prosecution has shown negligence, in many different respects. Three aspects of criminal negligence (as stated on jury instructions) #1 With the act (of Propofol in a home), is it the direct cause of Michael Jackson's death, and #3, is it the natural probable consequence of the act (the death).

-Chernoff states that it's easy in hindsight to say that Murray is a lousy doctor, but the prosecution witness doctors have never walked in Murray's shoes. It's easy to judge when people have a miniscule amount of compassion, but do not question his motives. Murray's biggest personality defect is his also his greatest strength; he thought he could help Michael Jackson, he thought he could help him sleep. But Murray was wrong, he was a little fish in a big dirty pond.

-Chernoff states that Murray had no idea why when he came back in the room, Michael Jackson looked like he was dead. Chernoff states that Murray should not have been expected to call 911 first, but to try to revive the patient (Michael Jackson) first. Chernoff states that Dr. Steinberg stated that maybe two minutes for revival, after that, it's a felony not to call 911.

-Chernoff states that Murray injected Michael Jackson with Flumanezil, runs down and gets Kai Chase, and then says that Chase got Prince I (Michael Jackson's oldest son), not Murray.

-Chernoff states that Steinberg stated that Murray performed substandard CPR, but it's based on testimony that the compressions were done on the bed. Chernoff states that compressions with Murray's hand behind Michael Jackson's back, and one hand compressing Michael Jackson's chest is not a violation of standard of care. Chernoff states that the prosecution stated Murray deviated from care from the standard of care because he did not provide sufficient for Michael Jackson , but Chernoff states that an ambubag was on the floor. Chernoff states that every single thing Murray did, the prosecution claimed that it was a deviation from the standard of care.

-Chernoff states that the prosecution brought in Michael Jackson's kids to gain sympathy. He states that the prosecution brought in Nicole Alvarez for no reason. He states that the prosecution wants to paint a perfect villain and a perfect victim, but there are neither. Chernoff states that the only reason that the fact that Murray helped with the press release at the time of Michael Jackson's death was because the defense brought it into testimony.

-Chernoff states that it is believable that Murray wanted to back to Michael Jackson's house from the hospital the day Michael Jackson died because his car was there, and it was believable that he wanted to go eat. What is not believable is that Murray wanted to go back to the house to get some cream, that Amir Williams was so disturbed by that, that he locked the house down, but never mentioned it to the police.

-Chernoff plays the voicemail from Frank Dileo to Conrad Murray again (6/19/09 stating that Michael Jackson had an episode, he was sick and Murray should get a blood test on Michael Jackson)

-Chernoff states that Michael Jackson was under tremendous, abnormal, impossible pressure from AEG. Chernoff concedes that giving Propofol in the home was not an appropriate thing to do. But Murray gave an uncontrolled substance, not Demerol, to Michael Jackson . Chernoff states that when Murray went home, the other life of Michael Jackson took over.

-Chernoff repeats Steinberg's testimony that Murray giving Propofol to Michael Jackson was "like a baby on a countertop". Chernoff states that this was insulting Michael Jackson, as if Michael Jackson was a baby, couldn't make contracts for himself, couldn't raise his children for himself, because he was just a baby. Chernoff asks if Murray was supposed to watch Michael Jackson all the time to save him from himself?

-Chernoff states to take this case away from Michael Jackson, in a psych unit, and some patient kills himself, overdoses. If jury is going to hold Murray responsible, don't do it because it's Michael Jackson. This is not a reality show, it's reality, and it's how it affects a real person and the people who love him.

David Walgren Rebuttal Closing

-Walgren states that they are not on trial because the victim is Michael Jackson. -Criminal gross negligence, giving Propofol, which is known for respiratory depression, as a one man operation, no safety measures, nothing. Bizarre, unethical, unconscionable behavior that has never been seen before, and that is why Murray is on trial. - Murray's patients who were witnesses had the benefit of a hospital, a team, monitors and were being treated for heart conditions, Michael Jackson did not have any of those benefits. Michael Jackson was being treated for insomnia that Murray knew nothing about.

-Walgren questions why the witnesses that were called who were Murray's patients were patients from over a decade ago. Walgren questions why none of Murray's current patients were called to testify.

Walgren: "Poor Conrad Murray. Everyone is just working against him." Defense blamed Elyssa Fleak, Alberto Alvarez, Shafer, AEG, Randy Phillips, Michael Amir Williams, Kai Chase. "Poor Conrad Murray." Walgren states that witness Mr. Ruben states that Murray was grieving, Walgren states that is because it's about Murray and nobody else.

Walgren states defense contends that Alvarez and Fleak are lying, Shafer is a cop, Kai Chase failed to get security, and "if allowed more time I'm sure they would find a way to blame Michael's son, Prince." Everyone is to blame except for Conrad Murray, according to defense. If Alvarez wanted to lie, he could have done a lot better than a bizarre story with an IV bag and Propofol inside of it. Walgren states defense is claiming it's a conspiracy between LAPD, bodyguards, and others to pin this on Murray. Poor Conrad Murray. Everything Conrad Murray did in his treatment was bizarre. Waited 20 minutes to call 911, bizarre. Gave Propofol in home setting for 60 days, bizarre. Lied to EMT's and UCLA doctors about giving Propofol, bizarre. Is it surprising that Murray had some usual setup for the saline bag? Walgren states nobody knows, but that Michael Jackson was sensitive to getting all of the medical stuff cleaned up each day so the children did not see it. Everything Murray did was bizarre, and none of it was consistent with a trained competent medical doctor, who was putting his patient first.

Walgren states defense blames Michael Jackson, that Murray left him alone. Michael Jackson sought out Propofol to sleep, but only one doctor said yes to administering it. Poor Conrad Murray. Michael Jackson is dead. Poor Conrad Murray. Nobody knows what it's like to walk in his shoes. Walgren: "You got that right. Because I haven't seen a doctor in this case that said they would ever do what Conrad Murray did. Ever. Including the defense experts."

Walgren states that defense closing arguments said nothing about Dr. White's testimony because it was junk science. Shafer on the other hand, did this pro bono, and showed true science to show how Michael Jackson died.

Walgren states that Murray had a legal duty to provide the standard of care for his patient, Michael Jackson . If Murray hadn't have left the room, this wouldn't have happened. If Murray had attached a monitoring system to Michael Jackson, this wouldn't have happened. If Murray knew how to effectively revive a patient, this wouldn't have happened. The law says that causation only be a natural and probable consequence. If you administer Propofol in a bedroom, a natural and probable consequence is that there could be death. It's a respiratory depressant, it has unpredictable effects as both Shafer and White says, it's dependent on your fasting, how much food you ate, other drugs in the system, how dehydrated you are. It is entirely foreseeable and predicatable that death would occur. White, defense witness stated that if he had a patient that liked to push Propofol, he would not leave him alone.

Walgren states that Alvarez could have easily made up easier lies. There's no evidence that Alvarez had any animosity toward Murray, thought he was a good doctor until Michael Jackson died. Alvarez nor Fleak have any position in this case, no reason to lie.

Walgren states that Shafer provided all graphs and data to the defense at their request. Shafer told the truth. Walgren states Michael Jackson 's fingerprints were not on the syringe. Alvarez fingerprints aren't on the saline bag. Conrad Murray's fingerprint is on the Propofol bottle found in the saline bag.

Walgren asks the jury to evaluate the lies Murray told: Murray lied to Ortega, Gongaware, Phillips, Jorrie that MJ was in great health. Murray emailed Bob Taylor in London and lied about MJ's health. Michael Jackson lied to EMT's, to UCLA Dr. Cooper and Dr. Nguyen. Murray lied to Tim Lopez, about the Propofol being shipped to his clinic rather than Nicole Alvarez apartment. Murray lied when he said he insisted on an autopsy, when he played no role in that whatsoever. Murray lied when he said he got a social group together for the family at UCLA, when it is UCLA protocol. Murray lied when he said he pulled Katherine Jackson aside and asked if there was anything he could do, she asked what happened, and he said he didn't know. Poor Conrad Murray.

Walgren states law is clear about causation. Defense theory does not fit causation. Murray said he knew Michael Jackson was dependent on Propofol, Murray said Michael Jackson liked to push the drug, and Murray was the one who gave Michael Jackson the valium, midazolam, Lorazepam and the Propofol and abandoned Michael Jackson.

Walgren concedes that the People cannot prove exactly what happened behind the doors. But jury knows what happened every night, Propofol being shipped, and that Michael Jackson died. It was a foreseeable and predictable consequence, and what is unusual is that Michael Jackson lived as long as he did receiving Propofol in this setting.

Walgren states that if Murray was so concerned, why did he record Michael in his bedroom? This was supposed to be a relationship based on trust, and Michael Jackson clearly trusted Murray. Murray brought Propofol into the house, administered, abandoned Michael Jackson, failed monitoring, failed to call 911, Murray is responsible. Murray is criminally negligent not because this is Michael Jackson, but because he behaved in a criminally negligent way. Murray was a substantial factor in Michael Jackson's death.

Walgren asks to jury to consider all evidence, and that he trusts that the jury will find that Murray was criminally negligent, because this was a pharmaceutical experiment in a bedroom. Walgren asks the jury to come back with the only right and true verdict in this case, and the only just verdict in this case. Walgren asks that the jury come back with a guilty verdict for the solitary count of involuntary manslaughter based on Murray's actions and his actions alone.

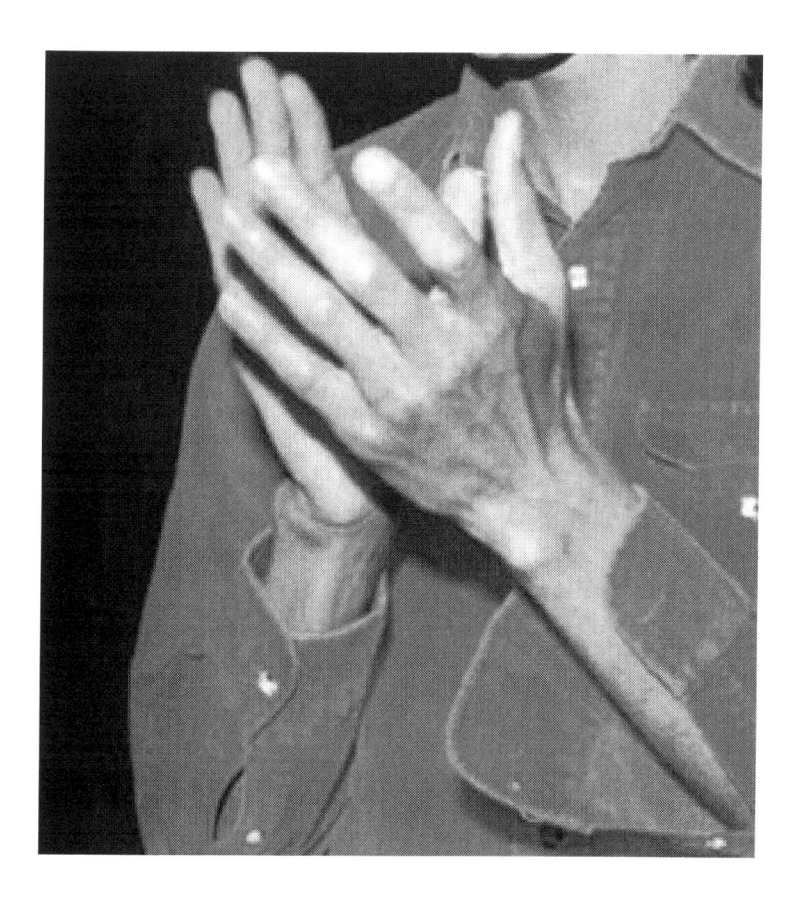

320

Printed in Great Britain
by Amazon.co.uk, Ltd.,
Marston Gate.